THE
POWER
WE
SHARE

Other books by
Elyse Guttenberg

Sunder, Eclipse and Seed

Summer Light
Daughter of the Shaman

Elyse Guttenberg

THE POWER WE SHARE

MURPHY DOME PRESS

Library of Congress Control Number: 2020914317

Cover art copyright 2020, Fiona Jayde http://fionajaydemedia.com
Murphy Dome Press logo from 744th Aircraft Control and Warning Station, Murphy Dome, Alaska, 1953

The Power We Share/ Elyse Guttenberg
www.elyseguttenberg.com

ISBN: 978-0-9992049-6-2 (ebook)
ISBN: 978-0-9992049-7-9 (print edition)

Published by
Murphy Dome Press
P.O. Box 81622
Fairbanks, Alaska 99708

To Sophie and Henry

tikkun olam

Sea Fever

I must go down to the seas again, to the lonely sea and the sky,
And all I ask is a tall ship and a star to steer her by;
And the wheel's kick and the wind's song and the white sail's shaking,
And a grey mist on the sea's face, and a grey dawn breaking.

I must go down to the seas again, for the call of the running tide
Is a wild call and a clear call that may not be denied;
And all I ask is a windy day with the white clouds flying,
And the flung spray and the blown spume, and the sea-gulls crying.

I must go down to the seas again, to the vagrant gypsy life,
To the gull's way and the whale's way where the wind's like a whetted
knife;
And all I ask is a merry yarn from a laughing fellow-rover,
And quiet sleep and a sweet dream when the long trick's over.

by John Masefield

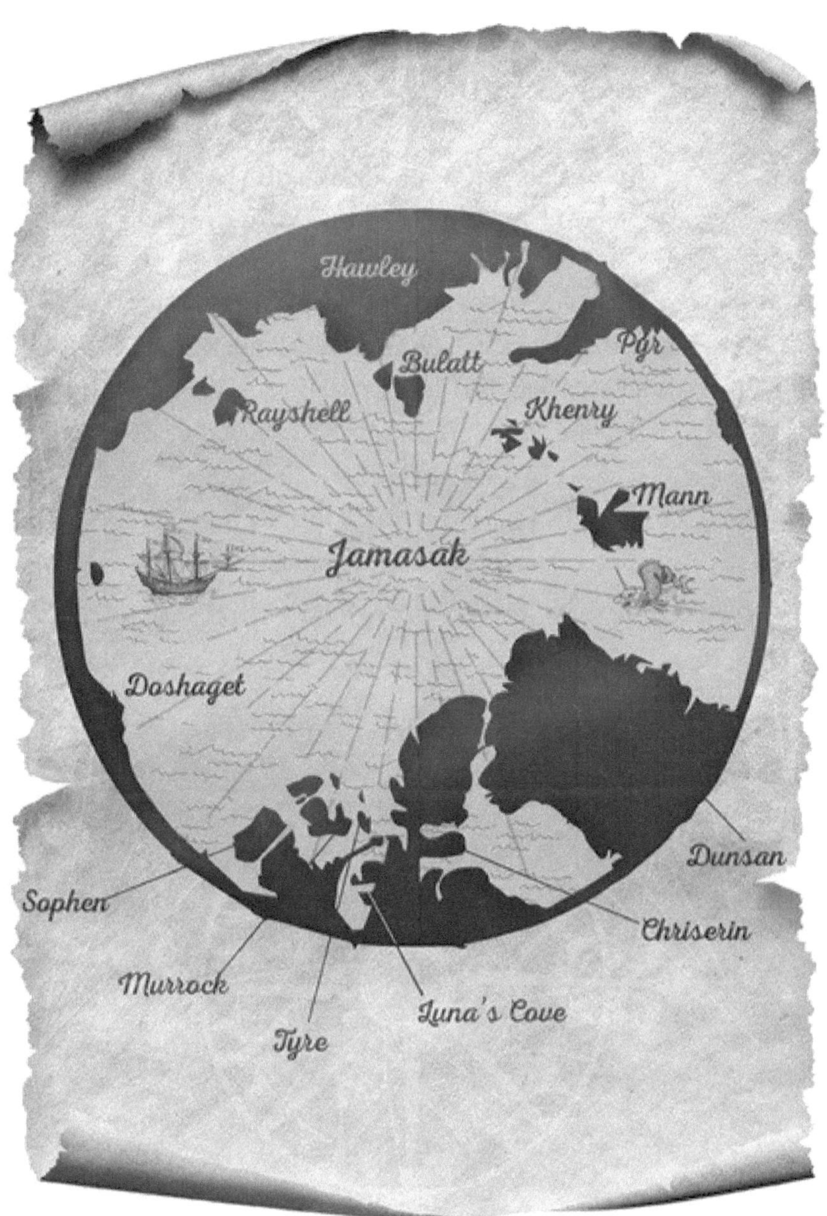

Hawley
Bulatt
Pgr
Rayshell
Khenry
Mann
Jamasak
Doshaget
Dunsan
Sophen
Chriserin
Murrock
Luna's Cove
Tyre

**Those of Us Who Are Not Witches Give Birth
to Sons and Daughters Who Are**

We are One People
From the Living Stars Who Traveled the Dark Lights
Raised High the Isles, Bequeathed us their Gift
We are Sons Born Ready to Prove Our Craft
Daughters to Master Our Own
We are Water that Births Us
Fire that Cleanses Us
Sky that Sustains Us
Ice that Surrounds

We Rejoice in the Power We Share

1

Equinox

Wherein Molly Sinclair is a Pirate and a Witch

Molly Sinclair followed the young lady around the ballroom floor. Her necklace looked perfect. Gold chain, sparkling gems, and with no sign of a locking spell on the catch, it shouldn't be difficult to steal. Her dance partner wouldn't matter. He was a foppish looking man with no rhythm, and she kept glancing past his shoulder as if she couldn't wait for the waltz to end.

She turned to see if any guards were paying attention. There were two at a nearby column, but they weren't looking her way, and one at the fountain was too busy watching the women to be a concern. The music faded and she smoothed her clothes and trailed a cautious ten steps behind the dancers as they left the crowded floor.

Molly had chosen low boots over white stockings for the evening, fitted trousers that reached just below her knees and a brocade surcoat that was a perfect match to the clothes worn by other guests—the men, not the women. They wore flashing jewels that smelled of wealth and sleek gowns that showed off their breasts. Hers were hidden beneath a layer of tight undergarments and she wasn't particularly pleased with the fit.

A serving boy wove through the knot of guests, his tray heaped with seaweed wrapped scallops and rounds of lobster. Molly paused and helped herself to one of each and searched the hall for her brother.

She didn't see him and glanced to the run of tall windows. Stars glimmered, and the moon was clear in the autumn sky. There wasn't a hint of a fog, but that was all right. Evan still had time. All he had to do was craft his spell and hold it while she worked hers and they'd be safely away from the governor's ball before anyone noticed they'd been robbed. She wasn't worried about being recognized; she'd lengthened her nose and squared her chin, changed her copper hair to an unassuming brown and looked nothing like her real self.

The young lady she'd been following took a seat beside a silver haired woman who seemed bored with the evening. They waited for the gentleman to leave then turned their attention to a younger man leaning against a chair. Molly coughed to lower her voice then stepped forward and asked for the honor of a dance.

The lady, Devra Loam, looked Molly over and beamed with pleasure. She glanced at her companion, gathered her skirt, and walked daintily beside Molly to the floor.

Candles and oil lamps lit the jade columns and spacious hall. Richly-dressed couples moved toward the center and guests clustered around tables laden with food. A spell-infused fountain bubbled with scented water and goldfish swam upward through the streams.

Musicians raised their lutes and the lilting notes of another waltz began. Molly took her partner's hand and the steps brought them out then together. Molly was taller than Miss Loam—taller than most women in fact—and she glanced inconspicuously at the necklace around her throat. The gems seemed real, and her left arm was clear of any guild mark which meant she was human, not witch. Perfect. She wouldn't notice Molly's spell.

Devra Loam inquired whether the gentleman—Molly gave her name as Hake Quartell— was enjoying himself and Molly answered with a simple, '*yes.*' And did Mister Quartell live nearby? '*Not actually,*' Molly replied. Miss Loam seemed disappointed. Molly executed another turn and studied the back of her neck. Gems hung from a ribbon, the ribbon from a gold chain and just above that, tucked in her plaited hair, was the smallest enameled shell Molly had ever seen. And inside the shell… Molly searched for a hint of magic and felt it. A locking spell too simple to be a problem, holding it all in place.

Quickly, before the dance ended, she blew a short, firm breath and this time as she brought Devra Loam around, she fixed the pattern of gems and gold, bezel and chain firmly in her thoughts, concentrated, and a moment later a second necklace, scarcely different from the first, circled Miss Loam's throat. The real necklace slid into Molly's hand, from her hand to the pouch on her belt and she was done. The music ended. Molly led Miss Loam back to her seat and fled into the crowd.

She and Evan needed to be careful. The governor clearly expected trouble. Just an hour ago on their way to the ball, they had ducked into an alley to avoid the soldiers patrolling the docks and avenues leading to the palace gates. They were stopping everyone, human or witch, they didn't seem to care.

Evan didn't like it. All those soldiers in stiff uniforms, muskets and swords polished to a shine. There was no good reason for it, he said. But her brother didn't spend his nights with his hair tucked under a hat and hunched over a mug of ale hoping for a useful bit of chitchat. And her chitchat said it was no more than folks expected, what with the nephew's ship finally anchored in the bay.

She warned Evan not to get cocky, provoke some guard into demanding they push up their sleeve, show their guild mark if they had one. He did. She did not.

What? Me a witch? Oh, no sir. Just a shopkeeper trying to get by. I did purchase a guild spell. Keeps the place safe when I'm not there. I can show you the papers if you like?

Arrogant fools, that's all they were. Too interested in the money they squeezed from common folk to follow the governor's latest rule for the day. And with enough power to make her life difficult.

A view opened to the upper landing and a line of guests crowding the entry to greet His Honor the Nephew. There was a holdup though she couldn't find the source. Men craned their necks. Women whispered behind fans. The line was through the arch and into the evening air and these were not the kind of people used to waiting.

She recognized the governor, Harkin Navarr. He was near the railing and shoulder to shoulder with a young man that, though he looked nothing like Navarr, must surely be the nephew. The governor's wife stood a few steps back. She was a large woman, dressed in an emerald gown that fit low across her chest and tight across her middle, a marked contrast to Navarr's tall, spider-thin assistant Jeron Scrud who—if the town gossip was true—was seldom far from his side. Behind them, two guards stood near the top of the stairs, two more at the bottom and another at the glass doors where she had told Evan to meet her.

He wasn't there, but she saw him beneath the row of windows along the southern wall. The view was open, and she could see the stars. Stars, but no fog. She hid a sigh.

There was plenty of time. If nothing else, her brother looked convincing in his guard's uniform. He carried a pistol in his belt and a short sword with a jewel in the pommel. His black hair was caught in a short, neat tail and though his cheeks were smooth he was tall for his age and she doubted he'd draw attention. Unless, that is, they caught him crafting a fog, arrested him and took a closer look. Because if that happened... No.

They weren't going to get caught. They'd done this before, and their plan was sound. And though she would have preferred Evan not be here at all—he was fifteen to her twenty-one— she couldn't pull off the heist without him. Strong as her magic was, there were too many spells involved and she needed his help to hold them together.

All they needed was to relieve the guests of as many jewels and spells as they could carry, replace them with replicas, then sail away on the *Fish* and find a port on the other side of the isles and do it all over again. And again, after that until they had enough gold salted away to live free of the guild and the governor and king and all their bloody laws regarding witches and humans and who could craft or sell what spells to who and for how much and where. Damn their threats and lies; she wanted no part of it all.

She caught Evan's eye and motioned toward the quarter moon. Evan answered with a nod of his own at a woman wearing an elaborate gold headpiece and from her to a pendulum clock marking the time.

Molly didn't answer. She refused to be drawn into a trap. Lecture Evan like a parent and they'd end up bickering like children. It wouldn't be the first time a night's work came to naught.

She had just picked out a likely dance partner when she glanced to the upper landing. An oversized chest she hadn't noticed before rested on the floor in front of Navarr. The curved lid was open. Iron bands outlined its rim.

Scrud signaled and the next two guests stepped forward. The man was long faced with a sour expression, the woman irritated at the delay. Scrud nodded and they moved to the stairs while Navarr peered into the chest for a look at the pouch the woman dropped inside.

Curious, Molly watched the next couple, but her view was blocked by Navarr's nephew. What was his name? The Honorable D… Devon Something or Other. He was taking a good deal of time chatting with the lady next in line.

Molly hadn't bothered to remember the string of titles the nephew inherited when his mother died. She had been on the wharf talking to a sailor when she learned of the visit, and before the night was over, she'd heard at least three versions of the story.

He either had or had not been a ward of the king in Jamasak but lost his arm to a shark when he was young. He had singlehandedly sunk a Night Waterman ship and the king honored him with a posting on a western isle. Or else it was a guild ship and not one of the black market vessels and, furious at the bungled job, the king shipped him off to his uncle here on Murrock. Judging from tonight's pomp, she doubted that version was true. Same with the shark. From what she could see of the nephew, both arms were intact.

He was tall, with hair as black as Evan's hanging over one eye and he wasn't as old as she had pictured. As soon as word got around that a ball was to be given in honor of Darlit—no, Davit, that was his name, Davit Lake— she had spent most of her time thinking about how to get her share of all that wealth gathered in one place, and little about the nephew at its source. Other than the color of his hair, she really didn't know much about him. It didn't matter. She already didn't like him.

The willowy lady was replaced by a teetering old fellow. Davit Lake slapped him amicably on his shoulder and something flashed then fell into the chest. Off the man went, and an equally distinguished gentleman took his place. He received the same warm slap and another pouch fell into the chest. Scrud retrieved it and tipped the contents into his palm as the governor leaned over to see.

A clock chimed, and Molly turned. It was later than she'd realized. Evan was no longer at the windows but thankfully, neither was the moon.

His fog spell had worked! The town, harbor and distant ships were cloaked in a wash of gray. She glanced over her shoulder, but if anyone noticed they didn't seem to care.

Evan had a more difficult time crafting spells than she did. Sometimes they worked, sometimes—no matter how carefully he followed the guild's instructions—they didn't come right. But maybe, finally, just as she'd promised, he'd turned a corner.

Streetlights along the wharf had turned to yellow blurs. Red tiled rooftops were difficult to see. She needed to get back to work or they'd have little to show for the night.

The next dance was a lively gavotte and Molly's new partner yielded a pair of sapphire earrings. Followed by a hefty purse full of coins from a man who bumped into Molly without so much as a pardon me. And a woman who gave up a brooch of pearl flowers in a field of rubies.

But the odd thing Molly noticed as she replaced each item with a replica and pocketed the real one, was that for all the jewels she'd found, other than the locking spell in Devra Loam's hair, she hadn't come across another shell the entire evening. The small, ornate shells with instructions for spells inside could be worth more than the finest gems. She hadn't found any to steal, and she should have.

The musicians lowered their instruments and Molly glanced to the landing where the line had dwindled to an end. Scrud closed the chest. He passed a rod through brass loops and twisted a key. Two guards stepped forward and grunted as they lifted the chest and waddled away.

Molly's purse had grown heavy and she should have been pleased. The jewelry would fetch a fine price, but she had hoped for at least a few good spells to sweeten the deal. Stolen spells could be difficult to sell— she needed someone discreet—and she needed the money they'd bring.

Except, how was it that so many pompous, wealthy merchants, guild masters and nobles could prance around in all their finery and nary a spell among them? Her plan had been to steal anything valuable she could manage, but anything should have included everything, jewels, coins and spells alike.

She started around the long table, past a middle-aged couple who glared in annoyance, and on to the food in the center. Pheasant. Roasted goat. Quail. Floating candles illuminated the display. She tried a bite of mango topped with cheese and glanced to the balcony. The nephew at the root of the fuss was gone. The governor and Scrud talked in a corner. She took another bite then paused at the couple's angry tone.

"Humiliating," the woman said.

Molly glanced at the man. He was dark, with a pinched nose and dainty lace on his sleeves. "They have no right," he agreed. "It's robbery. I wonder if the guild knows."

"I don't remember the invitation explaining a need for caution."

Molly had hidden in an alley with Evan before sneaking into the palace. They carried documents she had forged herself. She'd received no invitation.

"We won't get them back. Not so much as an empty shell. I'll wager they're in it together, Navarr and Scrud and the guild."

Scrud. Of course, Molly realized. The heavy chest on the landing. The smug look on the governor's face. They must have ordered the guests to drop any shells they'd brought into the chest. They were worried someone would harm the nephew, or if not harm, maybe steal something valuable. No wonder the only spell she found was tucked into a shell so small, no one noticed it was there.

"Oh. Excuse me." The woman's voice was suddenly high and false. "Your Excellency. Sir. We didn't see you." The man jostled Molly and she turned.

Her first thought when she found Davit Lake so close she could have drawn his pistol was to hope her vest was tugged flat over her breasts. Her second thought was that the governor's nephew couldn't be much older than she was herself, and though his hair really was the same dark shade as Evan's, his eyes were chestnut brown. Evan's eyes were blue. "Please," he insisted. "No need for ceremony. Davit Lake will do. And you are—?" He held out his hand, but the man was already hurrying away.

Lake chuckled and dropped his hand. "I didn't catch their names, did you?" He glanced at Molly, looked her over. "I've been stuck for hours on that damn landing. What are you eating? Anything good?"

"I think it's shark," she said flippantly, then froze. Her voice was high, and she sounded too much like a woman. She coughed and tried again. "Crab's over there."

Lake laughed. "I'll take the crab and pass on the shark. I had more than my share on the ship coming over. What's in there?"

He nodded toward a flagon and Molly turned. She felt his gaze linger on the back of her head a bit longer than she liked, and she quickly found the drink and raised it to her nose. "It's wine, Your Honor."

"Rum would be better. And no more titles, please."

Molly couldn't tell whether he was serious or testing her and if he was, what was he after? She held out the flagon and noticed her hands.

Narrow wrist, slender fingers. It didn't matter than she spent most days climbing rigging and stowing sails. Her hands looked half the size and twice as soft as his and he'd catch her working a spell if suddenly, she added gloves to her disguise.

Instead, she changed the wine to rum. It was a simple thing—grapes made wine and sugarcane made rum and both were mostly water. Change the water and the drink would change. Change the drink, and Davit Lake wouldn't notice her hands. She drew a breath, let it out, and the spell was done.

Lake took the flask and nodded his thanks, until their fingers grazed, and they pulled back in surprise, both at the same time. Lake's touch was warm, oddly so, and he must have noticed as well. He frowned as he set down the flask, stared at his hands then wiped them on his thighs before finally taking a drink. She tried not to panic. *All he sees is a young man,* she reassured herself. He wasn't looking at her. He had no reason to be suspicious.

"That's better," he said. "You seem a regular fellow. Do you mind helping me a bit? That bearded man with the wide belt over there. Is he anyone?"

Molly wasn't sure how she'd ended up talking so casually with Davit Lake, but if the governor's nephew decided she was a regular fellow, she wouldn't contradict him. "That's Beren Mace," she whispered back. "Owns Murrock Isle's largest shipyard and half the trade shops along the wharf."

"Human shops?" Lake seemed impressed. "Must be either a crook or a genius. And that one?" He nodded toward another man, stoop backed but impressive in his fine clothes."

Molly hesitated. She didn't know the man and didn't want to lie more than necessary. "Isn't he one of the governor's captains?"

"Looks a mite old for the job, don't you think?"

"When did you arrive?"

"Day before yesterday with the tide. I've hardly spoken to anyone beside Scrud. And my uncle, of course."

"Of course. And your ship, it's returning to Jamasak?" She waited, hoping for a hint of the routes she and Evan ought to avoid. She was confident the *Fish* could out sail even a king's vessel, but she'd just as soon avoid being hailed, especially if there were witches on the crew.

"We came in through the sound," Lake said. "Heavy winds the entire crossing." He looked at her again. "What did you say your name was?"

Molly smiled blandly then, "Melvin Goodeye," she said, pulling the name out of the air. She wasn't always careful with her disguises but was relieved now that she'd taken extra time with her spell. She'd kept her height, which worked well for pretending to be a man, but changed most of her face and hair. A few hours from now and he'd never see Melvin again.

"Who's that?" he nodded toward a woman in a red gown. "Quite the dress. And quite the lady inside."

"Don't know," Molly said flatly. She didn't have time for this. She needed to reach Evan, tell him about the chest. At the very least she wanted a look inside. If the stars were with her, she'd steal a few. The whole the damn thing if that was possible.

Lake raised a brow. "A woman like that? I'd want to know her if I lived here."

Molly hadn't been listening. "Yes, well," she backtracked. "I haven't been here all that long myself."

"Clever you to manage an invitation. Are you human or witch?"

Molly shot him a glance. "Human," she lied.

"As am I. Though we aren't all as useless as they say." His smile, she noticed, was a bit crooked, and though his tone was light, she couldn't tell if he was joking. "If nothing else," he continued, "they need someone to buy their damn spells."

The man laughed too much, Molly decided. It wasn't that his voice was unpleasant—it was low and easy—but she wasn't in the habit of trusting people she couldn't read.

"What do you say? Is there a tavern you'd recommend?"

"A tavern? Yes. There's um, the Gold Key Inn. It's cleaner than some. But I'd have thought a man in your position would have someone to show you around?"

"Too many!" Lake laughed then, abruptly: "Join me, why don't you? I'd love to slip away, and it'll be our secret. You wouldn't be opposed to sharing a table, would you?"

"Tonight?" Molly stiffened. "No, sorry. I don't think I can manage that."

"Tomorrow then? Excellent. The Gold Key. I'll find you." Lake dipped his head, turned and walked into the crowd.

Molly stared after him. She took a moment to shake off her surprise then turned and hurried in the opposite direction. The guests were mostly gathered on the far end of the hall and she picked out a column in a rear corner, checked that no one was watching, and slipped behind.

She was done with Melvin Goodeye for the night—he'd served his purpose—and she needed a guard's uniform to get near the chest. She shook off her encounter with Davit Lake and thought instead of the guards positioned around the governor's palace. Most of them had grey hair, rounded bellies. She didn't have time for a spell that strong but could at least change her clothes.

She pulled her attention inward, breathed deeply and the fine fabric of Master Goodeye's surcoat changed to the coarser blues of a uniform. Another breath and the trousers loosened, the shine on her boots was gone and the fancy heels flattened. She tried not to think of the long night still ahead, focused her thoughts, and by the time she stepped from the column, she was a guard, gaze lowered, and already annoyed with the uniform scratching at her neck and arms.

She made her way unnoticed around the fringes of the crowd until she reached the grand stairs and mounted the first step. The guards nodded indifferently, and she climbed another and peered across the hall. There was no sign of Davit Lake and that was good. The last thing she wanted was another drink with the governor's nephew. She looked again and saw her brother snitching a bit of food from a server's tray.

"Evan," she whispered. She pursed her lips and blew a tiny spell and, as if his name was a thing with weight and substance, her message carried over heads and across the hall.

He looked up and—no matter the face or clothes—recognized her. He gestured excitedly toward the window. *The fog! I did it!* He blew back his response. *Are you ready? Are we leaving?*

Not yet. Meet me on the landing. There's a chest.

What chest? He frowned and nodded toward the sky. *I can't hold it forever.*

Only a while more. Repeat the chant. It will hold.

He made a face but looked to the window and did as she asked. He joined her a moment later and listened intently as she explained the spells locked in the chest.

No one stopped them as they mounted the stairs. At the far end of the landing, the two guards stood in front of a narrow door, the chest between them on the floor. The one on the right, a balding, heavy man, pressed his hands to the small of his back. The second guard was younger, pock faced, impatient. They switched sides and bickered as they shuffled through the door. Molly held Evan back. "Wait," she said. "They'll drop it off and we'll go in after."

But the moments stretched. The guards didn't return. "All right, then," Molly said, and they sauntered across the landing, checked that no one was following, then opened the door and stepped through.

The room was a narrow rectangle, poorly lit, no windows. A gap in the floor opposite opened into shadows. Molly drew her pistol, a small flintlock already loaded and primed. Evan slipped his short-sword from his belt. They heard voices below, indistinct but loud enough the guards couldn't have gone far. Molly bolted the door behind them, and they followed down to a narrow, timbered passageway with torches flickering on the walls. They hesitated then caught voices and a screech as the chest scraped walls.

The ceiling grew lower as they continued, the passageway surprisingly long. They must be circling the palace hill, Molly realized, and though Navarr obviously made use of the tunnel, the timbers lining the walls looked as if they'd been rotting since long before he became governor.

The murmurs grew louder. "Take a break," the older guard grumbled. "The thing's damn heavy."

"Keep moving. I'm not losing any money because of you."

"The money will keep. I gotta catch my breath."

Evan peered around the wall. "They're stealing it," he whispered

"Did you see their looks?" The older guard laughed. "Nearly pissed themselves having to give up their precious spells. All that wasted money."

"They'll have more to worry about if the guild finds any spells weren't registered."

"They can't find out. We're stealing it, aren't we?"

The younger guard snorted. "Not sure that's the right word but come on. Rest time's over. We need to move."

Molly pulled Evan back. "We'll rush them and find the way out," she whispered. "Ready—"

"Wait!" Evan grabbed her arm. "The fog. It was there. You saw it. I crafted the spell exactly the way the guild says."

Molly gave him a look. "Of course, you did," she said.

"And if it's not there when we come out, it's not my fault?"

"I saw it," she answered carefully and peered around the wall. "And we'll make it to the *Fish*—"

"Except I'm not going back to Hayden Hall. You need me. Admit it."

"Evan, be reasonable—" She stopped. The guards were moving. She switched her pistol to her left hand and drew her cutlass. "Not now, all right? We need to disarm them. Take the chest."

Evan let it go. He nodded, drew himself taller, and they leapt into the passage. The two men spun in alarm and dropped the chest. The younger one reached for his pistol; the heavier man pulled his blade.

Evan charged past Molly and lunged at the older guard. Their short swords clashed, and they danced back and forth in the narrow space.

Evan parried then went low and struck the guard's thigh, not deep enough for a serious wound but enough to make him stumble while the other guard glared at Molly and fumbled with his pistol.

She advanced with the trigger back; the muzzle aimed at his chest. The man frowned and looked confused. He glanced at the flintlock and cocked hammer, his partner fighting with Evan, and went down on his knees and set his gun on the ground.

"Take it," he said. "Don't shoot."

Molly blinked in surprise. She kicked the gun aside and it hit the wall and came to a rest. The man's gaze darted across her face, her hands, belt and weapons. Evan's face was still his own, but she was Melvin Goodeye, young and not so threatening as she'd have preferred and yet the man looked afraid. He was a guard, not a soldier, more used to collecting bribes than fighting real thieves. This was going to be easier than she'd imagined.

She replaced her pistol and turned to Evan, but she was too trusting. The guard leaped from the floor and struck her hand. Her cutlass flew, and she spun to face him, but he had already snatched up his gun. He tried to cock it, but not fast enough.

Molly sprang at the man. She rammed her knee into his gut and heaved him backward. He was skinny and weighed hardly more than she did. He fell and the pistol arced, hit the wall and exploded. Her ears rang as she waited for him to rush her, but the tunnel was suddenly quiet.

She glanced to Evan and found him leaning into the older guard as he forced him against the wall. "Stay down Scritt," the man rasped. "I'm not dying over any damn cogs."

The younger guard, still on the floor, looked surprised "That's it? You're giving up?"

"Yeah, and it's my say so. They're not going to kill us." He glanced past Evan to Molly. "Are you?"

"Not today," Molly said as she retrieved their weapons. "How do we get out of here?"

"That way," the older guard answered. "The tunnel follows the hill. You'll feel the air. There's a door." The younger one said nothing.

Molly glanced ahead. The tunnel was shadowed, and she couldn't see any break in the wall, but the men were too cowardly to lie. She sliced through the older one's belt, motioned Evan to do the same and tied their wrists next. They cut off the guards' sleeves and gagged their mouths, hurrying to be done. "Their ankles, too," Molly said, but Evan had stopped. He was staring at his hands, frowning as he closed then opened them again.

"We need to hurry," he said nervously.

"Yes, but their feet—"

"Molly. The fog." He gave her a look that was suddenly older than his years and she nodded, braced herself, and they picked up the chest.

It was heavy, but not as much as she expected, and it banged awkwardly against the walls as they jostled forward. A few turns later and the air cooled; the outline of a door appeared in the wall. They set down the chest and Evan ran his hand around the timbered edges, up the sides and along the top. His fingers felt something, an indentation with a smoother edge inside. He pressed it, but nothing happened. He tried again then, frustrated, stepped back, glared, and gave a sudden hard kick to the door.

There was a thud of ancient wood. Dust filtered down, but that was all. He kicked again, harder, but the sound was the same. Dull. Unyielding. "They lied," he murmured, "It's sealed."

"Maybe," she said, and stepped around the chest and stood beside him. She raised her hands toward the door, and felt the breeze on the other side, the cooler air and the pull of the sea. They tried together this time; they put their shoulders to the door, counted and heaved, and heaved again. Bits of mortar, sand, flakes and grit flittered down and the door burst open.

They found themselves outside under the night sky, the air sweet after the stifling tunnel. She took a breath and felt her strength return. The moon was high over the dark sea. Its light caught on the masts and yards and outlined the ships in the harbor below. Palace Hill rose behind them. Ahead stretched a field of shadowed boulders and sparse trees, and beyond those the outlying houses and the winding down to the harbor.

Evan glared at the wispy clouds as if, just by staring harder, he'd force them to thicken and gather, hide their ship from prying eyes. He was about to say something when a voice called from the dark.

"Anyone there?"

She pushed Evan into the shadows behind her. "Cassaway? Scritt?" a man called. Heavy boots pounded the ground somewhere off to the right, nearer the trees.

"Soldiers," she whispered. "But how did they find us?"

Evan stepped around her to see. "The two in the tunnel, they warned the governor. I'm sorry. We should have tied their legs. Or… What if these are Night Watermen? The coachmen at the palace were taking wages. Said they saw a ship. A flag with a coiled serpent. Thieves. Someone talked? They were double crossed?"

A branch snapped in the opposite direction and trees swayed. Shadows changed and figures stepped out, one after another, they raced across a corner of the field. Molly caught a flash of silver. Muskets flared and dirt exploded. A woman cried out, then silence again.

"If those are Night Watermen," she said, "then who are they fighting?" *And what in the star's name am I doing,* she wondered, *dragging Evan into harm when I promised to keep him safe?* "Let's run for that rock, then the tree. Skirt the long way around, aim for the road."

They hunched low and started moving, darting as they run. The chest was less awkward outside the tunnel and they quickly reached the nearest house, but they were seen.

"The chest," voices shouted. "There it is."

They squirmed under a fence rail, dragged the chest behind them and ducked behind a trough.

A horse saw them, snorted and pawed the ground. "Over there! "A woman shouted, and a shot blasted the rail near Molly's head. The horse reared, and Molly pushed Evan down and scanned the yard. A small shed stood to one side. Pigs asleep against the fence. A wood pile and a wagon in the rear. A wagon?

She tapped Evan, pointed and they crawled toward it while the soldiers—Night Watermen or whoever they were—raced past them to another house.

Evan found a bridle, harness and traces while Molly pulled the wagon around, but the wheels creaked and from somewhere, not far, a soldier shouted. Someone stumbled and another shot rang out.

Molly fought for calm. The two sides were shooting at each other and chasing her and didn't seem near to giving up. She was tired from crafting so many spells, and her hands were shaking. She paused and shook off the last of her spells and Melvin Goodeye and the guard's annoying uniform were gone, and she was Molly. She straightened, shook out her hair and breathed freely again.

She turned her thoughts from the confusion and gun shots, the shouting in the thin night air, and focused instead on the wagon. She pictured the wheels, oak and ash; that's what they were. Trees that were growing before she was born. Wooden spokes and metal hub... She smoothed them and turned them and tied them together. She slicked the oil and straightened the axle and the wagon rolled forward without a hint of noise.

Quickly then, they hitched the horse, tossed the reins into the wagon bed and carefully swung the chest inside. That too made not a sound. They climbed in and crouched low.

Molly felt for the reins, found them and tugged and the horse pulled onto the road, but that was all the time they had. Bullets sprayed the wagon. The horse took fright and they raced wildly down the hill, past white stucco houses, honking geese and barking dogs, taverns shuttered for the night. The people chasing them were on horseback now and bullets whistled over their heads until suddenly, thankfully, the wharf was in sight. She twisted around to show Evan and he sat up. Blood dripped from a gash across his cheek.

Her stomach lurched, and she scrambled around the chest. She had no more time for magic, barely had time to think. If anything happened, it would be her fault. They had only each other. She saw his hands and stopped. They were cupped in his lap, a tendril of white smoke rising through his fingers. No. Not smoke. Fog. A tentative, misting, lick of fog rising in the air.

"I can't get it thick enough," he said, not looking up. "Just… I'm trying…"

"It doesn't matter," Molly said as the road gave way to the clatter of wood and decking. Seagulls screeched, and she spun to see the wharf and dead ahead the governor's flagship *Corona* anchored in the water. Its sails were furled. Merchant vessels and fishing boats bobbed closer in to shore. And the *Fish*, her ship, their ship, waited not far off the *Corona's* starboard bow.

She slid into the seat, grabbed the reins and guided the horse to the last piling where their dinghy was tied. They leaped from the wagon and grabbed the chest, Molly on the right and Evan with his free hand in a fist. They lowered the chest into the boat and glanced back to find the soldiers clamoring toward them.

They jumped, and Molly pushed off. The boat surged ahead as a volley of bullets shattered the oily water and the *Corona* sprang to life. Lights blinked on. Sailors scrambled from below and an alarm bell clanged.

"Load the cannons," a voice cried. "Weigh anchor." A ball burst from a swivel gun and exploded in the water. The spray hit, and Molly dug her oars into the water and pulled. The *Corona* loomed above them, so close the sailors could have caught them in a net.

"Fire!" the gunners called, and grapeshot spewed from a cannon. The waters shook, the dinghy lurched, and Molly glanced back to find Evan standing in the stern, balancing as he cupped his hands.

Evan's fog flowed from his fingertips. It washed over his arms and across the water and swallowed their boat, the *Corona*, and every scrap of debris between the wharf and the deeper sea. It turned shapes into shadows and shadows to a blur.

"Fire away!" an officer called, but the gunner's shots flew blind. "Where are they?" a voice roared through a bull horn. "What in all the stars…?"

Molly rowed silently alongside the *Corona's* hull. Cannon fire blasted above her, bursts of yellows and hot reds. One arced over their boat, another off the port bow, a flare and then nothing.

By the time they reached the *Fish* the fog was so thick she could hardly see the chain as she hooked the chest and raised it, hand over hand. She raced up the ladder, jumped to the deck and guided the dinghy in. Evan came after, his brow still furrowed as he worked to hold his fog, just a little longer now while Molly took her turn.

She raised her hands toward the mainsail, not clasped as Evan held his but pointing and ready, familiar and strong. The *Fish* was their ship, built by their parents, with spells in every board and line and spar and cleat. She nodded toward the foresail and down it came. The mainsail next. Molly pointed, and the sails shook free. Blocks clattered. Lines grew taut. The anchor rose, and the capstan turned. The rudder shifted and out of the harbor they sailed.

The stars were no longer visible through Evan's fog, but they were there. Haldin and Riva in the north, Teair and Estair in the south. Once, the stars had walked the isles. Men and women, they were gone now but their gifts remained, and their blood ran through Molly and Evan's veins and for that, she was very glad.

2

The Fish Being a Caravel of 190 Hands and 60 Tons is Deemed too Small to Ply the Seas

The oak door leading to *Brittle's Trade and Craft Brokery* was laced with iron crossbars and a rusted grate at eye level that was closed from inside. Molly peered through the grimy window alongside the door but saw only the reflection of Auklet's rooftops behind her. Two days had passed since they sailed out of Murrock's harbor. They'd spent the night hiding among the Gap Rocks and the next day, when the sun cleared the horizon, there wasn't a ship in sight.

The evening at the palace may have had a disappointing start, but it hadn't ended that way. She and Evan had taken no serious wounds, and it wasn't likely that the governor's *Corona* could have found them among the rocks. The area was difficult at the best of times. In the dark it was treacherous and foolhardy.

The next day, they'd sailed into Auklet on the nearby isle of Tars, paid the harbor master the usual bribe and hoped they wouldn't be boarded, at least not too soon. They'd walked the wharf, heard talk of a theft back on Murrock, but not any search. One day more, two at the most and the chest would be safe in her cellar and she'd bring Evan back to Hayden Hall and apologize to the teaching masters for keeping him so long.

She pushed open the door and was surprised to find customers inside. The street had been quiet and the shop unremarkable from the outside. Yet here it was, well stocked with barrels of marlin spikes and brass fittings and open shelves with items sorted by size and use— musical instruments, weapons, jewelry and more. The dark wood smelled of lemons and oil.

A woman leaned over the glass fronted counter opposite the door and bargained with an older, round faced man, Brittle, most likely. He was clean shaven with white hair that curled below his ears and round spectacles that made him look more a grocer than a pawnbroker and Molly wondered if that wasn't intentional. Legal business out front, black market in the alley behind. She hoped they wouldn't take long. Evan was alone on the *Fish* plotting ways to change her mind and prevent his return to Hayden Hall.

The woman inquired about the workings of an astronomical clock and Brittle fussed with a key. It was a complicated thing with faces for the constellations and moon, and a ring to show the ice that circled the isles and closed them in.

The clock chimed, the woman smiled and the other customer, a sailor from the look of his clothes, seemed equally impressed. Until Brittle named a price and the woman's face crumpled. She murmured her excuses and the sailor took her place.

If the pawnbroker was selling unregistered spells, Molly couldn't tell. She guessed the clock and musical instruments were human made and as to the shells she'd glimpsed, the witches' guild permitted used spells to be sold so long as the cogs inside—the written instructions with the chant, object and gestures required to make the spell work—were registered and the guild received their cut of the sale. Only master witches were permitted to craft new spells and those were sold only in sanctioned guild shops. If Brittle had any, he was breaking the law.

The sailor pulled out a plain, wooden shell and set it on the counter. His hair was pulled back in an untidy gray braid and though his clothes were old, his arms were massive. Molly sidled closer. He flipped the catch and turned it toward Brittle. "It'll twine rope, sir. Any length. I'm not asking much. Two coppers will do."

Brittle looked but didn't touch and the man grew concerned. He drew a tiny scroll from the shell, slipped off the thread holding it closed and smoothed it on the counter. "You can read the cog yourself, sir. Thread's the object, gesture's written down and the chant goes, *Ladder to the sky, anchor to the sea, right sides a circle—*" The thread began to grow. It thickened and lengthened, the size of a needle, a worm.

"Stop it," Brittle ordered. "You're wasting the spell. Did you steal it?" The man didn't answer. "Do you even know how many times it's been used? Or what's left?" He glared and the man lowered his sleeve and covered his guild mark. "Oh. I see," he said, less harshly. "Crafted it yourself, did you?"

"You know me, sir. I just need some money to tide me over till I find work."

Brittle glanced sideways at Molly. She wore no disguise today, unless the fine dress and stylish jacket of a wealthy merchant's daughter could be called a disguise. She lowered her gaze and stared innocently at the glass shelves.

Brittle turned back to the sailor. "I'll take it," he said. "But put the damn thread away before there's nothing left to sell. And be careful where you show these. I don't want the guild poking around." He pushed two coins at the sailor than added a third, and the man whisked them from the counter and hurried away.

"Sorry to keep you waiting," the shopkeeper said. His smile was lighthearted and easy again. "What can I do for you?"

For all his avuncular looks, Brittle seemed to know what he was about, and Molly decided to throw a few fancy spells in with the more common ones, pretend she didn't know the difference. She'd been through this often enough and knew when to hold out, when to give in. She wanted her money, but she had Evan to think about and wouldn't take foolish risks with someone who, for all she knew, might run to the guild as soon as her back was turned. "I was strolling by and saw your sign," she said.

She peered through the glass counter. The top shelf held a bird's nest with four red eggs, the size of her fingertip. And beside the nest some sort of flat, brass instrument that was rusted and in need of cleaning. There were markings on the face, but she couldn't make them out.

She caught a glimpse of Brittle's reflection as he searched her arm for a guild sign. She let him look and turned her attention to a small sphere suspended above an onyx stand. It was a perfect replica of the isles, complete with real water and ridges of white ice crafted to stay in place. Tiny domed palaces rose in the center where the king's court in Jamasak would be. "It's beautiful," she said. "Is the ice real?"

"I think it's crafted, but not real rim ice. And there's no cog to go with it if that's what you mean. It doesn't do anything."

She had wondered but wasn't about to let on. "And that one?" she pointed to the brass instrument.

"It's not for sale. Measures the stars; at least that's what I've been told."

She took a closer look. The flat brass circle was near the size of her open hand. There were four quadrants in the center and two pointers. But the oddest part was the engravings, the figures on the outer ring. A fish, and what looked like a ram, a crab and other shapes. "It looks complicated. Why go to all the trouble of measuring stars when anyone can a hire a witch or purchase a cog? What does it say?"

Brittle watched her over his spectacles. "Your guess is as good as mine. It's old, though. The woman I bought it from claimed it was a true relic. Said her parents found it floating near the rim."

Molly stiffened. Her thoughts flew to her own parents and the *Ice Warden*, and an image of tattered sails, riggings heavy with frost. *It's not true*, she reminded herself. She had no proof their ship had wrecked, but it was better than her other fear. That her parents had abandoned her and Evan at Luna's Cove and went off in search of... What? She never really knew. Or what treasure was so important they left her and Evan to fend for themselves.

Brittle was watching her. "Pick it up if you like. It's old, but it won't break."

"No." Molly said. "Thank you." The visit was taking too long, and she still hadn't gotten to business.

"I do get a few ladies missing jewelry," Brittle offered. "Or… If you don't see something you like… Perhaps you have something to sell? We have generous terms, and discretion, of course."

"Of course," Molly said. She set a pouch on the counter, her hand firmly on top.

"Registered?" Brittle asked. He did not look down.

"Some, not all." She had been careful to bring only spells she had stolen herself, none that could be traced to the chest. For those, she'd wait to decide if she trusted him, then return in a few days more.

He cocked his head. "I'd be careful if I were you, ma'am. They're hounding anyone looks like they might know about that thieving last night."

"Thieving?" Molly feigned surprise. "What happened?"

"Nothing doesn't happen every night, except this time the governor's called foul. Some spells went missing from the palace and he's blaming Night Watermen. Everyone's pointing a finger at everyone else. But if you ask me, not every thief's a Waterman and not every Waterman's a thief."

Molly thought of the shooting outside the palace, how chaotic it seemed. Evan thought they might have been Watermen, and it was possible, but more likely his imagination. Watermen were usually at sea, not on land. And they weren't thieves so much as black marketeers. Buying. Selling. Cheating the guild. "Night Watermen?" she asked innocently. "Were they involved?"

"Wouldn't know," Brittle said. "I'm more interested in keeping my head down, staying safe."

"They think they're free agents," she said suddenly. "But all they do is harass good people. If I was governor, I'd find them and torch their ships."

Brittle looked surprised. "Right, then. Well." He cleared his throat. "Why don't you show me what you have, and I'll give you an idea of its worth."

"Thank you," Molly said, collecting herself. "I've never done this before." She loosened the drawstrings and tapped out a ring and a chain bracelet and a few spells. A few seeing eyes and a rain cog, a spiked ball and a miniature knife that grew into a dagger when she set it down. Brittle picked it up, ran his thumb along the edge.

Molly grew impatient. She was supposed to be down at the wharf. She had broadsides to post before she could get back to Evan, a crew to hire and a new base—a home—to build. Someday. When she had the money. Soon. "Maybe I could come back later?" she offered.

Brittle noticed the ball and scratched his chin. "That's a replicator, isn't it? They're hard to come by."

"And worth a good price."

"If it mimics things as well as the last one I sold. Any idea where it's from?"

"Family heirloom." She smiled.

"Heirloom? Of course. It's best to keep the guild out of your business." He watched for her reaction, but Molly didn't reply. He fingered the spells. "I could sell the seeing eye for you, but you won't get much. This replicator now, it's worth more. But there's a risk—"

The front door closed, and Molly spun about and caught sight of the sailor as he passed the window. He'd been inside, eavesdropping! She thought of the chest on the *Fish*. "I'm sorry," she said suddenly and scooped everything back in her pouch. "It's late. I should be going."

"What? Wait!" Brittle called. "Why don't you leave those things with me? Or if that's a problem—"

Molly stopped at the door. "The cogs work, sir. I guarantee—"

She reached for the latch just as the door swung open. She stepped back, lost her balance, stumbled and grabbed for the door just as a tall man in a wide brimmed hat hurried in. "Brittle!" he called toward the counter and though his face was hidden, there was no mistaking the voice. Davit Lake. This time, she remembered the name.

The governor's nephew stood a scant few inches away. He caught the look on Brittle's face, cocked his head and saw her. Molly pushed a loose curl from her eyes. It slid back across her brow.

"I'm sorry," he hurried to apologize. "I didn't see you."

"My fault entirely, excuse me." She stepped wide, but he moved toward her and, left to right, they danced a few steps. She felt awkward and annoyed and stopped moving. Davit Lake stared bemusedly at her. *He doesn't recognize me,* she realized. *Melvin Goodeye. He knows only Melvin.*

Her clothes were different, her face. She had dressed Melvin in trousers and a fine surcoat and now she was in a dress. His nose was longer, his chin squarer, his hair brown, while today, she was Molly. Dressed in expensive silks and impractical red shoes, but still Molly.

And neither was Davit Lake outfitted in the bright, gaudy clothes of the palace ball. He had on browns and muted colors, ordinary clothes no one would notice in a crowd.

He'd be looking for a man, a guard, she told herself. *Not a well-dressed woman.* She glanced down at the low-cut bodice, the curl of copper—her real color—hair, and her face grew warm.

Lake's hand remained on the door, his arm blocking her as he helped himself to a longer look at her eyes and hair, the curve of her neck, her shoulders and breasts.

"If you're coming in, close the door!" Brittle shouted.

Lake ignored him. "I didn't mean to startle you."

"You didn't. I'm fine." Molly tried again to step around him, but he moved with her.

"Davit Lake," he offered. "Have we met before? You're—?"

"Leaving." She looked up, met his eyes and quickly looked away. If he wouldn't let go of the door, she'd move it herself. Impatient now, she drew a breath and felt the air around her. It was electric, charged with energy and she started a spell, turned it toward the door, the handle, shaped it, and—

Lake yelped and pulled away. He frowned and stared at his hand and Molly's focus withered. She thought of the wine she'd changed to rum when they met in the palace, the way his fingers warmed on the flask. That time, they'd both pulled away. This time, she was surprised her spell had been that strong.

Once outside, she paused on the landing, her back against the door. Her heart was racing, but instead of hurrying away she put her ear to the door, tried and failed to hear anything. Damn the stars but she wasn't thinking clearly. It was coincidence his coming here. She hadn't given him enough credit. His uncle had sent him searching for the chest, and a pawnshop was an obvious place to try. She should have kept him talking, found out what, if anything, he knew about the other thieves.

*   *   *

Davit watched through the window until she disappeared around a corner. "Who was that?" he asked. "A customer? She seems familiar. Do you know her?"

Brittle shook his head. "Never seen her before and didn't catch her name. Didn't catch her anything. She's smooth, though, I'll give her that. Have I ever told you, you have the worst possible timing? A few minutes earlier and you could have asked her yourself. A few minutes later and I'd have had her spells. Could have sold them pretty quick."

"Did you see her eyes? I made her jump, didn't I? She couldn't have recognized me, unless she'd been at the ball? I don't think she was. I wouldn't forget a face like hers."

"Step back," Brittle ordered. "Get your elbows off my counter."

Davit moved aside as Brittle leaned over, his face a hair's breadth from the glass. He sniffed, wrinkled his nose, move to the left and sniffed again.

"You have no idea how ridiculous that looks. What are you doing?"

"Patience," Brittle said. He rummaged below the counter and brought out a small, black shell. He opened it and a sprinkling of sand spilled across the glass. He murmured a few words, drew a finger through the grains then licked it. "Humph." He rubbed his nose. "Nothing. Not a trace. She said she wasn't a witch but if those spells were family heirlooms, I'm a princes' ass."

"What does it matter whether she's a witch? You're not. I'm not. Wouldn't want to be." Davit frowned. "What sort of spells?"

"If she's a witch that's her business. If she's lying in my shop, it's mine. But look here." Brittle came around the counter and held out Molly's spiked replicator.

"What is it?" Davit reached for the ball but pulled back. "Nope. Not touching spells I don't know about. She gave it to you?"

"Not exactly. If I see her again, I'll tell her I found it on the floor."

"You're giving it back? Why not sell it to Watermen? I thought you like their money."

"I do. I will. But not until I've got her trust. Where there's one spell, there's more."

"But what if she found it? Or someone else stole it and she's selling it for them? What is it anyway?"

"A replicator, though I doubt I can work it without the cog's instructions." He pulled off his apron, tossed it to a stool. "Must be one of those days, nothing goes right."

Davit glanced to the window. "Depends what you're looking for."

Brittle followed his glance. "Easy for you to say. How many times have I been stopped by a guild rat while you, they take one look and doff their hat and remind you to be careful, sir. Night Watermen been seen, sir. They never give you a hard time."

"Did you see her eyes? She nearly punched me. You'll tell me if she comes back, won't you? Or if you learn her name? I'd hate to think I just fell in love with a married woman."

"She looked like a thief, that's what she looked like. And I'll wager you a day's profit that either her silk purse was stolen from the governor—your uncle, sir—or she knows something about it."

"She's too pretty to be a thief," Davit said. "At least not a common thief. And my uncle, sir, is no smarter than a horse's ass."

*　　*　　*

By the time Molly reached the sea wall it was almost noon and the usual crowd of people hoping for work had already gathered. Men and women stood in line at the tables and jostled their way to the wall to check the postings for day laborers and dock workers, sailors and cooks. She elbowed her way toward the wall and read a few of the broadsides. '*Stolen Cargo. Payment Available for Information leading to Detection and Arrest.*' The date was old; it wasn't the chest.

'*Opportunity Available,*' read another. '*The Following Guild Halls Encourage Young Witches to Test. Apply. Apprentice: Winder Hall. Hark Hall. Gavrin Hall, etcetera*'

And this one that was riddled with holes from all the times it had been pulled down and tacked back up. '*Any Witch Engaged in Selling or Trading Non-Registered Spells Shall Be Subject to Punishment, Censorship and Trial. By order of—*'

She glanced over her shoulder and saw a few soldiers, but none nearby. And a man in front of a tavern across the road. She looked again and was certain he was the sailor from Brittle's shop, getting ready to drink his money away, though that was his business, not hers.

There was often trouble on the streets above the wharf. Sailors and dock workers, human and witch alike; they cursed and spat and elbowed each other for the chance of being the first to find paid work, or if not that, a few meals in exchange for labor. Fights broke out and guild rats disappeared when you needed them. At a table to Molly's right, a woman with white hair promised to settle complaints for unpaid wages. To her left, a few boys—couldn't have been more than twelve—pestered a man with a sign calling for work on a fish tender.

She found an empty spot on the wall, opened her satchel and pulled out the broadside she had crafted that morning.

Attention
Crew Members Desired
Must be Registered Seamen, Ready to Sail
~Bosun, Carpenters, Barrel Makers~
Male or Female ~ Human or Witch
Kapreil Family Traders
Gin Isle

She rather liked the name, she thought as she pinned it up. She'd thought of it just that morning. And Gin was far enough, she'd wager there wasn't an officer here in Auklet would go to the trouble of inquiring whether the Kapreil family did in fact exist. They didn't, but she'd be long gone before it became a problem.

She read the required wording at the bottom: '*Said owners agree to comply with all regulations etc., etc. All vessels weighing more than fifty-five tons will be crewed by human and witch, both and together.*' She checked that she'd gotten the harbor master's name correct then stepped back and was surprised to see a few men and women already vying to read the post. They looked as if they could use a bath along with the promise of a day's wage. She caught the flash of a witch's mark peering from under one man's sleeve, another on a woman's arm. And not far behind, a soldier strolling by.

He stopped to question an older man leading a donkey by a rope while passersby averted their eyes and hurried away. She thought of Governor Navarr barking in outrage when he realized the chest had been stolen. Late night guests refusing to leave until they'd been compensated and him trying to explain that it was all for their safety. Protection. She pictured them early the next morning, pounding at the gates. His breakfast interrupted. Wife harping at his incompetence.

What she couldn't puzzle out was how—and why— the two guards in the tunnel hurried so quickly back to the palace and warned Navarr? If they were stealing the chest, why turn themselves in?

The only thing that made sense was that they hadn't run back at all. They had planned it out ahead of time, hired, or conspired with the people waiting to take the chest. But who were they? And what about the second group shooting at them? At her?

"That notice stamped and dated, ma'am?" Molly winced and smoothed her expression. She hadn't seen the guard approach.

Her father used to tell her that before she was born, there were fewer soldiers in the towns. Guild officers yes, guards and sentinels and sailors in uniform yes, but fewer men and women actually trained to fight.

The same was true for vessels; they seldom used to carry heavy guns, certainly not near harbors so inconsequential as those on Murrock or Tars. There was no need. The king ruled half a world away in Jamasak with his council and astrologers. Guild halls regulated the crafts. Governors kept order in the towns. There was the black market Night Watermen, but not so many as now, and human trade and witches' craft shops carried on their business side by side.

By the time she was ten her father allowed her to accompany him on short trips aboard the *Ice Warden* while Evan, only four, stayed safe with their mother in Luna's Cove. Their ship was fitted with swivel guns on the weather deck and four, four pounders below. But her father tensed when they came in sight of another vessel and warned her to wait below until he knew whether they were merchants or privateers, Night Watermen or guild.

The world, he said, was changing. The thousand years the stars had promised were coming to an end and no one knew anymore where truth ended, and falsehoods began. Too much had been lost with time. The king, the governor and the guild, everyone, was in an uproar. What was apparent was that there were fewer master witches and fewer cogs to sell. And with fewer sales the guild couldn't afford their ships and manors. But as much as her father mistrusted the guild, he worried about being found by Night Watermen more.

Time went on, and the changes grew stronger. Molly was seldom allowed in the towns anymore, and more of her parent's conversations revolved around the king's newest galleon or some governor's growing fleet.

Human trade shops grew wealthy smelting iron and manufacturing gun powder, while the last of the witch's privately-owned craft shops were taken over by the guild and suddenly, there were beggars on the streets. Her parents, Senesh and Esty Sinclair sold the unregistered spells they crafted in secret and she and Evan were left to hide in the safety of Luna's Cove while their expeditions to the rim grew more frequent.

And for what? Chunks of broken-off ice? Is that what they wanted? The stars had shaped the world with magic. They created the isles to be a haven, safe and temperate and warm, protected by a ring of ice, the boundary that hemmed the world and never changed, never melted. Except that sometimes, more often of late, it did. And when people found a floating pan or craggy tower of rim ice, they hauled in whatever chips and bits they could carry and sold them where they could.

Was that what her parents were doing when they disappeared? Gathering rim ice so they could keep hiding on Luna's Cove and run from the guild? The Cove was safe. They'd warded the tiny isle with spells to prevent anyone from approaching. No wave could carry a ship toward its beaches. No wind would fill its sails. The shoals and reefs were treacherous. Rocky pillars stood close and sharp. It didn't matter. Molly was done with hiding. She wouldn't repeat her parent's mistakes.

They'd taken the *Ice Warden* but left her and Evan the *Fish*. It was fast, but she needed a second, heavier vessel for hauling cargo. She meant to fill its hold, buy, trade, sell and steal until she had enough money to build a home in Doshaget or Sophen, right in the middle of Pyr or Hawley if she liked, it didn't matter so long as it wasn't under the king's thumb, and they no longer needed to hide.

She turned and faced the guard, a smile pasted on her face.

He was a short man with a chest band strung with shells and a log book in the crook of his arm. His brown hair was plaited with tiny beads that clacked as he moved. "Can I help you?" she asked.

"Looks like you're hiring. And your papers, they're all in order?"

"Yes, sir."

"And your ship?"

"Yes sir. It's owned by the Kapreil Family Traders. Papers are signed by the Harbor Master. You can see it right there."

"I can, and don't get cocky. If you got a ship, you'll have a crew and I'll need the roster. If all you've got are humans, just the names will do. You got witches, I'll need the halls where they apprenticed." He flipped open his book, found a pen.

Molly rummaged through her satchel and drew out a paper. It held the same forged signature and counterfeit seals that allowed the *Fish* entry into most ports where she traded. She handed it to the soldier and did her best to look composed.

"By order of the king, yeah, yeah. You're licensed to take on cargo bearing ten barrels of oil, salt pork, hides and bolts of cotton, wool and spices." He glanced at Molly's arm, found no craft mark and continued reading. Molly stared at the side of his head.

What she had thought from a distance were beads were seeing eyes, common on soldier's uniforms. A few were gray, others with pupils like cat-eye slits, none larger than the tip of her finger. The seeing eye nearest Molly blinked awake and memorized her face, height, clothes. What it saw a captain would later see. Nothing would be lost, nothing forgotten. "I'm sure you'll find everything in order." She wondered if she should have changed her face as well as her clothes when she started out that morning, but she'd thought the low-cut neckline and lapis pendant would give the guild rats—men and women alike—something other than stolen spells to think about. It had worked for Davit Lake, hadn't it? And the odd look he gave when their fingers chanced to touch? He'd stared at his hand, not hers. She was safe.

The soldier frowned. "These papers are for your cargo, ma'am. The notice says you're hiring a crew? I need the names. It's a simple request."

A spell, she warned herself, though she already had an idea. *A quick, simple spell.* "Excuse me. Wrong paper," she apologized and reached into her satchel and found a clean sheet of parchment.

She pictured the letters she needed, the curl of an r, the down slanted y, the details of name, craft and hall invented on the spot. Names he wanted, and names he'd have. She tapped a finger and words appeared. Black flourishes. The ink already dry.

"Here we are, crew's registry," she said, but suddenly, out of nowhere, the sailor from Brittle's shop was at her side.

"Sorry I took so long getting back, ma'am," he said.

Molly hid her surprise. The sailor was taller than she remembered, cleaner, and not drunk. He carried a pistol and a dirk with its handle wrapped in tiny shells and he placed his hand familiarly on her arm. She opened, then closed her mouth and didn't pull away.

He glanced earnestly at the soldier. "Name's Cobb, sir. Macklin Cobb. We don't have a full roster as the lady says, which is why we're hiring. I'm out of Hark Hall on Dunsan isle." He glanced sideways at Molly.

The soldier looked confused. "Then you do have new hires? Just not their background?"

"I can row back to our ship, sir. I know exactly where the papers are." He leaned toward Molly and whispered, "This would be a good time to pass him a coin."

His voice was level and frank, but she wondered what he wanted. Most people wanted something these days. Food. Work. A place to hide. Information about illegal cogs he could turn over to the guild in exchange for a few month's freedom.

She didn't think he'd do that. He could lie, that was apparent, but she needed to make a quick decision and she surprised herself by trusting him. Aloud, she said, "That's a generous offer, Mr. Cobb. And you'll be properly thanked as soon as we're done."

The soldier glanced suspiciously between them. "You know, don't you, there was a theft at the palace last night? A few guards were killed."

Molly grimaced. She'd heard cries in the field but didn't know anyone died. It wasn't her bullet, but it could have been. The shooting was wild and random. She wasn't afraid to use a gun. She'd kill if she had to, to protect Evan most of all. She'd do anything for her brother.

She passed the soldier a coin and it disappeared in his belt.

"Yes, sir," Macklin said. "News like that travels fast, and folks are saying there were witches involved. Couldn't have been me. I used to be a weathercrafter, but not anymore." He pushed up his sleeve and held out his arm. "And anyway, we were all shipside last night."

The soldier grunted, and Molly saw the web of hideous burn marks he'd covered at Brittle's shop. "And how long would that take?" the soldier asked. "The rowing, I mean."

"I can be there and back in an hour. Two at the most."

The soldier glanced past Molly to the tavern across the way. A woman in a red dress stood in the doorway, her arms wrapped around a man. "Tell you what," he said. "Seeing as I can't just stand around waiting, why don't you come find me when you've got those papers? Tomorrow will be fine." The seeing eyes in his hair blinked shut and without waiting for a reply, he hurried across the road.

Molly waited till he was gone then reeled on the sailor. "And what would you have done, Mr. Cobb if he accepted that offer?"

"Him?" Macklin laughed. "Wouldn't happen. He's lazy as a dog and hasn't got the rank to care. Did you notice, he didn't ask the name of your ship, or where you're sailing. But, if you don't mind my asking," he said, more seriously. "I am looking for work. I wasn't making that up."

Molly watched as a woman seated at one of the nearby tables pushed a paper toward an eager young man and handed him a pen. "Macklin Cobb?" she asked. "That's your real name?" The sailor nodded, and Molly glanced to her broadside. *Crew members desired. Registered seamen, ready to sail.* Not a single person had glanced at the posting since the soldier walked up.

Sail what? Molly asked herself. Her plans weren't fully formed, but they were nearly all she thought about. She wanted that second ship. One hundred and fifty tons. Lateen and square rigged like the *Fish,* but heavier to carry cargo. She needed that second ship and a crew to sail it. She'd need a bosun to take charge of the ship's stores, the cordage and sails and oil. A carpenter and a skilled cooper, navigators. She knew it sounded backwards, assembling a crew before she had the ship, but she wanted to be ready.

In which case… She turned back around. She could start with Macklin Cobb. He had already proved himself useful, and she could use a good weathercrafter, though she wasn't sure how much of his craft remained. She'd never worked with someone who'd lost their mark. "Do you mind if I ask about those scars, Mr. Cobb? You lost your craft?"

"I didn't lose it," he said firmly. "The guild took my livelihood, not my craft. I'm as useful as any rigger, sail master and navigator combined. You won't regret taking me on. But you want to know what I did? It's simple. I sold a spell to the wrong person. I guaranteed some noblewoman, fifth cousin of a cousin of the king, that I could bring a storm. I should have known not to trust the stink of her Jamasak perfume. But I wanted the work and the money was good and I signed my name.

"The lady wanted a storm raised. Needed it to coincide with the arrival of a certain captain undercutting her business. Buying and selling wine. Olives and sugar cane and pearls. His ship was bursting with cargo and slow, but I didn't know he had witches on board and fool that I was, I assumed I would have been told.

"My storm struck, but his witches found a channel and sailed through. I raised a second wind, stronger than the first but, another oversight on the lady's part. She never told me she'd sent a fighting ship on the same course and it was caught in my storm. Slammed into the rocks, the vessel sank and next thing I know the guild drags me into a hall and cuts out my mark, so I can't sell a cog.

"The stars give, but the guild takes away. Or at least they try. I can still calm a wind or raise a storm, end a drought or find a current. Just can't let the guild find out. And if I can't sell a spell, I can't earn a living. Can't pay for a room. Can hardly afford a meal unless some shopkeeper is kind enough to hand me a mop and toss a coin. Problem is these days, there's too many witches willing to push the same broom."

Molly glanced about. The crowd had disbursed, and no one was in earshot. "And if I offer you a berth, I expect you'll want to hear about the nature of the work?"

Macklin shrugged. "Not necessary ma'am. Or, at least not yet. Here's the thing, and I don't expect you to discuss your business with every hand, and I'm not asking how your ship came in yesterday without a crew but smooth as any landing I've seen, and that with a wind blowing strong. But take me on and I'll work without wages for a week and if you're satisfied, sign me up for more. If not, we shake hands and go our ways and no one's the wiser."

Molly stared in surprise. She was always careful with the *Fish*. She made sure it appeared unremarkable, at least from shore. But if he figured out that she sailed without a crew, others might notice as well. "You lied to that soldier," she said. "How do I know you're not lying to me?"

"Fair question but look at it from my side. I lied to that guild rat, and you didn't flinch. You pretended to know me and lied that you have a crew. You don't, do you?"

Molly glanced to the street. There was a woman selling sausages from a cart. A lone girl calling, "Bananas, ripe bananas for sale." Two well-dressed gentlemen passed by, their ivory walking sticks tapping in a matched staccato rhythm. Any one of them could be spying. Nor could she shake the feeling that Davit Lake had followed from Brittle's shop. He could be anywhere, watching from an alley.

She looked Macklin in the eye and lied. "I do need a crew," she said. "For a second ship I mean to buy. The ship you saw me on, the *Fish*, it runs on spells, cogs that are registered and paid for. The sails are made in a trade shop. The hull is maintained by a stonecrafter that cleans the algae. And there's a shipbuilder I know takes care of the chinking. The Kapreil family spares no expense."

Macklin seemed impressed. "Then let me help you. I know this town. I know the witches and the humans and who's a drunkard and who'll be grateful for the work. And I'll do it in half the time it would take you alone, and if you're not satisfied put me off at the next port."

Molly considered the offer. She liked the man and wanted to give him a chance. He was blustery and straight forward and his eyes seemed honest. "I'll do that, Mr. Cobb," she said. "But if I find that you lied or cheated me, or that you aren't the weathercrafter you claim, I won't just put you off at the next port. I'll put you off in a jolly boat and the stars take you where they will."

3

Of Hayden Hall Witches' Guild
Apprentices, Journeymen and Masters

Molly tossed her purchases over the rail and climbed aboard the *Fish*. "Evan?" she called. There was no answer and she called again.

Macklin dropped his duffle behind her, glanced about and nodded appreciatively. "How old did you say your brother was?"

"Fifteen. And he's here, somewhere." She glanced at Macklin. She wasn't sure she'd done the right thing, allowing a stranger aboard. She was only beginning to realize the effort it would take to keep up the ruse and pretend her spells were purchased. "He's probably asleep," she said offhandedly. "Why don't you settle yourself below and I'll find you in a bit."

Macklin cocked his head. "If you mean to leave under sail, ma'am, I could check—"

"No need," she said. "We're fine."

"Then we'll sit out the tide?"

She looked to the rigging, the topmast. Evan often sat there, his legs dangling in the air. He liked to watch people, miniature figures far below, coming and going about their business, but there was no sign of him there.

"I could cook up some dinner? Clean the galley?"

"Not necessary, just… It's a bit tight below. Find yourself a place for your hammock."

Macklin gave her a look. "Right then. I best be going."

Molly waited until he disappeared through the hatch. She didn't think Evan had run away; their dinghy was still there, covered with a canvas sheet. He wasn't perched on the bowsprit, and not sulking among the coiled lines where he hid when he was small.

Their parents had built the ship. They layered it with repair and transmute spells that took care of everything from chinking to clearing barnacles and tarring the lines and Molly trusted the ship with her life. The *Fish* was sixty-five feet, a caravel with a lateen sail on the mizzen mast and two square sails on the main, a forecastle and double stern castle. She was built for speed and maneuverability and her figurehead, a giant blue and white winged fish, looked as if it could leap for the sky. Wooden bubbles issued from its lips and its scales were large as a fist.

It was shortly after she and Evan left Luna Cove's hidden shores that she realized one of them had to come up legally through the guild, serve their time as apprentice, journeyman then master, and receive a mark. Legally. Documented. Registered. She enrolled Evan in Hanna Hall, purchased her first safe house on the far side of the isle, and added his fees to the reasons she kept thieving.

She knew the risks and what would happen if they were caught. Not about the stealing—that could be resolved with a few gold pieces, but if the guild learned the kind of witches they were. They'd be shipped off to the king in Jamasak and locked away in prison. Punished for being what they were. Or…

She thought of Macklin's arm. The guild had cut out his mark, scarred him and ruined his chance for a normal life. They'd do the same to Evan. Or worse. She heard stories, terrible stories of kidnapping and secret rituals at sea, in the dead of night.

"Evan!" she called again.

"Over here." His voice, thin as a boy's, came from above. She shielded her eyes, found him settled on the main mast's top yard where she'd just searched. He leaned precariously forward, waved something for her to see.

"What have you got?" she called, but she already guessed. She glanced to the deck and saw the stolen chest at the base of the mast, its top thrown back. She tried to sound calm. "Why don't you come down," she called. "I can't see from here."

He winced as he stepped along the yard, teetered then caught himself. By the time he reached the deck Molly was kneeling over the chest and Evan was grimacing, his left arm pressed tight against his side, right hand in a fist. "It's sharp," he said. "I'm going to put it down."

Molly peered inside the chest. A few of the shells had opened and objects fallen out. There were trinkets and stones and knives. Flowers that were infused with a spell rather than carried in a shell. There were combs to hold women's complicated hairpieces, flickering lights and tiny shoes to help someone dance all night.

"I tried to stop it," Evan said. "As soon as I got the chest open. I tried a create and destroy spell that I had gotten to work once before. No, twice. I thought at first it was a shell, but it didn't open. It's the whole thing."

"You should have waited till I got back."

"You were gone so long. It got away, but I caught it again." He crouched beside her and slowly spread his fingers. A small, spiked gray ball rolled to the deck, then stopped.

"It's a replicator," Molly exclaimed. "I brought one like that to the pawnshop."

"The spikes are sharp. It hurt."

Molly heard Macklin singing below and glanced to the hatch. *There's a wind, west wind, took me far from my home, and the dear sweet maid who cried when I roamed…*

Evan froze. "What's that?"

Molly winced. She had hoped for more time to explain, but now with the chest open, she wasn't sure where to begin. "That's Macklin Cobb," she said tentatively. "He's going to stay with us for a while."

But the stars called me on and there's gold to be found, and the wind, north wind, took me far from my home…

"Stay with us? What are you talking about? Who is he? Does he know about the chest?"

"No, and I'm not going to tell him. A guild rat was questioning me, and he distracted him. He lives here. He can help hire a crew."

"But you just met him."

"Yes, but it doesn't matter," she insisted. "He's a weathercrafter. He—" She caught herself and stopped. "Give him a chance, Evan. We talked about hiring a crew. You know that. You agreed. But… Why don't we look inside the chest for now, see what we find?"

Evan gave her a look, then shrugged and moved nearer. Molly pulled out a walnut sized shell encased in gold then dropped it as a dagger crawled up the side, as easily as if it were a snake slithering through grass. The dagger began gnawing back and forth, sawing the rim until she tapped it. The blade stiffened, the sawing stopped.

She pried the dagger loose and looked for a sign to show which guild hall registered the spell, but there wasn't any.

"Look at this." Evan laughed and held out a soft looking ball and Molly set the dagger aside and took it.

When a customer walked into a guild shop and purchased a spell, they paid their money and gave their name, and went home with the spell encased in a shell. Ornate shells if they could afford the price, simpler ones if not. The shells themselves weren't magic. They housed the spell a master witch infused with their craft and sold to the guild in the form of instructions: the chant, object and gesture necessary for the buyer to work the spell. The shells were locked in drawers or tied onto belts, chest bands, jewelry and carried wherever their owners went.

"It's moving," she said as the ball eased its way up her sleeve. Her arm grew warm. The ache in her shoulder began to fade. A pleasant sensation stretched from her fingers to her neck. "It's a soother," she said. "Imagine Navarr's guests, stuck in those stiff chairs, furious to have their soothers taken."

Evan reached for another. "This one's ugly." He held up a marble-sized eye without lid or lashes. "Who'd bring that to a ball?"

"Anyone who could afford it," Molly said. "It's for spying on your neighbors. Turn it over. Sometimes there's a mouth on the other side and it can speak as well. Maybe that's why Navarr collected the spells, he didn't want someone spying on his nephew?"

"I've seen them at Hayden Hall. A few apprentices made them. I never tried."

"See if it works."

Evan stiffened. "Why? There's no cog with it. If I can't work it out, you'll say that proves I should go back to my studies."

"No, I thought it would be fun. That's all."

Evan wrinkled his nose. "I suppose. But if nothing happens… You won't say a word?"

"I swear on the stars."

"Well. Maybe." He took back the eye and rolled it around his palm. It was glass-like, hard and translucent. "If it's a seeing eye, it might have something to do with navigation. But that could be navigation by any of the crafts. Fire or ice, water or sky. I'll try sky."

Molly held quiet.

"I'm not sure if I should try an attract and repel, repair and transmute, or create and destroy spell. I remember it was in the guild's list, in the Grimoire, but I need a chant."

He murmured something, too softly for Molly to hear, then dipped his forehead and blew on it. Nothing happened. The eye didn't move. It didn't blink or sway or reveal hidden secrets.

"Something else?" she suggested. "A different chant?"

Evan tried again. "I already have the object," he murmured. "It needs the chant and the gesture to finish the cog. I should change one element at a time." He scratched his head, tried to remember the guild spells, then circled his finger around the eye. "*Out of day to see, through night to hear.*" He hesitated as the air began to move—nothing clear—but a ripple, like steam from a kettle.

Molly held her breath as Evan tried again. "*Day to see and night to hear. Eye to search and mind to find.*" The eye began to rotate. It turned a full circle and a moment later a miniature *Fish* floated between Molly and Evan. "Of course," she laughed. "It sees the *Fish*. I wonder if it remembers what we said."

"I could try a different way," Evan said, but then he stopped. He opened his hand and dropped the eye back in the chest and the image of the *Fish* blinked out. "It doesn't prove a thing," he said. "You craft spells, and no one forced you to apprentice. I hate Hayden Hall. I can't do half of what they teach anyway, and I won't be a parrot, if that's what you want. Chant. Object. Gesture. Chant. Object. Gesture." He rose and walked angrily to the rail.

Molly stayed where she was. A wind had come up and the ship moved with the swells. "Evan, please." He didn't turn. "You have to go back. It's not just about learning spells. You'll figure them out. It's about being legal, protecting the *Fish*. It won't be much longer. But Master Ossian doesn't take kindly to truancy."

"Ossian doesn't take kindly to anything I do."

She stared at his back. How was she supposed to answer her brother when she was right, but he wasn't wrong? When every choice she made began with keeping him safe?

She rummaged through the chest and pulled out a glossy shell painted with waves and wind, probably a weather spell inside. She shook it. Shells were sometimes keyed to the owner's touch but this one opened easily. She unrolled the scroll and read the cog: *Wind be clear, and wind be free, taste of sky and taste of sea. From the (insert direction) in calm or gale, raise the current, set the sail.*

When it came to guild spells others had made, she could work them well enough, the same as anyone. But when it came to crafting the guild-sanctioned spells apprentices were taught in the halls, she wasn't half as skilled as Evan. Oh, she could repeat the chant, add the correct gesture and once in a while hold a spell longer than a moment but beyond that… No. Compared to what Evan was learning as an apprentice, her methods were wild.

Crafting spells the way her parents taught worked far better for her than any guild method. It was because she had never apprenticed, never memorized their spells or had a teaching master guide her lessons the way Evan had. And if they were difficult for him, they were near impossible for her.

Do it this way, her mother used to say, and Molly could almost see Esty Sinclair standing nearby, hands flat on the *Fish's* planks. Her hair, except for the one tight curl falling to her forehead, would be pulled back. And she'd be wearing her red vest with the laces Molly used to pull, and around her neck the gold chain with the chip of rim ice, so clear Molly could see through it to the other side.

To ward the Fish, you need to concentrate. Close your eyes, but only if you want; there's no rule. What matters is that you focus, but not on yourself. Go deeper. Think of the oak, the living heart inside. Feel the grain and the knots where sap once flowed. And then, because it isn't a tree any longer but a board, feel its angles, its history. Feel the surface where the carpenter's plane smoothed the wood. Think of the dowel holding the boards together and the way they touch. And when you have those things firmly in your mind's eye, feel the board's strength. Let it be whole. Let it be well. And then pull back. You are Molly Sinclair. You crafted the spell, but it isn't yours. The board is part of the Fish. Your work is to make it whole. Now release, and you're done.

Molly could speed the wind. Raise a current. Turn a sail. Light a fire. Ease a boulder from a hill. Grow a seedling. Open a lock. Not all at once, but fire, water, sky or ice. She worked them all. But a guild cog? Hardly ever.

She needed Evan to understand that for all his mishaps and frustration, he was better at learning them than she would ever be. She was too old to apprentice. Evan still had a chance. And once he had a legal charter… She stopped. Macklin was singing again. She wished he wouldn't.

There's a wind, east wind, took me far from my home, and the arms of the maid I called my own. When she favored me with kisses than I asked her to be my missus, there's a wind east wind took me far from my home.

But a moment later she heard another sound. She turned and saw the replicator Evan had left on the deck. It was rocking and she reached out, tried to pick it up, but the spikes pricked her hand. "Ouch!" she cried.

Evan spun about, and the replicator started rolling. Molly reached for it, but the ball shot away.

"Where's it going?" Evan called. It sped over a coiled rope and across the decking, rolling and spinning and driving itself around stacked barrels and hatch covers.

Molly ran after it and Evan scrambled on hands and knees, nearly caught it then missed as it disappeared into a mouse-sized opening behind a barrel. "Did you see the spikes?" Molly laughed.

"It looked like a sea urchin. Do you think it's alive?"

She knelt and felt behind the barrel, but nothing was there. "It can't be," she said. "It's a guild spell, that's all."

They rolled the barrel aside, but the spiked ball wasn't there, and they were about to give up when they heard a ticking sound and turned to see one of the curved barrel staves peel away from the others. It hit the deck and rolled itself into a ball again, spiked and brittle and noisy. Behind it, the barrel stood intact.

The ball whirled across the deck, struck the mainmast and stopped. Evan eased toward it, but his shadow crossed the replicator and quick as a nod, the needles folded in on themselves. One moment it was a spiked ball, the next it flattened itself against the smooth wooden plate— a base with four sides, holes and bolts and rings that secured the mast. Try as they might, they couldn't pry it free, couldn't tell where the real plate began, or the replicator ended or if it was there at all.

Evan grew thoughtful. "You should copy it," he said. "Figure it out and craft one of your own. Think of the money it would bring."

Molly didn't answer. She couldn't tell whether he was serious or starting another argument about Hayden Hall. He didn't want to go back—she knew that— but he'd be strong someday, though it would be in his own way, of course. He was different from other witches, and so was she. Same as their mother was different. Same as their father. Same as their mother's mother. And for all she knew, through earlier generations as well. And there lay the root of their problems.

By every history she'd read, by every law and sign on every guild shop wall, that wasn't supposed to happen.

The Star's gift of magic, the ability to craft spells, was carried within a witch's blood. It continued through the mother's side and skipped a generation. A child, male or female, born to a human mother could be either witch or human. The child of a witch could only be human. But the crafts returned in that witch's grandchildren. So it had been since the stars first walked the isles. Except in the Sinclair family and per-haps—Molly didn't know—in other craftborn families where witches were born of witches and the gift had not waned with the passing of time. It grew stronger.

It was the reason Molly's parents wouldn't risk bringing her to a guild hall to be tested in their dome of the stars where the truth of a witch's blood was revealed. The dark lights that spilled across the evening skies reacted to witches. They found them. Touched them. As if the lights were curtains rippling on unseen winds, they reached into the small domes with their four pillars made of ice, found a witch's arm and marked it.

And in the guild halls where the even the strongest witches were able to craft only one of the four elemental spells, ice or water, fire or sky, the masters would be very interested to learn that she and Evan could craft any of them. All. And there were other things they'd demand to know—how many times could their spells be reused. How many could they craft in a day, and how strong were they? How did they do it? Had they taught themselves? Or was it their blood?

It was the reason they were renegades. It was the reason for everything she did.

Records were kept. Archived by the guild and the king. Tracked by astrologers and clerks. Centuries spent tracing bloodlines, libraries filled with genealogies and the names of witches who apprenticed, became journeymen and masters. The names of their brothers, sisters, mothers and grandmothers.

She could forge papers until the stars returned, but one of these days they'd be caught and imprisoned. It would be easier if one of them was legal. She was too old. It had to be Evan. All that was required was four years as an apprentice, two as a journeyman, and after that one master spell worthy enough for the guild to sign his papers and they'd be free.

Evan sighed. "It wasn't my fault it got out of the chest," he said. "And you couldn't catch it either. But I'm tired of arguing. You want me back at Hayden Hall? All right. I'll go. But I'll do it my way. I'll craft a spell so strong, Ossian will sign my charter right there. He'll see I'm worth more than his fees, and you will, too. There's always another way, Molly. You just don't want to see."

He turned to walk away, then changed his mind and sank to the deck, drew up his knees. Molly sat beside him. He was getting taller, she noticed. Her legs were only a little longer than his. She felt protective and worried, just as she had in the early days on Luna's Cove when they finally accepted that it was the two of them, alone together. "Remember how we used to bring our blankets outside and sleep on the sand?"

Evan nodded. "We used to dribble sand in our hair and pull crabs from the shallows. And sometimes we'd sleep on the deck, right there." He pointed to the quarter deck. "And you used to tell stories about the stars."

"You'd pick out one of the constellations and that's whose story I'd tell." Molly tried to remember. "And the stars looked down from their ships and saw a paradise so beautiful, a land so lush and fertile—"

"Remember how we used to laugh at that word, 'lush?' You used to say it so funny. Lussshhh. Go on. Do the rest."

"I will if you let me," she elbowed him in the side. "They saw a paradise so beautiful, they turned their ships and sailed the river of dark lights down, down, down to the isles. And the very next day when the sun rose in the sky, they pulled from it the magic of fire and used its heat to push back the water and warm the air and raise the isles."

"I always used to wonder about that part. How could they raise the isles, when the guild says they already found them?"

"I don't know. Just… The story's so old it's a wonder it makes sense at all. And stop interrupting. I'm trying to remember… They raised the isles and cooled the fire with ice and created the rim to circle the world and stand, taller and stronger than anyone could see through or over or around and keep the isles safe for a thousand years."

"So, the ice was already there, but not the isles?"

"I told you, I don't know," Molly laughed. "But afterward… They built the first dome of the stars in Jamasak, so the dark lights would find them again and know who they were. That part was magic, but the next part is real: they dwelt in the homes they built and married with the women and men they found there, good people who were comely and tall, and they gave birth to a thousand years of witches."

Evan stopped her again. "That's us, isn't it? We're one of the generations?"

"I suppose," Molly said thoughtfully. "We must be."

"How do they count it, the guild? If we're craftborn do we count as one generation, or if everyone else skips, grandmother to grandchildren, are we two generations? What does it mean?"

Molly looked at her brother. "I don't know. No one does. But the stars were here. They were men and women, real as you and I. They came here. They shaped the isles. They're gone but we're part of them. Their descendants, their legacy. Something has to be true."

Evan grew silent, then shrugged and punched her playfully in the shoulder. He rose after that and Molly watched him walk away. At least this time, she told herself, he was talking about the stars rather than claiming she didn't want him underfoot. It wasn't true. She missed him when they were apart, even sullen and angry, she'd rather he was with her on the *Fish*. Who else could she speak openly with, or be herself, not have to hide? Who else shared her memories and hopes?

The day was growing late, clouds speeding by. She listened to the sound of wood creaking and waves lapping against the hull and Macklin, singing again. She rose and locked the chest then crafted one spell to lighten the load and another to keep it silent as she dragged it to her cabin. And one more when she had it pushed into a corner. An invisibility spell, stronger than the others and meant to last. Macklin would have to trip over the damn thing to find it, but three spells was enough for now.

* * *

A harried looking man with a collar embroidered with Hayden Hall's guild emblem—a coracle skimming the waves—stopped Molly's carriage at the gate. She leaned out the window and he looked over her silk dress, the gem encrusted netting that almost but not quite contained her hair and the dagger she'd placed prominently in her waistband. He stepped back and waved the driver through.

Situated on the cliffs atop Mann Isle, Hayden Hall was a meandering stone and timber structure surrounding a large courtyard. Additions stretched like the arms of a starfish from its core. The masters' residencies, teaching halls, stables, barns and outbuildings were in the rear. Molly had seen little beyond the main hall, but Evan described the way each wing opened onto kitchen gardens, then fields which ended in a crumbling stone wall. Trees rose above, cliffs fell to churning water far below.

Stepping from the carriage, she was surprised to find the courtyard bustling with wagons, carriages with two, four and six horses and people, most of them wearing what looked like their best clothes, milling about. When last she was here, there were only a few delivery wagons, the usual array of masters, wardens and apprentices going about their errands. Nothing so busy as this.

She turned to take Evan's arm, but he was already walking away. They had left Macklin alone on the *Fish*, an idea Evan didn't approve, but they'd been surprised to find so many guild ships in the harbor, and more than a few with heavy guns, and she wasn't willing to leave her ship unmanned. It had been ten days since last they were here; six since they stole the chest, three since Macklin came aboard and Evan still didn't trust him.

She lifted her skirts and hurried after him. "What's going on?" she whispered.

Evan glanced to the main hall. The broad double doors stood open. Miniature witch-crafted trees that hadn't been there a few weeks ago lined the outer walls. Mangoes and cherries hung from the same branches. Roses opened then closed then opened again. A line of well-scrubbed boys ran past. One skinny girl sat on a bench and tossed a stone into the air and lit it with a rainbow of colors. "New applicants," Evan said. "The testing. I forgot."

"But the equinox was two weeks ago. Shouldn't they be gone by now?"

"Ossian won't care so long as they pay the fee. But I've never seen so many at once."

Eight times each year, young witches travelled to the guild halls to be tested; on the equinoxes, solstices and four cross quarters. They came with letters, documents to prove their supposed craft. Some knew only that their maternal grandmothers had been witches. All paid an exorbitant fee for the privilege of standing inside a dome of the stars and waiting for the masters to open the roof. And when they did, and if the dark lights appeared, and if the candidate's blood contained so much as a whisper of a memory of the stars, then the lights found them. The first sign, little more than a shadow, of their craft appeared on their arm and they were accepted, along with their payment, into a hall.

For new apprentices it was a hazy flush of color. Four years later when they became journeymen, they entered a dome a second time. Guild wardens opened the roof and the dark lights shone and another, more definite sign of their craft—ice or water, fire or sky—appeared on their arm. The visit was repeated when they became a master.

Much later, with each new spell the guild approved, a gem was added; a curving row embedded along the side of the face but set by the guild this time. With a knife, not magic. Opal for the first master's spell, then obsidian. Followed by sapphire, emerald and lazurite. Ruby for a sixth—there were fewer of these and few also of corundum—and lastly diamond, for those who became high masters and wore the mark from chin to temple.

Their carriage pulled to the side to wait for Molly's return. and two men rode up on horseback. There was a flurry of activity and an older, round faced man, one of Hayden Hall's many wardens, rushed to greet them.

The riders dismounted and slapped the dust from their cloaks. "Do you know them?" Molly asked. They looked overheated and irritable as they leaned together and whispered.

"Guild masters," Evan said. "That one with the silver raven insignia is from Sommer Hall, on Bulatt. The peony would be from Pyr. Their ships were in the harbor just now."

"But why so many masters just for a testing?"

Evan gave her a look. "They let us serve food," he said. "Not discuss policy." A line of boys sprang past and he turned to watch. The one in the lead was taller and faster than the four chasing him and they didn't seem to care if they mussed their clothes. The tall boy ran with his chin high, his laugh clear above the others. And he wasn't just racing, he was leading them, glancing over his shoulder to see if they followed as he darted around a watering trough and headed toward the dome.

He was near enough to the entrance, he could have touched one of the ice pillars. He darted close, then away, then in again as if it was a game and he didn't care that it was forbidden.

The boy bent over, hands on his knees, breathing heavily. He looked up and, out of the entire courtyard, his gaze locked on Evan's, but only for a moment and the boys were on him again. He sprung from their reach and raced off, shouting as he led them behind the long row of carriages.

A new one had just pulled in. Its dark wood gleamed, and gold lanterns swayed from the roof. One of the drivers, a woman in a red frock coat, placed a stool beneath the carriage door. An older woman stepped out and behind her a girl with unkempt, shoulder length hair the color of wheat jumped to the ground and surveyed the yard. She had an improbable look about her, as if she had purposefully dressed in plain clothes rather than silks and refused any attempt to brush her hair.

The woman raised her voice to scold the girl, except she was already too far off. She stepped to the center of the yard, leaned out to watch the boys running by, and caught sight of Evan watching her.

Molly touched his arm. Heron Sanders, First Warden of Hayden Hall motioned them to follow. Evan glanced at the master, rolled his eyes and the girl dipped her head in agreement.

Sanders was a short, barrel-chested man, ungainly in his loose robe and pinched velvet shoes. He led them through a corridor and into the high-ceilinged hall where long rows of trestle tables were being laid for dinner and apprentices on ladders fitted candles into globes. "I hope you're not hungry," he said. "We're feeding a dozen masters tonight, and the cooks will cut off your hand if you so much as touch the table."

Molly pretended to admire the silver candle stands. "Why so many masters?" she asked.

"For the testing, of course. They always come."

"He's lying," Evan whispered. "Families come. Not masters."

"Of course," she said, trying to sound impressed. "No wonder there were so many guild ships in the harbor. All those cannons."

"I hadn't noticed. We're almost there." Sanders cleared his throat.

"Who are they fighting?"

He gazed appraisingly at her. "There is no fighting, my dear. Unless you're thinking of pirates? Night Watermen? There's been scuffles of late. And as to the applicants, they're here because the king called for witches. And if the king wants witches, Hayden Hall will provide them."

He glanced at Evan. "We're crowded you know. Much more since you've been gone."

Molly didn't trust him. Sanders had a tuft of flyaway gray hair and large ears that made it difficult to take him seriously. She glanced at the line of gems embedded along his jaw and upward toward his ear. Opal. Obsidian. Sapphire. Emerald. Lazurite and ruby. Only Ossian, with his faceted corundum had more.

The narrow corridor widened as they reached the solar. High backed chairs formed a waiting area outside the door, but Sanders didn't ask them to sit. He knocked, waited for a reply, then entered the high master's quarters.

Ossian Rangor was seated behind a bare, ornate desk. Its sides were carved with sea horses and twining strands of kelp and wide-eyed carp. Ossian glanced briefly at them and returned to the papers in his hand. He was a tall, olive skinned man, gray haired, clean shaven. His eyes were dark, his brows ragged, nearly white. Sanders motioned for Molly and Evan to sit then took his leave.

Twenty years ago, when the isle's former king, Seym Makken, passed away and his eldest son died following a sudden fever, Artice Makken had taken the throne. He was forty-five, the second of four brothers, and in short order called for a new alignment of the High Council. He replaced entrenched astrologers with younger men and women, turned governors out of their palaces and deeded their landholdings to those he trusted more. He maintained the ancient laws which decreed that while the isle's kings and queens could be either witch or human, the High Council would be comprised only of witches, the governors only humans.

Safe in his palace in Jamasak, in the very center of the isles, he replaced most of the high masters. Ossian, who had raced skimmers with Artice in their younger days, was given Hayden Hall on Mann Isle where rich veins of copper, gold and iron ore enhanced the guild's wealth.

Ossian rode to its doors in full regalia and handed his papers to Geon Isillan, an elderly watercrafter who considered himself fortunate to be granted a ship and allowed to leave with his wife. But these days, Molly questioned whether any guild master held more than a shred of allegiance to the king who placed them in power.

Evan was growing impatient. He tapped his foot, leaned to the side and tried to see through the tall windows to the dome and the boy and girl he'd seen there.

Ossian continued to read. Warm though the day was, he wore a fur collared jacket with Hayden Hall's coracle stitched on the chest. The coracle was repeated on the wall above his desk, to the right of the King's symbol—a sun between two hands— and on the left, a conch shell, the sign of the governor of Mann.

King. Governor. Guild. The three legs upholding Jamasak's rule. But as Molly thought about it, large as the crowd in the courtyard had been, she hadn't seen a single ship carrying the king's flag. There were guild flags, and merchant vessels flying the flag of one or another isle, but none with the king's insignia.

Her gaze lit on the words carved into the walls above the banners, the same words inside every dome and taught to every apprentice.

Those of Us Who Are Not Witches Give Birth
to Sons and Daughters Who Are
We are One People
From the Living Stars Who Traveled the Dark Lights
Raised High the Isles, Bequeathed us their Gift
We are Sons Born Ready to Prove Our Craft
Daughters to Master Our Own
We are Water that Births Us
Fire that Cleanses Us
Sky that Sustains Us
Ice that Surrounds Us
We Rejoice in the Power We Share

Molly was growing anxious. When she came to get Evan, she promised they would be gone only a few days. She had invented an elaborate story about an elderly uncle who asked to see him one last time. Ossian hesitated until she pushed a purse across his desk. She'd need a fatter one this time, and a way to convince him to blame her, not Evan. He had been apprenticed here six months; the longest he'd spent at any hall and needed only two seasons more to be a journeyman.

Ossian's chair scrapped the floor and Molly stiffened then rose as he motioned them forward. "I see your brother has decided to grace us with his return." He raised a brow. "How long has it been?"

"Ten days," she said, though she wondered whether he really cared. "The equinox tides were high, sir. I had hoped to return sooner."

Evan nodded. "We were caught in a storm and thrown off course. It was days. I'm sorry. We needed to hire a crew—"

Molly kicked his foot.

"Sorry?" Ossian snorted. "Sorry is what a child says when he spills a cup of milk. Sorry has no place in an apprentice's vocabulary. So, unless you're here to buy back your charter…?"

Molly stiffened. "It's my fault, sir. Not his."

"Of course, it's your fault," Ossian said flatly. "You're the one took him out, aren't you?" He rose and looked to the window. "So many applicants and nowhere to put them. The king wants witches, but has he offered to house or feed them? Or even care how well they're trained?"

Molly held out her purse. "If there is any way I can be of help—"

Ossian took the purse and dropped it in a drawer. "You may go," he said. "I have a dozen masters to entertain. And stay out of trouble. If you can."

"Of course," Molly said. "It's different here than at Evan's last hall."

Ossian looked up, suddenly interested. "Which hall was that?"

Evan kicked Molly's foot. "Eltiem," he answered first.

Ossian shot him a glance. "That would be Master Yarrum. I'm curious. In what way was it different?"

Molly wanted to take back her words, but it was too late. "Perhaps I misspoke," she said. "I didn't mean they teach differently. I wouldn't know of course. Just that the climate is…Wetter."

Ossian rifled through his papers. "That's odd," he murmured. "I asked Sanders to bring me a full list of apprentice charters. I don't see yours. You're how old?"

"Thirteen," Evan lied. Fourteen was old for a boy or girl beginning their apprenticeships, fifteen unheard of.

"And this is your second year? Eltiem was first?"

Evan nodded. There had been close calls before, masters looking into Evan's claims, but none had been successful and, the way Molly figured, it would be nearly impossible for Ossian to verify his claim. And if Master Yarrum were to walk in at that very moment, he wouldn't remember an apprentice from a year ago. Ossian could send an inquiry, but even at full sail with the weather cooperating and winds holding steady, it could take weeks for a ship to arrive, longer if there were passengers or cargo on board. He could send a message spell but that required caring once they left the room.

He started to speak but there was a rap on the door and Heron Sanders entered, breathing heavily. "You wanted to know when the masters from Khenry arrived."

Ossian scowled. "So soon?"

"He was seen on the wharf."

"He'll drink my wine and steal my apprentices. Though some—" he glanced at Evan. "I'd give away. But keep him happy, and drunk, and out of my way. And find this boy a cot. Are there more applicants?"

"Nine, and a few look promising. One of the girls is Cai Makken."

Ossian raised a brow. "Here? Now that is interesting."

"Yes, and she's bound to pass. Our astrologers predict more lights than usual for an autumn sky."

Ossian turned to Evan. "I give you three months to make something of yourself, Mr. Sinclair. Look across that yard and tell me there isn't another boy hoping for your bed. Now get out. I don't have time for this."

Sanders dipped his head and herded them through the door. Once in the corridor, he pointed toward the chairs. "Wait there," he said curtly. "I'll have someone take you to the yard."

They remained standing. Sanders started away and Molly turned back around. Ossian's door hadn't closed, and she could see—they both saw—the high master. He was still at his desk and he looked angry. He shook his head, muttered and pounded the surface.

The air began to waver. Books appeared on the desk, hazy at first, until the edges sharpened. They had been there all along, and not just books. Papers emerged, piles waiting to topple. There were goblets and open carafes. Pens. Inks. Boxes. An hourglass. A small animal skull of some kind with oversized eye holes and small, sharp teeth. Everything cluttered and dirty.

Until he looked up and saw them. His words fell away. His face darkened.

It's a chant, Molly realized. *He's crafting a cog.*

"Sanders!" he shouted and further along the corridor the head warden turned back around. He took in the open door, Molly and Evan peering inside, and rushed back and blocked their view. "I told you to wait," he snapped.

"Is there a problem?" Molly probed.

Sanders narrowed his eyes. "Never mind. You'll wait where I can see you."

They held back a few steps before following. "What was that?" Molly whispered.

"Cleaning his desk with a cog? Doesn't make sense."

"We embarrassed him. His dignity."

"I didn't see any dignity in there. I saw greed."

Sanders glared and waited for them to catch up. When they reached the main doors, he paused and surveyed the crowd. There were more guild masters now than families and he noted which of them were standing together and who eyed who.

Molly coughed to get his attention. "What did Ossian mean?" she asked, "about Evan having three months?"

"It means," Sanders said without looking at her, "your brother is fortunate in his timing. Fortunate you have sufficient funds while he's shown so little aptitude—"

Evan tensed. He pulled his hands into fists and Molly shook her head in warning.

"The king wants witches," Sanders continued. "And that requires our apprentices find their craft. Water, fire, ice or sky. Find yours, young man. That's my best advice." He raised an arm and hailed one of the masters, a woman with dark skin and huge, dark eyes. Her braids were shot with flickering lights and a row of gems snaked along the side of her face.

Molly recognized most from the insignias on their clothes. Some were from near the archipelago. None from Jamasak.

"They've enough forest to build a wall around the entire isle," the woman said. "But ask for a decent straight grained timber for a mast, and they laugh."

"Even so," one of the men said. "Where's Ossian's proof?"

"He hasn't any," the woman replied. "Anyone can see the king needs us more than we need him."

"Exactly my point," another man said. "I heard they charted twenty young witches in Doshaget."

"I don't believe it."

"Twenty humans," he laughed. "Only half passed, but they sent them to Jamasak just the same."

Sanders saw Molly staring and glared. "The carriages are there," he said pointedly. "And you, Mr. Sinclair, already know the way to the apprentice's attic. Go. Now. And take my advice and make yourself scarce."

4

A Leak in the Sea

Everything was in order when Molly climbed from the rowboat she'd hired to carry her back to the *Fish*. Macklin had run up the governor's flag while she was gone and—so far as she knew—no one had hailed the ship. What she couldn't be sure of, was whether Macklin had gone through her cabin.

The man was no one's fool and by now, every longshoreman, tavern keeper and fishwife knew of Navarr's stolen chest. Macklin had been alone on the *Fish* for hours with little to do but explore and poke about the cracks and crevasses. He was below deck, singing again.

> *Oh, it's work the till and roam the sea,*
> *Brave sailors you must be.*
> *Human and witch stand side by side,*
> *Brave sailors chart the sky.*

She made her way to the lower deck and found him standing over a water barrel, back bent and his face in shadows.

> *Set your course and raise the sails,*
> *Empty a keg and don't you fail.*
> *Face the ice and dare the Stars,*
> *Brave sailors wandering far.*

He lifted the lid and stared inside. Had he not heard her? Her footsteps echoed through the decking. It was difficult to hide.

Wives and husbands left at home,
Little children all have grown.
Tide turns in and the years pass by
And it's never a master would abide
The wanderer's life long gone at sea,
Witch and human sailors we.

She was planning to tell him about the spells. It was one thing to lie to a stranger, another to keep the lie going for days and weeks. But this business of confiding in people was new to her. She seldom spoke longer than a few minutes to anyone beside Evan.

He turned finally, cocked his head in surprise. "You're back! Excellent. And the young sir? He's settled? I was like that myself at his age."

She glanced to the heavy guns and his hammock and duffle packed between. She tried to remember what exactly she'd told him, and what she'd left out. What if he came up on her unaware and found her crafting spells? When, not if.

She walked past him, between the rows of cannons and patted one of the muzzles. "We've these six-pounders," she said lightly. "All cast with reinforcing rings."

"Aye, Evan showed me."

"Right. Of course. Did he tell you we named them after the stars? This one's Haldin and Riva's over there. Teair and Estair. Shorr and Ameil. Husbands and wives, just as they settled the isles."

She felt awkward, and annoyed at herself for feeling that way. How long before he discovered that the spells that kept barnacles from building up on the keel weren't purchased? Neither were the spells that prevented shipworm from attacking the oak. Or the weapons that never needed cleaning. The powder kegs that weren't troubled by salt or damp. The ship's figurehead, the flying fish that opened its eyes and steered through a storm.

The *Fish* was far from the only ship in the isles to rely on spells, but sooner or later Macklin would notice that her spells never ran out, yet she never stopped by a guild shop. Nothing rotted, and the lines were always tarred, the wind in her favor. A human crew required five sailors just to maneuver a large cannon into place, load and aim, fire a shot and swab the bore. She couldn't forge a guild receipt every time she needed to turn the whip staff or raise the anchor. No witch could run a ship alone. "We'll anchor here tonight," she said. "Wait till morning then sail for Auklet."

"Aye," he said. He glanced at the powder horns hanging from their pegs, the cartridge cases, kegs of gunpowder.

"You've trained as a gunner?" she asked.

"Experienced more like. I've picked up a few tricks. And I'll do most anything when the need arises. These haven't been fired? They look clean."

"They are. Oiled and ready."

"And well hid on the outside. There's nothing to see but the swivels."

"It's an attract and repel spell. They're built into the ship. The spells, I mean. Not the guns." She shot him a glance, turned the conversation. "I told you, didn't I? I'm looking for a ship to buy. A cargo ship, to earn more money. Have you heard of the *Red Star*? She tied up at Auklet a few week's past."

"You don't want that one. The hull's in poor shape and the owners keep delaying the work."

"*The Perihelion* then, with the king's sun on her prow?"

"Now there's a ship. I sailed with her crew, two seasons back. She's seaworthy and then some. I didn't realize you were interested in something so large?"

"I am. I will be," she said. "Soon. I'm looking for land to buy. A few buildings. Or a house. On a waterfront. Maybe near Sommer. I'm not sure. I'll know when I find it."

*   *   *

They hadn't been long at sea when Molly shut the cabin door securely behind her then walked to the corner and kicked the invisible chest. It was exactly as she'd left it. She glanced through the windows.

Hayden Hall, perched though it was on the isle's cliffs, was too far now to see. Daylight was fading and the first evening stars showed in the sky. She listened to the deck creak, the waves lapping the sides. The moon would be up soon and more stars. She stood here sometimes at night and imagined she could hear them talking to each other, talking to the wind and the currents, and to her as well.

She wished she could hear them, just once. Real words spoken by real women and men. She wished the stars would come down as they had in the first days and walk the sun-drenched beaches and climb the hills and maybe she would meet one and maybe they would be husband and wife, the way the guild said it happened a thousand years ago.

She hugged her arms across her chest and tried to picture what it would be like to kiss a star. Not the sort that flickered in the night sky. He'd have to be real, like one of the First Stars who came to the isles, otherwise how could she kiss him? She laughed at the thought. How could he beget the first of fifty generations of witches?

And what did that feel like, she wondered, kissing a man? She had never done that before, never wanted to. But then, if she'd never met a man she wanted to kiss, how could she say she didn't want to? If a man who was a star showed up and wanted to kiss her, he would have to be handsome, tall and maybe with curly hair, and make it dark. She liked that. She liked dark hair and brown eyes and his lips had to be soft, his arms at least as strong as hers. She touched her finger to her lips and raised her chin to where a man might be if she was going to kiss him—

Macklin knocked, and she spun about, her heart beating wildly. She opened the door and he hurried in. He was breathing hard.

"It's the lower deck ma'am. I think there's a leak." Water dripped from his hair and his boots were soaked.

"What? Where?" *It's not possible,* she told herself.

"I went below to check the bilge and there's water everywhere. A leak in the hull. I'm heading back. Just wanted to let you know."

Her thoughts spun as she remembered the cannon fire bursting around the *Fish* as she and Evan fled the *Corona*. She pictured splintered boards and ragged shards, damage she might have missed when she checked.

"I'll hook up a sling, climb out and fix it with canvas and tar. If you'll just tell me where there's hemp and a mallet. I think we're in luck and the leak's near the waterline." He turned to leave.

"No, wait. You must be tired. I'll go." She moved to stop him. "There's ale if you like. In the galley. Help yourself."

She couldn't have him standing over her while she crafted a repair. It would be impossible to hide. He'd ask questions, and they'd turn to Evan. Her parents. Luna's Cove. Her gold was there, and more than that; the hope that her parents would someday return. She'd left signs, messages telling where she was. She wasn't ready to talk about it with a man she hardly knew.

"I could heat the pitch," Macklin offered. His voice was tight and hard. "You brought me on to work, ma'am, not drink."

"You've earned a rest. I'll be fine." She tried to recall what he said when they first met. Hold his wages till he proved his worth? He stepped nearer. She was tall, but he loomed over her.

"I see. You thought your spells would hold. Of course." He'd carried a lamp and sat it down, took in the cabin's rosewood carvings and wainscoted walls. If he'd found the chest while she was gone, he'd glance to the corner and hope she didn't notice, but he didn't. He walked past her writing table, past her bed and stopped a few scant feet from the hidden chest. "Is that one of your Kapreil ships?" He nodded toward a tiny ship, a reproduction of her parent's *Ice Warden* mounted on a shelf. It was a beautiful miniature with a carrack's smooth planking and oar holes, its sails neatly furled.

She took a breath, let it out. How in the star's name was she going to explain herself to a crew she'd never met when she couldn't bring herself to tell Macklin, a man she wanted to trust?

She swallowed, steeled herself. "There is no Kapreil family," she said. "That was a story I told to keep the officer away. I'm sorry—"

"Of course." Macklin looked at her. "I understand. I'm just grateful you took me aboard."

"Yes, well…"

He took another step and she took two. She planted herself in front of the chest.

"What are you doing?" he asked.

"What do you mean?" She tapped the chest with her foot to make sure it was there.

"All this dancing. Are you done?" He grabbed her arm, but she jerked free.

"Stop pretending," he shouted. "Who are you with? The guild? The king? That paper you showed the guild rat? It was blank till you touched it."

"It was a boughten spell," she said, then winced at herself for lying again. He'd find out. Of course, he would. Boughten spells gave out. The Sinclair's did not. In every family the star's gift skipped a generation. In theirs it did not.

"I don't know who you're working for, but you're a witch. Same as me. Same as your brother. What I can't figure out is what craft you used to steer the ship and ease the wind—don't think I didn't see that little trick. You could be a weathercrafter. Or a water. But how can you be both when your arm says you're neither?"

"What about your arm? You beg me to take you on then demand answers to questions you won't answer yourself."

"Look here," he said, and his voice softened. "I'm not ashamed of what I am, but I hate the guild for what they've done. I'd join the Night Watermen if I could find them—" His eyes narrowed. "Is that it? You're a Night Waterman? I've heard of them hiding children from the guild. It would explain why your arm's not marked."

Molly's pulse quickened. She heard her mother's voice, warning again. *Never let them see what you are, Molly. They'll try to buy you and when you refuse, they'll imprison you. Try to run and they'll chase you. Try to hide and they'll come after you. They'll find you and syphon your blood if it would help them understand what they lost, and what we—you—have.*

She and Evan had waited at Luna's Cove for nearly three years after their parents disappeared. The hidden cove was rich with fresh water and food, fruit and shellfish and goats and wild turkeys. They slept in the small house or sheltered under trees, walked the empty beaches and watched for their parent's sail.

They climbed the hills and looked to the south where, on a clear day, it was possible to see the ice, a ragged blue and white wall taller than any mountain range. But there was no sign of the *Ice Warden*, no sign of their parents, no way to learn where they'd gone.

The ice that circled their world was impenetrable. It could not be bridged or tunneled. It was too thick to pierce, too high to see over. Astrologers and navigators had tried. They knew that the constellations that moved through the night sky did not end at the rim, but they also knew that while their witches could raise a wind or beguile the currents, they could not see beyond the ice.

She and Evan took to sailing further out and their excursions lasted longer, a day and then a week. But they kept returning to Luna's Cove, less frequently as time went by but enough to assure themselves their parents hadn't returned. They expanded the small house each time they came back, and the caves and tunnels as well. But mostly they lived aboard the *Fish*, using different names in each new port, changing their pennant.

They kept to themselves and for a while, lived on the gold Senesh and Esty left behind, but time wore on. The gold dwindled. Until one day, she realized that not only were she and Evan waiting, they were hiding—the same as her parents had always done. Wait, and hide from the guild. The two things she swore she was done with. Someday, she'd be free.

And Macklin wasn't the guild. He was a witch and she needed to trust him.

Tell the truth. Say the words. It was neither her parent's spells, nor hers alone that guided and maintained the *Fish*; they were twined together. Spells to steer and track the currents, trim the sails and check the caulking. She worked them the way human crews worked the watch; some by day and some by night and many, if not most, so near to rote she hardly thought about them at all. Except now, with Macklin aboard, she had to reconsider.

She met his gaze. "All right then, I'm a witch. I've known what I was for as long as I've known how to run and climb."

"That's a start. I'm not your enemy, Molly Sinclair. I'm not here to turn you in and I won't—I couldn't if I wanted to—steal your craft. But if you never apprenticed, how'd you learn so many spells?"

"My grandparents taught me." *Say the word*, she urged herself. *Say it.* She clenched her hands, held them at her sides. "They were witches, all of them."

"All four? You should be proud. And strong, I'd think."

Say it. Or there'll never be an end to hiding. "You haven't asked about my parents."

"They're gone, aren't they?"

"Yes, though I don't know where. They were… are… witches." She paused and was surprised to feel relieved. "Both of them. Craftborn. They couldn't risk bringing me to the guild."

"Craftborn?" He blinked, then frowned. He glanced about the cabin as if seeing it for the first time. "Always heard they were treated like princes," he murmured. "The few ever found."

"Prisoners more like."

He studied Molly's face. "I never thought of it that way, but, of course. The guild would never share power, or control."

"Which is why I lied. And why I need a crew, to run a cargo ship. I need gold. I need to find a corner of land and build a safehouse where I can come and go as I please."

She thought about that for a moment, the smaller isles she and Evan visited, and the towns, Backsid and Skendall she'd enjoyed. Roads crisscrossed the countryside and there were deep water harbors and shops and farms, and people less suspicious of newcomers. She'd walked the streets and climbed the hills and picked out a few possible locations, wooded parcels not far from the waterfront where two, even three large houses could be built nearby each other.

"No disrespect ma'am, but if you don't mind my asking, you have the resources?"

"Almost. It's taking longer than I hoped. But—" Molly paused, but there was no going back, nor did she want to. She turned and opened the chest. The invisibility spell faded. The evening light reached into her cabin and the shells and soothers and seeing eyes shifted and woke.

Macklin blinked. "So that's where they are," he said. "Right under my eyes. And the governor a hundred miles away." He paused then, "Did you steal it, or buy it?" he asked.

"Rescued it, more like. From the thieves who stole it from the governor."

Macklin laughed. "You're a wonder, Molly Sinclair. Oh, and by the by, there is no leak. I needed to get your attention."

Molly nodded, then grew serious. "I hate the guild," she said. "I hate what they've done to us."

Macklin stood over the chest. "Aye. I've got a lifetime of that."

"I'd plunder their ships if I could. Thumb my nose and take their gold and buy a town, a city, a world where I could spit on their star-cursed laws."

He stopped rummaging. "Board a guild ship? You'd do that? Pit your weapons against theirs?

Molly stared through the cabin windows. She'd been a pick pocket and a burglar, fought with swords and knives, fists and spells, and if taking a guild ship on the open sea was part of being free, then yes, she would do that too. She wouldn't run as her parents had, wouldn't confine Evan to a life hiding on Luna's Cove. "Yes," she said. "I'd do that. Whatever it takes."

Macklin stood. "The more you talk, Molly Sinclair, the more I like what I hear. And I'll help you find that crew if you'll let me. Though not the folks I had in mind when you first mentioned a ship; they're too afraid of the guild. But there's one man I'm thinking of, Troth Edda and his mate Tribolt, and Nick Sculpin, a young fellow. Once he trusts you, he'd jump off the masthead if you so much as hinted at the need." He chuckled. "It will be a pleasure to see his face when I ask if he'd like to play at cat and mouse with the guild.

"Oh, and there's Brigit Rest. Now there's a woman can right any sail, track her prey and load a cannon all at once. They've no love for the guild, but you'll have to pay their wages up front. Can you do that? I won't ask if you can't make good on your promise. I'm not trying to be harsh, just it's a lot you're asking."

She put out her hand and Macklin took it. "You find this crew," she said. "And I'll pay them, and we'll win our prize. The money, the ship, the land I mean to buy. They won't regret the choice."

✷   ✷   ✷

Nothing on the outside of *Brittle's Trade and Craft Brokery* had changed since Molly's first visit and she might not have returned if it weren't for Brittle himself.

He'd been lying about his spells and which were registered, stolen or used. The floating globe with real water? The red eggs? They were easily worth a month of a sailor's pay and she doubted he'd tell where they came from.

The streets behind her were busy with wagons and carts, men in ragged vests, others in silk, women hurrying by. She looked much the same as the first time she stopped by. She wore a green dress that was flattering but not conspicuous. Her hair was down, and the face was hers; she needed the conversation to return where they'd left off, not start with new introductions. She checked her pistol; made sure the ivory handle showed above her waistband and stepped inside.

Brittle was seated behind his counter and fortunately, the shop was empty. He lifted his gaze, returned to his ledger then quickly looked again. "Miss? Ma'am! You're back. Excellent. Come in." He scurried around the counter to greet her.

She had considered taking the stolen spells to a different shop, but she needed the money, and couldn't trust that another pawn broker wouldn't go straight to the governor. Broadsheets describing the suspects—two male guards—were tacked to the seawall and there was a reward for information. If Brittle suspected anything, he would have turned her in by now.

She smiled, businesslike. "I have to apologize. I left in something of a hurry. I believe we were in the middle of a conversation?" The layered smells of oiled wood and spices came back to her, vials of cinnamon. A basket of lavender. Candles and well stocked, surprisingly neat shelves.

"And my apologies as well." Brittle pulled a rag from an apron pocket, wiped his hands. "I would have sent a message, but I didn't have a name. Miss—?"

"Jenin Rose," she said, offering a name she sometimes used. "I sailed in with the *Lode Star*. Four masts. Blue paint on the stern. She sailed under the king's flag?" She pointed vaguely toward the harbor.

"The *Lode Star*?" Brittle repeated. "No, I can't seem to recall."

"It's already sailed. Equinox tides, you know."

"Of course. And you'll be staying here in Auklet? Which means we can look forward to a long and I hope, profitable, friendship?"

There was a noise out back, a crate falling or someone unloading a pallet. Brittle scowled and glanced over his shoulder. "Excuse me," he apologized. "I'll be just a moment. Don't leave." He hurried into the dark rear of the shop.

Molly followed part way around the counter. She peered toward the back room, but it was poorly lit and difficult to see. She made out a stack of small casks, lumber against a wall, a shadowed corner that might hide a stairwell to a cellar. She caught the faint sound of keys rattling and hurried back around the corner.

"Oh, there you are. I was just admiring the case." She moved to the shelves, picked out a large, enameled shell and set it on the counter. "May I?" she asked and opened it without waiting for a reply.

Inside, a goldfish swam around a white lotus in a pond no larger than the circle between her thumb and finger. She touched the water. It was real. "Very nice," she said, trying not to sound impressed, though she was.

Brittle took it back, closed it and set it aside. "You know what I said to myself when you walked in? I said, now there's a woman appreciates fine things. Expensive things. But maybe she's not looking for baubles today? Maybe she's more serious than that?"

He stepped onto a stool and brought down a package. It was thick but not large and he pulled back the velvet wrapping. Inside lay a book, a red volume with a leather catch. He spun it for Molly to read: *By Order of the First Congress, Queen Esteray Sofeil, In Consideration of Celestial Occurrences and their Influence on Corruption Within the Ice.*

Molly kept her hands at her sides. It was a Grimoire, but thicker than she had ever seen, and older. *The King's Grimoire*—the current version— was slender. Before the King's, the guild had released the Black, before that the Gold. Red came earlier. Evan would know if there were more. She did not.

Her parents had shown her Grimoires; the guild's collected and organized corpus of accepted spells. *Try them,* they said. *Scribble notes in the margins if you like. See what you can do with them. There's no harm.* And she had, until she realized that her own methods of crafting spells worked better than the guild's memorization technique and she lost interest and returned to experimenting.

"Thank you, but no." She pushed the book back at Brittle.

"Not even a peek?" he cajoled. "They say cogs were different in the old days. That almost anyone could do them."

"Anyone who was a witch," she said wondering if he was trying to talk her into buying the thing. "They said people could fly or make someone ill. I hope you're not trying to frighten me." She tapped the glass in front of the brass instrument she'd noticed before. "Tell me about this."

"Ah. Good choice. Let me show you." Brittle pushed aside the Grimoire and lay the instrument on the counter. It was discolored and most of the markings rubbed away. "Touch it, go on. It's old but it won't break."

Molly nudged the dial, but it was too rusted to move. He had said it was used to measure the stars, find your location at sea. "Were these numbers?" she asked.

"It's a thought, though I don't know. But I'll tell you what I did hear." He lowered his voice, leaned closer. "Most folks think it's from the other side."

"What other side?"

"The other side of the ice, of course."

Molly tensed. She refused to be distracted. *He doesn't know who I am*, she reminded herself. *Doesn't know anything about my parents sailing near the ice, mapping the rim. I won't be pulled in to fables about another side.* She looked up, challenging him. "You said it was a relic, that it was found encased in ice? But rim ice doesn't melt."

"Why don't we put this away," he said, returning the instrument to its shelf. "Let's not get drawn into other people's gossip."

"Which gossip is that?"

"Nothing serious, just about the king. His witches and castle."

"What castle?"

Brittle's eyes sparked. "Ah, finally. You're interested. Perhaps now you'd like to trade? My gossip for your spells."

"I'm listening. You first."

Brittle cocked his head. "Seeing as I like you, and it is just gossip… Folks are saying the king's building a new castle. A huge thing on the far side of Jamasak, not the palace. No one knows exactly where. But it's got magic crafted into every turret, cliffs warded to keep it hid. Cannons to keep it safe. And you know who's going to live there?" He leaned across the counter. "Witches. He's rounding up witches. Pressing them into service. Old masters. Young journeymen, anyone, so long as they can craft a cog." He watched her closely. "Doesn't that worry you?"

"I'm not a witch," Molly said indifferently.

"So you said." Brittle seemed disappointed, but only until Molly set her purse on the counter.

She opened the cords and spilled the contents across the glass. She'd brought spells from the chest this time, expensive looking shells along with a few she'd gathered in other ports.

Brittle flipped through them. He touched one, ignored another. His manner revealed nothing. Piles emerged as he checked the shells for names on the bottom and inside the lid, and made certain the instructions for the chant, object, and gesture were included. *To disguise a pebble as gold. For a warm sun, or rain. To speed a crop. Turn salt water fresh. Silence a messenger spell. Speed an arrow. Sharpen a blade. Repair a sail. Navigate at night.*

He kneaded the small of his back. "I suppose for this lot here…" he pointed at the larger pile. "I'll go three bronzes."

"What? For the whole thing?"

He smiled. "Three bronzes each."

Molly looked him in the eye. That was more than she'd expected but she wouldn't let him know. "They're worth four times that," she said.

"Perhaps, but I've got to make a profit."

"If you're not interested…" She reached to scoop up the piles.

"This one now," Brittle peered closer to read the tiny print. "Dries gun powder. Use three times." He straightened, met her gaze. "For this I'll give you three."

"Three bronzes?" The cog wasn't rare; she'd crafted similar spells herself.

"Silver. Or throw in this—" He indicated a cog for sharpening a sword. "And I'll make it gold."

"Gold? I accept," Molly said quickly. "One gold for the drying spell and sword sharpener and an additional three silvers for each in the pile there. Anything else?"

"I don't think so, unless, any chance you have a replicator? Didn't you have one last time you came in?"

"I did bring one. I thought… It's not here?" She frowned at the piles. "I must have left it behind."

"Well then," he said. "I imagine we're done for the day."

"But there's still these and—" she stopped as Brittle set first one gold coin in front of her then another. "Spells change hands," he said, adding a third. "Money makes friends."

"Yes, of course," Molly said. "I see," though she wasn't sure she did.

"You're new here," Brittle explained. "And I was telling the truth when I said I like you. There's plenty of witches need money and plenty of humans want cogs. So, if you happen to come by a few more, I promise a fair deal."

Molly nodded. She was almost afraid to answer and risk having him change his mind and take back the gold. It was more than generous, more than she could have hoped. She gathered up the remaining shells, closed her purse. She stopped at the door and stared at the handle before turning abruptly around. "Actually, there is one thing. The governor's nephew?"

"What about him?" Brittle remained indifferent.

"I was wondering if you knew where I might find him."

"Governor's nephew? Let's see…" Brittle picked up his rag, rubbed a spot on his counter. "Young man? Dark hair? He made quite the stir at the palace. You met him there?"

"I met him here," Molly said, her face reddening. Whatever else Brittle might be, he was infuriatingly good at bargaining. "The *Lode Star's* captain asked if I ran into the gentleman, to please pass along his greeting."

"Now that I think about it, he did mention a tavern. He may be the governor's nephew, but he likes a drink, same as anyone. Gold Key Inn. That's what he said.

Molly opened then closed her mouth. The Gold Key Inn was the tavern she recommended to Lake the night she stole the chest. She never thought he'd actually go there.

Brittle was still talking. "Becca Gray, proprietor," he said. "It's on Gurdji Street, halfway down. You'll see the sign. Two keys crossed over an open door. Day after tomorrow would be best. And late. Late is good."

"Late. Of course. And thank you, Mr. Brittle. I'll pass your name along to the *Lode Star's* captain. Perhaps he'll stop by."

5

The Stars Give and the Guild Takes Away

The apprentices' attic was bare. The bedding perfectly smoothed, no clothes strewn about and not a boy to be seen. Evan stepped back to the corridor and made sure he hadn't mistaken the stairwell leading to the narrow hall on the side of the ancient building. Silent or not, it was the right place, complete with the *Rules of the Apprentice* he wanted to snatch from the wall every time he walked by:

Apprentices must obtain Permission prior to Crafting new Spells
No Apprentices allowed in Craft Halls without Supervision
No Spells may be removed from Craft Halls
Spells may not be Sold, Bartered or Granted to others
No First or Second Year Exceptions

He tossed his duffle to the mattress beneath the window and stared at the view toward the cliffs. This was the one place in Hayden Hall where Evan thought he had gotten the better deal. He had the only opening window, with a ledge leading to the lower roofs and an easy drop to the courtyard and trees beyond.

He liked to look out and imagine he was back on the *Fish*, not stuck in a guild hall memorizing cogs. Before his parents disappeared. Before his sister took it on herself to decide he needed a witch's charter. And maybe he wasn't good enough to be a high master yet, but he'd wager anyone he could craft spells better than Heron Sanders. Sanders the worm-tongued. Sanders the pot-bellied dog who jumped every time Ossian so much as glanced his way.

Why couldn't Molly understand? He didn't need a witch's charter. Didn't need their useless cogs. He'd craft his own spells the way she did, learn at his own pace, in his own way, just as she always had.

He looked more closely about the room he shared with Ross, Drew and Jak, the three apprentices already sharing the attic when he arrived. They'd probably been put to work in the kitchens or mucking out the barns. With so many visiting masters about, Sanders would want every hand set to work, so long as troublemakers like him stayed out of the way.

He frowned suddenly and jumped from his bed. Where was his Grimoire? It should have been on his nightstand, or at least on the shelf above his bed? On a whim, he searched under Jak's bed. The boy's assorted keepsakes—rocks, a ball, tattered books from home—were still there along, along with dried out, smuggled food. But no Grimoire.

He sat up, brushed his hands. Who would steal a Grimoire when every new apprentice was given a copy the day they enrolled? They were stacked in cupboards, displayed on stands, used as threats and promises. *Learn this by tomorrow or miss your supper. Craft this cog before continuing to the next.*

He crossed to the wardrobe and found his clothes in a rumpled heap on the bottom. He scooped them up and his Grimoire fell to the floor. Curious, he carried it back to his bed, untied the cord and opened to a random page.

The formal script was difficult to read; the curling outline of one letter trailed into the next. There were illustrations, but only a few helped—the position of a hand, right or left, palm upward or down. The correct way to execute a gesture. The proper shape of an object. He turned to the beginning.

On one side was an illustration of the king's palace in Jamasak, the center of the world, with its glass domed towers, walkways and intersecting roofs, balconies and open courts. And in gilded letters on the following page:

And so, it came to pass that the Stars looked down from the Sky and saw a paradise so beautiful, they turned their ships and sailed the River of Dark Lights down to the isles.

And when the sun rose in the Sky, they pulled from it the magic of Fire and used its heat to push back the water and warm the air and raise the Isles. They crafted a land of summer and bound winter in its rim.

They cooled the Fire with Ice and raised the glaciers to rim the world and keep it safe. And for all the generations that followed, humans gave birth to witches and witches to humans, the promise of a thousand years fulfilled and marked by the Dark Lights themselves.

And the Guild grew to protect the crafts and the line of Kings and Queens in Jamasak protected the Guild, and for half a hundred generations the Grimoires were compiled so that the Crafts, the greatest of all the Stars' Gifts, would not be forgotten.

A bell in the courtyard rang and Evan glanced through the window. The autumn days were growing shorter and evening had settled in. He craned his neck and caught a hint of the waves moving beyond the trees. Molly would be gone by now, back to whatever she did while she was free of him, except that Macklin would be there. He wondered how that was going.

He returned to the Grimoire and paged through the four sections. Stonecraft for those whose strength was ice. Woodcraft for witches born with fire. Watercraft for water. Weathercraft for sky. Pages and pages of cogs sorted by craft and divided again by type.

He searched for a replicator spell similar to what Molly used for stealing jewels. He had tried it on his own a few times, but one of his rings came out solid as a marble and another, a necklace, looked convincing but kept falling apart. He didn't care that apprentices weren't supposed to craft cogs without teachers present. How else was he supposed to learn?

The spell should be somewhere, listed under ice or water, fire or sky.

Annoyed, he flipped back and forth but couldn't find the replicator spell. He ought to at least remember whether it belonged in the attract and repel, repair and transmute, or create and destroy subdivisions under the main sections.

Molly thought he wasn't trying hard enough, but he was. Master Emmit, one of the few teachers who didn't go out of his way to berate apprentices, often explained that a witch who was a sky might use an attract and repel spell to change an object, while someone who was water, might use a different spell for the same result. A drop of rain, for instance could fill a well. But so might mud, or a leaf, a tear. The permutations were endless and Evan often scribbled notes in the margins.

But where were his notes? *Try repeating twice if sand,* he'd written, and *gesture left instead of right.* He even included Molly's suggestions, gestures and chants that achieved the same end without their rules.

His stomach knotted and he shut the book. The answer was in front of him. He couldn't find his notes because this wasn't his Grimoire. It wasn't even the same volume. It was different. Changed. He shifted it from one hand to the other, guessed at the weight and fingered the paper.

He stared glumly out the window. The carriages and guests that filled the grounds earlier were gone, visitors to the inns, masters to their rooms. A guard at the gate was asleep in his chair. An apprentice lit a lamp with a cog-light and the walkway brightened. A shadow moved and he watched it disappear then emerge further on.

The shadow became a figure, someone crouching behind a bench. He saw it again, nearer the dome of the stars. Shaggy head, narrow shoulders. Whoever it was waited until the cog-lighter passed. By then, Evan remembered the boy he had seen earlier that day, the one who raced the other candidates around the dome.

Quickly, before the other boys returned, he pried open the window, squeezed through and felt for the ledge. With his back pressed against the wall, he inched along then jumped to the lower roof and found the line of rusted handholds. He scurried down and dropped the last few feet to the ground.

The courtyard was darker than it seemed from his window, but the sky was clear and the moon out and he could see shadows and movement. He wasn't afraid of being caught; the masters were too busy entertaining their guests to worry about one small infraction. Crouching low, he peered around the corner and saw the figure slinking toward the dome. He launched from the wall and ran at the boy. He didn't have a plan, didn't know what he was doing except that he was going to catch him and find out what was going on. He pounced on the boy's back. "Got you!" he hissed.

"What the—?" The boy jerked and spun about. He was taller than Evan but near the same weight. Evan wrapped his arms around the boy's shoulders and clung to his back and they fell to the ground and rolled with the boy first on top, then Evan. He straddled his hips and pinned his arms to the ground. "What are you doing?" Evan demanded.

"Me? You're the one knocked me down." The boy tried to spit but Evan ducked then shoved his head to one side. "You're stealing gems from the wall, aren't you?"

The boy gagged. "Was not!"

"Was too. I saw you." Evan squeezed his clenched fist. "What have you got? No lying."

"You sack of cod."

Evan grabbed the boy's hand and pried his fingers apart, but his hand was empty. He shifted his weight and the boy slammed his knee into Evan's gut. They rolled and this time the brown-haired boy came out on top and pinned Evan by the shoulders. "Rat," Evan snarled. "Damned guild rat."

The boy lifted Evan by the shoulders, slammed him down. "Who are you? Sander's boy? I saw you watching me."

Evan faked a moan. The boy eased his grip and Evan rolled free. The boy jumped aside and rubbed his jaw. Evan felt the back of his head: no blood, just a deep pounding ache.

He cocked his head, glanced about and suddenly, their expressions changed. The boy's mouth twitched. Evan smiled then laughed and a moment later they were chuckling and brushing the dust from their sleeves and trousers. "What's your name?" the boy asked.

"Evan Sinclair," he said then, "Shh. Wait—" He turned and listened. The lamplighter was gone. A cat perched on a wall, but that was all. "What's yours?" he asked.

"Reed Marshall."

"You just get here? With the other candidates? Are you going to apprentice?"

"You know another reason to eat the scraps they call food? You?"

Evan shrugged. "I've been here a while. You look old to be signing a first charter."

"You don't look like a twelve-year-old yourself. What's that fuzz on your lip?"

"It's just dirt. I'm fif—" He caught himself. "Thirteen."

"Yeah. Me too. Thirteen. Want to see something?" Evan nodded and Reed dug beneath his belt and brought out a dark, finely cut gem, a ruby, large as his fingertip.

Evan reached toward it then stopped. "That belongs in the dome," he said. "Throw it back."

Reed made a face. "It's not like I pried it off the wall. It fell and rolled out. Or something. It's been here for days, maybe longer. It's not my fault no one saw it."

"You know what they'll do if they find it?"

"Kick me out." Reed shrugged. "My father wallops me, and I go back to sliming fish. Wouldn't be the first time."

Evan gawked at him. "You were kicked out and you came back?"

"Sent back. It's not even a good story. My family owned a shipyard. We had a few bad runs. My older brother ran off and joined a Night Waterman gang. Next one married his girl. That left me, the only one turned out to be a witch. But right now, I'm thinking this hall might be more fun than the others." Reed's eyes danced. "How much do you think we could get for this?"

"Whoa," Evan held up his hands. "There is no 'we.' Put it back."

"I will if you go inside the dome with me."

"Are you crazy?"

Reed laughed. "Sure. Maybe. Don't you want to see what happens? Maybe the roof will slide back, and the dark lights will mark us. Or... Forget the dome. Let's take it to the Night Watermen, join a crew."

"Are you always like this? One scheme after another?"

"It's not a scheme. The Night Watermen will sign us to their Free Charter and we'll never need the guild again. I dare you to step inside."

"I will if you put it back."

Reed nodded, and Evan followed him up the steps to the entrance, an opening between ice pillars in the low, circular wall. He wasn't afraid, though his mouth was dry, and he couldn't shake the feeling of being watched.

Then, suddenly, they were inside. Evan slowly turned about. The dome was small; the size of a garden deck. The interior walls were covered in gems and colored stones, mosaics of men and women riding the dark lights as if they were a river. Stepping from boats. Raising the isles. Closing the ice.

Evan had stood beneath a dome of the stars before. The first time was at Hanna Hall on Rayshell isle where Molly took him to be apprenticed the first time. Witches were supposed to have one craft, not all, and he was terrified of being found out but nothing out of the ordinary happened. The lights passed overhead, and the masters opened the dome roof. A few lights streamed down and marked his arm the same as they marked every witch their first time with a smudge. His was blue, a hint of the star's blood in his veins.

But here, now... The walls, everything inside this dome was more beautiful than most of the others. The eight outer pillars of rim ice were filled with stones and pebbles, particles of dust caught inside. *Within Ice all earth is contained,* the guild taught. The pillars support the domed roof, the visible canopy of sky. And they were there, the constellations moving above his head, changing along with the real stars. *For Sky is the home of the Stars and the center of the Dome is Fire, and surrounding the Fire is a ring of Water, just as the isles float on water, all around.*

"See, that's what I don't get," Reed said. "First time I stood inside one of these, it went pretty much like they said. It was a vernal equinox. The roof opened, right down the middle and dark lights appeared in the sky. A band of white, nothing spectacular. But when I walked out, I had my mark. But the next time? I snuck in on my own, and nothing happened. The way the masters talk, you'd think I'd get blasted."

"Maybe a guild master has to be there?" Evan said. "Or there's a secret spell that summons the lights?"

"Rubbish. The only reason the guild shows up is to collect their fees."

"Maybe the lights didn't come because it wasn't solstice, or a cross quarter?"

"Or maybe the domes are broken? Or the lights worn out? You ever think about that? Everything gets old. The generations pass. Isn't that what they say? I don't mind if you keep the ruby. It fell off by itself. No one will know."

"No! I don't want it. It doesn't belong to me." Evan stepped toward the entry. He heard something; he was certain this time. It came from above, not rain, but a tap tapping sound. "Do you hear that?"

Reed listened. "I don't hear anything. Wait... Now I do."

"It's not rain. It's pebbles or something. Someone's throwing pebbles. Put the gem down. By the wall."

Evan glared until finally, Reed set the stone on the ground, but near the entrance where he could reach it if he wanted it later. He followed Evan down the steps and back to the courtyard. The shadows along the paved stones had grown longer but nothing else moved. The noise was gone.

* * *

Molly eased back the cover plate and peered through the spyhole for a look at the crew. The *Fish's* crew. Her crew. At least if the next few hours went well it would be.

No sooner had they returned to Auklet when Macklin started rounding up every witch-born sailor he trusted. It took longer than he'd guessed, what with half of them drunk and the other half not wanting to be found. One woman owed him money, saw him coming and stole a horse right out of a stable with the farrier just a few stalls away. Another was missing at sea. Another in prison. Another had found work at a guild hall and Macklin talked his way out of that conversation before it began. There were five in the end and they'd agreed only to hear her out, and Molly was nervous. She'd never hired witches before, let alone a pack of thieves whose loyalty she couldn't trust.

The cellar below her house was a good place to meet. She had leased the residence half a year ago and though it was farther from Hayden Hall than her other safe houses had been from his previous schools, it promised security.

The houses were useful for scouting missions and retreating. For times when it wasn't wise to store stolen goods on the *Fish* or sail back to Luna's Cove every time she had gold to hide. This latest house promised enough trees to ensure privacy, and land to keep curious neighbors away.

She had agreed to the lease when the caretakers, an elderly couple, showed her the cellar. It was reached through a tunnel beneath a shed in the rear gardens and wasn't easy to find. The tunnel led to an underground passage and one door leading upstairs, a second into the cellar where she stood now.

It was time.

She opened the door and the talking ceased. Only Macklin remained at ease. He leaned against the far wall with his arms folded, a cautious look in his eye. A cutlass hung from a peg above his right shoulder, a set of matched flintlocks above his left and more weapons Molly had mounted on the walls beyond those.

Macklin nodded toward a stool, but Molly remained standing. She approached the nearest man, held out her hand. "Niles Tribolt?" she asked, and the man nodded. He was taller than she'd expected, and she tried not to stare at the swath of shells dangling from his chest band. "Glad to meet you," she said.

"Same to you, Miss Sinclair."

"Molly," she said. "Let's save the formalities for strangers and leave the titles in the halls."

Tribolt looked to Macklin. "She is young," he said. "But you didn't say she had a grip." He pulled a yellowed paper from his vest, unfolded it and held it out. "Says here I'm a master witch out of Pyr. I work with wood, ma'am. Molly. Masts, barrels, crates and coffins. I build them up and tear them apart and fix them when they're broke."

"And he talks too much," the next man said. "Leave her alone. She doesn't care about the color of your piss."

"Oh, and you do?" Tribolt snickered. "That's Troth Edda. Calls himself a carpenter, but only because he never says anything worthwhile."

"What?" Troth exclaimed. "Stop squawking and you might learn a thing or two."

Molly frowned until she glanced between them and realized they were laughing. Troth Edda's hair was white and long and braided, and it was impossible to tell his age. He wore a vest with no shirt and there were scars on his arm, paler than Macklin's and reaching above his elbow.

A woman stepped forward. She was dressed in ship's clothes, the same as Molly; linen shirt, dark trousers and tall boots and there was a pistol and double-edged dagger on her hip. "Name's Sally Yarrow," she said. "Navigator and—"

"Not just a navigator," the youngest man, Nick Sculpin if she guessed correctly, interrupted. "One of the best. Don't let her soft eyes fool you."

Sally ignored the comment. "Navigator and watercrafter. Pleased to meet you."

"We could use a navigator," Molly said. "And if Macklin wants you and you're willing, I'm pleased to have you aboard." She glanced to see if Sally's arm was scarred, but her sleeves were turned down and tied at the wrist.

Nick reached toward Sally, but she swatted his hand away. His yellow hair was striking, and with his large eyes and teasing mouth, he was surprisingly handsome. He tried to get Sally to look at him, then stepped nearer when she didn't. There was a game going on, but Molly couldn't figure the rules. The next time Sally glanced his way, it was Nick who pretended not to see.

Tribolt cleared his throat. "And this," he said pointedly, "is Brigit Rest."

The gunner was a tall woman with muscled arms, a sharp nose and strong jawline. Her dark hair was cut like a helmet, close above her eyes and straight across her shoulders.

Macklin had warned her that Brigit refused to sign on without first having a look at the *Fish*. In person. On board. She wouldn't hire on any ship, she'd said, until she inspected its guns and knew how they performed.

They had no love for the guild, Macklin said, none of them, and she'd have to pay their wages up front. It wasn't harsh, just that her word was all they had, and she was asking a lot.

Molly moved to the center of the room. She leaned against the stool and launched, a bit nervously, into the speech she'd rehearsed for days. "Thank you for coming," she said. "Macklin will have told you the offer, so you know I need a crew. The *Fish* is mine, left by my parents, but don't ask for proof because there's no bill of sale, no record to show it was transferred to my name or my brother's." She paused. Their expressions were guarded, but no one stopped her or asked any questions.

"I'll pay your wages and set the terms, and I promise they'll be fair. I'll ask nothing of you I wouldn't ask of myself." She relaxed a bit. Brigit cocked her head and Tribolt looked dubious, but at least they were listening.

"Macklin is quartermaster," she continued. "His word second only to mine. If he sends a message while we're on shore, you answer. If he says we're to meet and you can't, you send word, or we sail without you. If we can't depend on you, you're gone. Your contract void. Everything depends on working together. On haste, and skill and—"

Tribolt snorted. "Macklin might be quartermaster, but I'll quarter him if he comes near me with a lash. I had enough whippings on the king's ships."

"And the guild's," Nick added. "I swore I'd never sail for a captain that beats a man or woman too sick to work."

Macklin stiffened. "We don't do that here," he said firmly. "Maybe on a guild ship, or for all I know under a Night Waterman flag, but not if I have a say."

"Night Watermen don't whip you," Nick said. "But they'll punish theft among the crew."

"If you know so much about Night Watermen," Sally said, "What are you doing here? You could be rich."

Nick smiled. "What's the use of being rich if I can't spend money on my favorite woman?" Sally didn't answer.

"They've a code," Troth said. "Theft among mates is treason."

Night Watermen? Molly glanced at their faces. Why were they talking about Night Watermen?

"And they share their take," Troth said. "While me, if I want to eat, I have to work a human trade. It's years since I sold a spell."

"Tell us about the wages," Brigit called. "Macklin wouldn't say."

"Aye," Tribolt agreed. "Or how long we'll be gone? We've a right to know."

"And the route," Nick said. "And what if the ship's wrecked? Night Watermen take care of their own. If a man loses his hand, they help. Wounded or whole, they take care of their own."

Molly thought of the shooting the night she stole the chest. The bullets had been real, but the entire episode was chaotic and bumbling, from the time the guards in the tunnel dropped to their knees, to the gangs chasing each other—and her— outside. "Enough," she said loudly. "Night Watermen are thieves, afraid to come out in the day. I'll wager not one of you has met them."

Nick shrugged. "It's not like they'd anchor in plain sight. The best way I know to find them is you find people who know the right people. Sooner or later, you'll have a lead."

"I've met them," Tribolt said. "One of them robbed me at knifepoint. A huge man. Ugly as mud."

Troth snickered. "They don't hurt old men."

Tribolt puffed out his chest. "You saying I'm old?"

Molly glanced at Macklin, but he shook his head and stepped back. She pushed her way between them. "Enough! Stop this! We are not here to talk about Night Watermen. We've battles of our own. Sign on to my crew and you'll be free to stay or leave. There'll be no lashing, no shackles, no blockhouses. But I'll put you ashore if I hear you gossiping in the taverns and find out I can't trust you. I'll expect you to sign an oath, not just for your service but for your silence. You're never to say our names, not mine and not anyone here. Are we agreed?"

"Sounds fair," Troth said. "But how are you going to do that? Stop us, I mean? Far as I can see, we're all witches here except you, and why the secrecy? I don't mind signing an oath, if it's fair."

"Not so fast," Brigit said, "Fair or not, I have questions about your ship and Macklin's been stingy with answers. The masts look sound, the sails and rigging hale, but that's from a distance. The only weapons I saw were a few light swivels and meanwhile Macklin's bragging about gold. I'm not opposed to thieving—he told us there'd be some—and I've been known to take risks, but why expect us to fight without heavy guns?"

"I have weapons," Molly said. "But you won't see them until you sign on. And when you do, I promise a ship that's the finest in the seas, with enough spells crafted into her deck to sail twice around the isles and more. But tell me, you're witches, yes?" They nodded and Molly swallowed. She'd get through this, one word at a time. "You apprenticed and came up through the halls?"

They frowned and exchanged glances.

"And proved yourself with a master's spell? One, if not more. Put out your arms," she said. "Show me."

No one moved. They glanced at each other, at Molly, at the floor, until finally, Macklin pushed up his sleeve and thrust out his arm. They looked to his scars then shrugged and did the same. Macklin was sky and his arm was the worst, a maze of welts and scars where the guild cut his mark away. Brigit's arm showed fire. Nick Sculpin, sky. Sally Yarrow, water. Tribolt's arm was marked with a blaze of fire running from this elbow to his wrist. Troth Edda was sky, the same as Nick.

Brigit's arm was scared though not as bad as Macklin's and she thought of her brother and the haze of blue that appeared on his arm the first time he entered a dome. The color was faint, with no hint of which craft sign would—should—someday appear. But if the guild tried to do to him what they had done to Macklin and cut his arm, she would kill them. She would kill anyone who tried.

Brigit's eyes were cold. "I sold a spell to a pig farmer," she said.

Molly could feel her mistrust, sharper than the others. "And?" she prompted.

"And she was rich and puffed up on the meat she and her husband sold. Until one day her pigs took ill and she wasn't so haughty then, wringing her hands and wailing to the stars. She found me through the guild, which was fine, and it was simple enough to craft a spell. It worked, but once the pigs were healthy again, she wouldn't pay for the spell." The other nodded. Stories like hers weren't rare.

"She claimed the pigs improved without me. I waited, registered a complaint and when the guild didn't answer, helped myself to a few trinkets she left around her house. Next thing I know, it turns out she was a *royal* pig farmer and soldiers show up and I get dragged to a dome.

Some folks say it's the lights that open the roof when a witch steps inside, and maybe it used to be true but it's not anymore. The guild opens it with a lever. Not even a cog. Watch them; there's always someone off to the side. This time, they didn't even bother. They just held me and pulled their knives, but I fought back and got away, so don't talk to me about secrets."

Molly didn't. Not yet. "Macklin says you're a gunner?"

Brigit pulled back her hair and Molly saw the gems embedded along her jaw. Opal. Sapphire. Emerald. Lazurite. Ruby. "Fire spells," Brigit said. "Attract and repel. Create and destroy."

Molly held out her arm and Brigit flicked a glance. "Smooth as a babe. What are we supposed to see?"

Molly drew a breath. "That wall," she said. "Watch." And for a moment, she heard her mother's voice: *Never let them know what you are, Molly. You'll remind them what they're not, and they'll be afraid.* She wouldn't keep that promise anymore. Her parents believed in hiding. She did not.

She'd mounted three crossbows high on the wall. Below them, a row of long swords, cutlasses and rapiers. Daggers below those. There were blunderbusses with flared muzzles and a muskatoon; three pistols with short barrels and two long, all primed and loaded and checked just a few hours earlier to be sure they wouldn't fall or explode, go off half-cocked or fail to release.

"The dagger at the end," she said. She nodded and the blade flew from the wall. It shot across the room, a blur spinning through the air. It arced then came down point first in the floor in front of Tribolt. He fell back and laughed.

"Next," she called, and Sally jumped aside as a saber sped from the wall. It pierced the floorboard within an inch of the first and held there wobbling.

Molly nodded and the next sword dropped from its hook. It hovered in the air then spun. A dagger followed, then another. Troth and Tribolt and the others nodded and laughed at the display. Brigit did not.

"Excellent performance," she said, clapping her hands. "You bought yourself a cog. And what? You want us to believe you're a witch?"

"She's a witch," Tribolt crowed. "Without a mark. Make them hover. Call a wind, or… What are you? Sky? Fire?"

"The handle's wood," Nick said excitedly. "She could be fire."

Brigit stood over the saber and pried it free. "She bought a spell," she said. "Any human can do that."

"True enough," Molly said. "But where's the shell?"

"You opened it before we got here. A shell proves nothing." Brigit lifted the blade and swung it. "You whispered the chant when you walked in. What about the pistols? Are you going to show us what they can do?"

"You're daring me?" Molly said. If Brigit was trying to provoke her, she was doing a good job. She nodded toward the smallest flintlock, a silver handled gun with a gleaming mechanism. It shot from the wall and spun, end over end. She opened her hand to grab it, but Brigit was faster. She snatched it and turned the muzzle directly at Molly's chest.

Molly froze. "That's two cogs," Brigit said, a bit surprised. "I'll give you credit. Not every human can juggle two at the same time."

"And not many witches, either," Nick said.

Brigit cocked the trigger. "It's loaded. I wasn't sure. There's no shame in being human, but lying to us, that's something else, especially if you want our trust. Maybe you want to explain how you stole so many spells, because that's a better story than the one you're trying to sell." She lowered the gun, but her finger hovered near the trigger.

Molly held Brigit's gaze, but she focused her thoughts on the gun, on the iron casting and the smooth bore inside. It probably wasn't safe taking her focus off Brigit, but this was important. She let the room fade, stared at the gun and thought about the powder and wad and ball. She pictured the salt peter, the smelting and heat that had gone into its making and she reversed it. She separated the elements, one from the other. And suddenly, Brigit cursed as the metal grew hot. She glared at the gun then dropped it. It hit the ground, softened and bent.

Brigit blinked and hurled herself at Molly. They fell together and latched on to shoulders, arms and neck. Brigit shoved Molly's head against the floor and Molly kicked at her from behind and they rolled again. Brigit raised her fist toward Molly's face but suddenly, Macklin was standing over them. He grabbed Brigit's arm and hauled her from on top of Molly.

"Stop it," he ordered, and he kicked the gun into a corner and picked up one of the stray knives and tucked it in his belt. "Both of you! All of you, back away. There's no guild cogs here. The only spells in the room are the ones Molly crafted, and if you don't believe that get out. Get out now."

No one moved.

Molly straightened her clothes and glanced warily at Brigit. She didn't blame her for doubting, and if she had to be honest, she trusted her more. But she couldn't say that, not yet. "Macklin's right," she said. "There's no boughten cogs here and I am a witch. I've no love for the guild and what they've done to us. I'm just… Used to hiding."

Troth nodded. "Not every witch enters the guild. There's plenty families can't afford the fee."

Tribolt said, "Aye, but their craft's hit or miss. Didn't look that way with yours."

Molly said, "I buy spells, sometimes. Mostly I keep moving. I stay away from the guild and spend most of my time on the *Fish*."

Tribolt laughed. "Throw me to the seas for a fool if I wouldn't do the same."

"Not yet," Brigit said. "Plenty of witches buy spells they can't craft themselves, and most of us try to stay away from the guild. You want us to swear silence? Why? Where's the rest of the truth, Molly Sinclair?"

"There is more," Molly said, and steeled herself. *I'm done with hiding. I want a home. No secrets.* "My parents were renegades—"

"Night Watermen?" Sally asked. "I knew it."

"No." Molly stopped her. "Not Night Watermen. My parents sailed alone and free. The Night Watermen harassed them, same as they harass everyone."

"That's not so," Nick said. "If your parents were renegades, the Night Watermen would have left them alone. I hear they'll treat with the few renegade pirates that don't want to join, so long as they don't interfere. Unless there's something else? Were they guild? Or royals?"

"Of course not! All the years we were growing up, my parents sent me and my brother below whenever their ships came in sight."

"Whose ships?" Nick pressed her. "Night Watermen or guild?"

"They hid you because you were witches?" Brigit asked.

Molly glanced between them. "Both. Or Night Watermen. I don't know. I don't know why they did what they did. They left."

"And went where?" Brigit asked. "To who?"

Molly's stomach twisted. She could answer, but only part of the question. The full answer, she had never known.

"Tell them," Macklin urged her. "Before we have a spat and everyone leaves."

"Tell us what?" Tribolt asked.

Molly took a deep breath, let it out. "That I'm a witch."

"We already know that," Brigit said. "What else?"

"And so is my brother." She glanced at Macklin. "And so were they."

She said it simply and quick, then watched as Brigit's expression changed. Understanding moved across her face. The others were equally surprised, then thoughtful, then something else. *Wait,* Molly warned herself. *Give them time.*

"That's it?" Brigit asked, more calmly than Molly expected. "You're craftborn. That's why they hid you. That's why the secrecy and pacts. If they find you, it's worse than for us. They'll string you up and bleed you dry and sell your blood to the highest bidder."

"Or keep it for themselves," Macklin said.

Brigit glanced to the whitewashed walls and plain floor, the weapons strewn everywhere. "So, you need a crew and there's thieving involved. You have a plan?"

"I do, yes," Molly said, and relief washed through her. "Sail with me and I promise a fair share of our earnings, equal split, whatever the prize. From this."

She held out her hands and an image appeared, the spell coming easily. Water shimmered blue and silver. And riding the waves, a perfect likeness of the merchant vessel *White Lily* with high castles fore and aft, proud as the sea itself.

Sally reached out but her hand passed through the ship. It was an image, nothing more. Nick laughed, and Tribolt nodded.

This was the right thing to do, she promised herself. Telling them what she was. Bringing them aboard the *Fish*. They would be free someday, all of them. It was more than just the promise of freedom from the guild, and it wasn't for her alone. It was for all of them.

"We'll be taking the merchant ship, *White Lily*. I first saw her two weeks ago, not far off the coast of Tars. She's caravel built, a hundred and fifteen feet long, twenty sailors aboard. She's flying under Samsid's flag, an orange pendent with a black tern, but what's more important is that she's like a deep-water port, doing business offshore. A ship comes in, cargo changes hands, the ship leaves. The *White Lily* seldom makes land. She'll be fully loaded, heavy and slow. There'll be gold. The harbor master will meet it, collects his fees and then he's gone and that's their mistake, and our fortune."

"Guns?" Brigit asked.

"Eight small cannons, firing three-inch balls."

"When?" Troth asked.

"Soon. You'll wait in Auklet till Macklin sends word then we'll gather on the *Fish*. Not here. Forget you saw this house."

"Equal shares?" Troth exchanged a glance with Tribolt. "What's that mean? You take your cut, and we divide the rest?" He watched her closely; they all did.

The question mattered. She had turned it over in her head a hundred times. The answer was always the same. "Equal shares," she said. "Seven ways. I meant what I said. We have enough skill and craft between us to board the *White Lily*, take what we want and send her back to Jamasak and a blight on any one who dares come after. Are you in?"

Troth glanced along the faces. "Seven. That's what you said, seven *equal* shares?"

"You heard correctly."

"I'm in," Tribolt said, and he pulled one of the daggers from the flooring, sighted down the edge.

"I'm in," Troth agreed, and Sally Yarrow nodded, then Nick after her and Brigit too. Molly crossed back to the door and pulled out another paper she had waiting, along with a pen and pot of ink. She brought it back and passed it around for them to sign, then took the pen and signed in a flourishing hand.

6

Wherein Two Balls and a Tankard of Ale
are Infused with Curious Magical Properties

The waters outside Murrock isle's east harbor looked choppy to Davit Lake's eye, with none of the calm he promised Brittle for the crossing.

There was a chill in the air; not a deep cold—the isles never felt that—but the sails were huffing as the ferry pulled near. If Brittle was conscious, he would have spent the hours below deck gray faced and moaning the entire way.

It had taken days for Davit to convince his old friend to board the ferry. He had sent a dragonfly with an invitation in the governor's own voice. A different one returned. Brittle complained about his stomach, legs, the shop, until Davit had enough. He'd come over to Auklet himself, he said, and wipe the damn counters and cheat the customers, if that's what it took to convince Brittle to tell Navarr about the replicator he found outside his door. Outside. That was the story they settled on. It kept their hands clean, and suspicions away from the girl with the copper hair. That was important. She was innocent, caught in the middle, and he was certain this entire mess had nothing to do with her.

Simple lies were best. It was one of the few things Davit was sure of anymore. Throw the governor a crumb and with luck, he'd learn something worth passing back to the king. His days were already filled with lies, and he needed to keep the two sides looking the other way.

He'd seen Navarr's temper, though never directed at him. Quite the opposite. Since arriving from Jamasak, Navarr had trusted him, spoken openly, made it clear that he was to be included in everything: policy and decision making. Private conversations. Well, perhaps not all his private conversations. Davit didn't need to be that close.

The governor enjoyed Davit's company and playing the part of his uncle to please the king. He was convinced that spying on the guild and reporting back to the capitol would bring him nearer the king's inner circle. It would bring gifts and invitations. A welcome in the wealthiest royal households. Navarr's wife, the good lady Beatrice was unaware of the ruse, but even the thought of her ill-tempered company on a coveted trip to Jamasak couldn't darken Navarr's hope.

It made Davit's job much easier. There were factions these days, splinter groups within the guild that shifted with each new moon and the king needed him—and others—to ferret out the plots. Navarr opened doors it would have taken months for the king to crack.

The mission required subtlety. While the guild halls assured the king that every witch they sent him had been tested and proved a master, his astrologers were less convinced. They believed the guild was cheating, lying, possibly even sending him weaker witches while keeping the strongest at the halls and trading their cogs to Night Watermen in exchange for guns and ammunition. It wasn't far from the truth.

The guild had grown powerful. Distanced from Jamasak and a king they seldom saw, they had been tightening their hold over the crafts for years. But no matter how many astrologers studied the skies, the gift of the stars was changing, and no one could read the future. Except for the one thing that even the poorest fishmongers knew: controlling the cog trade and who could or could not be chartered as a witch, was more important than ever.

The ferry docked and an oarsman tied up and most of the passengers disembarked before Davit caught Brittle's eye. A ferryman helped him walk, and by the time they reached him, Brittle was huffing and patting the sweat from his brow. "I don't know why I let you talk me into this," Brittle grumbled. "You could as easily have shown him the replicator yourself."

"And have Scrud questioning how I came by the thing? No. You're much more convincing."

Brittle handed the ferryman a coin then glanced warily at the horses hitched behind Davit. "What's this? First you send me across the straits in a broken-down excuse of a ship and now I'm to ride a horse instead of sitting in a coach? What happened to those manners you learned at court?"

Davit laughed. "Complain all you like, but we both know you wouldn't miss a chance to peek inside Navarr's palace. Legally. And look at you, trussed up like a fop."

Brittle tugged his red surcoat over his belly and brushed a hair from his shoulder. His boots were buffed, his hair tied back with a ribbon. A rich man's sword hung at his side. He poked Davit's velvet coat. "Don't tell me this nephew business isn't going to your head."

"I'm supposed to look this way. You are supposed to—"

"I know. You told me. Act like a greedy, fawning pawn broker. Which I am. Now help me up on that horse and remember, you promised me a very indulgent meal when we're done."

Brittle had never been inside Navarr's palace, never seen the inner courtyards and tiled fountains where Davit had lived for more than a month now, and which had been the residence of every appointed governor in Murrock for hundreds of years. And by the time the attendant guided them through the wide gates he was definitely impressed.

The courtyard was a maze of plantings, miniature trees bearing fruit, ferns hanging from tiled roofs. They passed through a second courtyard, this one lined with rows of low fountains and a glass dome overhead. Brittle turned constantly, eager as a boy to see the canaries, parrots, and flittering hummingbirds.

There were more people in the next hall, clusters of men and women, merchants and astrologers, guild masters with shells clanking as they moved. Brittle elbowed Lake. "Dithering astrologers. I can't stand their arguing. Who's that woman over there?"

"Master Annas? She's one of Navarr's treasurers, and those two with her are auditors. Play dice with her and you'll die a pauper. Now pay attention. I didn't bring you here to gawk."

Brittle huffed. "I am paying attention. There are two doors along the east wall, neither guarded. Two to the west, but the soldiers are anxious to be off duty. One fellow just handed them a few coins and they let him slip through."

The attendant stopped at a door, rapped, and a moment later, they were inside the governor's private solar. The walls, cornices and frescoes were heavily carved with birds, seashells and schools of fish. Davit had been here before, but the furnishings had been stripped and he stepped back in surprise to find so many spells hidden in the mantel, the window trim and candelabra overhead; so many he actually felt them, like a burn running along his skin.

His hand had been on the wall and he pulled it back. It was warm, oddly so, and the feel of it reminded him of the girl he'd met in Brittle's shop. Jenin Rose, but he didn't want to think about her. Not here, where there was so much hidden magic. This place had nothing to do with her.

"Watch where you stand," he whispered to Brittle. "There are tracking eyes that can drop on your shoulder, follow you for days. And don't touch the lamps. Scrud will know in an instant if you're hiding spells."

"I'm not, but…" Brittle stopped. "That's the governor?"

Harken Navarr and his assistant Jeron Scrud stood at the far end of the long, narrow room. Navarr was naked to the waist, his black trousers tied with a sash. He stood with his hands raised, his pale, paunchy torso leaning oddly forward. He was sweating, his white hair pasted across his forehead.

Davit stepped wide of the candelabra and flipped the edge of his collar down. A twice-hidden seeing eye blinked awake.

Navarr lowered his hands and wiped them on his sides. "So!" he called. "You found your pawn broker? I trust you weren't accosted in the halls?"

Brittle bowed. "It's an honor to meet you, sir. To serve the isles."

Navarr mopped his brow. "Is it true? There were pirates in your shop?" He sounded excited and childishly impressed. "What did they say? Did they steal anything?"

"If you mean Night Watermen, sir, it's possible. I wouldn't exactly know." Brittle glanced at Davit. "They'd be disguised."

Navarr laughed. "No, I don't suppose they'd introduce themselves. I like that. You're honest. Scrud, do you hear? He's met real Night Watermen. Not those useless mercenaries we hired."

Mercenaries? Davit and Brittle exchanged a glance.

Scrud nodded. "It's just as you said. Sooner or later, they'd show their faces."

"I'm sorry," Davit said. "Who are we talking about?"

Navarr said, "The louts I hired to steal my chest. Both of them. All of them. The two inside, then one batch to steal it from them, a second to grab it from them."

"I thought you suspected Night Watermen?"

"Of stealing the chest? Nonsense. Real Watermen would never have given up. But I don't know who the two were that got away. They're the only ones I didn't hire."

Scrud frowned but Navarr kept talking. "It was my own idea and you see, of course. I couldn't have my wife knowing I want—no, need—those spells."

"Right. Of course," Davit said, though he didn't at all see.

Scrud said, "Excuse me. Sir—"

"Yes, well," Navarr straightened his shoulders. "Enough of that. Come in, come in. There's food. Cheese. Wine. Help yourself. But first, wait. Stand there." He waved them away from the platters. "I want you to see this."

Scrud moved to face the governor. He was taller than Navarr and far thinner; his opposite in build, demeanor. He wore a plain brown shirt, loose at the neck, a sheathed dagger at his hip. He wore no jewels, carried no shells, at least none that Davit could see. Even so, he didn't trust him. Scrud was a witch and though there were no gems on his face and he'd never seen him craft a cog, he was certain the governor would employ no less than a master.

"I'm ready," Navarr called. "Give them here." He raised his hands and for a moment Davit thought they meant to wrestle. Instead, Scrud tossed two small blue rubber balls toward the governor, one after the other.

"Juggling?" Brittle whispered. "What in the seas—?"

The two balls stopped midair and hovered above Navarr's hands. Shaking a bit, but hovering. Navarr's face lit up. "You see," he cried. "Scrud's worth a dozen guild masters, a hundred."

Davit frowned as he touched his collar and nudged the seeing eye to make sure it was awake and watching. He didn't like what he was seeing, what it meant.

"Concentrate," Scrud urged. "Hold the ball. There now… Raise your hands… The ball is the object. Your hands, the gesture. Your thought—"

"Which hand?"

The balls sank. Scrud quickly reached in and tapped Navarr's elbow. "The right one, but it doesn't matter. Feel them. Use your thoughts as if they're a wind and you're lifting the balls. Hold them. That's it."

Brittle shook his head. "But he's human," he whispered. "How's he doing that?"

Davit glanced uncomfortably from Navarr to Scrud. He watched the assistant's hands, his eyes and lips to see if he was gesturing or muttering a chant. Harkin Navarr *was* human. He should not be able to keep two balls—or one, or anything—floating without a purchased spell to hold them. Simple or complicated didn't matter. Raise a wind or freeze a rain. He'd heard of human witches. He didn't want it to be true.

The governor couldn't be a witch. Mistakes like that weren't made. It was the law that maintained the balance of power. The kings and queens in Jamasak were sometimes witch, sometimes human. The guild and High Council were always witch. Governors always human. Thus, it had been since the last of the stars died and the Makken family took the throne.

And Harken Navarr, who was governor for the simple reason that he was married to the wealthy daughter of a distant cousin of the king's wife *was* human, tested by a law decreed so long ago, no memory could find the source.

Davit too was human. He had been tested. As a young man, he had fostered in the manor of Rickjay Lynx, another of the king's many cousins. Davit's own parents were long gone, killed during a skirmish he barely remembered and his heritage in the crafts was unknown. But he'd stood beneath a dome while his foster parents watched from a viewing stand eating grapes and sipping wine with a hope they didn't try to hide.

They had fussed over him and cautioned him to stand still and clear his thoughts when the dome opened, and he had. Or at least, he tried. He kept his feet still, but curiosity was difficult to check, and he couldn't help but look up and watch as the dark lights, a plain band of white, reached across the sky and revealed… Nothing. He was twelve years old and the dark lights took no note and passed him by. He was human, not witch and afterward while his foster parents squeezed his shoulder and told him not to worry, there would be great things in his future, Davit hid his relief.

The balls wobbled. Navarr tensed and they fell and Scrud chased them while Navarr crowed with delight. "Did you see? They were floating. Longer than a minute, wasn't it, Scrud?" He stopped talking and slipped on a shirt and a pendant bearing Murrock's radiant sun. "I've been practicing an hour a day. Gets me away from my duties. And also…" He speared an olive with the tip of a knife. "From my wife. Are you married, Mr. Brittle?"

"Never had the privilege," Brittle said. "Though I've heard your wife is an uncommon beauty."

"Uncommon!" Navarr laughed. "I'll give you that. She thinks I'm keeping some pretty young girl back here, but if she knew what I was really dandling, she'd be far more surprised. Did you see, Davit? It was magic. Mine!"

"The governor's come very far," Scrud said, his bland voice revealing nothing.

"I'm impressed," Davit said. "You work well together."

Scrud dipped his head. "Without the governor's natural ability, no amount of lessons could achieve such confidence."

Navarr beamed. "Imagine what king Makken will say when I present him a gift of magic? It will mark a new era. The Grimoire open to all. I was born human, but the world is changing. Magic accessible to all. Well, perhaps not all. We wouldn't want that. But think of it. I'll join the High Council. The first human witch."

Davit pulled back. "You'll tell the king?"

"Of course. When I'm ready. Too soon would be a risk."

Davit nudged Brittle toward Scrud then drew Navarr to the window. He lowered his voice. "I meant to tell you, sir, the king is very pleased with your work."

"You heard from him?" Navarr looked delighted. "How? When?"

"A messenger spell. Just recently." He glanced to the ceiling. The tracking spell had turned toward Scrud and wouldn't hear their words.

"Then you'll understand why I can't let the king know until I've mastered a few more spells. It won't be long. I'm almost there. But I'll need proof when I reveal myself." He nodded toward Brittle. "Your man there? My money will keep him quiet, but you haven't told him you're not really my nephew?"

"No, of course not," Davit lied reassuringly. He was good at wearing masks, playing with the truth. He'd been doing it since arriving in Murrock. Since his first day in Jamasak with the king. The Night Watermen had taught him well and burying the truth was second nature.

"Good," Navarr said. "And he'll have his gold as soon as I have that replicator." He turned, then turned again. "Did he say anything else? The king?"

"He was pleased with your report," Davit said, and that too wasn't entirely a lie. He had sent the king a tally of guild ships in Navarr's harbor, the number of spells bought and sold, and though the number was lower than a year ago, Navarr kept only an appropriate share and sent the remainder to the king. Navarr thought the king wanted him to spy on the guild; the king suspected Navarr of cheating him and sent Davit to find the truth. But as far as he could see, Navarr cared about little more than juggling toys in the air.

They returned to the table and Navarr poured wine. "Master Brittle," he said. "My nephew tells me I can trust you."

"Yes sir, thank you. I believe we have the same goal."

"Oh?" Scrud raised his brow. "And what might that be?"

Brittle nodded toward the balls. "Power, sir. Magic. Gold. However you want it served. You want yours. I want mine. No less does the guild and the king, and I'll wager the Night Watermen as well."

"You'd put a wager on thieves?" Scrud studied Brittle's face. "And do you mind my asking, are you witch, sir, or human?"

"Me?" Brittle chuckled. "Human, of course. Witches have their craft and I have my shop. I do all right for myself."

Navarr rolled his eyes. "Leave him be, Scrud. We have business to discuss. You mentioned a replicator. Is it here?"

Brittle pulled out a pouch. He tipped it and out fell the small, gray, spine covered ball he'd stolen from Molly. It hit the table with a clink, rolled and came to a rest.

Navarr reached toward it, then hesitated. "You worked it?"

"No," Davit answered, his hands tight at this sides. "I didn't want it running out, in case it was already used." Which was half true. Purchased cogs had a limited life span, and Davit didn't like using cogs, didn't trust them and didn't want to grow dependent on them the way so many humans did. Nor did he like the way he felt the few times he did use them. Sometimes he grew dizzy. Sometimes his heart pounded, as if he'd climbed a hill. Or his hands shook, or he needed to rub his eyes to clear them. Most people never complained, and he didn't. Not aloud. He just worked harder to get things done.

Navarr touched a spine. "It's sharp," he exclaimed. "Tell me again how you found it?"

Davit suddenly wanted to be gone. "Yes, well," he started. "Once we knew the chest was missing—"

"Stolen." Navarr corrected.

"Stolen," Davit agreed. "The pawn shops seemed an obvious place to start. Enough people were already searching Murrock, so I sailed to Tars and a sailor pointed out Brittle's shop. But we don't know who dropped it."

Brittle said, "Any help I can give…"

Scrud reached past Navarr and picked up the spiked ball. "No shell," he murmured. "But there's a guild mark. The letters J and L. Loam? Is that right?"

"There's a Jace Loam." Navarr made a face. "He was at the palace that night. All red faced and angry. It could have been his. What if he's plotting with the guild?"

"Loam is guild," Scrud reminded him. "He's a warden in another hall."

Navarr turned on Brittle. "Your payment, if I remember correctly, was contingent on learning exactly how this works."

"I told you what I know. The girl came in. She was hoping to pick up some money. She left. I wouldn't know how it works."

Davit's eyes widened. Brittle had agreed not to mention the girl. She had nothing to do with the theft.

"Girl? I thought you found it outside?"

"Right. I did." Brittle glanced helplessly at Davit. "But a girl brought it to my attention."

Scrud scowled. "How can you be sure it's a replicator if you haven't seen it work?"

"She told me."

"Outside," Davit added. "She never came in."

Scrud glanced between them. "This is pointless. The governor wants his chest back. That's more important than any one spell."

"No," Navarr disagreed. "What I want are spells that work. For me to practice with. What if the guild sent the girl? That would be worth telling the king."

Brittle stared at his feet. "Perhaps. She was interested in money."

Davit wanted to strangle him. Navarr was impossible and Brittle was talking too much. And right now, he wanted to protect the girl. "She found it," he said. "She couldn't have known it was stolen. And if the guild sent her, why would she sell it?"

"Or, what about real Night Watermen?" Navarr asked. "Not lone pirates or thieves. She might be with them. I could send a few men, in case she returns?"

"To my shop?" Brittle's eyes widened. "No, it wouldn't help. It could take days, weeks until she returned. And I remember now. She gave her name. Jenin Rose. She had a berth on the *Lodestar*."

Jenin Rose? Davit stared at Brittle. He'd never said the girl had a name.

"The *Lodestar*?" Scrud repeated. "There's a *Lonely Star*, out of Bulatt I believe, and the harbor records cite a *Trade Star*. The girl's bound to be working with someone."

Navarr brought his fist down on the table. "I want her arrested. She's our link and I want those cogs. Scrud can't make enough and I can't simply walk into a guild shop and buy a hundred. Follow her and she'll lead us back to the chest. She'll be too frightened to protest."

He looked pleased with himself. "We'll turn her over to the king. That's what we'll do. You want to be paid, Mr. Brittle? You know what she looks like? Find her. I'll pay you double. No. Triple."

"Triple?" Brittle scratched his chin. "She was young." He tried to remember. "Brown hair. She wore it up. Down. No up. Yes. And I think her eyes were blue."

"Brown," Davit corrected. "And her hair is copper, a dark copper."

Scrud looked at him. "I didn't realize you'd met her?"

Davit blinked. "I didn't. Brittle told me."

Navarr pounded the table. "Damn it, if I want to find out what the woman looked like, I'd ask her maid. Can you find her?"

"For triple the money—" Brittle looked away from Davit. "I'll deliver her into your arms. She's a renegade. Not my concern. I have it on good faith that she'll be at the Gold Key Inn in Auklet. Tomorrow night."

Scrud whispered a few words and Navarr nodded. "My assistant… Well, actually, Scrud's more my tutor. In the crafts. Magic. Oh, never mind. Scrud here suggests you bring a tracking spell. I'll supply it. You need only touch it to a corner of her sleeve and we'll find her."

Scrud opened a drawer in the table and pulled out a small, smooth shell no larger than a pea. He held it toward Brittle, but Davit stepped in, took it from his hand.

"I'll do it," Davit said. "I know the place. The ale flows and so does the talk." He glared at Brittle. "I'll find her. I give you my *good faith*."

*　*　*

The directions Brittle had given Molly for the Gold Key Inn were excellent. What he hadn't described was the reek of alcohol as she neared, kitchen scraps so old, even the cats mewing on fences kept their distance.

She came around a corner and caught the rush of voices. Men in low hats and rough coats stood shoulder to shoulder with women carrying pistols and knives and bandoliers heavy with spells and all of them, the lucky ones at least, with their arms wrapped around someone's waist. She hadn't decided yet whether she was right to trust Brittle, or if the kindly looking pawn broker with the sharp eyes had sent her into a trap.

In the weeks since she and Evan stole the chest, she'd sold exactly five spells out of the fifty or more inside, not counting the few of her own she sold Brittle. She'd met Macklin and hired a crew, but there were questions that gnawed at her, and she wasn't comfortable leaving them unanswered.

How was it that the governor's soldiers were already on the streets when she and Evan stumbled from the hidden door? Unless the two guards they'd fought in the tunnel were double crossed? They could have told someone their plans, and that person, hoping for a reward, warned the governor ahead of time and they were ambushed. But that didn't account for the other band shooting at them.

And how was it that the governor's nephew showed up at the one pawnshop she'd visited? Only two people knew she was going there, Evan and the woman who'd given her Brittle's name in the first place, and neither made sense. She was missing something and no matter how she looked at it, her thoughts circled back to Davit Lake.

She squared her shoulders and tugged her vest flat over the curve of her breasts then elbowed her way inside. She was dressed in the same clothes, the same face Lake had seen her in at the palace, the young up and coming merchant with the square jaw. She'd fit in well enough at the Gold Key, but she needed to jog his memory and the real Molly wouldn't do.

I'm Melvin Goodeye. I believe we've met? She practiced the name. *I'm Melvin Goodeye. What a coincidence. We met at the Governor's ball.*

Candles stuttered in iron brackets and the floor was scattered with straw and no one looked up as she made her way in. The large outer room held three long rows of trestle tables, and not an empty chair in sight.

Melvin Goodeye. She repeated the name and a red-faced woman carrying an overloaded tray raised a brow. "What 'cha say?" the woman barked. "Mussels and goat cheese? See the sign? You want to sit, you gotta pay."

"Is there drinking water?"

"Water will cost you. And don't be wasting a seat if that's all you want."

Molly held out a coin. "I'm looking for someone. A young man. Tall. Black hair. Probably well dressed?"

The woman set down the tray, looked her over, and the coin disappeared between her breasts. "Sounds too pretty for me, but I'll keep my eyes open, in case something come up." She unloaded a foaming pitcher and passed mugs along a table.

A circle gathered around a large, dark skinned woman playing a concertina and a few coins hit her bowl as she sang. *Oh, we'll sail through the isles, the star-wrought isles and it's many a wonder we'll see. For the day stars return we will always yearn, for the river of light set us free. Oh, the river of light set us free. So, we'll raise high our glass and we'll drink to the last...*

Molly wove her way through the outer room and into the next. It was darker here and the tables were pushed in wherever they fit. Further back were alcoves where men and women, partially hidden behind beaded curtains, visited in private.

She found Lake almost immediately, alone at a table with a clear view back toward the entry. He hadn't noticed her, and she hovered behind him, coughed then jostled his shoulder. Lake pulled his attention from the door and looked her over. "Do I know you?"

She pulled over a stool and sat. "Melvin Goodeye, sir. We met at the palace the night the chest was stolen. Everyone's been talking about it—"

He cocked his head. "I remember. I was hungry and I'd been on that damn balcony for hours. You gave me a drink?" He motioned and a kitchen boy came by with wine.

Molly slid her stool closer. Lake's words were slurred; his eyes shot with red. He was drunk and looking for someone. She didn't have much time.

Lake poured, and pushed a goblet her way. "Just please, don't turn into some fawning jack-a-dandy. I've had my fill of those. Oh, and the wine's no good till you've had a few."

She raised the goblet and watched as two men appeared at the entry. They were dressed in the blue uniform of the governor's personal guard and carried long swords and pistols, powder horns over their shoulders.

A third guard was more interested in teasing one of the serving girls. He glanced at Lake then quickly looked away.

Molly sipped the wine. She winced at the sour taste and set it down. She didn't know who Lake was waiting for, but maybe that would help keep his attention from her. She liked his face, she decided. It was narrow with a strong chin, and his eyes were dark. He looked less like the governor than the first time they met but then she remembered, it was Navarr's wife he was related to, not the governor.

He turned and Molly snapped around. Was he married, she wondered? Engaged? Not that it was her concern, but it would be useful to know ahead of time if he was climbing through some noblewoman's window.

The serving boy set two fresh goblets in front of them. "You've hardly touched your drink," Lake said. "Come on. It's not so bad as that." He lifted his wine and motioned Molly to do the same. She sipped then took a little more. "You have a sweetheart somewhere?" he asked.

Molly nearly choked. "No. Travel too much. You?"

"Nah. Same thing. Travel. Though I wouldn't object. Meeting someone, I mean."

He glanced over his shoulder and Molly stole the chance to dip her small finger in the wine. She drew it out and flicked a drop of the red liquid back inside. The wine sizzled. Bubbles gathered. Alcohol evaporated and only the safe, red taste of grapes remained. "Me neither," she said, drinking it down. "Nice looking girl, there." She nodded toward a woman across the room.

Lake followed her glance. "Nice breasts," he agreed. "You want to get introduced?"

Molly colored and shook her head and the next moment, when a serving boy refilled her drink, she drank it down without bothering with the spell. "So, that chest?" she said. "I'll bet the governor would pay a fine sum to get his hands on the rats who robbed him?"

Lake shrugged. "You haven't by any chance seen a young lady come in? Shapely. Well dressed. Tall for a woman. Hair sort of…" he paused. "There's a curl sits here, on her shoulder."

Molly frowned and wondered who he meant. She reached for her drink, then stopped. The wine was safe, wasn't it? She couldn't remember if she'd repeated the spell; it had to be crafted with each new cup. But Lake kept glancing about, and she couldn't risk being seen. "So," she said. "You're looking for the thieves? Night Watermen?"

Lake stiffened. "Why would I do that?"

"The thieves?" she said, confused. "Aren't you searching for the chest?"

"How did you know that?"

"You said so," she answered. But had he? She wasn't sure. She wrapped her hands around the goblet and drank.

A woman entered and Lake watched her move through the crowd, until she pushed back her hood and black hair tumbled free. He leaned heavily back in his chair. "Wrong color," he said. "I might have missed her, and I'd never know."

"Know what?" she asked uncomfortably.

Lake refilled their goblets. "Damn inn's too dark," he said. "Even if she was sitting right there, you'd hardly see the red in her hair. She'd be wearing a green dress. Or, well, maybe not here."

Green dress? Molly stiffened. He couldn't be talking about her, could he? She hardly remembered what she wore in Brittle's shop. And now, suddenly, she didn't feel well. She hadn't eaten dinner and the pipe smoke and odors from the kitchen weren't mixing with the wine. She had to think clearly, stay alert. "This girl," she asked. "You think she's involved with the theft?"

"That's just it," he said. "She's not. She can't be." The men at the table behind him were singing and he joined along. "*I had a little lady, and she was very fine, I put her in my cupboard, she drank up all my wine. Come on. Sing. I put her in my closet, she came out dressed in red.*" He nudged her arm, but instead of singing, she took another drink.

"I led her to my chamber, she sat down on my bed. I reached above her stocking, she laughed and then she said…"

Said what…? Molly couldn't hear the words. Fine rhymed with wine and red rhymed with bed. But she didn't know what came next and suddenly the floor, table and walls were moving, rolling like the seas. Her stomach heaved and she searched for an exit, but the guards were still at the door, hands on their pistols, seeing eyes braided in their hair.

Lake offered to fill her drink, but she hardly trusted herself to answer. He was schooled, pampered. And she hadn't missed the way the young women—and a few of the not so young ones—moistened their lips when he looked their way. "I think… The wine is getting to me," she said.

"This tavern is getting to me."

"I need some air…" She stumbled to her feet.

Lake snatched a bottle and two empty goblets. They tried to move but the crowd had tightened. A circle of men knelt on the floor and argued over a pile of shells. "Four," a man cried, and he slapped his knee in delight. "I'll trade my blunt-weapon for your no-voles."

"No, you won't," another man protested. His nose was dripping, and his eyes bloodshot. "That spell ain't worth the shell you stuffed it in. I'll give you the fire-starter but that's all."

"I rolled a four," he snarled. "And your fire-starter's no more than a toy." The man was full of bluster and drink and he started scooping the shells into his arms while the others shouted, and someone kicked him from behind. The shells spewed across the floor and he fell against another man who pushed him back then punched him in the face.

The fighting spread. Someone slammed his fist into another man's jaw and the man reeled and fell against Lake. He knocked over a chair and a woman kicked him in the shin.

Another man, his shirt half torn, came up on Molly. He tried to shove her aside, but she shoved back. He grabbed a glass bottle from a table, lifted it but she punched him in the stomach and his arm hit a post. The bottle shattered and glass shards flew. Someone grabbed her arm and she spun to find Lake, pulling her away.

"This way," he warned as a pistol shot rang through the tavern. People startled, shouted, scrambled to get away. Davit pushed her away from the door and back toward the galley where kitchen girls looked up from plucked chickens and boys chopping onions stopped and gawked.

They swerved between tables, upset a barrel of potatoes and tripped over a dog until finally, they were outside. The skies had opened and there was a sudden downpour of rain. Molly winced as heavy drops pelted her face. They were soaked, instantly, but Lake shook his head and laughed, and Molly stared at him then laughed as well. But it lasted only a moment before the door burst open and a rush of men and women erupted from the inn.

They ran into an alley between low buildings and Lake went up one side trying locked doors and Molly tried the other. She found a door that groaned and nearly moved, but the hinges were rusted, and when she tried to clear her thoughts and reach for a spell, she couldn't stop one of Evan's repair and transmute spells from announcing itself, front and center in her drunken thoughts. It wasn't supposed to work for her, it was a guild spell, but oddly, the hinges creaked, and the door shuddered.

"Not this one," Lake called from a door nearer the street. "Maybe now?"

The tumult of noises grew louder. There was brawling, and gunshots, probably on the front side of the inn.

She tried again, flattened her hand against the rusted latch plate, repeated Evan's words but in a different order this time and the door moved. She pulled back and frowned. The spell—a guild spell—was working and she didn't know why. Didn't know much of anything just then except that nothing stayed still anymore, not the ground, nor her thoughts, nor magic, or the world. Maybe she was drunk; she didn't know. But the world kept changing and Davit Lake seemed to be there every time it did.

He joined her suddenly, put his shoulder to the door and pushed with her and it opened. They tumbled into the quiet of a small room. She slammed the door behind them, and the world went black. "Where are you?" she whispered.

"Here." He tapped her shoulder and Molly jumped.

Melvin. He thinks I'm Melvin. Just another young merchant trying to grow rich. She felt her way forward till she reached a wall and then another door. It swung open and they found themselves inside a large well-stocked shop. There were cluttered tables and rows of shelving lit by outside street lamps. "It's a guild shop," she said, "I can't remember the last time I've been in one."

Lake cleared a space on a counter and pulled out the bottle of wine and two goblets. "You haven't missed a thing," he said. "I never liked these places."

He peered into a box full of bracelets with settings made to flip open, hold a cog inside. There were hairpins and glass vials with scrolls. Molly pulled one out and held it to the light. "Says it's a weathercrafter spell out of Nance Hall on Chriserin. I wonder what it does."

"I'm glad I'm not a witch," Davit said.

"Oh? And why is that?" She put the vial back.

"It's obvious, isn't it? They're hunted. Controlled. They have no freedom. The king uses them. The guild grows rich off them. Humans either fear or envy them. They can hardly live a life of their own."

Molly stared at him. She had never heard anyone, witch or human, say that before.

"They have the most precious gift of all and what does the guild do? Use them to make baubles, trinkets and toys. The stars gave us a land of bounty and when it's gone? Pfft. They'll have nothing. They won't know what to do. Not me. I'm glad I'm not a witch."

"Me too," Molly said awkwardly. "They can't work unless the guild says they can. Can't walk down a street without carrying their papers. Can't even sail their own ship without following some land-loving guild masters' rule."

"It's no better with the Night Watermen," Davit said. "A witch joins them, that's it. Can't go back." He looked embarrassed now, they both did, as if they'd said too much.

They drank in silence and wandered separately along the shelves. Davit started singing.

> *Flow like a river, shine like the sea,*
> *hasten the dark lights that set us all free.*
> *Sharpen your sword and strengthen your hand,*
> *human and witch and woman and man.*
> *Raise high the rafters, hasten the grain,*
> *thousand year star light shine upon us again.*

"You have a nice voice," Molly said. "What's the song?"

Davit shrugged. "Not sure it has a name. Just something I always knew. Haven't you heard it?" She shook her head.

He chose a painted shell from a basket and read aloud: "*Rain. 3 Tms. Qrtr. Section. Chant: In all the east, there comes a feast, of water, rain, and flood. Object: Vial included. Gesture: Press hands upward, apart. Repeat.*" He held it toward Molly. "It's yours for two silvers."

She shook her head and picked another. "*Light a fire, light a lamp. Three stones, included. Gesture: touch charcoal.* Is this the best they've got?"

"You can start a fire with your coal, and I'll put it out with my rain."

Molly laughed, then caught herself and stopped. She had absolutely, definitely, drank too much. She couldn't tell if he was joking or serious or hinting and if he was hinting, at what? "I'm not a witch," she said firmly. "You want to try a spell, go ahead."

"Me?" Their eyes met and darted away. "I'm not a witch. And anyway, aren't the cogs supposed to be registered before they'll work? I guess. I mean, I don't know."

"What do you mean you don't know? Haven't you ever bought a spell before?" She took a drink and watched him over the rim. She changed her mind. She didn't like Davit Lake, she decided. What sort of human never purchased a spell? Unless you were a governor's nephew. In which case he was pampered. Spoiled. Arrogant. She'd never trust anyone like that.

"Of course, I've bought spells. Plenty of times." He reached into an open shelf, pulled down the first thing he found: a tall, rectangular block of ice just large enough to lift with one hand. It sat on a footed stand, finely carved with fish and lacy strands of kelp. "It's heavy," he exclaimed and held it toward her.

She touched a finger to it, pulled back. "It's warm," she said.

"Yeah, I felt that, too. It's not real. But… Seems like every time I touch a cog lately, it turns warm. You think the guild's up to something?"

"Nah, the guild's too weak and busy fighting each other. If you're feeling something, it's probably the cog itself, the magic."

"You felt it too, the warmth, didn't you?" He watched her closely and she tried not to squirm.

"Maybe. I'm not sure. I mean, I'm not a witch, but sometimes, more often lately, when I hold a cog… I feel something. Warmth, maybe. Like the memory of the sun if it's a plant, or something that was once alive. The separate minerals inside a rock. The rocks in a mountain, the mountain on the land. The touch of water. Windblown across the rim—" she paused.

"I never heard anyone talk like that before. Not about spells, not about anything." Davit stared at her, then grew embarrassed and looked away.

"Maybe you should put it down," she said. She meant on the counter, but Davit pulled the block against his chest and slid to the floor. Molly set the wine goblets down, then the bottle and sank down beside him. Their backs were against a cabinet, legs straight out and shoulders nearly touching. Davit held out the block so they both could see. There were constellations inside. They shimmered with light, a perfect replica of the early winter sky. "It's not real," she said. "I thought it might be."

"It's crafted," Davit said, turning it around. "Look, there's a sea on the bottom, dark lights in the sky. I wonder how they got all those colors inside? It's almost like I can feel them, the colors. But that's not possible."

"Anymore than I feel warmth." Molly squinted and thought of her parents standing at the prow of the *Ice Warden* as they sailed too near the ice. Twisted mountains of sheer white cliffs rose ahead of them. The way forward was dark. Frost and fog clouded their way, and the ice narrowing around them.

What were her parents doing so near the rim; that's what she wanted to know. *The Stars cooled the Fire with Ice and created the rim to circle the world and keep it safe.* Safe? They'd been safe in Luna's Cove. For two people who spent so much time hiding, what were they doing? She glanced at Davit. He was still talking.

"You ought to see all the toys the king keeps in Jamasak. Tricks and gadgets and everything a game. His astrologers tell him anything he wants to hear."

Tricks and gadgets? Macklin had said nearly the same thing.

"Sometimes they find it floating, the rim sky. Everyone wants a piece. They sell it. The king could outlaw it but so long as he has enough, he doesn't care about the rest of the world, and the Night Watermen thrive on his folly."

Molly wrinkled her nose. "But you're one of them. Royals. You lived in Jamasak. How can you talk that way?"

She waited but instead of answering, he looked at her. His eyes moved from her face to her hair. Her mouth. He knit his brow. She stiffened and looked away "Did anyone ever tell you, you have beautiful eyes for a man?"

"No."

"I know what you mean. I used to get teased."

Molly couldn't imagine anyone teasing him. His eyes were too deep and his voice, when he sang, made her chest ache. "What in the seas would anyone tease you about?"

He stared at the bottom of his goblet. It was empty. He tipped it, waited for a drop. "Actually, I was fostered. I wasn't always 'one of them.'"

"Doesn't seem to have done you any harm."

"Then what am I doing drinking with strangers when I could be in the palace, all those noble women fussing with my hair. Anything left in that bottle?"

Molly shook it. "I don't think so."

"Just as well."

Well? She didn't feel well. Her stomach felt as if it was being squeezed to her throat. "It's hot in here. We ought to be going."

Lake was watching her again. She reached toward her hair then caught herself. A girl would do that, not a boy.

"Aren't you a little old," he asked, "for your skin to be so smooth? But… I'm sorry. That wasn't polite. I couldn't grow a beard myself until I was past eighteen. And my legs, they weren't as shapely as yours, just skinny."

Molly touched her face; her cheeks were smooth. Melvin Goodeye's square jaw was gone and her hair. Damn the stars, she could almost feel it growing longer. Her disguise was fading, and she was too drunk to keep it strong.

She slid lower, away from his side, and stared at their legs. Four of them. Stretched out side by side. His trousers were long, black and plain but hers were the same kind she wore to the ball. Fitted. Silk. They reached just below her knees and the white stockings… Oh. Her legs. He'd been staring at her legs. Her calves. Ankle. Narrow feet. She pushed herself from the floor. "I think I'm going to be sick," she said and before he could answer she was out the door and halfway down the alley.

7

Declination of a Grimoire

Evan hoisted himself to a window in the journeyman's study hall and peered inside. The hall was in a three-story tower with only a few windows at ground level and he needed to stand on a rock to see inside.

It was early and no one was about. He jumped down and hurried around to the door. There was just enough time to steal a messenger spell and make it back for lessons in the apprentice's hall before anyone realized he was late. Except... The door was locked.

He should have expected it. Ossian was being his usual annoying self, afraid that with so many visiting masters about, someone might be tempted to snoop around the outbuildings, find something they shouldn't.

It was impossible to miss the whispers and conspiracies. One hall failed to pay the king's tax. Another lied about the number of newly charted witches. Or cannons forged. Spells crafted. With all the furtive glances, it was a wonder the masters spoke to each other at all.

He searched the grass until he found a stick with a crimp in the end. He'd learned a spell for opening doors at his previous hall. It was a basic repair and transmute spell taught to first-year apprentices since it concerned itself with objects that already existed rather than the more difficult create and destroy spells reserved for second year apprentices. He ought to be able to get it right.

The spell required a stick that resembled a key; that was the object. The gesture was easy, a circle in the air then point, as if turning a key. The first part of the chant, *Thus I open, thus I close,* fit his purpose, but he couldn't figure out what the second part, *I am driven, in repose,* had to do with opening a lock.

And how did master witches come up with these chants, anyway? Separate the cogs into elements and they could be so outlandish, he wondered if crafting them had more to do with luck than skill.

To work, a spell needed to be refined to its basic essence; the chant, object and gesture of the cog. New spells were brought to the guild and tested to be certain the witch's power was infused—transferred into the cog— then registered, packaged in a shell, and sold. Multiple times if it was strong enough. The rarer the spell, the higher the price. The best were catalogued and taught to apprentices.

He closed his eyes, gestured with the stick and said the words. Nothing happened.

He scowled, tried again: *Thus I open, thus I close, I am driven, in repose,* but there was no click in the mechanism, no scrape of a hinge.

Sometimes—often— he wondered if he was the problem, not the cog. That maybe the lock, or the fog, or whatever spell he was trying to work didn't like the sound of his voice. Or sensed somehow that he was impertinent, or annoyed. That he'd as soon thumb his nose at the guild as spend another day in their hall.

He glanced over his shoulder. He could still make it back to morning lessons before the teaching master realized he was missing, but he had to hurry or one of the older journeymen was bound to come across the field and find him. Or maybe Molly was right, and he just needed to keep at it. The spell had worked before; he'd used it on other doors. He was too impatient and needed to pay more attention to the words, the gesture. Stop trying to rush.

He shook off his annoyance, tossed aside the stick and closed his eyes. He quieted his thoughts and instead of worrying whether he said the words correctly, focused and sensed his way inside. That was what Molly did and she never memorized cogs.

He wrapped his hand around the latch and felt the cold hard touch of metal and then further in, the point where copper and zinc ended, and pliant wood began. He sensed the points where the wood was intersected by bolts: each element true to its nature, and its nature as open as if he was seeing it in the clear light of day. The wood held warmth, a buried hint of sap in the grain. He felt the human hand that shaped the latch and planed the wood, smoothed the edges. He sent his thoughts deeper. Yes. There. He had it! The metal turned. The bolt slipped. The door creaked. He just had to be patient and focus.

He glanced to the stairs that curved along the tower walls, saw nothing and hurried to the master's desk and opened a drawer. It was filled with empty shells and he rummaged through them until he found two halves that matched. Next, he ran his hand along the outer edge of the desk. This wasn't the first time he'd sneaked into the building and he knew what he wanted. He flipped a catch and another drawer sprang open.

Inside on a velvet cushion lay a row of sleeping dragonflies. Their wings caught the morning light. Their legs were thin but strong. He picked one from the end and carefully tucked it inside the bottom half of the shell. A wingtip fluttered and he nearly dropped it in surprise. He closed the shell, then the drawer, checked that he'd left no footprints behind, and raced from the tower.

Outside again, the daylight was growing. He heard waves crashing on the rocks far below and the wind rustling the treetops. He stopped in the high grass, crouched low to hide. He opened the shell—the dragonfly hadn't moved—and held it to his lips. "Messenger," he whispered, and heard the tiniest scratch of insect wings. 'Messenger' was the chant. The dragonfly was the object.

"Molly?" he said quietly. "I have an idea. What if we went back to Luna's Cove? I know I complained, but we're not kids and it doesn't have to be the way it used to be. We don't need a legal charter and even if we had one, something would go wrong. Molly, I can't wait two more years. I won't make it. I'm learning cogs, but it's taking too long.

"Reed, he's new, too. He gets them the first time and so do some of the others, but the masters don't let us try anything on our own, and it takes me too long. Also, my Grimoire with my notes is missing."

A bell rang in the distance and Evan looked up. Reed had promised to hold the door, but he needed to hurry.

He pursed his lips and blew. The dragonfly unfolded itself and lifted its head over the rim. "Fly," he said. "Find my sister. Tell her what I said. Molly, get me out of here. Please!"

The dragonfly stretched its cramped wings and angled upward. Evan raised the shell higher and the wind changed. The dragonfly rose. Its jeweled wings whirred, and it sped higher until it caught a current and veered away and Evan raced across the field.

*　*　*

"You're just in time," Reed whispered. "Old Crotchety hasn't said anything that makes sense."

Janken Tarr, the teaching master, stood at a slate table in the center of the hall. Her voice was small, and her words disappeared into the rafters overhead.

"You see that?" Reed asked mischievously. "The King's Charter up there on the wall. What if tomorrow, there was just an empty frame instead?"

Evan started to answer but there was a girl close by on his left, and she poked his arm. "Quiet," she warned. "It's not worth getting in trouble for talking."

He'd seen the girl before. Cai. That was her name. He liked the sound; it was simple and straightforward. He had seen her in the great hall with the other new apprentices, everyone waiting at the long table for a heap of stew. One of the servers, a gawky town boy, got in a row with her about the mutton but the boy stopped when she mentioned the kitchen scraps he was stealing.

She was older than most of the new apprentices, but so was Reed and for that matter, so was he. He'd ask her about it sometime; she didn't seem shy. Boys were tested for their apprenticeship at twelve, but girls came differently into their craft, younger and at any time really, so it didn't matter whether she was ten or twelve or fifteen, like him. Except, he'd have to lie.

By the time most families pulled the guild fee together, magic had long been a part of their daughters' lives. Spells came easily to their lips, while boys suspected, but weren't certain until the dark lights found them. But though a girl might know she was a witch, a mark appeared only when she entered the dome.

Except for him and Molly, it hadn't happened that way. Evan's craft came early for a boy. He was seven the first time Molly called their mother to hurry, come see what he'd done.

They were in Luna's Cove, playing near the water's edge. Evan had dug a small hole in the sand and the sea came up and filled it with water. He crafted another hole, then another, long ropes of miniature oceans. He'd turned broken shells into perfect tiny ships with masts and sails and anchors and raised a wind to sail them back and forth in pure delight.

Molly was younger, hardly more than a toddler the first time she crafted a spell and there wasn't one spell, like Evan's. There were many. The rain she brought. The salmon with scales that changed colors. The too-hot afternoon when she turned water to ice. The rocks she slid from the hill. The day she steered the *Fish*.

Evan looked up. Janken Tarr had been talking. "And what is the purpose of an apprentice's first year?" she asked. She was a short woman, with large ears and a long neck that didn't fit the rest of her body.

"The first-year apprentice must watch and listen," they all responded.

Evan glanced at Cai. He liked the way her hair barely reached her shoulders. Brown hair cut so uneven, it looked as if she hacked it with a knife. She saw him looking and smiled, and Evan flushed and turned away.

"And what is the purpose of an apprentice's second year?"

"The second-year apprentice must take the lesson of the first year and practice. With ears to hear and eyes to see."

"Excellent."

Reed poked Evan in the side. "Good thing I got here in time or I'd never know."

"And now again," Tarr said. "Year one to observe. Year two to remember. Year three to practice. Year four complete. For those of you hoping to earn your journeyman's status—and I'm sure that means all of you. It certainly means the families who invested in you—you must first commit to memory the pages of your Grimoire. You will repeat each spell until you can recite them in full."

"Cog, cog, cog," Reed bobbed his head like a chicken pecking corn.

Evan chuckled and tried to be quiet, but Cai slipped in beside them. "Is that the best she can do?"

Tarr clasped her hands and paced. "All witches have within them an affinity for a particular element." She turned, walked back again. "A young girl enters a room. She's hardly more than a child but the adults sense a change. The room grows warm. Picture the mother as she looks to the hearth. The fire flares, yet no tinder had been struck. The father rises from his bench. He's curious. He orders the child to go out and return and again the room changes. A warm breeze strokes the mother's cheek. She's not a witch herself, nor, as far as she knows, is her older child, a bright girl with no sign of a witch's inclination. Her own mother was a witch, a woodcrafter though she never mastered, and she knows immediately that her daughter carries the star's blood in her veins."

"How much longer?" Reed whispered. "I'm hungry. I need to do my business."

"I was in Marce Hall," Cai whispered. "They lecture forever before they throw you a crumb of a spell. Sugar to salt. That was my first one.

Everything was fine until I got caught changing it back to sugar and hiding it in my room."

Reed made a face. "Where'd she come from?"

"Shh," Evan warned. "I don't want to end up scrubbing floors all week."

Tarr brought out a tray filled with assorted beakers, casks and spoons. She braced her hands on the table. "Sugar," she announced. She pointed to the first cask and spooned a small mound onto the tray. "Water." She pointed to a pitcher.

Evan looked at Cai. "How did you know she'd pick that spell?"

"Lucky guess." Cai smiled.

"Eventually," Tarr said, "You will all learn to transmute sugar into salt, but those of you who are watercrafters will do it more quickly." She paused as the door abruptly opened and Beryl Islandor, the warden in charge of the warehouse, hurried inside. Her gauzy robes lifted behind her and Evan jumped aside as she pushed her way through.

Islandor had sharp shoulders and white hair she wore in a nest of braids. She held out a note and waited as Tarr broke the seal. "Finally. Something interesting," Reed whispered.

Tarr's expression was tight as she and Islandor whispered back and forth until finally, the warden nodded, took back the scroll and hurried from the hall.

Tarr cleared her throat. "It seems we are done for the day," she announced. "Master Ossian has called a meeting with our guests. You're free to return to your rooms. You may move around the attics and upper floors but stay clear of the grounds and great hall. I suggest you use your time wisely and study your Grimoires."

"I'll bet there's a war," Reed said.

"All-out war? That's not possible," Evan said.

"Is too. What do you call the battle between the Night Watermen and the king?"

"That's just fighting," Cai said. "But this won't be about gold. It's about whether the halls can stand together against the king."

Reed snorted. "Since when do you know so much?"

She met his gaze. "I listen. Which wouldn't hurt you to try."

Tarr rapped on her desk. "You'll find copies of the most recent Grimoire in your rooms. I suggest, if you want to earn your journeyman's mark…"

"Junnyyyyyminnn," Reed mimicked her voice. "Maahhk."

"Shh." Evan elbowed him. "What's that she just said?"

"Part of a new decree," Cai said.

"…A year's reprieve," Tarr continued. "It will be difficult for most, impossible for some. A feat worth striving toward for all."

"What reprieve?" Evan asked.

"It means," Reed said, "that instead of scrubbing floors you get to bark like a dog."

"Three years instead of four?" Evan asked as soon as they were outside. "Is that true?"

"You still have to prove your craft," Cai said. "They wouldn't let you test for journeyman if you didn't know what you were. And you still need a spell to prove yourself."

"Three years," Evan said thoughtfully. "Ossian hinted about that."

"Difficult for most. Impossible for others," Cai said. "That would be me."

Evan stopped where he was. "Why? You knew everything Tarr was going to say. You'll learn in no time."

Cai looked away. "No time. That's the problem. I won't be here long enough."

Reed had hurried on and Evan and Cai were walking alone, shoulder to shoulder toward the main hall. It was the nearest he had ever come to being alone with a girl who wasn't his sister and he would have felt shy, but Cai was different. The way she talked. The things she said. They were real. Honest. "But you just enrolled? You can't leave so soon?"

Cai shrugged. "Didn't you notice I'm a little old to be a first-year apprentice?"

"For a boy maybe, but it doesn't matter for girls. And anyway, so what? I'm old, too."

"At least your family doesn't move you from hall to hall just when you meet people."

"Hey!" Reed pulled a carrot from the kitchen garden and waved it in the air. "Come on. We're free!"

Cai slowed and Evan matched her pace. "That's not true what you said, about moving all the time. I move too. I've been here five months. Eltiem before that. Hanna before that."

Cai looked surprised. "All right," she said. "But I doubt it's for the same reason." And suddenly, she leaned forward and kissed him on the cheek. A small kiss and then she was running toward Reed, shouting for him to wait. Evan stood where he was, hand on his face, until she glanced back, and he ran after her.

*　*　*

Tucked into the peak of Hayden Hall, Evan's attic was an odd shaped room. All angles and corners with one narrow window facing the sea, another looking toward the main gate and further away, the town and harbor. Evan sat with his back against the wall waiting to be sure Ross and Drew were asleep. Jak, the youngest of the three, had closed his eyes an hour ago, his book slipping from his hands.

Evan moved his candle to the sill and eased the Grimoire from under his pillow.

He wasn't as angry as when he first discovered his copy was missing, but he was worried about his notes inside. They could be incriminating. He couldn't remember whether he'd written Molly's name in the margin or just an 'm'. And he wasn't sure what happened after the books were collected. Were they scrambled together with no way to know which copy belonged to whom?

He ran his hands over the soft leather. *The King's Grimoire. Volume 2.* The calligraphy was nice enough; curling letters with embossed designs of the sun and moon. This one had more illustrations, and it was thinner all over, though the colors were sharper.

> *The King's Grimoire*
> *Granted and Codified by Artice Makken,*
> *King in Jamasak, Lord of the Isles*
> *Descendant of the Thousand Year Reign of Stars*

The next page was a picture of the dome of the stars in Jamasak with a perfect map of the constellations, and familiar words,

> *Those of Us Who Are Not Witches Give Birth*
> *to Sons and Daughters Who Are*
> *We are One People*
> *From the Living Stars Who Traveled the Dark Lights*
> *Raised High the Isles, Bequeathed us their Gift*
> *We are Sons Born Ready to Prove Our Craft*
> *Daughters to Master Our Own*
> *We are Water that Births Us*
> *Fire that Cleanses Us*
> *Sky that Sustains Us*
> *Ice that Surrounds Us*
> *We Rejoice in the Power We Share*

The words were the same as in his missing volume. And the words on the next page were the same as those carved into the walls of every dome and every hall. *Water that Births Us, Fire that Cleanses Us, Sky that Sustains Us, Ice that Surrounds Us.* An entire page for that single line. And on the facing page:

> *And Ice is the Greatest of These*
> *For With it the Stars Raised the Isles from the Sea*
> *And Crafted the Rim Which Circles the World, Protects Us and*
> *Unites Us*

Destroys Fire, Embraces Water, Shatters Stone, Moves Metal
Contains Earth, Reflects Sky

He leafed through the sections until he found the one on watercraft. Evan had often wondered whether that would prove to be his craft. Water spells weren't difficult; he and Molly used them to steer the *Fish,* though they used other spells as well. They navigated with sky, used warm air crafted by fire to steer; raised the anchor with water, used sky to repair metal fittings.

Or, maybe he wasn't better with water. Most of the *Fish's* spells had been placed there by their parents. He and Molly simply renewed them. But if he was to leave Hayden Hall a year early, he needed a spell worthy enough to become a journeyman. And if he needed to memorize a few cogs to get there, he would do it. He would do anything to be done apprenticing.

The major divisions were still there. Create and destroy, repair and transmute. Attract and repel or finding and hiding as the apprentices called them. And further down, within each category, the spells were further divided depending whether the witch had an affinity for ice or sky, fire or water.

But this was new. At the bottom of a page with an attract and repel spell— *To Turn a Ship in a Storm*—an alternate chant was listed if the first didn't work. What was that about? An assumption that a chant might not accomplish its goal? Was he now required to memorize an alternate list?

He looked to the other boys; they were still asleep. He closed the Grimoire, blew out his candle and slipped fully dressed from the blankets. He pulled on his boots and squeezed through the window to the outside ledge.

The sun had long since set and the night air was cool. The moon was nearly full, but directly overhead and he cast no shadow. Clinging to the wall, he felt his way to the inside corner, shimmied up the bricks and onto the long, low pitched roof. From there to the nearest chimney then down again on the far side of the hall and along another ledge.

He hadn't made a sound. The visiting masters were in the main hall in another wing, eating and drinking. He pictured them in their robes and finery, arguing over what price to set for their newest spells. Something to quiet a barking dog? Roast their meat to perfection? He snickered. That could be useful.

The masters at his previous hall used to say that in the oldest times when the stars still walked the isles, witches could do fabulous things. They could fly or turn invisible. Heal an illness or end a drought? Evan wasn't sure how much he believed, but he did know that these days, cogs cost more and did less, far less than even he remembered.

He found the window near Reed's bed, tapped the glass and a moment later Reed appeared, squinting in surprise. His eyes were barely open, but he motioned Evan to wait while he pulled on his clothes and tucked a knife inside his belt.

He climbed out and left the window open behind him. "How did you get here?" he asked. "You must have grown up climbing trees?"

"Rigging, more like. But I've been thinking—"

Reed stopped him. "Don't do that," he joked. "It's more fun to act first, think later."

A horse neighed and in the forest beyond the wall, an owl called, and another answered. Evan glanced down. The ground below their ledge was lit by yellow cog lights. Shadows stretched to the great hall. "Hey," Reed swatted his shoulder. "Don't look so serious. Where are we going?"

"I'll tell you along the way. But be careful. It's narrow and the stones are crumbling." Evan paced off the distance from memory. Sixteen steps back across the roof. Corridor. Stairs. Then the girls' side. Twelve steps. Corridor. Stairs. And then, finally an open window, dimly lit on the other side. They climbed through and Evan glanced along a narrow corridor. "This way," he said. "It'll take us to the library."

"That's all? You woke me for that?"

"There'll be Grimoires. Old ones. I'm looking for a cog. Something stronger than in the new volume."

Reed thought a moment. "I get it. But won't the masters be there?"

"No. They're in the great hall. They'll be there for hours. Shh. What's that? "A light flickered then disappeared.

"Who's there?" Reed whispered, then, louder: "What are you doing here?"

Evan whipped around. Cai was standing not a foot away. "Close the window," she warned. "You want to get caught? And move away from the stairs. Sound carries."

Evan did as she asked. When he turned back around the hall was lit by a pale light floating above her hand. Cai wore a hooded cloak over a shirt, trousers and soft boots. She carried a few shells on her belt and chest band, but none made a sound as she moved.

"You followed us," Reed said.

"Maybe." Her eyes flashed. "Maybe I used a tracking spell?"

"Maybe you didn't." Reed glared at Evan. "Did you tell her we'd be here?"

"No," Cai answered for him. "Did you see that last ship that came in? It had two gun decks, fully armed. The law says no more than five masters are allowed to meet outside Jamasak, but there's more than a dozen here and no one cares." She turned to Evan. "Where are we going?"

Reed's eyes widened. "She's not coming, is she?"

"The library," Evan said and before Reed could protest, he started for the stairs.

"Not that way," Cai said. "That leads to Sander's rooms."

Reed said, "He's in the great hall. Evan saw him."

"Well, that won't last. They hate each other."

"Where did you hear that?" Evan asked.

"My grandmother is a guild master. She forgets I'm in the room and likes to talk."

Reed rolled his eyes. "Half the apprentices I know claim to have a guild master in the family. It doesn't prove anything."

"It does when they're on the High Council. Diamond mark. Eighth degree. Jamasak Hall. I do hear things."

"You made that up. No one gets near the Council unless they're related to the king."

Evan stepped between them. "That's enough. It doesn't matter who her grandmother is. We're here, together."

Cai shook her head. "Not until he stops acting as if he's the only witch that was ever harassed by the guild. My grandmother is Ania Makken. I'll be happy to stand here and recite my lineage, but if you want to find the library, we don't have much time."

"Royal, are you?" Reed looked uncertain. "Makken, fakin. It's all the same to me." He glanced at Evan. "You heard her. We don't have much time."

They followed Cai in the other direction. She counted off three doors and stopped at a fourth. She pressed her ear to the wood, heard nothing and stepped inside.

They slipped quietly into a small room with a four-poster bed draped with a canopy. There was a desk with paper and brass stamps, a washstand and in a deep alcove cut into one of the walls, a statue carved from black marble. It was life-sized, the figure of a man dressed in ceremonial robes. It caught what little light reached the alcove and seemed to flow in waves of gray and black and darkest blue.

"Behold Haldin, the first of the stars," Cai said. "His nose is chipped and an ear's missing, but he's seen a lot of solstices go by. Push his arm."

Evan approached the statue. A stream of water spilled from its hand to its bare feet. The stone was smooth and cold, and Evan barely grazed the arm when it swung down and the wall behind the statue slid aside. A landing appeared and a stairwell leading into darkness.

"How in the seas did you find that?" Reed asked, his sarcasm gone.

"I didn't." Cai answered. "But I did spend the better part of an hour in the kitchen and if you ask the right question, people talk."

Evan entered first. The stairwell was steep and dark, and they walked one behind the other until they came to a small landing and a door. He felt Cai's breath warm on the back of his neck and startled, nearly bumping into her as she stepped past him and reached for the door. A moment later they were inside the library, shoulder to shoulder and gazing upward as they turned to take it in.

Evan glanced from the glass domed roof to the heavy beams that spanned the upper walls. He took in the shelves, eight walls packed floor to ceiling with so many books, he wondered if he could pull one out. A heavy wheeled ladder leaned against each wall and there were couches and red leather chairs in the center of the room and more chairs and couches filling the corners and nooks. He moved to the nearest shelf and ran his hands along the books and read the spines.

Reed crossed to an end table and picked up a block of ice. "You've got to see this," he called. "It's rim ice and it's filled with…" He turned it for a better look. "Rusty nails?"

Evan pulled himself from the books to see what Reed had found. It was ice, smooth and unmarred on the sides, jagged on top and filled with the oddest assortment of rusted brads, a strip of canvas that might once have been part of a sail, a shard of wood that could have been anything, a handle, a hammer, a spike. "It's junk," he said, surprised.

Reed said, "I never saw rim ice where I grew up. But I thought it was supposed to be grand, filled with… I don't know… Amazing things? The ice in the dome, sometimes there's pebbles inside, flakes of… I don't know. What is it really? I never thought about it before."

"Rim ice is rare," Evan said. "Or… Finding it is." He had seen ice, free floating pans and jagged formations that had broken off the rim and managed to reach Luna's cove. It wasn't surprising, Luna's Cove wasn't far from the rim. But it was also his and Molly's secret, and he didn't mention it here.

Cai touched the block then put her finger to her tongue.

"What are you doing?" Reed yanked it away.

"I wanted to see if it was real. Have you ever wondered which came first? Ice or the isles?"

Evan drew back. "What if it's from the other side?" he asked.

Reed gave him a look. "There is no other side."

"You don't know that." Evan scowled. "And since when are you so eager to believe everything the guild tells you?"

"All right, all right." Reed set the block back on the table. "You don't need to go all serious on me."

Evan turned away. He shouldn't have said anything. He didn't know what he believed about the so called 'other side' except that talk of the rim—the edge of the world—always reminded him of his parents. If they were dead, he wanted their lives to mean something. And the *Ice Warden*, too. He hated to think of their ship ending up as a shard of wood displayed in some suffocating guild hall.

He returned to the shelves and rolled one of the ladders into place and climbed the first rung. He pulled out a volume, pushed it back and tried another. He had never seen so many books. Never known so many existed or what they could possibly be about. *The Decrees of Doreen Makken the IV. With a Ship's Bell: Crafted Rigging on the Star of Jamasak.* It gave him an odd feeling to realize how little he knew; how childish it was to assume that he and Molly knew everything about the isles there was to know. The truth was, except for Luna's Cove and the halls he'd attended, the forays they'd gone on, his life was guarded and small.

And what was he doing dragging his friends here in the middle of the night, risking their apprenticeship when they hardly knew each other? He wasn't sure about Reed, but he could tell Cai trusted him. They thought alike. Had the same ideas, though she was smarter, quicker. He liked that about her, liked a lot of things.

She saw him looking at her. "I'll keep watch at the doors," she called. "You keep searching."

Evan nodded, climbed another rung and a word jumped out: *Grimoire.* It was a thick volume with the same dark binding as his missing copy. He glanced to Cai—no one was coming—and pulled it out. The leather had lost its smell, but it was clean, the binding smooth. *The King's Grimoire*, it said and below that, *Volume One, by the hand of Master Ettian Farway, scribe.*

Volume one? The one in his room was Volume two, the same as his missing copy, though they were different. He wrapped his arm around the ladder to steady himself and opened the book to find the same line drawing of the palace in Jamasak, but a different, longer list of cogs. The instructions were different, too. Confusing and less specific with only part of each spell explained. He kept reading.

Where a chant in a current Grimoire was written, '*The wind must rise the seas must churn, into the sunlight your gaze now turn,*' this one said, '*To change a wind, envision the desired direction.*' How was he supposed to memorize that? Or the human who purchased the spell? How were they supposed to know what to do? Where was the object? The gesture?

The shelves continued, row after crowded row of books in no order he could discern. The highest ended at the point where the fretwork of beams and glass dome began. He left *Volume One* partway out so he could find it again and climbed higher.

The ladder slid an inch along its track, and he wobbled then steadied himself and a moment later he found another Grimoire, a black one. There was no *King's Version* in the title, just the two words, *Black Grimoire.* His heart was pounding; he had hoped but hadn't really expected to find an older volume yet here it was, already in his hand.

He glanced down and saw Reed shaking a bottle. He made out a tiny ship in a storm of white caped waves. Reed stopped shaking and the ship leaned to starboard, righted itself.

Evan was about to pull out the *Black Grimoire* when a smaller book caught his eye. The binding was gold and it was pushed further in against the wall. The teaching masters spoke of three Grimoires. The *King's* in all its versions, and before those a Black, a Gold, and long before that, a Red. This was gold, and in better shape than he dared hope.

He opened to a random page. *Philosophical Arguments on the Nature of the Isles. Declination, Positioning and etcetera.* And the next page: *Coronal Activity and Seasonal Correlation to the River of Lights. Solstice. Equinox. Cross Quarters.* He flipped ahead: *The Collection, Recording and Dissemination of Information.* What information? He flipped back, searched for the cogs and tried to make sense of what he saw until suddenly, Cai called out.

"Evan?" Her voice was low, urgent. "*Ssst!* Masters. Hide. Up on the beams."

Reed was already half way up another ladder and climbing toward the heavy timbers that bridged the walls below the dome. Cai leaped for the rung below him, her hands at his heels. A moment later, the doors flew open and a line of robed masters streamed into the library. Reed caught hold of one of the beams and scrambled on top. *Hurry!* Cai motioned. *Move!*

Evan slipped the gold Grimoire back in its place and noted the location. If they were caught, it was better to pretend they were a few empty-headed kids, mucking about where they shouldn't be. He'd come back later, find it again.

But when he tried to push the book further into the shelf, it wouldn't go. He drew it out and pushed again then glanced below, counted four, five, six heads. Heron Sanders entered last and closed the doors.

He felt along the back of the shelf and touched something. Another book? He pried it free and stared at the faded red binding, so much smaller than the others. *Grimoire,* the cover read. Nothing else. No mention of a version or a guild hall or which king reigned in Jamasak when it was bound.

"Ssst!" Cai called again.

The masters milled about the room and settled into chairs. A few stood around a table with a decanter and goblets. They did not look up. Ossian held the bottle Reed had played with a scant minute ago. He shook it and tiny men and women clung to the mast as waves splashed across the deck.

Evan pushed the book back in place. He hoisted himself over the timber, tucked in his legs and inched toward Cai and Reed.

One of the masters, a younger woman, handed Ossian a goblet. "Stop pacing," she said. "You've nothing to worry about. Your wardens are everywhere."

Evan leaned out and saw Beryl Islander, Sanders and Ossian then guessed the others by their insignias. The eight-sided wheel of Sophen would be Master Clay. Zak wore the lily of Doshaget. A third man came into view and Evan recognized Tygner of Hanna Hall where he'd apprenticed until the wardens caught him pulling pranks and Molly refused to pay their fees.

Tygner's voice echoed inside the dome. "Your suspicions don't trouble me," he said. "It's what we do about them that matters."

"And how long we wait," Ossian said, "Another season while Artice Makken strengthens his navy?"

"If there's a war," one of the masters said. "We'll never win."

Evan reached the opposite wall and Cai grabbed his sleeve and pulled him in. "They're talking about the king," she whispered.

"He wants his witches," Tygner said. "There's nothing new."

"And he'll have them," Ossian said. "As promised. But what they're capable of, and what he does with them is none of our concern."

"It's certainly nothing we can control," Sanders said, and the others nodded.

Tygner said, "And when they take his blood test? What then?"

Beryl Islander raised a glass. "We have nothing to hide," she said. "Though I wouldn't presume to speak for the other halls."

"You talk around the truth," Tygner said. "But you won't face it."

"What truth is that?" Ossian said. "Families are hungry. They send their sons and daughters but keep the brightest at home."

Marice Marc, a young master with yellow hair, approached Ossian. "I'm not familiar with your astrologers," she said, "But mine speak of conjunctions, that the star Naiga is too near Saffa, that it doesn't bode well for the dark lights."

"Which we see for ourselves," Tygner said dismissively "What is your point?"

"There's no shame in being human."

Ossian glared at them. "Of course not. But neither should we waste time arguing. Whatever is happening among the stars, down below, the tides have turned. We have an ally. Or, should I say, a mutual enemy in the king."

Reed shifted his weight. The timber where they hid was no wider than their shoulders and blocked by a larger, angled beam. Reed pulled in his leg but a corner of his cloak dipped below the edge. He grabbed it, but not before Ossian caught the shifting light.

He looked up, waited, but the sound did not repeat. He pulled a shell from his belt, opened it and a wind emerged, a gust. It sped across the library, wheeled from one wall to the next. It rustled curtains. Lifted rugs and set the candles to flickering on their stands.

Evan pulled back just as a sprinkling of dust sprayed from Ossian's shell. Weightless pinpricks of silver, the dust blew into corners and cracks and wherever it reached, shadows appeared. Beryl on a couch. Marice sipping wine. Sanders beside a table. The dust revealed their shapes.

Evan held his breath but so far as he could tell, there was no hint of their shoulders or knees, of Reed with his arms crossed, Evan and Cai holding tight to each other's hand. The dust didn't reach their beam.

Ossian lifted the open shell. There was a whistling sound and the wind carried the dust back and it settled into its shell. Evan heard a snap as it closed, and then voices, the masters rising from their seats, setting down their drinks and finally, walking out.

"That's it?" Cai whispered. "Just that one finding and hiding spell?"

They waited to be sure the masters weren't coming back then ran. Down the ladders and through the hidden door and up the stairwell. Not until they were safely past the statue and out in the corridor again, did they speak. "Did you hear that?" Reed said, catching his breath. "What did it mean?"

"It means," Cai laughed, "they haven't got a decent spell between them. That dust never reached the dome."

Evan watched her smile. Joyful. That's what she was. Joyful and alive. She glanced at him, dipped her head. "He was trying to scare them," Evan said. "All that talk about fighting and the king."

"I'd be scared. If I believed it," Reed said offhandedly. "And you'd think he was an apprentice, using a shell when he could have crafted his own spell." He hurried to the end of the corridor, peered around the corner.

Evan stayed back. He looked to Cai.

"I might be an apprentice," she whispered. "But I didn't need any shells to find you."

"I'm glad you did. Find me, I mean."

"Apprentice," Cai said.

"Apprentice," he whispered back.

8

In for a Penny, In for a Pound

Auklet's harbor master Layf Neppit was proud of his position. It had fattened his purse, thickened his middle and taught him to appreciate the status accumulated through twenty years of service at the pleasure of the king, the Far-Away-King as Neppit preferred to call him rather than Artice Makken, Descendent of the Stars. "So long as he doesn't show his royal face in my harbor," Neppit joked to his assistant, "I'll call him any damn thing I please."

Neppit reclined in his chair, long stemmed pipe smoldering on his desk, stockinged feet resting alongside. He had just closed his eyes when his assistant rapped on the door and announced a Miss Sally Yarrow accompanied by her servant. "She's crying, sir. I don't know why."

"And I don't know why in the bloody isles you think you can—"

"You'll want to see her." The assistant winked and gestured rudely, and the harbor master straightened and looked to the door.

Macklin Cobb entered first. He was dressed neatly but plain, as a servant ought to be. Sally Yarrow, entering behind him, was far more memorable. She had chosen a red dress for the task at hand. It was fitted at the waist with yards of satin that were short enough to offer a peek of her well-turned ankle and low enough for a teasing glance at her soft, powdered breasts.

One look and Neppit was into his boots and rushing to greet her. He shooed his assistant from the room while he sucked in his belly and buttoned his waistcoat. "I have to apologize for my office," he said. "I wasn't expecting so lovely a visitor."

"Oh, no. It's perfect." Sally glanced to the windows. The shutters were open, the view to the harbor as close as a tax collector could want.

Macklin said nothing. He kept his gaze deferential and low and walked quietly behind Master Neppit and paused at the wide desk.

Sally dabbed her eyes. "I've heard so much about you, your kindness toward the ladies." She pressed against Neppit's leg and threw in an extra sigh in case he hadn't heard the first.

Neppit took her arm and, with his gaze on her freckled breasts, led her to his couch.

There was little of interest on the desk and Macklin moved to the run of shelves below the windows. Lower down were bills of laden to approve, taxes to collect, names to record, week after week and month after month, all dutifully labeled and stacked. The upper shelf held a spyglass and a ledger opened to the current week. Macklin turned to block Neppit's view and scanned the headings. Ship. Owner. Dates and nature of the cargo. He ran his finger down the page.

Behind him, Sally held out her hand and Master Neppit kissed her fingertips. They sat and Sally took his squat hand and rested it on her chest. "You must help me sir. My fiancée's ship hasn't been sighted in days. It can't be lost, can it?"

"Of course not," the harbor master reassured her. "A lovely girl like you shouldn't worry." He glared at the back of Macklin's head before putting his arm around Sally's shoulder. He was delighted and a little surprised when she didn't protest.

She leaned toward him. Her heart was racing, though not for any reason he guessed. "You wouldn't object, would you, if my man looks through your window? In case…" she sniffled. "In case my fiancé made port and—how can I even think it? —didn't care that I was waiting? All alone. But if his ship docked, you would know, wouldn't you?"

"You poor dear," Neppit cooed. He waved his hand for Macklin to go on, search for whatever in the seas his mistress required so long as he minded his own business, not theirs.

Sally rewarded him with a peck on his cheek. Neppit leaned closer and she tried not to grimace as his lips grazed her neck. She breathed heavily, and he pulled her in. She squeezed his knee and Neppit moaned. *Hurry!* Sally signed and Macklin loosened the handkerchief around his neck.

The seeing eye hidden in a fold of the fabric woke and opened its lid. Macklin found the entry for *White Lily* printed near the middle of the page. Registration. Ports of call. The seeing eye blinked. Date of arrival. Blink again. Macklin adjusted his scarf. Mooring fee. Guild tax. Tug fee. He passed those by.

Sally coughed. She reached toward the knife inside her boot and glared at Macklin. *Hurry you sot, or there'll be a mess to clean.*

He glanced at Sally, tried not to stare, and turned back around. Tonnage. Guns. Number of crew. Blink. Blink again, then found it: the full cargo list. Shells, blasting powder, tea, rum, gold. He closed the book, folded his handkerchief and the seeing eye returned to sleep.

Sally rose and startled the harbor master. She smoothed her skirt, pushed a stray bit of hair behind her ear. "We'll just be going," she said briskly.

Neppit looked confused. His cheeks were flushed and blotchy. "Wait. What?"

"Don't bother seeing us out," she said. "You've helped enough."

"Wait! Where are you going? Jamiss!" He barked at his assistant, but by then Sally and Macklin were too far to catch the words.

They reached the street and Macklin laughed. "That went well," he said.

Sally swiped the back of her hand roughly across her mouth. "That's because he wasn't pawing at you. Let's get out of here before he sticks his face out the door and I shoot the man."

*   *   *

The sky held dark though morning was near. Molly felt it with each breath, as if a wave was gathering inside her. The crew felt it as well. They were spread along the *Fish's* deck, on ratlines and perched on the yards waiting for Molly's signal that the merchant vessel *White Lily* was in sight. Only Brigit remained below, checking that their cannons were ready, rammers and sponges, projectiles and spells all in place.

Molly gripped the rail and watched for a lantern flare or the ring of a distant bell. If there'd been no run-ins with pirates or marauding Night Watermen, and if nothing was amiss, the *White Lilly* would be anchored in north and east of Tars. Her cargo was due to be downloaded to a barge later in the day. Precious cargo picked up in the towns of Samsid and Treest and carried to Auklet where it would be offloaded, and their travels started again. But not before Molly and her crew paid their little visit.

Troth jumped to the deck. He'd left his concertina in its case near the binnacle and he picked it up and pulled a few notes. Molly nodded her approval. The *White Lily* was far enough away, the sound wouldn't carry. Nick joined him, singing. His voice was low and sweet, and Sally moved in to listen then caught him watching and quickly looked away.

Molly looked away as well. She was captain; she wasn't supposed to stare at the dueling lovebirds, but it was difficult to feign disinterest. She had seldom—no, never—seen anyone fall in love. If that's what this was. She thought it might be, though she wasn't sure what it would look like, or how they would know.

Macklin pulled out a mouth harp, sat on a barrel and played as Nick sang.

"*He's a sweeter lad than I am, Mistress Sigh. Dressed in silks and handsome britches, Mistress Sigh.*" He glanced meaningfully at Sally. "*If he takes you to his bed, then be warned you'll never wed. So, beware the fancy sailors, Mistress Sigh.*"

Sally fixed her gaze on the water and refused to look his way.

Nick moved on to the woman's verse and raised his voice an octave. It would have been silly, but his voice was too pure to ruin even a bawdy tune like that. "*If I take you to my bed, Mister Lie, will you cover me in kisses, Mister Lie? When the flush has left my cheek and the children's cry is bleak, will I find you at the tavern, Mister Lie?*"

And lowering his voice again: "*I'm a better man that he is, Mistress Sigh. If you take me for a husband, Mistress Sigh, from your kisses and our home, I will never need to roam. I will hold you as a treasure, Mistress Sigh.*"

And the woman's answer: "*I will draw my own conclusions Mister Lie. In my bed or if I'm wed, I will see the babes are fed, and be damned your moonfaced pleading, Mister Lie.*"

The verse ended and Molly's thoughts returned to the vessel they were about to plunder. She was tense, but confident, too. They had planned carefully. At the very moment Sally and Macklin knocked on the harbor master's door, Brigit and Nick were adding spells to smooth the cannon's chambers, and in another part of town Troth and Tribolt were cutting the locks on a warehouse door and riding off with a wagon full of enough gun powder to face an entire fleet.

They had checked their spells and refined their plans and drilled and drilled again. Macklin raised a wind. Tribolt worked the sails. Sally fixed their position. Brigit started her fires. Nick and Troth put them out.

The *White Lily* was one of five carracks registered to a mercantile family out of Samsid. She was a three-masted vessel, ten years old, with a wide beam which allowed her to carry a heavy cargo but made her slow, and—if nothing went wrong— the odds of the lighter *Fish* out-sailing her were very good.

And afterward, when the stolen cargo was safe aboard, they'd make for Luna's Cove, divide and store the prize, then sail east, maybe for Khenry and the small towns on the archipelago there. They'd sell whatever remained and see if there was any land worth looking at. She didn't expect the *White Lily* to bring in all the money she'd need, but it was a step along the way. They'd be honest folk someday, wealthy, but not flaunt it. Pay their taxes with one hand, thumb their noses at the guild with the other. But most important, they'd have a home they wouldn't have to leave, on streets they could walk without having to hide.

She hadn't yet mentioned Luna's Cove to the crew, but she would, soon. They had been surprised, but less suspicious than she expected when they learned she was craftborn. With luck, Luna's Cove would be just another piece to her story. And though she hadn't heard from Evan since she'd jumped the wall at Hayden Hall, she thought he would approve. She hoped so. She was doing something, more than merely talking.

And finally, a hint of morning light touched the horizon. Molly scanned the waters with a spyglass and the hump of a ship appeared. A mast took shape, dark against the brightening sky. She made out the ship's castles, higher in the stern and—she narrowed her eyes— an orange pendent with a black tern fluttered above the mainmast. Samsid's flag. It was the *White Lily*, anchored north of the sound, exactly where it was supposed to be.

Macklin was on the quarterdeck waiting for her sign. "Raise anchor," she called, and he nodded toward Troth. "Raise anchor," he repeated and Troth, already at the capstan, set his hand to the winch's bar. Troth was the oldest member of the crew, but he was lean and strong and his movements as elegant as a younger man. He touched off a spell and slowly at first, creaking, and then faster than two or three sailors on a human crew could manage, the capstan's bars began to turn. The line drew tight and far below on the rocky bottom, the anchor pulled free and rose.

"Lay aloft and loose all sails," Molly called, and Nick was ready. Turning in the crow's nest, he gestured at the foresail, the mainsail, the lateen sail as well. Lines pulled and canvas fell and waited to catch the wind.

The wind was Macklin's job. He reached for the rail and felt his way forward, like a blind man searching for a scent until he found what he needed: a chill on his forehead and face. A wind not so strong he couldn't shape it; not so slight it couldn't speed the *Fish*.

Molly felt it too, the shudder of wind and cooler air. A pair of orange beaked puffins swerved and changed course and flitted above the waves. Gulls squawked and circled, avoided the ship as Macklin's wind brought the *Fish* nearer the *White Lily*, a mile now and closing.

Brigit loosed her spell. It darted up the stairs to the aft deck and flew from line to line exactly as they'd practiced. Flames—or more precisely, the illusion of flames—swept upward along the masts and reached for the bowsprit and sails.

A half mile away, on board the sleeping merchant ship, the second mate waited for the bell to signal the end of his watch. His thoughts were on his empty stomach and the kippers he hoped to coax from the taciturn cook. He paced the larboard deck, turned and stopped as a flash of light caught his eye. Puzzled, he waited until he saw it again, not a lantern but a flame, yellow and bright and low on the water where no light ought to be. "Fire!" he cried, and he ran for the bell and sounded the alarm.

Molly's heart raced as tiny figures rose from a hatch and pushed their way to the *White Lily*'s rail. "Raise anchor," a voice called. "Loose the sheets."

She swallowed her excitement. "Wait," she told her crew. "We need them near. We need to locate their witches." She checked her weapons. Two wide bore pistols. Extra powder horn if she needed to reload without a spell. Knives strapped to her calf and in her boots and belt. A pocket pistol inside her vest. Loaded. Halfcocked. Ready.

"We're in range," Brigit said behind her. "I can bring them to their knees and we board after. Say the word."

Molly shook her head. The *White Lily* was drawing near, but slowly now and she needed to be patient. Brigit might be experienced, but this business of taking a ship was new to her. The cannons were in range but shoot now and she risked sinking the *White Lily* and losing the cargo, and the trust her crew had put in her, as well. "Ready the guns," she said, "but hold to the plan. We board first then find their witches."

She glanced at Macklin; he carried pistols and a boarding ax. A grappling hook waited beside his feet and hers, and Nick's and Troth's as well. Sally adjusted the rudder as the *White Lily's* bow began to turn and the *Fish,* with its sails billowing smoke, slipped through the waves to meet the oncoming vessel, an eighth mile and closing.

It was full light now and Molly picked out a lone figure on the forecastle, a woman, tall and straight backed, a bullhorn in her hand. "Jump," the woman shouted. "We're lowering our boats. Whose flag do you fly?"

Molly cupped her hands to her mouth and, doing her best to cower and look frightened, glanced to the flames shooting across the sails. "Can you help?" she shouted. "We need a doctor. We've injured people on board."

A second figure joined the woman at the *White Lily's* rail and Molly recognized the captain she'd seen on shore. His white hair billowed in the wind; he wore a short jacket with bright buttons. The woman passed him the bullhorn and the ship continued to slow. A third figure, more heavily armed, stepped in alongside.

They conferred for a moment then, "State your name," the captain called. "Who are you? What flag do you fly?"

Molly looked to her crew. "No one answer," she warned. "They're suspicious."

"Too suspicious," Tribolt agreed. "They're wondering why we haven't jumped."

Molly crouched below the gunwale and made her way to Macklin. His wind had slacked; they should have been closer. "Someone's slowed it," he said tightly. "They've a witch on board, maybe two, but I can't find where."

Molly glanced at the flames. They licked the air and blazed with color but anyone paying attention would realize the fire hadn't spread past the initial burst. She caught Troth's attention. "We need a decoy," she said. "Can you buy us time?"

He thought a moment then motioned to Nick. The younger man shimmied down the mast. "Get me a board," Troth said. "Or a rope. A rope will do."

"They're loading their swivel guns," Tribolt warned.

Nick unrolled a coiled rope and Troth hacked off two, then three ragged lengths. Anyone watching from the *White Lily* would see only the clouds of smoke and blaze of flames consuming the ship, not the man peering above the gunwale as he chucked a few lengths of rope overboard. Troth gestured again and the ropes began to change They stretched and split and shaped themselves, first into rafts and then into three small, square sterned boats, the size of ordinary rowboats.

Simple things, they bobbed and rose and—Troth nodded a third and final time—the fibers split and wove themselves, knotting and twisting until shapes appeared, the outline, the suggestion of sailors huddled close for support. Their heads were bowed, shoulders pressed together, sodden clothes black with soot.

Across the waves, the *White Lily's* crew paused, and the captain shouted to bring the injured aboard, then he turned and climbed below. He had barely disappeared when the *Fish* bore down on the *White Lily*. Guns blasted and sailors screamed as they fell. The captain raced back to the rail, shouting for his crew to change course, pull back, hard to port, but it was too late.

Brigit's shot exploded from the fore guns and hurled across the water. A second cannonball hit the *White Lily's* rail. The deck burst into a rain of shards and debris and a man was killed, a splinter through his back. The captain was slammed back as men and women shouted and raised their arms to shield their heads. A third cannon burst, chain shot this time. It shredded canvas and tore the ropes and the *White Lily's* sailors lurched for their swivel guns.

Molly reeled as one of the women turned a swivel straight on at the *Fish* but Brigit was watching. She pointed at the distant gun, gestured, and the volley exploded midair. A second swivel aimed high and Brigit pointed again. The shots hung suspended for a moment, then fell and splashed uselessly into the waves. The *Fish* remained whole, unharmed.

Molly readied her grappling hook. She had practiced this, wrapped sheeting around the barbs and taken aim, hefted and swung till the weight of the shaft, the timing and release was familiar, like something she had always known, and knowing it, wasn't afraid.

She hurled the hook straight on for the *White Lily's* rigging, yanked hard and felt the barbed flukes bite.

A moment later and she jumped and sailed across the water and lit down on the *White Lily's* rail with Macklin a heartbeat behind her. She glanced over her shoulder to be sure that Nick made it, then Sally with a dagger in one hand, double barreled pistol in the other. Troth and Tribolt landed with boarding axes and cutlasses raised. Brigit jumped last and for a few brief moments it seemed the *White Lily's* merchant crew was too confused to fight back. They gaped at the rippling flames and waiting for the fire to reach and take them all. When it didn't, when they realized they'd been tricked, they cursed and drew their swords, cocked their pistols and started shooting.

A blustering, red-faced man turned his gun on Molly, but she fired first. Her pistol dislodged, hit his leg and he crumpled backward while another man jumped to avoid tripping over him. He raised his cutlass and Molly drew her dagger. He lunged but she jumped aside and came in quickly with her shorter blade and slashed his arm. His cutlass fell and she kicked it aside then smacked his head with the butt of her pistol.

Off to her left, a sailor raised his ax above Macklin's back, but Molly saw and fired first. The man fell and Macklin wheeled to fight another. There was shooting everywhere, officers barking orders, sailors pulling mates from beneath ruined sails, men and women groaning.

The *Fish's* crew was outnumbered but the *White Lily* was unprepared. Tribolt grabbed for the halyards just as a sailor lunged at him. He raised his ax, slashed, and the man fell overboard. But when Tribolt paused to gauge the battle, he slipped. His feet went out and he cursed then stared at the deck in front of him.

Molly followed his gaze and turned to find him crab walking backward, revulsion on his face. The deck in front of his feet was moving, undulating with black orbs. They crawled toward him. Crab-like creatures, eyeless but toothed, repulsive with nail-thin legs that clinked as they came.

Behind him, Sally shouted as a man twice her height swung his blade. He was slow and she dodged then went for the opening below his arm. But her sword bent as she rushed in. The blade sagged as if it was clay, too soft to hold its shape. Sally stared in surprise then threw the useless weapon aside. The man swung and she whirled and pulled a second knife from her belt. Again, it crumpled and she feinted right and left, evading the man's blade until somehow, thankfully, her blade stiffened again and held.

Molly shouldered her way toward a door. Until now, her crew had held the advantage, but no more. There were witches aboard. Somewhere. Hiding. With the last of her flintlocks cocked, she searched what seemed to be the captain's quarters. Well apportioned and neatly trimmed but no one inside. She tried a smaller cabin. Bunks. Sea chests. A writing table, but no one there.

She swept through the aft cabins and found a woman loading a gun, a pale-faced man drinking rum. Passengers. No hint of a witch's craft, no sign of any spells. She raced back for the weather deck and stopped short.

The fighting had paused. Men and women gazed upward as twilight passed over the sky. In place of daylight, hundreds, thousands of lights, pin pricks of color began to burst and fall. A shower of sparks shot toward them. For a single moment it was beautiful and mesmerizing, but Molly backed away.

Witches were doing this. The spiders attacking Tribolt. Sally's blade suddenly useless and now, cog-fire falling from above.

Nick shouted and slapped as they burrowed though his clothes and burnt his shoulder. Troth tore at his shirt and Sally shouted, but none of the *White Lily's* crew were touched.

Molly pressed up against the castles' wall and sent her thoughts below and along the decks. She searched for a touch of power, magic and found… Nothing. And again, nothing wherever she searched. Until, finally she heard something. A murmur, as if someone whispered in her ear. Not from the lower decks but nearby. She forced herself to wait, move slowly.

She didn't see the woman at first. She ducked behind the mainmast, around the binnacle. She passed Macklin as he punched a man across the jaw then found her, a woman in plain clothes; human and covered in shells. On her chest band and in bulging pouches. Slung over her arm and hanging from cords. Scores of shells. Oval and round and small and large and dark as a pistol shot and all of them—save for the pile of empty shells littering the deck—loaded and ready.

She scowled in anger. What sort of ship owners had so little regard for their cargo they trusted it to a human armed with spells? Were they hoarding pennies? Afraid the few witches they might have hired wouldn't be strong enough?

The woman snapped open a shell, murmured, and high overhead, another round of cog-fire flared.

Molly stepped forward and the woman spun about. She was purposefully unremarkable; neither young nor old, nor tall nor short, her face easy to miss in a crowd. Her gaze shifted to Molly's pistol and she seemed surprised to find someone come up on her, unaware. "Lay down your weapons," the woman ordered. "You can't win."

Molly didn't shoot. She answered with a nod and the first, the simplest unlocking spell that came to mind. She'd used it not so long ago…

There was a tinkling sound as one, then another, then dozens of cog-fires cooled and rolled uselessly about the ship. And not just the cog-fires but the rest of the woman's shells, from around her neck, her belt and chest band and piled at her feet. They opened and bits of parchment and fabric fluttered away. Sticks and pebbles and tiny vials and leaves scattered uselessly about. The spells faded. The sky brightened and the woman backed away.

Molly had expected to feel victorious and elated but she didn't. She wanted this battle to be over. She wanted to claim her prize and be gone.

She scanned the deck and grabbed hold of a dangling rope and swung past Macklin locked in an embrace with one of the *White Lily's* sailors. Past Tribolt as he brought a barrel down on someone's head. She landed in front of the captain, released the rope and aimed her pistol. "Yield," she said. "Yield and I'll spare your crew."

"Yield?" The captain gawked. "Who are you?"

Molly searched for a name. "Rista Marsh," she said. "Captain of the *Meridian*."

The fighting slowed as first one sailor, then another lowered their weapons to listen. The captain carried a sword and a gun, but he was a merchant not a soldier, and she suddenly wondered if he even knew how to use it. "Yield," she said, louder. "And your crew will be spared, Captain…?"

He snarled as he glanced past Molly, took in the ruined deck, the slashed sails and fallen sailors. "Kasz," he said tightly. "Captain Hugo Kasz. And you have illegally, against all charters and laws of the King boarded a merchant ship. While your vessel and that—" He gestured toward the *Fish* which, though flames still licked at the sails and rigging, was obviously not in danger. "What is that, some sort of mirage?"

"My ship is no concern of yours, but you have a crew to protect and I suggest you do it."

Kasz started to speak then hesitated as he caught sight of the woman who'd been armed with the spells. He looked confused, then surprised.

"Tell your crew to lay down their weapons," Molly said firmly. "No one will be harmed."

Kasz straightened his shoulders. "What? You steal a few spells and think that's enough to save you? You Night Watermen can't hide forever."

Night Watermen? She stared at the captain. *Is that who he thinks we are?* All the more luck to her if the king hears it was Night Watermen, and not renegade pirates thieving in the southern seas.

In any case, his dithering was annoying. They had talked enough, and her left arm ached and her ankle felt as if she'd twisted it running. She looked for Macklin, found him watching from a crate beside the mizzenmast. She caught his attention and glanced meaningfully toward an upended barrel and a few ruined bits of blackened cog-fire.

Macklin nodded. He understood. He turned, motioned for Troth then Tribolt to be ready. He picked out the rest of their crew and they quietly stepped back, away from the *White Lily's* sailors. The ship dipped suddenly into a swell.

Molly grabbed hold of the rail. She closed her eyes and lifted her face toward the sun and felt its heat, the strength of its rays reaching down from the sky and into the water, into the ship, and across her face, her body and arms. She drew it in, the light and heat, and let it push away the exhaustion. Clouded days or clear, the sun was still there. Through rain. Inside the night. The sun was still there and her craft, like the sun, was still there.

She opened her eyes and picked out a barrel nearby the mast; she pictured the tiny shots of cog-fire fallen against the base. The barrel staves growing warm. Drinking in the sun's heat. She focused and sharpened its rays and a moment later, tendrils of grey smoke mingled with the tang of burning wood.

The captain saw the smoke and stiffened. "What's going on?" he demanded. "What are you?"

"Night Watermen," she answered. "You found us out, and I won't offer again. Call off your crew and the terms will be fair."

"Fair?" he snarled back. "And what does fair mean to a pack of thieves? You're in no position to discuss terms."

Fair? Molly's thoughts turned. Evan wouldn't find this fair, not when he'd been left behind with the guild and missed the fighting. And if her parents were here, she'd tell them they were wrong to hide when they could have fought for their freedom, not run.

She had said she needed a second ship, and she did. But the *White Lily* was here, beneath her feet and suddenly, she didn't want to settle for stealing their cargo then go back to waiting and hiding and waiting again, until she had enough prize money to buy that second ship. There was no glory in fighting a merchant captain. And she didn't need to wait to buy a second ship, when she was standing on its deck.

Nor did she want this simpering man to leave with his cargo taken but his ship intact, pretending he had saved his crew. The owners would put it in dry dock, grumble about the cost of repairs then back on the seas it would go. They'd find another human to work whatever spells they'd bought. And where would her crew be, except hounded by the guild and waiting again.

"Fire!" Macklin shouted. "Fire on the deck."

Molly smiled. "What does 'fair' look like?" she asked the captain. "It's this ship in trade for your lives."

The barrel broke into flames and the captain's eyes widened. There were ropes nearby and lines. One spark and the fire could spread… Molly didn't move.

The *White Lily's* crew grabbed for buckets, filled them with water and hurled it at the barrel. Off to the side, Macklin quietly reloaded his pistol. The rest of her crew, unnoticed, picked up a few stray blades and slid knives into their belts.

Kasz looked suspicious. "You'll let us keep the ship?"

"No," Molly said. "We'll keep the ship, and we won't kill you."

"And the cargo?" he sputtered.

"Remains with us. I'm sure you'll do everything in your power to convince your employers you took the high ground."

"They'll never believe me."

"They will when you remind them it was their choice to buy cogs instead of hiring witches. Their ship's still afloat. They can fight me, win it back. You have five seconds, Captain. You are what? Twenty miles out of Auklet?"

"You'll be found. You won't get away with this."

"But you will," Molly said. "Think about it. You aren't abandoning your ship. You're saving your crew."

Kasz shook his head in disgust. He glanced fore and aft, from his crewmates to the masts, the hatch, and back to the fire. It was growing, enveloping the barrel and threatening the deck and nearby ropes. He'd lost three of his crew, and more were seriously wounded. They looked pale, and exhausted.

"Captain Marsh." He addressed Molly in a different tone. "Might I have a moment with my second mate?" Molly nodded and Kasz and an older man in a blood drenched jacket huddled in conversation. A minute passed and though the fire was nearly gone now, Kasz gave the word, and though there was grumbling and narrowed eyes, the *White Lily's* crew threw down their pistols, dirks and cutlasses.

The pile grew until, last of all, Kasz unbuckled his belt and dropped his jeweled sword atop the mound. Shells and cogs and seeing eyes followed until finally they were done. Molly allowed them time to attend their dead and they wrapped the three sailors in torn sail cloth and the *White Lily's* crew gathered tensely about. The day was wearing on as they spoke their farewells and, with Brigit guarding from behind, gave the bodies to the sea.

It was a brief and somber affair after that. Brigit held her guns on the crew while Sally and Nick lowered the *White Lily's* two long boats—but no oars— into the waiting sea. Tribolt tied the crews' arms behind their backs and steered them into seats. The captain climbed in last. Macklin gave a shove and the boats heaved into the waves.

By the time Macklin climbed back on deck, the mood had changed. Nick had found a piglet down below and held the squirming thing triumphantly in his arms. Sally danced with a bottle of wine in one hand, rum in the other.

"We set course for Luna's Cove, my home," Molly announced. "Two days toward the rim, south by south east." She felt excited again, not for the fighting that was behind them now, but for what lay ahead. "We divide everything, spells and guns and gold, as I promised, and we'll make plans. We'll repair the *White Lily* and when we're done, we do this again, but better next time." She paused as she caught the question on everyone's face. "These sailors weren't our enemy," she said. "It's the guild we're going after. The guild and the king, and the gold and dignity they tried to steal. It's ours. Our lives. We won't let them steal it again."

9

A Confusion of Slips

The hidden door into the library opened at Evan's touch. Reed nearly knocked him over as he hurried inside, and Cai closed the door quietly behind them.

No lamps were lit, but the moon showed through the glass roof, and it wasn't difficult to see. Reed walked straight to the block of ice he'd played with the first time he was here. He squatted down, tapped the frozen sides. "It's got to be real," he said. "Else how would all those nails get inside, and why would they waste so many spells keeping it solid?" He glanced at Evan. "Tell me again what we're looking for?"

"A Grimoire," Evan called. "Small and red. It's on one of the high shelves. Up there."

Cai stepped back for a better view. "And you think those old spells will still work?"

"I hope so," Evan said. "I can't stay here. It's stifling and I feel like I'm lying, every day." Her shoulder brushed his and he stopped. Cai was dressed in black leggings and boots, a tunic that fell just past her knees, the hammered dagger in her waistband in easy reach. She smiled and a tiny, perfect crescent appeared on each side of her mouth. His heart jumped and he turned, hurried for a ladder.

He had intended to return alone to the library, but Reed had pestered him into telling his plan, and once it was out, he couldn't exclude Cai. Though now, he wished she wasn't here. Caught alone, he'd earn a box on the ears and a week's worth of menial duty, mucking out stables or pig sties, chopping firewood. He wouldn't care. But if Cai were dragged in front of Ossian—or worse, expelled from Hayden Hall—he'd never forgive himself.

"The day I'm a journeyman, I'm gone," Reed said. "It will be just me and the more spells I can sell, the better." He set the block back on the table, then bounced into one of the velvet chairs, jumped up and tried another. "I wonder if that's what they really looked like."

"Who?" Evan asked.

"The stars," Reed said. "Though I don't know why we call them that; they're supposed to have been real people. The guild wouldn't tell the truth even if they knew."

Evan said, "A thousand years is a long time to remember."

"And if they knew, who's to say they'd put it in a Grimoire?"

"They'd erase the truth," Evan said. "Every time they wrote a new Grimoire and hid the old. The Red, the Gold, the Black. A thousand years of history, forgotten.

"Enough talking," Cai said. "We're taking too long. Which shelf was it on?"

"This one," Evan said, starting up a ladder." He climbed a few steps, leaned back to check the angle then climbed down and chose another. Cai started up the ladder to his right.

He was twenty feet above the ground, nearly to the horizontal roof timbers when he found it, a tiny volume tucked in the shadows, exactly where he'd left it. He wiped a smudge of dust from the top, and it opened to the same page as before. *Philosophical Arguments on the Nature of the Isles.* The heading made no sense.

He looped his arm around the ladder rail, steadied himself. *As posited by Serifka; When considered as a whole, the color, degree and intensity of wind upon the Lights may infer an equal reaction in the crafts—*

Suddenly, "Hide! Now!" Reed had climbed the ladder behind Cai and was hissing and motioning him to hurry, move.

"What? Again?" Evan cursed and closed the book just as the library doors flew open. He tucked the book in his vest, saw Cai with one leg already over a beam, and Reed just behind her. He grabbed for a timber and pulled himself up.

Dressed in their formal robes, head pieces and sashes, the guild masters filed into the library. Ossian raised his hand and the lamps flickered to life. His heart hammering, Evan inched toward Cai and Reed. "It's my fault," he whispered. "I should have waited."

"They'll be gone in a few minutes," Reed whispered back. "Don't worry."

Evan peered cautiously over the beam as two masters sat on a couch and a third hovered nearby. There were six in all, four men, two women: Beryl Islander and Anista Sang of Doshaget. Master Tygner was the youngest; the others mostly white haired. The apprentices had been told that the visiting masters had gathered to witness the blood test, that the autumn equinox was one of the eight strongest nights of the year to view the dark lights but that had been weeks ago, and they were still here, still debating.

Harbrook, an older man wearing the colors of Hark Hall filled two goblets and handed them to the women. "There have always been apprentices, journeymen and masters," he said. "We can't simply wave our hands and rewrite a centuries old system."

"But if the system is broken?" Ossian filled his own cup. "If its very foundation is obsolete, where is it written that it can't be changed?"

Harbrook raised a cup. "Of course," he said. "That was a poor choice of words. The guild is not a system. It's the gift of the stars."

"Really?" Anista Sang said mockingly. "Your craft may be a gift, sir. The guild is not."

Tygner glanced between them. "Some would call that treason," he said.

"Not everyone," Anista said. "The guild and the Makkens rose together, decades after the First Stars were gone. That much is a fact.

Harbrook shook his head. "The guild may have written its charter," he said. "But the stars led them to it."

"They sound like us," Cai whispered. "Arguing over rules."

Ossian said, "If the Night Watermen can write their own charter, so can we. They seem to be the only people with sense any more. And whether our forebears were witches or humans, they certainly weren't stars as the guild claims."

Tygner turned on him. "Now that is treason."

"The stars we *see*," Ossian repeated. "That isn't treason. It's common sense."

"Enough philosophy," Anista said. "We have the king to deal with, and his witches."

"Another reason not to wait," Ossian said, and he turned, started pacing. "At the very least, we should agree on changes to our charter."

Evan shifted his weight and Cai caught a flash of red. "Is that the Grimoire?" He pulled a corner of the book out to show her, then put his finger to his lips. Below them, the master's kept talking.

"He wants more than witches," Tygner said. "He wants our halls and lands. I've been thinking; what if we narrowed apprentices' training? Say, to the same craft their grandmothers practiced?"

"I don't understand," Beryl Islander said. "We'd have fewer witches."

"It's a thought," Ossian said. "Instead of apprentices waiting to find their craft, it's given to them. Assigned."

"If it's known," said Harbrook.

"Of course, it's known. We'd have the records."

Tygner said, "They'll progress more quickly. We could save an entire year. Pass them along. Bring in the next crop. It's reasonable."

"As if reason always triumphed," Anista said. "Their inclination may be different from their grandparents. They'll protest."

"Let them!" Ossian said. "We'll ship them off to the king and it's his concern, not ours."

Anista nodded. "We treat with both sides. The Watermen and the king. We keep to the middle." She picked up the block of rim ice Reed had admired and held it toward a lamp.

Reed scowled. "Hey, that's mine," he whispered. "I was going to keep it."

"Shh," Evan warned. "What does she mean? Treat with both sides?"

"Shh yourself," Reed hissed. "You got your book. I wanted my ice." He reached for the book and Evan swatted his hand away.

"Shh, both of you," Cai warned.

Ossian stopped in front of Anista. "If there is a middle way," he said. "There is control, which the king fears losing, and the Night Watermen want, and which– if we don't move now and pit them against each other—we lose altogether. And I don't intend to lose this war."

Reed reached again for the book and Evan jerked away. His shoulder hit the vertical beam and his boot scratched along the timber. The sound echoed.

Ossian stopped. He looked up. "What's that?"

Evan stiffened but before he could catch it, the Grimoire slipped from his vest. It grazed the beam and pages fluttering, spiraled downward and hit the carpeted floor.

The masters stared. They rose and glared and searched the broad span of the dome. "Who's there?" Ossian demanded.

Reed crawled backward. He bumped into Cai and froze. Evan's thoughts darted and spun. He glanced to the hidden panel where they'd entered, but the masters were too near. The front doors were better. They were young, the three of them, they could run faster. Except for the ladders. The ladders would slow them down…

He stared at Cai. "I'll go first," he said. His voice was firm, serious. "You stay here. I won't let them find you."

"No, I'll go," Cai insisted. "They won't hurt me. I'm royal, remember."

"Who's there?" Ossian barked. "Show yourself! Someone, call the guards."

If they let you go, Evan wanted to say, *I'll never see you again.*

"Stop arguing," Reed said. "I'll go first."

Evan swallowed, shook his head. "No. You're both staying." He threw his leg over the beam and felt for the ladder. "Wait till they're gone." He stared into Cai's eyes. "Promise. Find me later."

He reached for her hand and their finger's touched. Reed put his arm around her shoulders and they watched as the masters dragged Evan from the ladder.

He didn't fight back. Tygner stepped in and smacked him hard across the face. He veered backward and when he gained his footing, Ossian loomed over him.

"It's nobody. A child," Anista laughed. "I was afraid it was one of the other masters, hoping to report us."

Ossian struck Evan's head with the back of his hand and the blow, though not hard, took him by surprise. He tasted blood and wiped his sleeve across his mouth. He twisted and tried to yank free, but the men tightened their grip. He moaned and let his knees buckle and slipped to the floor.

"Are you an apprentice, boy?" Tygner asked.

He didn't answer. He hated him. They were cowards, plotting in secret.

"Do you work here?" Tygner demanded. "Speak up. No one will hurt you."

Ossian shook his head in disgust. "Evan Sinclair, of course. He's an apprentice. One of mine, I'm embarrassed to say."

Evan caught a glimpse of the Red Grimoire half hidden beneath a couch, but Ossian caught the glance. He swooped down, narrowed his eyes as he read the title. He tucked it under his arm.

Tygner glared at Ossian. "And you expect us to believe you can control Night Watermen when you can't keep an apprentice in line?"

Ossian stiffened. He raised his hand and smacked Evan's head.

Evan reeled and gagged. There'll be a bruise, he told himself, but if that was Ossian's best, he could take it. So long as Cai and Reed weren't caught, he would take anything. He moaned and clutched his stomach.

"Is that what you were after?" Tygner nodded toward the Red Grimoire.

"It's old," Ossian said offhandedly. "He probably thought it was valuable."

Beryl Islander took Evan's chin and forced him to look at her. "Idiot boy. You thought you could sell it? Speak up." She let go, pushed him away.

"He doesn't know anything," Ossian scoffed. "There's one like this, every season."

Evan glanced toward the beams and caught a flicker of shadow, Reed's foot maybe, or an arm.

Ossian twisted a handful of Evan's shirt, and hauled him to his feet. He eyed the other masters. "If you'll excuse me. I'll deal with the boy. He'll be punished. And my apologies; we'll save our discussions for tomorrow."

Ossian shoved him ahead. They reached the door and Evan pretended to trip. He glanced to the dome and saw nothing. Cai and Reed were safe. "I can walk," he snarled, and Ossian pushed him along the corridors to his private chamber.

The last time he was here, the high master had taken Molly's purse and dropped it into a drawer. Evan would have sworn he wanted the money for himself, but he was no longer certain. Were they talking about a war to save the guild? Is that what they were planning?

The huge desk dominated the room and Ossian stepped behind it and folded his arms. "So. Mister Sinclair. How about we don't play games and you tell me why exactly you were hiding in the library?"

Evan stared at his feet and pretended to sulk. The longer he took, the more time Cai and Reed had to escape. "It was one of the town boys," he lied. "He dared me to steal a block of rim ice. I heard you coming and hid."

"Hmm," Ossian murmured, then, "No." Evan looked up. "That isn't it. I've spent a lifetime dealing with boys smarter than you. I'm not so easily fooled. And you are not so valuable as you think."

Evan kept his shoulders slumped, but he was only half listening. He didn't see the Red Grimoire though Ossian had it under his arm when they entered the room. He must have set it down, but there wasn't so much as a quill or bottle of ink littering the desk. It wasn't on a chair. He glanced at the candelabra with its grimacing turtles devouring each other's tails. At the shelves and silk curtains and crests mounted on the wall: the sun and hands, the nautilus and coracle. King. Governor. Guild.

It was a lie, wasn't it? Everything in the room carefully placed to underscore Hayden Hall's wealth, impress humans, intimidate apprentices, and send a message to the king. Ossian was in full control of Hayden Hall and Hayden Hall was in control of its craft. But it wasn't true.

He thought again of his last visit and Ossian's outrage when he caught him and Molly eavesdropping from the corridor. For a single moment, the desk that seemed immaculate was covered in a jumbled heap of papers, boxes, bottles and goblets, inks and pens.

Unless… Ossian was grumbling when they saw the desk. He swore and pounded on it. Or maybe not pounded, but rattled. Or maybe swiped? Ossian had looked up and saw them in the corridor. And suddenly, Evan knew.

Ossian hadn't been muttering; that was a chant. And he hadn't swept his hand in anger. It was a circling motion. A gesture. And the object… The object was the desk itself.

Ossian was hiding papers. He was using a cog, an ordinary cog, except he hadn't been able to get the spell right. He wasn't angry because they'd seen his desk. He was angry because they'd seen him trying to craft a spell and failing. The high master had no more control over his craft than Evan.

He inched nearer the desk. The Red Grimoire was there somewhere, most likely on the far side. He ran his fingers lightly along the edge until he hit on something round, low profile. A bowl?

Ossian raised a brow. "Nothing to say? Very well, I'll get to the point. I've checked with the masters at Eltiem Hall and it seems there are no records of anyone with your name."

Evan waited, his face a mask as he felt along the desk.

"Do you not know what happens to apprentices who defy the guild? Do you want to live as a human? But then, you aren't much more than that, are you?"

Evan shrugged. "If it's money you want—?"

"Ah, so you can talk. Sadly, for you, I doubt you've enough gold to offset the trouble you caused."

"You've been through my room," Evan said. "You searched my clothes. Stole my Grimoire."

Ossian chuckled. "Stole your Grimoire? You have no idea what you're talking about. Your notes however, those were interesting."

Notes? Evan forced himself to stay calm. He risked a small step to the left, searching…

"What is it? A family fortune? Your ship? Your sister?"

Evan looked up.

"Ah, so it is your sister? Those were her initials in the margins. What was it you wrote? *M's unlock*, on one page? *M's echo*, on another? Interesting. We keep records, you know, and your sister hasn't purchased any spells in months. She might have stolen them, but my guess is she crafted them. I can think of what an *unlock* might be, but an *echo*? You'll have to show me that sometime. The point is, your sister is a witch and she's not listed in any hall. She's a renegade. Not the first; don't give yourself airs. It's common, more among girls than boys. Eventually—inevitably—they sell a spell, and we find them. But if you're hiding her, and she's hiding her craft, and you're offering money, what else are you hiding?"

"I already told you; if you want gold, you'll have it."

"Ah. You skip right to gold?" Ossian shook his head. "Is she really your sister? Or Night Watermen? One of their spies?" Ossian stopped. There was a knock, and he glanced irritably to the door.

Evan tried to think. He couldn't keep hunting and pecking along the desk. He needed to do something. Focus.

"I think I'll send you to the king. Yes. That suits my needs. He's paying for witches. I'll apologize later for your lack of skill. It will take months before they notice. And you needn't be afraid. In Jamasak, they say, even the lowest beggars are fortunate enough to eat." He glanced at the door. "Come in."

Evan breathed deeply. He wanted to close his eyes as Molly often did, but that would cost time. He settled for shutting out Ossian's threats and Sanders' voice behind him now. He pictured the small red volume, the brittle edges. He pictured it, and then saw it.

Papers were strewn across the desk. Stacked booklets and sheaves, rolled parchments all gray and brown except for one small book near Ossian's hand; the Red Grimoire. He lunged across the desk, grabbed it and ran for the door.

Ossian shouted and Sanders blinked then darted after him, but his robes caught underfoot, and Evan was halfway down the hall before Sanders left the room.

Evan grabbed the railing and jumped and nearly fell the first flight of stairs. He paused on the landing long enough to tuck the Grimoire inside his vest and choose a direction. Reed and Cai would have fled the library by now, but where would they go?

He hesitated. Try for his attic, gather up clothes and climb out his window? But his roommates would run and fetch a warden. Better to hide in the fields until dawn. Slip back and find Cai. Figure something out.

He vaulted the remaining stairs then slowed as he reached the great hall. It was late, but no one would pay attention to one more apprentice fetching a drink for a master. He had a minute, no more than that, before Sander's called the alarm.

He slowed and crossed from an archway to a bay window. The hall was crowded for the late hour. Wardens and masters slumped over abandoned games of Storm, while yawning servants cleared platters. He moved past the hearth and along the trestle table with its picked over roasts and fruit turned brown in the air. Two ancient masters, a man and a woman sat with their chairs pulled close, talking. Neither had been in the library.

He saw something, a flicker, out of the corner of his eye. It disappeared but a moment later he saw Cai and Reed waving from the far end of the hall.

He quickened his pace, but his foot struck a chair and a hound yelped. A goblet spilled and suddenly there were guards, running and shouting and sweeping into the hall. A man lunged for Evan's shoulder, but he shoved him aside and raced from the hall.

Reed and Cai ran ahead. "Hurry!" Cai called. "The doors! Outside!" Evan caught up and they sprang through the next hallway, pushed through the outer doors and tripped across the shadowed yard.

The sky was dark, and they ducked behind the nearest carriage shed and clung to the wall. Evan caught his breath and listened as boots pounded the flagstones.

"They'll never catch us," Reed laughed between breaths. "We're faster. We'll outrun them." He found a pebble and threw it hard in the opposite direction. The guards took off and Reed pointed to the next building, an empty guard hut and they darted through the shadows then crowded inside.

Reed poked out his head, searched for the next place to hide. "Wait!" Cai pulled him back. "We need a plan. We can't keep this up."

Reed leaned over, hands on his knees breathing hard. "I haven't had this much fun in weeks," he gasped.

"This isn't fun," Cai whispered. "We need to think. And be quiet."

"You be quiet," Reed said.

"Stop it," Evan whispered. "Cai's right. We can't just play cat and mouse."

"We can break into a storehouse," Reed said. "Wait them out. then run away."

Cai peered around the corner. There were guards, six, eight, ten, maybe more, running toward the craft halls. Pistol shots rang out. She pulled back. "We have to think," she told Reed. "Not pretend."

Evan touched her arm. "I have to get past the gates," he said. "They aren't looking for you."

"Oh no, you don't," Reed said. "You're not leaving me behind."

Cai held Evan's gaze. "Reed's right, we're in this together but we need a plan. Do we know anyone in town who could hide us?"

"We don't have time for plans," Reed said. "We need guns. Swords. Weapons."

Cai leaned out again. "They're moving toward the stables," she said. "Do we have any money?"

They felt their pockets and pouches, pulled out two silver pieces between them, a few coppers, no gold. Cai handed her coins to Evan. "You take it," she said. "In case we're separated."

The guards split up. A few circled toward the outbuildings. Some returned to search the main hall, others toward the barns. "Can we at least agree to jump the gate?" Reed asked.

Evan looked from Reed to Cai. Her face was lined with shadows. Wisps of yellow cog-light touched her hair. She turned and held his gaze until the shouts and pounding bootsteps fell away.

"How about this," she said. "Reed and I go out and pretend we don't know what's going on. You jump the gate, start for town. They don't know we're together."

"No!" Evan said. "They'll shoot before they know who you are. They won't care."

"No, it's a good idea. I like it," Reed said. "We'll be a decoy." He leaned around the corner. A few guards stood outside the main hall. They turned constantly, listening, flintlocks cocked and ready. He pulled back in. "Except it's me first," he said. "I'll run out and holler. Cai, you stay with Evan."

And then suddenly, he was gone. "Reed! No!" Evan grabbed at his shirt, missed.

Reed raced into the open yard. He waved his arms and darted wildly back and forth, leading them away from the hut, away from the gates.

The guards cocked their pistols and ran at the shouting figure.

Reed darted behind the fruit trees that lined the yard, from there to the well house. He ducked low behind a water trough. A stone bench. A statue of a star. A moment later he was in the open courtyard again. He jumped out and jeered at the guards. "Looking for me?" he taunted and skipped from side to side.

The guards spun and caught Reed in the light. He flapped his arms, daring them to fight. He had just enough time to glance over his shoulder, motion for Evan and Cai to run when their guns flared.

Pistol shots fractured the night. They came from the courtyard and hall windows. Bursts of light and noise. Evan grabbed Cai's hand and they ran along the shadowed wall, ducked behind a bush and ran again.

"Come get me," Reed teased. His voice was clear and strong, but with the next shot someone grunted—not Reed. The cry was too low and from the wrong direction. A guard then? Caught in the cross fire?

Evan and Cai lurched ahead then waited behind a bush. They found each other's hands and looked out, afraid of what they might see.

"Over here," a guard shouted. "Scoth's down."

"We got the boy," called another. "It's bad. I think he's dead."

Time stopped. Evan stared at Cai. Her face was shadowed and dark. She put her finger to her lips. *Don't say it. We don't know. Not a word.*

He held quiet. Reed couldn't be dead. She was right, and they had to keep going. Think clearly. *We got the boy.* He pushed aside a branch and peered toward the courtyard and the one place with any hope of hiding. He nudged Cai and she followed his glance.

"The dome?"

"We can hide inside. Nothing will happen. No dark light. Nothing."

"I know. But..." She hesitated. "I never told you. That first night? That was me, throwing pebbles at the dome."

"I know. I mean… I wanted it to be you. Who else would be out at that hour?"

"You," she said, and they shared a smile, but only for a moment.

Evan dropped to a crouch and tried to see Reed as the guards pressed tightly around, but it was impossible to know whether they were checking for wounds, or if he was dead. Cai tugged his sleeve and reluctantly, he turned away. They took off running, low and fast. They darted from tree to bench to shrub and finally into the dome.

They leapt between the columns and ducked low inside the shoulder-high wall. Instantly, the world turned quiet. The acrid smell of gun powder and the noise and angry voices receded. They sank to the floor and leaned back. "Do you think he's all right?" Cai asked.

"I don't know," Evan said. He ran his hand along the mosaic tiles behind him. The stones were smooth in parts, rough in others, just as he remembered from the last time he'd been here, with Reed. Reed. What if he was dead? He pushed the thought aside. The entire wall was covered with stones, lapis and mother of pearl, semi-precious stones cut and shaped into images of men and women.

He thought of the masters in the library. They said the guild had come into power long after the First Stars were gone. So how could any artist know what they looked like? The statues in the courtyard. The black marble Haldin. Any of them. All of them.

Rays of light emanated from the figures' hands and Evan wondered if they were supposed to depict the exact moment they raised the ice and bestowed the gift of magic on the isles. Not knowing bothered him, but not knowing how to find real answers bothered more.

He drew his knees to his chest. "That night you threw the pebbles?" he asked. "Were you following us, or did you see us by chance?"

"Following," Cai said. "I saw you with your sister."

"How did you know she was my sister? You'd only just arrived."

"I saw Sanders call you over, and knew you weren't one of the applicants, then later I asked around. One of the cooks said your sister took you out for a few weeks and another that she must have paid Ossian a pretty penny to take you back. And besides, you look alike. I was curious. Are you angry?"

"No. I'm glad you were. Curious, I mean." He looked up. "You hear that?" There was shouting, men's voices.

"He's not moving," a guard called then, "He ain't dead. Poor kid. He was probably trying to run away."

"They all do that. Some of them anyway. Wouldn't you?"

The guard snickered. "What, and give up the chance to let the guild run your life? I'll buy my cogs thank you, and work for my wages. Pick him up by his arm there, that leg looks ruined. And be glad you're human, not witch."

Evan had been holding his breath. He let it out. Reed was hurt, but alive and they were safe, at least until Ossian realized they shot the wrong apprentice. He glanced at Cai. The fire at the dome's center lit her eyes and there was a smudge of dirt across her cheek and her hair was stuck with leaves. He wanted to reach across and brush them away. He wanted to tell her that he had never known someone could look like that, sad and wise, brave and gentle all at the same time. He didn't know if he had the words, and this wasn't the right time.

"I should never have gone back for that book," he said. "Reed wouldn't be hurt, and anyway, the old Grimoires are useless, just like the masters said. Cai, I have to go back. I can't leave him there."

"I know. But… Listen. Hear me out. I'll go. I'll find out what's going on. But not you." She touched her finger to his lips before he could object. "They don't know I'm here. And you're no help to Reed if you're dead or arrested. And you're no help to me if I have to save both of you."

She reached across his shoulder and felt the nearest pillar. "It's cold," she said. "And you can see the silt and tumbled rocks inside, like the ice in the library."

"It is the same. It's supposed to be cold."

"I know, but…" She stopped, started again. "How is it we're even sitting here? I was taught there's supposed to be a wind, something magic that keeps the domes locked. Except on the equinox and solstice, or if the masters let you in."

"Where did you hear that?"

"In my last hall. I heard that if you lie to the guild about your craft, the dark lights will strike you down, and that's not true either. They ought to at least keep their lies straight."

He stole a glance at her profile, sharp chin, the straight line of her nose and high forehead. He was so used to being alone. He had never spoken with anyone but Molly about things like the guild or ice or how the dome worked. He hadn't known it was possible. "I always wondered," he said, "If we carry the star's blood and we're witches, why do we need the guild?"

"We don't. Not really. The dark lights are different. They just are. They find us, mark us. They know we're here."

"The guild says they can take our craft away but that's not true. Macklin Cobb, he's with my sister. The guild tried to cut out his mark. His arm is all scarred, a mess to look at, but he still has his craft. They can't change that."

Cai grimaced. "That's horrible," Cai said then, "My mark's yellow. What's yours?"

Evan pushed up his sleeve and Cai did the same. They held their arms out; Evan's was a blur, a tinge of blue that reached from his elbow to his wrist and faded at the edges. Cai's arm was marked with yellow, but paler than Evan's. "It's supposed to change," Cai said. "When we become journeyman and our craft is stronger, the outline becomes more distinct."

Evan sat back. "If that even happens anymore." He rolled his sleeve back down. "The world is changing."

"Yes, but something has to be true. The lights are. We're still here. Our crafts."

Evan nodded. "You ever wonder what's out there?"

"Beyond the stars?"

Evan shook his head. "The rim. Do you ever want to go there? Find out?"

"Whether there's anything on the other side? If there is another side? Yes. I'd want to know. Wouldn't you?"

"No," he answered sharply. "Not if it meant leaving someone behind." He blinked. He hadn't known he was going to say that. He wasn't sure what he meant.

He reached for Cai's hand and she moved nearer. She leaned her head on his shoulder and he breathed in the smell of her hair. It was like morning, fresh and warm and light. He wanted to stop time and stay there forever, but Cai brought him back.

"You haven't chosen your craft yet, have you?"

"Chosen?" Evan snorted. "That's another thing the guild makes you do. As if you look up one day and say, oh, I'm a fire. I'm ice. If you're supposed to have only one craft, how can you choose? Or they tell you to find it, as if it was lost." Their shoulders were touching, their legs side by side. He tapped her foot and she tapped back.

She smiled suddenly. "Watch this," she said, and scooped up a loose clump of mortar that had fallen from the wall and held it in her hand. She blew and the grains began to change. They melted and filled her hand. Gray turned to white, to a wisp of smoke then suddenly a ball of fire hovering in the air.

Evan climbed to his knees and glanced over the wall. Nothing moved. The soldiers hadn't returned, and the grounds were quiet. He ducked back down and watched.

Cai waited till he was settled, then blew again and in place of the fire, a cloud appeared. Rain fell and water puddled in her hand. "That first one was fire," she said. "And this one's water. And now ice." No sooner had she spoken when the water froze. A disk of ice sat in her hand. "And finally, sky." She smiled and the ice thawed. It melted then evaporated and disappeared. "Fire. Water. Ice and sky. Why should I choose one when I'd rather have all? And I'll wager you do, too."

Evan nodded. He was impressed, but tired also. The moon was far to the west now and the night seemed endless. He felt shy suddenly; he lowered his gaze and stared at his hands. "Is that why your family sent you away? Because you weren't like everyone else?"

Cai drew back and Evan's stomach knotted. He'd upset her, said something wrong. He reached for her hand. "I'm sorry," he said. "I didn't mean that. We're different, you and I. Yes, I want them, all the crafts, but… You don't have to stay here, do you? You could run away, pick an isle and never come back?"

"Maybe you can. But it's not that simple. Wealth doesn't buy freedom, not where I come from."

"No, you're right. That was stupid of me. But, Cai. It's nearly light. I have to go."

"I know." She squeezed his hand and they wound their fingers together.

The moment stretched and Evan let go of her hands and held her face and she let him. She didn't pull away. She angled her face, awkwardly at first, this way, then that. She hesitated then leaned in.

He closed his eyes and felt the light pressure of her lips against his, the warmth of her breath, her skin so soft. The kiss lingered and deepened. He stopped thinking and stayed there, holding her as long as he could.

When at last they pulled apart, Cai blinked then smiled. "I have an idea," she whispered, and she kissed him on his lips, a quick one this time. "Wait here. I'll be right back." She peered around the pillar, made sure no one was about. "Promise you'll wait?"

Evan's heart was still racing but he nodded and watched as she sauntered across the deserted yard as simply as if she was a dairymaid going about her chores. She swung toward the stable and a horse whinnied as she disappeared inside.

Evan pulled back, waited, then grew concerned. He peered over the wall, saw nothing and crawled to the entry just as Cai whistled. Horse's hooves clomped and a moment later a wagon appeared. It slowed in front of the dome and Evan leaped in the back.

Cai hurried around and quickly piled loose hay over his legs and torso then dragged two gunny sacks against his side. Evan took one last look: she had found an apron somewhere, tied it over her trousers and made it look like a dress. Nothing that would stand up to scrutiny, but with a straw milkmaid's hat hiding her face, he almost didn't recognize her.

Cai glanced right and left then jumped to the seat and led the horses toward the gatehouse. The wagon stopped and Evan heard Cai's light voice then a lower one answering; muffled laughter back and forth. Then finally, the wagon jolted and started forward. It rolled past Hayden Hall's heavy gates and down along the road.

The next thing he knew Cai was banging on the sideboards and daylight had come. They had reached the waterfront, and the wharf was already filled with the morning bustle. Fish wives dragged carts and sailors called to their mates and with so many visiting masters still in port, there were vessels of every size and shape and flags of every color, and all of them bobbing and pulling against their anchors.

Evan jumped out and came around to the front of the wagon. Cai, still seated, reached for his hand. "Listen carefully. You're to find the *Swift Pace* and sneak on board," she said. "Anyone asks, tell them you're picking up a package from Captain Karron. He's my uncle. Zen Karron, on the *Swift Pace*. He's always tied on the fourth slip. Remember. The fourth." She pointed along the wharf. "Once you're on board, stowaway till they reach Carillon, on Pyr. He'll be getting off. It's his estate. I've been there dozens of times. Follow him and I'll find you. You have that?"

Evan repeated the message. "Fourth slip. The *Swift Pace*. The captain is your uncle Carillon."

"No, Karron is my uncle," she corrected. "Get off in Carillon. It's a large town, and they'll send a carriage to bring him home. If you get lost, ask around. Hide on the grounds and I'll find you."

"What if I'm caught? What do I say?"

"Invent something. Tell him Ossian mistreated me, and I couldn't get away. They blocked my spells, and I sent you to explain. That will work. My family is very proud. But hurry. Karron's a Makken, but he's not terrible."

"Get off in Carillon. Right. I can do that. But Cai, don't wait. It isn't safe."

"It's safer for me than you. But don't worry. I'll be there as soon as I can."

Evan started away. The dock was a jumble of longshoremen, sailors and beggar boys, barrels and crates piled too high to see above. He raised his collar and lowered his eyes. *Find the Swift Pace. Stay on till Carillon. Karron is the uncle.*

He passed an older woman who stopped to light her pipe; two men arguing over a bucket of fish. He stopped abruptly. He hadn't said goodbye. He turned and ran past the woman, around a cage full of doves, a tangle of nets. "Cai! Wait!" he shouted.

The wagon was already moving but she heard him and pulled back on the reins and Evan grabbed the wagon's side. "What are you doing?" she asked, then lowered her voice as a guard noticed her and smirked. "Hurry. It's a large ship. You can hide most anywhere. Just… Send a message. As soon as you can."

"I didn't say goodbye," he called, then jumped to the wagon step and Cai leaned over, pressed her lips to his. "You're my luck," he whispered. "You'll find me, right?"

"Of course," she said. "I already found you once, didn't I?" She reached behind the seat for a blanket, grabbed it and threw it his way. He snatched it from the air, and she smiled one last time then called to the horses.

Evan stood in the middle of the road and watched until she disappeared. Then he bundled the blanket against his chest and started along the wharf, counting the ships. *Wind Speed. Simgin's Race.* That was two. Both near the same size as the *Fish. Night Hold.* Three. And there it was. The *Swift Pace* in the fourth slip, just as she said. It was a sturdy merchant vessel, larger than he expected, though the paint could use freshening and there were barnacles at the waterline.

He held back as sailors boarded the ship. A woman on the foredeck barked an order and a sailor spit out his wad of chew and hurried to the gangway. Another woman raised a heavy duffle to her shoulder and climbed, followed by a man, short and skinny, dragging a pair of milk goats by a rope. Evan rolled his blanket into something approaching a package, tucked it under his arm and fell into line.

10

With Eyes that See

Molly stood on the *Fish's* aft castle, the wind at her back as Sally worked the tiller. Two days more and they would reach their family's home on Luna's Cove, though it could take longer depending how hard they pushed the *White Lily*.

It was a day and a half since they'd taken the merchant vessel. The *Fish* had escaped damage, but the *White Lily's* mid-deck was a wreck, boards shredded, and sails torn. She and Sally had returned to the *Fish*, while the others remained aboard the *Lily* seeing to repairs.

Brigit's task was below, acquainting herself with their newly acquired guns and powder stores. Nick took on mending the sails and Tribolt—when he wasn't sneaking a swig of Captain Kasz's choice rum—rearranged the ballast. Troth examined the hull while he and Tribolt bickered more than since the ship was taken, good natured but endlessly.

Macklin was assigned to sorting the prize. It was tedious work and he didn't claim to understand the varieties of silk and lace or the value of saffron versus pepper, but the crew trusted him to be fair. Equal shares, Molly promised. The risk had been theirs, and so would be the reward.

Their spells eased the way and kept the ships sailing in tandem, but the crew was tired and stretched thin. Macklin had nearly fallen through a jagged hole in the middeck and the mizzen mast needed to be replaced. Luna's Cove would provide the necessary tree, but they'd need to mill the wood and it was difficult to say how long it would take.

She looked across the water to the *White Lily* and saw Nick. He was carrying a cask of what she assumed was rum and even at a distance his manner was infectious. He set down the cask and Tribolt whooped at the discovery and Troth helped pry off the lid.

Nick donned a feathered hat, but it kept flying off and she was certain he was drunk. His crooning carried across the waves. *I'll roam the sea, the foaming sea, a lovesick lad am I. Without a kiss from one sweet miss, I'll climb the ropes and dive—* He stopped and pulled out a pistol, shot it skyward then turned and waved at Sally.

Molly thought she'd ignore him but instead, Sally hung over the *Fish's* rail and waved back. She watched as they played back and forth, waving then turning aside, preening then ignoring each other, until something in the distance caught her eye, the hint of a straight line, narrow, vertical, far out to sea.

She frowned and crossed to the binnacle and pulled out a spyglass and this time, there was no mistaking the line of a mast, hazy, but a mast all the same.

She remained calm. The vessel was too large for a fishing boat. A merchant ship, then? With its long beak, it was large enough to be a galleon. But whose? Not the king's? She'd never seen a royal vessel this far from Jamasak. And though Luna's Cove was protected with more spells than anyone could purchase, she didn't like having her whereabouts known.

She lowered the glass and the ship disappeared in the haze. It could be a guild ship? One of the wealthier halls? She hadn't thought about the guild masters in a while. She still didn't believe they converged on Hayden Hall simply to attend the equinox blood test. But why else were so many masters there at the same time? She hadn't heard from Evan in a long while either. She should send him a message. It was difficult not to worry.

Or, what if instead of a guild ship, they were about to be hailed by Night Watermen? There would be a tale. Molly Sinclair and her crew fighting off the fearsome, secretive black marketeers. She'd avoid them, of course. They allowed a bit of independent piracy outside their web and were said to be more interested in buying and selling than stealing, but there were plenty of stories of that as well. Stealing and forcing pirates into their ring, taking and selling bribes and protections. And while she was confident of the *Fish's* performance there was the damaged *Lily* to consider, and this was not the best time to encounter a vessel of any stripe.

She raised the glass. The sails were distinct now, not a mirage at all. Cannon ports ran from bow to stern. The ship, whatever it was, carried more heavy guns than the *Fish* and *White Lily* combined. She called Sally and handed her the glass.

The navigator it at once. "Two points off the port bow," she said. Her voice was firm, not panicked. "She doesn't seem to be in a hurry."

By the time they maneuvered the *Fish* alongside the *White Lily* and crossed over, the entire crew was at the rail. Nick climbed to the crow's nest. "She's a galleon," he called. "And big. Three masts, square rigged. She's flying a white flag with a five petaled flower. Says *Oracle* across her bow. Wait." He took a longer look. "There a second flag. Blue and gold. The king's pennant," he called. "She's part of Makken's fleet."

"Can't be," Macklin said. "It's not grand enough."

Tribolt said, "You think they heard about the *White Lily* so soon?"

"It's possible," Macklin said. "If this *Oracle* was already nearby. Best thing is to keep out of their way."

Brigit said, "Except if we've seen them, like as not they've seen us."

"They've seen us," Sally said. "They're changing course. The current's with us and we can hasten it with a spell. How much further to that cove of yours?"

Molly glanced at Macklin. The day they'd met, he'd offered to work for free until he proved himself. She had found the offer intriguing, practical and reasoned, but also desperate. Macklin had no work; wasn't permitted to sell his spells, and neither could Brigit, or the rest of her crew and the thought made her angry. It reminded her of another promise she'd made. Join her and the next time they took a ship they would leave merchant vessels in peace and find themselves a fat guild vessel and take their prize. No one objected.

Her thoughts raced ahead. "What if we don't run," she said. "What if we meet them head on? Isn't this what we talked about? If that's a king's ship, they don't deserve to pass by."

Macklin cocked his head and Brigit waited for more. "What if we go after them?" Molly said, and the words sounded right. "We raise a wind, use it to our advantage. Think of it, two ships in as many days? If we're attacked, we use the *White Lily* to draw fire and retreat on the *Fish*."

"Take a king's ship?" Macklin looked uncertain.

"Yes. Or at least the cargo, for now?"

Macklin glanced along the rail. One of the *White Lily's* swivel guns had been blasted from its mountings, another was damaged beyond repair. "It's risky," he said thoughtfully.

"I won't run," Molly said, and she was surprised how calm she felt. "We'll outmaneuver them. Fight smarter. A king's ship will assume they're invincible. They'll be cocky."

"Cocky is good," Brigit said. "They'll underestimate us."

Molly glanced across the *White Lily's* deck then higher, through the ruined sails and back to the *Fish's* spars. An idea took shape and she pictured the sails from a different angle. "What if…" She started slowly. "Instead of engaging the *Oracle*, we disguise the *Fish*, hide her in plain sight? Macklin, stand over there. What do you see?"

"Masts," he said. "Yards and shrouds and sails. Some ruined, some whole. I can hardly see the sky."

Molly stepped back and forth. With the *Oracle* behind her, she could place the smaller *Fish* directly behind the *White Lily* until it nearly disappeared. Most of the *Lily's* damage was to her port and they could turn her about so the *Oracle* saw only her better side. But they would need a mass of canvas to hide the *Fish* and keep her in place.

"Picture yourself on the *Oracle*," she said. "You've sighted a ship. It's hazy and there's a masts and ropes are chaos. There's a breeze, five knots. They're coming near. What's your first thought?"

"We're a merchant vessel, headed for port." Nick said.

"Going about our own business," Macklin said, "No threat to them."

"And if the wind changes?" Molly asked.

"They'll assume we have witches navigating. Nothing unusual there."

"All right then," Sally said. "So now we're one ship, not two, and they're not expecting a fight. We wait till we're close and what? Open fire?"

Molly thought a moment. "Or… What if… What if we send an invitation and they come to us? We invite the captain to dinner? You—" she looked at Sally. "You invite him. If you're willing, that is?"

"What?" Macklin said. "Kidnap him?"

The ship was distinct now, a stain against the sky. "Ransom," Molly said excitedly. "We capture the captain then exchange him for whatever prize they're carrying. I mean to send a message. I want them to know who we are. All of them, the guild. The governors. The king. I want it known. We are free witches. We will not run or hide."

"I'd do it," Nick offered. "I'd put on a dress. A bit of rouge. They'll never know from afar."

Sally folded her arms across her chest. "The stars will come home before anyone believes that." She studied the oncoming ship. "All right," she said stiffly. "But this is the last time I pretend to be a giggling maid. You hail the ship, Molly. I'll invite the captain, but that's all, and I'll shoot any man who so much as tries to touch me in a dress."

Nick bowed. "Dinner with the prettiest navigator in the isles."

"Be quiet or I'll make you hold my fan," Sally snapped. "Wait. A parasol. That's better. Find me one and I'll hide a pistol inside."

Sally and Molly hurried to the captain's cabin where'd they'd already found a trunk near to bursting with women's clothes. Molly pulled out the first dress she touched. It was blue silk and lace with silver threads stitched through the sleeves. Sally grumbled as she pulled it over her trousers and raised her arms for Molly to tie a sash and keep it from falling. She dug deeper in the chest and found a parasol with a fringe of lace, and Sally, with a foolish grin, hooked it daintily over her arm.

By the time they returned to the deck, the ships were tethered so close, they moved like dancers with no more than a shadow between. The *Oracle* had drawn near enough for Molly to discern individuals, some on the decks and more in the rigging. Nick counted two gunners at each of the cannonades, at the forecastle and quarterdeck, more sailors scurrying about.

One man stood out. He wore a dark jacket with a red waistband; two sailors in blue uniforms hovered at his sides. He scanned the *White Lily* with a spyglass and found Sally, waving as excitedly as if she was watching a parade. The man laughed and said something over his shoulder and took another, longer look.

Sally made a show of flipping the catch on a large filigreed shell. She pulled out a slip of parchment, read the chant, then pursed her lips, blew and a cloud of dandelion seeds flew toward the approaching ship.

The captain caught a few. He raised them to his ear and smiled as he listened to Sally's voice. *If it please the master of so fine a ship, you are cordially invited to join the captain and myself in libations and perhaps a game of Storm. I do so long for company to help the tedious miles pass. Signed, Sincerely, a Young Lady too long at Sea.*

The captain raised his glass for a better look at the young lady and Sally smiled obligingly. "You owe me for this," she said through gritted teeth.

Molly glanced sideways at her, at the way she fixed a curl and rested a hand on her breast. "I do. I owe you. I can't imagine it's easy."

"Damn well it's not easy. Though actually, it is. Too easy, and distasteful as hell."

"But how do you do it? Molly asked honestly. "He's gawking like a fool."

"His doing. Not mine." She studied Molly's face. "Wait. You've got someone haven't you? Back on shore? A fellow? I'll wager you haven't kissed him yet? You're blushing. I'll wager you've never kissed anyone."

Molly swallowed and didn't answer. Nothing was happening on the Oracle, though more people had joined the captain at the quarterdeck rail.

Sally said, "I've seen you watching me. I thought at first it was Nick, that you liked him, in which case I would have said, fine. There he is. But then I saw that the only time you looked at him was when he looked at me. And I'd know if you were in love with me."

Molly's eyes widened. "I'm not. And I've never kissed anyone. Who would I kiss? Why would I even want to?"

"Wait." Sally stopped her. "I'm sorry, I shouldn't have said that. We'll talk later, I promise. But you want my best advice.? All this business about clothing and pretending to be coy. Don't do it. Leave it to others. You think Nick cares one whit whether I bat my eyes or sway my hips? He's happy if I so much as talk to him."

A wave rose and caught them off balance. The ships scrapped each other but the sound didn't carry. They were all on the *White Lily* now. The *Fish's* blue-eyed figurehead was tucked in behind the *White Lily's* bow, the masts a confusion of shapes. It was impossible to discern the one behind the other.

Sally raised the spyglass. "Looks like the captain's conferring with his crew. And there's someone else. A cabin boy...?" She looked again. "He's holding a cloak and a hat. The captain's putting them on. It worked. He's coming."

A sailor blew a whistle. Orders were barked. Molly looked to Macklin. "It's time," she said, more calmly than she felt. "Raise the wind. Bring us near." When she turned back around, the cabin boy was gone, and the captain was at the rail. The crew worked the davit's chains and lowered a boat. Two sailors with muskets in the crook of their arms climbed down and the captain followed. It all seemed so easy.

The boat drew near. It was halfway there when suddenly, the *White Lily* pitched. It dipped into a trough and Sally, in her oversized skirts, fell forward. The bow lifted and Molly grabbed her arm. "It's all right," Sally said. "I'll smooth the waves."

"Not yet," Molly warned. "They'll see you and—" She stopped.

She felt something, a difference in the wind, a taste in the air. She looked to the Oracles' small boat, approaching. The sailors were swinging their oars wide. The captain scanned the water. But no, not the water. The oarsmen were turning, bringing their boat around. The wave that had pitched the *White Lily's* bow… It was crafted, not natural. The *Oracle's* boat hadn't felt it at all.

Two figures stood at the galleon's rail, a woman in brown and a man with a red sash. They waited until the rowboat neared the ship and though Molly couldn't make out their insignias, it didn't matter. They were witches and they'd found her out. The woman raised her hand and the *Oracle's* cannon ports lifted. Dark muzzles pointed. Sailors, witches and human, raced across the deck.

"Fire! Fire now!" Molly cried. Sally tore off the dress and Molly raced past her. By the time she reached the aft deck, Macklin was climbing the ratlines and the sky was growing dark.

Brigit's first cannon roared. The ball fell short, but the explosion rocked the small boat. The captain was thrown to the side then caught hold of the ladder just as Brigit's second cannon fired. Grapeshot struck the *Oracle's* rail and splinters burst and flew upward. Bloodied sailors toppled from ropes and cannon fire burst from her sides.

A ball exploded early, a burst of color and noise, but no harm until the next shot. It hit the *White Lily's* quarterdeck. Timbers groaned and the ship leaned heavily to starboard and behind it, the *Fish* recoiled and smacked hard against the *White Lily's* side.

"Craft a spell. Hold the wind," Molly called to Macklin. "Keep us in range."

The *Oracle's* captain was back onboard. He removed his cloak and Molly realized what she should have seen before. The taller man was the captain; the one in the boat had been the cabin boy. They'd switched places. They were buying time, and she'd been tricked from the start. And the sailors who waved to Sally; they were witches, the king's witches, with Jamasak's emblem—the two hands holding a sun—blazing on their clothes.

Another wind rose and Molly looked to the sky. Water sprayed and the waves began to churn. White caps broke against the hull. Molly fell back as the *Fish* and *White Lily* angrily ground against each other. She tried to concentrate, find a spell to align them and hold them safe together.

Brigit kept firing, shot after screaming shot. They pelted the *Oracle* and tore up the planking and it would have worked. It could have. Except that the *Oracle's* witches raised their hands. Five witches, maybe more. They stood in a line and pushed against Brigit's spell until each shot and cannon ball fell useless into the sea.

Molly spun about and found Macklin clinging to the topsail yard. "Can you see anything?" she shouted.

"They've sent a wind," he cried. "It's pushing us out of range."

Thunder cracked and Molly backed away from the rail as the air warmed. It grew cloying and thick. A smell like coal filled her lungs.

Lightning struck. A shot of silver fire; it hit the *White Lily's* topmast and exploded into sparks. Another bolt hit, erratic but sharp. It struck their mast head with a sound like gunshot. A crack and then that scent again, acrid and burning.

Sally grabbed a bucket and Macklin dropped from the ratline as everyone threw water and stamped at the growing fires. They hacked at smoldering ropes and heaved them overboard and threw bucket after bucket of water and refilled them with their craft and flung more water, but there were too many flames and too many *Oracle* witches keeping them strong, and the fires sprang up faster than they could put them out.

Until finally, Molly threw her bucket aside. "We can't stop it," she cried. "Cut us loose." She grabbed an ax from the bulwark and started running. "Retreat," she shouted. "Everyone, onto the *Fish*!"

She slammed the ax into a rope holding the ships together, ran to the next and cut through. At the last one, she raised the ax over her head and brought it down. The rope split, the ax buried itself in the board and the *Fish* was free.

She watched with relief as the *Fish's* bow swung away but when she turned to her crew, she found them standing there, buckets in hands, staring past her shoulder. "What are you doing?" Macklin called. His voice was low, strained.

"Retreat. We have to—" Their eyes stopped her and by the time she turned to see the *Fish*, her heart was thundering in her chest. The *Fish* was picking up speed and sailing hard on, around the *White Lily* and straight for the *Oracle*. Fifty yards and no sign of turning.

Fear closed her throat. "It isn't me," she said. "Who's on board? Where is everyone?" She spun wildly, counted off the crew though they were all standing in front of her.

Mounted on the prow, the wooden fish's eyes blinked open. The rudder shifted and held its course. The sails filled with wind and the *Fish*, her ship, Evan's ship, her parent's ship, raced dead on for the *Oracle*.

"I'm not doing it," Molly cried again. "It's them, their witches. It has to be."

But it wasn't. The *Fish* was twenty-five yards from the *Oracle* and their crew panicked. They broke formation and scattered. The sky cleared. The dark receded.

She stared at her crew. If one of them was moving the *Fish*, she would have felt it. And it wasn't the *Oracle's* witches. They seemed just as surprised, frightened and confused.

Fifteen yards. Fear gripped her and she started walking, following along the rail. Ten yards. The figurehead's eyes closed then opened.

And this time when it blinked, a phosphorescent light flared blue then green. It spread across the bow and along the keel. The light shimmered and dimmed then grew stronger as the *Fish* surged toward the *Oracle.*

The wake spread white behind it, and Molly thought of her brother and was glad he wasn't there to see or hear the sound…

…The wrenching crack that rose as the *Fish's* bow rammed the *Oracle.* There was a splintering as if lightning struck a tree, splitting it, ripping it asunder. The *Fish* reared upward, cutting through the *Oracle's* hull. The bow rose, impossibly high, forcing its way through tons of wood and iron until it came to a stop. It beached itself atop the *Oracle's* deck and hung there. Molly gaped at the sight.

The *Oracle's* main mast toppled; it split and caught in the web of lines and ropes. Sailors shouted and screamed as lines tore and shards flew. Canvas fluttered and collapsed.

Molly was only dimly aware of her crewmates as they stomped out the last of the *White Lily's* fires. She felt as if she was part of another world. Her world, the *Fish,* was gone. At any moment it would splinter and crack. The impact would have smashed the *Fish's* bow, broken its ribs and beams. Like sticks. Like so many bits and pieces of wreckage. Her life. Her ship. Her home. She felt numb and terribly alone. But then…

She looked again. Something was happening. Except… How could it? The wind was changing. Sails fluttered in disarray. She didn't dare breathe.

Against all belief, the *Fish* was backing away. With a wrenching, grating sound it pulled itself free of the *Oracle.* As if it could swim against the tide. As if the moon had no pull on currents and the crashing waves no more impact than a drop of rain, the *Fish* tore free of the *Oracle's* broken hull and sailed backward against the wind and began to turn.

"Look! There!" Macklin's voice filled with wonder. "Do you see?"

The *Fish* was intact. Unharmed. The phosphorescent light still covered the hull, but Molly was no longer afraid. The light clung to the boards It flared and spread along the keel, under the water and tracked along the ship.

Behind it, the *Oracle* was sinking. Men and women scrambled for safety. They fell from the rigging, some to the deck, others to the sea. The stern rose and the prow looked down. An explosion followed, not flames but a crack like gunpowder.

She heard cries; people trapped in the lower decks. And then different sounds. Axes and gun fire and then, climbing vertically from the lower hold, a line of men and women pushed through a hatch. They coughed and shouted. Some fell. Others jumped and swam for fallen spars and barrels and debris, anything they could hold.

Three small boats dropped to the sea. Molly picked out the captain clinging to a rope. Crewmen jumped and fell and dove into the water, emerged and swam for the boats. They hoisted themselves in and, sputtering and exhausted, lent a hand to their struggling mates.

"Look!" Sally pointed. She was holding Nick's hand. "There's fighting, on the one boat there."

The captain was arguing with someone. Long hair. A woman. She snatched at his hands and grabbed his arm, but a crewman yanked her down. There was a flash of silver; a spell, Molly realized. The captain was sending a messenger spell. The woman threw herself at him, but too late. The boat dipped. The captain fell against a sailor and a black dart—a messenger spell—

shot skyward.

The sailor shoved the woman aside and she clawed empty air and fell, over the gunwale and into the sea. A splash followed, and then nothing. The surviving passengers looked dazed. The captain lowered his face to his hands while other swimmers fought desperately for a grip.

Brigit aimed a gun. "Give the word and I'll shoot that man."

"Leave him be," Molly said. "The messenger spell's gone, and enough people have died for one day."

Halfway between the *White Lily* and the sinking *Oracle*, the *Fish* sat easy in the water. It lolled as if nothing had happened and the sea wasn't swallowing men and women whole. It would be near enough soon, they'd reel her in. The instant they reached Luna's Cove, she'd search every plank and beam and try to understand how, why, the *Fish* had rammed itself into the *Oracle*, then freed itself, unharmed.

The three boats were slowly receding when Macklin shouted. "Look! There. Someone's swimming."

Molly shielded her eyes. "It's the woman," she said, relieved for the moment to have something beyond the *Fish* to think about. "Throw a line."

Troth threw a rope and they watched as the swimmer grabbed hold. They reached for her arms and helped her aboard and Sally wrapped a blanket around her shoulders. The woman's face was bruised but she was strong enough to stand. Her dripping hair was long and black, her complexion dark, cheekbones high. She had a pointed chin and eyes that seemed to miss nothing. Her shoulders were broad enough, it was a wonder she was the one who'd fallen and not the sailor who pushed her.

"Mercy," she said. "I ask for quarter." Her shoulders shook and she coughed and coughed again.

"Who are you?" Molly asked.

"I'll tell you, but please—"

"No," Molly stopped. "No *buts*. What happened out there?"

"My name is Madinina," the woman said. She pulled the blanket closer. "Please, if you hold the stars dear, tell me first if I'm safe. And who are you? Who fires on a ship of the king's fleet, fully armed, his favored witches on board?"

Molly exchanged a glance with Macklin. They had fought two battles in two days, won the first and survived the other. Nick was limping and Tribolt's shirt was soaked in blood from a wound that wouldn't close. She was not in the mood for puzzles.

Macklin's hand hovered near his blade. "Forgive me," Madinina said. "I mean no disrespect. I've been held prisoner, weeks in the hold."

Molly narrowed her eyes. "Your captain released a message. Where was it sent?"

Madinina straightened. "Not my captain. And if you saw him send it, you saw me try to stop it."

"That's no answer," Nick said. Her grabbed her arm and twisted it behind her back.

The blanket fell away, and Brigit grabbed the woman's left arm and pushed up her sleeve. Her arm was dripping wet, and her mark… It was strange. Parts were jagged, but over those were the smoother lines of sky.

Molly stared. "I've never seen a mark like that."

Nick released his grip and Madinina rubbed her arm. "The day I received that mark," she said earnestly, "it was a solstice eve and I was standing in a dome. Lights whipped across the sky. Colors like a waterfall, like nothing you've ever seen. I was seventeen and my apprenticeship was done. When the roof closed, there were two marks on my arm instead of one. Ice and sky.

"The masters dragged me in front a tribunal. They couldn't decide whether I was strong, and a threat, or a mistake, which couldn't happen. They declared it a trick and denied my charter. I spent the next few years thieving and trying to get by. I was jailed, escaped, caught again and at some point, I never learned how, word got back to the king and I was sent for."

"Sent for?" Molly asked. "What does that mean? I thought you were a prisoner?"

"We were, though they used a different word. Tried to make it softer."

Sally spit to the side. "But you went along? Did their bidding?"

"Yes, but no. If I hadn't gone with them, they'd have slit my throat and left me in an alley and no one would have dared ask why. So, yes. They brought me to Jamasak and made sure I was aware that they knew my mother's name, my grandmothers'. They knew where I was born and where my family lived and every spell I'd crafted from the time I entered a hall. And not just me; they'd brought in others. Master witches, all of us. We were treated well enough, for a while."

Sally shook her head. "In Jamasak?"

"Never near the king, but on the isle and palace, both. The city was grand, though it takes an army of witches to maintain. All glass and sunlight. Domes and spires and viewing stands so high, you'd think you could reach the stars, except we were kept apart. King's favored witches. They kept telling us how fortunate we were to be chosen, so long as we didn't try to leave."

"You crafted spells for them?"

"For three months, but all they wanted was pyrotechnics and incendiaries."

"Is that what you were carrying on the *Oracle*? We heard explosions."

"I imagine so, yes, though we were kept in the hold most of the time and it was warded tight as shackles. They were afraid of us and up until a few days ago, we didn't know where we were headed. Before that, we followed the ice."

Molly frowned. "Weapons I understand. Incendiaries for a battle I understand—though I don't know who he's fighting—but what would the king want with ice?"

"It was more about maps. We were there to chart the rim and mark down anywhere the ice jutted into the sea or receded into caverns. Where it rose higher, or if any rocks were visible. If I was building a new castle, I wouldn't put it at the edge of the world."

"Maps?" Molly repeated. She thought of the way Macklin had marveled at her parents' charts when he came aboard, the outlined coasts and odd drawings of men with harpoons spearing mythological leviathans. Maps were information, and information was power. "So, this new castle is near the rim, and he needs incendiaries for a war, but with who? The guild? Pirates? I don't see it yet. Is there more?"

Madinina was tiring. She pulled the blanket back over her shoulders and sank against the bulwark. "I wish there was. We'd been sailing for five days when new orders arrived. The captain changed course. We were to sail for Murrock. That's where we were headed just now."

Molly tensed. "He had business there? With the guild?"

"With the governor, I believe. Harkin Navarr."

Molly looked to Macklin, but he was as surprised as she was. "How do we know you're not lying?" he asked. "You could have faked that fight and come here to spy."

"I did fake it. I want them to believe I drowned. The other witches with me, they're sure to be picked up, but I'll be free. If you'll have me?"

She glanced questioningly at Macklin and he nodded, as did Tribolt and Troth and Nick and Sally, one after the other and Brigit, too. They dipped their heads and cast their votes and Molly agreed. "It seems you have your wish." she said, "And we need to be out of here before whoever hears that message tries to find us."

11

Chant, Object Gesture

Evan counted ten, maybe twenty sailors scurrying about the *Swift Pace*, and all of them too busy to notice one more boy. The remaining crew would show up soon enough and though he wouldn't mind having a look at Cai's uncle, his first task was to find a place to hide until they reached Carillon.

He surveyed the weather deck while he had a chance and counted four breach loading swivel guns on the port rail, the same on the starboard, dozens of axes along the bulwark. The *Swift Pace* looked to be a hundred and fifty feet bow to stern and ropes were everywhere, and barrels of drinking water. He took note. Those were important. He couldn't walk up to just anybody and ask for water. He might be expert at sneaking around a guild hall, but this was different. He'd have to ration and steal and couldn't trust to the good graces of Cai's uncle.

He made his way to the lower deck, ignored what he assumed were officers' cabins and was about to check a storeroom when he heard voices. He grabbed a burlap sack and slung it over his shoulder as two sailors walked by. They glanced his way and barely grunted, then disappeared through a companionway. There were more voices and footsteps overhead and he was trying to decide whether to try the lower hold when a dirty, tow headed boy tripped on the ladder and landed with a thud.

Evan backed into the shadows and watched. The boy looked about his age and his face, on one side, was pink and scarred, his patched vest too large for his scrawny frame. And though no one had seen him fall, he kept glancing about as if expecting a box on his ears. He rose and opened a keg, filled two water skins and leaned forward as he walked away, dragging his left foot behind.

Evan waited until he was gone then helped himself to a drink of water and, with a thought, practiced mimicking the boy's limp. He dragged his right foot, then switched to the left. He dropped his head, caved his chest and matched the boy's meek demeanor. They might not look alike, but they were both slender and near the same height and age and pretending to be someone else—if he could get away with it—could be useful. By the time he had a reasonable imitation of a limp, he had picked out a corner to hide on the orlop deck below.

No one was about, and he hurriedly dragged chests and kegs into a corner and built a wall with a pallet to frame a door and close it in. He crawled inside and made a few adjustments. There was just enough room to stretch out and he lay with his head cradled in his arm and feeling the creak and groan of the ship as it rocked beneath him.

Stowing away was stranger than he'd imagined. Easy enough so far—he didn't think anyone noticed him—but he couldn't think of a time he had ever felt so alone. The darkness hemmed him in. Time was distorted. Sounds magnified, and the hull creaked as—it must have been hours—the ship pulled away. He felt the anchor chains echo. Listened to the beat of footsteps, loud and insistent. He switched positions, moved his head to where his feet had been and wondered how long it might take, a week, maybe two, until Cai's uncle stepped off the ship and into Carillon. It could be longer if they stopped to pick up passengers, or unload cargo. He could bear it. Thinking of Cai would help.

She would have to lie of course, arrange her own passage and maybe buy out her charter. And if they didn't want to stay there, they didn't have to. They could move on, find a place that suited them better. It wasn't as if he needed to decide now, and certainly not without Cai. He wondered whether she'd prefer larger towns, or a particular isle, or maybe she'd rather live on board the *Fish*?

The next time he woke the ship's bell was tolling. His chest was clammy, and his lips were parched. He needed to relieve himself. He wanted water.

He peeked from his tunnel and when he didn't hear any voices, climbed out. No one was about and he stretched his arms gloriously to the sides, jumped a few times then made his way to the stairs.

It was night; he had slept through the ship's bell and lost track. A few scattered lanterns hung from beams and men snored in swaying hammocks. Most of the crew was asleep but he passed a knot of sailors hunched over a game of dice, a woman carving a pipe, another man who hissed as he limped by.

They ignored him for the most, hardly grunted as he walked with his eyes lowered, head down. He made it to the weather dark and stayed long enough to relieve himself and feel the breeze, then hurried back below. Someone had dropped a cap near the companionway, and he pulled it low over his forehead the way he imaged the cabin boy might do, then wandered about until he found the galley.

There was the usual brick oven, coal box and bellows. The shelves were well stocked, and he filched a stick of pemmican, a biscuit and a few figs. Cooks usually went to sleep early and woke while most everyone was asleep, and he needed to hurry. He glanced over his shoulder then stepped onto a stool and felt around the shelves until he found candles and further on, a tinderbox and a chipped knife. He grabbed them and, on the way out, snatched a water skin and a second candle and hurried back to his cave.

Pleased with himself, he chewed the pemmican and thought of sending Molly a messenger spell, let her know he was safe, but… He stopped. This had all started with the Red Grimoire, and he hadn't looked at it since the library. Molly could wait; she didn't even know he was gone.

He lit one of the candles, sat up cross-legged and opened the book. *The Red Grimoire, By Order of the First Council, Queen Reilla Makken of Jamasak, To Combat Corruption Within the Ring of Ice.*

Corruption? Evan wasn't sure what he'd expected but it wasn't a lecture on treason. The pages were brittle, and the ink was faded and difficult to read. *Dividing the skies into quadrants, we come upon a factor of Celestial Navigation such that it is likely that during the winter Solstice Chinen and Gaylock did descend upon the Lights which are called by some the River…and thus descending made it possible that…*

Descending? What did that mean? It wasn't any help finding a cog for a messenger spell. He turned the page.

A witch born during Chinen's ascendency may better control Sky then one born during the summer months…

He turned again. *And so, applying these theories, it is likely that spells of Fire become more febrile, those of Sky more highly charged and thus better achieving the witch's intention… Therefore, if it can be shown that corruption, either within the Lights or Ice bear directly upon the craft bearer's intention…*

Corruption again? Evan frowned. His candle was burning low and all this talk about corruption made no more sense at the end of the book than it had in the beginning. Besides, he already knew his intention. He needed to send messages, one to Molly and one to Cai, but he had no dragonflies to carry them.

The candle sputtered then flickered out, but he didn't care. He was tired and with the light gone, he had no sense of up or down or corruption or intention, or anything beyond the world of his cave, rocking in the dark.

*   *   *

Evan woke to the sound of boots stomping overhead. Boots and darkness and a different feel to the rolling ship. The *Swift Pace* was no longer moving. They had docked! He stuffed the tinderbox, Grimoire and one remaining candle into a bundle, poked out his head, then hurried from his cave.

They had reached Carillon. Finally! He stopped at the nearest port hole and looked out. The sun had risen, and a town stretched in front of him. It perched above the harbor but… It was not, it couldn't be, the bustling city Cai described.

Rickety crates and crab pots cluttered the dock. Buildings, raised on stilts, looked no better than shacks. Cai had mentioned tiled rooftops, shops and buildings so close you could have jumped from one to the other. Further out to sea was a galleon with its sails furled and what looked to be a siege tower chained to the deck, the king's pennant flying above the mast.

He tensed as he climbed to the upper deck. He'd lost track of the days and didn't know how long they'd been sailing. A few days? A week? Maybe more? The crew was at work, riggers tightening the sails, sailors hauling crates from below. They paused and stared at the wharf as four heavily armed guards rode up with a wagon—a cage full of ragged men and a few women—and stopped at their ship. Evan remembered the boy he was imitating and pulled his cap lower and tapped a sailor's arm. "Excuse me," he asked. "What town is this?"

The man had been swabbing the deck. He paused and scowled. "Well it ain't Jamasak, is it?"

A door in the forecastle opened and a man in a red silk coat stepped out, adjusted his hat and started down the plank. "Excuse me," he asked again. "Is that Captain Karron?"

"Don't be an idiot," the sailor hissed. "That's Captain Shorn. And go on with you, unless you want your ears boxed again."

Evan peered over the rail as two men shuffling a large crate toward the plank paused to let Shorn pass. They opened the lid and Evan caught a hint of glistening wood and ivory. It was an instrument. A harpsicord. Shorn nodded his approval then approached another man, also dressed in red. They watched with mild disinterest as the harpsicord was carried onto the ship. Behind them, a woman in a brown cape counted off the prisoners.

Nothing's changed, Evan told himself. It's a detour. A change of crew. There'd always been a chance they would pick up cargo. One day more and the *Swift Pace* will sail into Carillon's harbor and he'll find Cai. "That man Shorn is talking to, the one in the fancy coat, who's he?"

"That would be Captain Edinin coming on for the next run. You've seen him before."

"Yes, of course. What I meant was, I thought we'd be in Carillon by now? Did Captain Karron go on ahead?"

"Karron? What's the matter with you? Karron's been gone these last few weeks. He's going to Carillon, not us. Why would the likes of him stop in a backwater hole like this?"

"Where are we?"

"Bulatt, idiot. You were right there last night when we talked about it."

Evan felt sick. "Bulatt. Oh. And this Edinin, what sort of man is he?"

"He's a lord high mucky muck. Same as they all are. And what are you asking so many questions for?" The sailor glanced over his shoulder. "Look, they switched off is all," he said. "And if you don't want a beating, best stay out of their way. They've got that pack of malcontents to deliver and everything's all hush hush and watch your back. Now get out of here. Find some work before you get us both in trouble."

Evan didn't move. "But if someone needed to get to Carillon, they could change ships at the next port, couldn't they? Where are we taking the prisoners? Are they witches?"

The sailor leaned on his mop handle but kept talking. "I wouldn't know but I suspect it's got something to do with the two ships that disappeared."

"What ships? What happened?"

"*Oracle* and *White Lily*. You must have heard this? The guild's rounding up every thief they can find. Holding conclaves and the king's off building himself a new castle and no one's supposed to know, but everyone does. And if you're looking to sneak off, it's your arse will get flogged, not mine."

Evan nodded and backed away. "I should go" he said. "They'll be looking for me. But thanks. Thank you. For talking, I mean."

With all the work above, it was surprisingly easy to slip back into his hiding place without running into anyone. He shifted the pallets and moved a few crates to make it less stifling and thought about crafting a breeze and brighter light but decided against it. There were witches on board. If there hadn't been any before, there would be now that they had prisoners to guard. And while he might risk a bit of craft, there was always a chance someone would notice. Caution was better. He lit his candle, leaned over its meager light and opened the Red Grimoire.

He needed to send a message to Cai, warn her that this passage would take longer than they'd hoped but he'd get to Carillon. He'd find a way, he promised, just as soon as he could.

He tried to be systematic with the book this time, not flip back and forth. There were no chapters, nothing resembling the attract and repel or repair and transmute sections of his own Grimoire. And no mention of cogs, though he did find references to craft bearers which he supposed meant any kind of witch.

But this sort of passage— *Regardless of Tegheth's postulation that a correlation exists between the hue of the celestial Lights and the position of each Star, a generations long inquiry Must begin*—made no sense.

Nor did this: *Since it has been shown that the individual craft bearer's affinities are revealed most strongly during the eight quarters, might not the guild make use of these same conjunctions to isolate gaps in the rim…*

Affinities? The teaching masters used the same word when they talked about whether apprentices leaned more toward ice or sky, fire or water, but he had never felt a pull, not in any one direction. Inclination. Affinity. Whatever they called it.

All he wanted was to send a plain, simple messenger spell to Cai. Chant. Object. Gesture. No wonder this Red Grimoire had been tossed in the back of a shelf and forgotten. Thrown away was more likely.

He blew out the candle and listened to the waves lap against the hull as the ship returned to the open sea. A whistle blew and someone called the soundings. He wondered if the new captain played the harpsichord he'd seen, or if it was being shipped to their next stop. But mostly, he wondered whether any of the stars showing in the sky tonight were the same as those who sailed to the isles a hundred generations ago. Or maybe, more like, they'd be their descendants. Or what if that was just a story that changed every time the Grimoires changed? Like this Red, or the Gold, or Black?

Volumes changed. Titles. King's Version One to Version Two. Maybe the simple explanation was best and the queen at that time was having trouble with her spells the same way he had trouble and she created the guild to compile a Grimoire. But in the beginning, in the Red version, they didn't include the spells, they only talked about them.

And maybe… What happened was that all the questions in the Red Grimoire turned into answers in the Black. And the answers—the spells—over time became no more than a list while the questions were forgotten? And maybe he didn't need a Grimoire anyway.

He and Molly had been crafting spells for years. Echo spells. Unlocking spells. The spells that steered the *Fish*. They were formed from their need, their intention. Maybe he needed to stop talking about giving up on cogs, and just do it.

He sat up. If Queen Reilla's Grimoire had nothing to do with memorized cogs, and Molly crafted spells without them, then he didn't need them either. The corruption that worried the queen wasn't piracy or theft, it was a diminishing in the crafts, even so long ago as that.

He cupped his hands to his mouth. "This is my message," he whispered. "I send it to you, Cai, wherever you are. *The Swift Pace isn't going to Carillon, and your uncle's not on board. I'm sorry. It's my fault. I'll make my way to Carillon. I miss you. I'll find you. There's so much I need to say.*"

He blew, and his words became the chant. His hands the object forming the message; his breath the only gesture he'd ever need. He blew again and his message sped away, out of the hold, away from the ship and over the sea.

*　*　*

He couldn't sleep. Barefoot and quiet as a shadow, he crawled from his hiding place and made his way aft toward the stairs. He couldn't go up; there were too many footsteps and noises and the new officers and passengers would be there, along with the captain he didn't want to meet. The lowest deck was a better choice. He'd at least be able to straighten his cramped legs and stare at something further than six inches from his face. A lamp flickered as he neared the stairs and he followed it then turned and walked a bit.

He skirted crates and shadows and ballast, chickens asleep in their cages, burlap sacks filled with more food than he could have stolen in a week. He peered in a barrel; it was full of flour. The next held barley. He was about to try another when he found himself in front of a narrow door with a wooden grill in the center and a heavy chain around the latch. He pressed his face to the grill and tried to see.

"You can bring me rum or go away," a gruff voice called.

Evan jumped. They'd loaded a dozen prisoners onto the ship, but this was the first he'd actually seen. Or not seen. At least not yet. He couldn't make out anything beyond the gloom inside. He swallowed and lowered his voice to sound brave. "Come around to the door where I can see you," he called.

The man snorted. "I'll come when you bring my rum."

"Sounds like you're the one begging favors, not me."

Evan heard a shuffle, and a face appeared at the grill. The light was poor, but the man laughed when he saw Evan's face. "You're nothing but a boy. What? Your mates dare you to come down? Did you bet? I can help."

Evan scowled. The man looked to be of average height with dark eyes that glared through the bars. His nose was wide, his hair gray at the temples. He might be dangerous, but Evan hadn't run away from Hayden Hall to be treated like a child. "What's your name?" he asked.

"Steff Conure. You?"

Evan told him. "What did you do to end up in those chains? Are you a witch? And the other prisoners?"

"Get me my rum and maybe we'll talk."

"Talk and I'll get your rum. Maybe."

The man, Steff Conure, laughed. "Oh ho! Don't you bargain hard? And I'll tell you, but only because you'll likely hear it in the morning. They're witches, most of them, and so am I. But the way it turns out, I'm too good a witch. Used to be they cared about that. Don't anymore."

"Who's 'they'? The guild?"

"That's another question. Bring me rum if you want to hear more." Conure stepped away and sank, out of sight, against the door.

He'd been beaten, Evan realized. Conure's lips were swollen, and dried blood trailed across his face and from the way he winced, there were likely more bruises beneath his shirt. Evan pressed his mouth to the grate, promised that he'd try, then searched the hold and was surprised when he came across a jug.

He hurried back and found the cell door still closed, but the chain was gone. "Stop gawking like an idiot," Conure called. "You bring my rum?"

Hinges squealed as Evan pushed open the door. A lamp above Conure's head barely illuminated the cell, but there was enough light to see by. He held out the jug and Conure grabbed it, pulled the cork with his teeth and took a swig. The cell stank from the goat that had been its previous occupant. Droppings mingled with hay, and there was the usual stack of ballast and kegs, sweat, and the stink of urine. Evan moved alongside the door so that a guard, looking in, might not see him.

"You're trying to puzzle me out, aren't you," Conure said. "A witch could have unchained the door with a spell. Or a human with a cog, but where's the shell? Did I lie? If I'm a witch, how come I don't free myself? Here. I'm pulling your leg. Have a drink. It'll clear your thoughts. Unless you prefer goat's milk?" Conure smiled crookedly and Evan smiled back.

It felt good to be talking to somebody—anybody—after so many days hiding or grunting a furtive reply when someone mistook him for the cabin boy. He put the bottle to his lips the way he'd seen other men do and threw back his head. The rum scorched his throat and he was pretty sure it tasted awful, but he got it down without coughing. He took another, smaller drink and passed it back. "You said you're too good a witch, so was that you? You unlocked the door?"

"Not bad for a start. What else?"

"You're not afraid of getting caught, and I'm wondering what sort of witch you are. If you're a stonecrafter you could have snapped the chain. If you're a woodcrafter, you could have opened the door. But stonecrafters are ice, and woodcrafters are fire, and ice is stronger than fire. So, I figure you're ice. But if you can open the chain, why not escape?"

Conure cocked his head. "And go where? We're on a ship, in case you haven't noticed and I'm not taking on the king's army for a thrill." He squinted into the bottle.

"Why were you arrested?"

Conure wiped his hand across his mouth. "I am, or was, a master stonecrafter and good guess on that one, boy. About half a year ago, on Hawley, I crafted a new spell. A lamp. Nothing exciting, but I brought it to the guild the way you're supposed to, took my pay and went about my business. Now, my turn."

"You haven't finished!" Evan protested.

"You haven't started." He narrowed his gaze. "So, here's what I'm thinking. For a cabin boy, you know an awful lot about cogs. You're not afraid to sneak around, steal yourself some rum, maybe from right under the purser's eye. I can't see your arm, but you can't beat me at my own game. You're a witch?"

Evan stiffened. Molly would be furious if he told Conure, a stranger, that he was a witch. He'd never told anyone—outside a guild hall—and neither had she. But Molly had never been a stowaway, alone and heading in the wrong direction. And Evan couldn't see how he was taking any more of a risk then Steff Conure. Besides, all Conure had to do was look at his arm. It told part of the truth, just not all.

"You're a journeyman?" Conure guessed. "You're not old enough to be a master. Or... Wait! Drown me for a fool. You're an apprentice. You've run away from your hall, haven't you? Good job, lad. Which one?"

Evan shook his head. "My turn," he said. "No one gets arrested for registering a spell. What happened?"

Conure dipped his head. "All right. One witch to another. I'm not ashamed. Except for the trouble it brought my family and I'm not ashamed of that, just would have preferred it never happened. You see this?" He turned his face, showed Evan the line of scars. "They took my gems. Used to be six of them. It aches at night, and I'd just as soon numb myself with drink as feel the pain. Or the memories.

"My spells made my wife a wealthy woman, and a respected man out of me. Seemed as if every hall wanted to buy whatever I had. The guild paid in gold and you'd have thought I was a lord out of Jamasak to see the coach we rode.

"We had a second child, a fat, laughing girl to go with our boy. She was all smiles and dark hair so thick, folks said she was a gift of the stars and we treated her that way. Problem was, it went to my head. I needed to sell more spells, so I sat down and figured what sort would bring the most gold. I had just sold a nice transmute spell, used fire to heighten the color of a ruby. But I went and sold a weathercraft spell to a farmer after that, a way to know if rain was coming and how much and when.

"Farmer liked it so much he started bragging and some snake of an underwarden notices that a stonecrafter was also peddling weather spells."

"What's wrong with that?" Evan said flippantly. "Lots of witches have two crafts."

"Oh?" Conure raised a brow. "Who?"

Evan shrugged and looked away. "No one really. Apprentices talk, is all."

"Yes. I suppose you do. And what kind of witch are you? You didn't say."

"I don't know yet."

"Of course. You're young. I keep forgetting. Which hall did you say you're from?"

"Hayden Hall. My turn. Why didn't you sell your spells to Night Watermen?"

Conure snorted. "Because it wasn't the guild buying my spells, it was the king. The guild couldn't match his price. And I was selling on the black market, but the king paid better. My turn. I've been at Hayden Hall. What's the master's name there? I forget."

"Ossian."

"Right. Not a tolerant man. He the reason you're creeping around in the dark? Because I'd say you didn't run away from your hall just to hire on as a cabin boy. You're a stowaway, aren't you? You alone? Who's helping you?"

"Of course, I'm alone. And I won't answer any more questions until you finish your story."

Conure laughed. "Cheeky, aren't you? But I like you, so I'll tell you more. I thought I was safe, my family cared for, everyone a friend. Except I was wrong. The king— his agents, not him, he doesn't know a thing—they were keeping track. They offered more gold. Wanted me to come to Jamasak and said I could bring my family along." He stopped. "You hear that? The watch changed. Someone's coming."

Evan flattened himself alongside the door. Conure curled on the floor and pretended to sleep and a moment later, a woman's face appeared at the grate. "Breakfast, your highness," she called. Evan held his breath as a plate clanked against the floor. And then footsteps, receding this time.

"You should leave," Conure said, suddenly tired. "Come back tonight. And bring more rum."

"I will," Evan said. "Thanks." His thoughts reeled as he made his way back to his cave. He slipped out once to relieve himself, but he was nervous about being caught and the hours moved slowly. He had an idea he wanted to tell Conure, about how they could both escape. Once on land, they'd find a way to reach Carillon. Two people traveling together would be better than one.

* * *

Nightfall came and he returned to the cell. Conure took one look at his empty hands, scowled and said nothing. He'd had visitors during the day. Broken iron rings that had been bolted to the hull now scattered the floor and his arms were covered in new bruises. "Are you all right?" Evan asked. "What happened?"

"Nothing that hasn't happened before. I'm just tired. You would be too if you weren't so young. You ever kiss a girl?"

"What?" Evan stepped back. He had forgotten how sharp Conure could be, how easily he caught him off guard. "I have," he admitted, and his face warmed at the memory. "Why?"

"No reason. Just wondered if you were old enough to understand what a man will do for someone he loves."

"I think I can," Evan said. "Yes. I can. Imagine."

"You ever hear of a press gang? You could be sleeping with your arms around your wife or drunk in an alley, it's all the same when they come. They beat you till you're half dead. Stuff a rag down your throat and a bag over your head so you can't call down a cog. And just when you think you'll never see the sun again, they pull it off and there's a soldier in front of you and he's all trussed up in a hat with peacock feathers and a badge with Jamasak's sun big as day, a pile of gold beside him. For the wife, they say and all you have to do is swear to the king."

"Swear what?"

"That you'll serve him in Jamasak. Count yourself among the strongest witches. Stupid me to think I could stand against the king."

"But what if we can?" Evan interrupted. "I don't mean the king. I mean here, now. There's just sailors and guards, and if we worked together? We could escape. Next time we dock, I'll sneak you off. I'll help you, and then you'll help me."

Conure looked surprised. "And how's that?"

Evan drew himself taller. "I have a plan. We'll need a few spells."

"What sort of spells?"

"An attract and repel spell to start with. We'll work together. It's what my sister and I do."

"Your sister? You didn't mention her. She a witch?"

"Yes. That's how we navigate and bring winds, hoist the sails, everything. I don't always get the spells right, and she's better at them. But we could do it, you and me together." He crouched beside Conure. "I've been all over this ship and I know how to hide. There are empty crates. I can get you inside one." Evan stopped. Conure was staring him. "I'm talking too fast, aren't I? But I've figured it out. We can escape. I'll show you something." He drew the Red Grimoire from his vest.

"A book?" Conure raised a brow.

"Not just any book. A Grimoire. It's ancient." He pressed it into Conure's hands, "There isn't a cog in it, anywhere. It's all about celestial navigation and corruption and craft bearers. The lists of cogs came later, then they took those out too."

"They didn't just take them away," Conure said coldly. "They were obsolete. Useless. They didn't matter anymore."

"What do you mean? Have you read it?"

"No, and I'm not going to get riled up about it. Tell me about this plan. You're going to put me in a crate?"

"Yes. You'll use your unlocking spell, and I'll show you how to use an echo spell so we can communicate. My sister and I use them."

"Never heard of it."

"You wouldn't have. It's one of our own. They're like messenger spells but across shorter distances. The captain brought a harpsichord on board and the crate is empty. The lid may be nailed, but I'll open it."

"Easy boy, I'm trying to follow. So, we've got a crate that sounds more like a coffin with me inside. What happens when they find this piss hole empty?"

Evan's eyes gleamed. "That's what I've been trying to tell you. We'll be long gone. I'll get Molly to bring the *Fish.* That's our ship."

Conure laughed. "This keeps getting better. You have a ship and a sister and a crew—"

"No crew," Evan interrupted. "At least not yet. It's always been just Molly and me."

"And you'll call her with one of your echo spells. But…" He paused and grew quiet then, "This ship of yours; it's not some little catboat, is it?"

"Of course not," Evan said indignantly. "She's two hundred hands and the fastest caravel you'll find. Lateen rigged on the mizzen, with eight heavy guns."

"All that and she's yours?"

"Yes. I told you. It's seaworthy, if that's what you're worried about. Our parents built spells into every part of the ship. We'll never be caught." He knew he was bragging but he was excited and growing impatient. A guard could return at any moment. They had to work this out and Conure wasn't listening.

"Your parents? I was wondering about them. They must be damn wealthy to have a ship with so many boughten spells?"

"They're not boughten." Evan nearly shouted. "I told you. They built the *Fish* themselves. Every nail and board and spell."

"Spells, too? And they're the shipbuilders?"

"No. I mean yes."

"I see. And where are they?"

"They're gone. And we don't have time for all these questions."

"I'm sorry. I lost my parents as well. But these spells, they didn't buy them so… They crafted them?"

"I already told you they did. Look, you don't have to come if you don't want to."

Conure pushed himself from the floor. "No, I do. I like your story. I think we can do something about it."

Evan had been holding his breath; he let it out, started pacing the small cell. "It might take a few days. I'm shut up half the night and we have to wait till I can scout around."

"Of course. And you'd better get going. They'll be checking on me soon. Stay quiet. Don't take any chances."

Evan nodded. "The crate first. I'll make sure it's still there. I've got a bit of food put aside. And water. We'll need more. I'll find out the ship's schedule, how long till it makes land."

* * *

Hunched in the dark of his cramped hole, Evan fleshed out his plans. There was little to carry. Cai's blanket and the stolen kitchen knife. Candle and tinder and water. The Red Grimoire and the clothing on his back. He lay his stockings out to dry. Rolled and rerolled the blanket. Poked his head out the door, listened, then pulled back in and wondered if Cai received his message. He lay there, planning and hoping, until hours later the ship's swaying lulled him to sleep. But instead of morning, Evan woke to the shouts of sailors kicking down his walls and door. Hands grabbed him in the dark.

He lurched out of sleep and howled as a boot slammed his ribs and another cracked his shin. He shouted and tried to roll over, but soldiers grabbed his arms and dragged him up the stairs and onto the deck and dropped him, face down.

He groaned and tried to see. It was dawn, but not yet light and there were boots everywhere. In front of his burning eyes and further out. Boots and legs stretching into darkness. He tried lifting his shoulders, but they kicked him back down. There were sailors and soldiers, uniformed men and women circling him. They had found him out. Someone saw him. Poor Conure. He would never be free. Cai—

They pulled him to his feet and when at last they stepped back, the ship's captain, Edinin from the dock, was standing in front of him. He was tall with long, slick black hair, a sneer on his face. And though Evan didn't recognize him at first, Steff Conure was at his side. He was dressed in a clean, stiff shirt. His hair was tied back, his eyes no longer bloodshot.

"That's him?" Edinin asked. "He's nothing but a cabin boy."

"Yes sir." A woman with wiry red hair agreed.

"And he's a witch?"

The woman grabbed Evan's arm and he jerked away until another sailor held him while she tore back his sleeve. The captain glanced briefly, unimpressed.

Evan gritted his teeth. His mouth was warm with blood and he spit a wad of pink saliva at Conure's feet. "Damn you," he cursed.

Conure started to say something, then stopped as the ship shuddered. All eyes turned as a fog, grey with a light all its own, began to move. It curled and massed across the water, rose and thinned and where it stopped, daylight flooded in and the sea appeared. The world changed.

"The king's armada," Conure said. His voice was flat, dry. "Behold your new home."

Evan didn't understand. The sailor holding him loosed his grip and he struggled to stand as the sea began to roll. Shapes stretched and changed as he watched—they all watched—and what he thought were clouds took on angles and lines. Sails, he realized, and ships. Hundreds of ships spread across the horizon where the fog had been.

The more distant ships were no more than a hint of their true size. But those nearest the *Swift Pace* were fully armed vessels, bright with paint and tall prows and gilded figureheads, and all flying Jamasak's pennant, two hands holding a sun. The largest ships were at the front of the line, galleons and five-masted frigates painted and festooned and all of them larger than Evan imagined any ship could be. Their sails blustered with witch-crafted winds and pale gauzy curtains were strung about their waists as if they were sailing to a royal fete.

Conure leaned toward Evan. "You're sharp for a boy; remember that and you'll get by."

"You sold me out," Evan hissed.

"The price was right, and you won't have it so bad, you and your craftborn sister, if what you told me is true. But I meant you no harm and thanks to you, I'll see my wife again. They were going to catch you anyway."

12

Pirates of Fire, Pirates of Ice

Molly woke with a start. Her heart was racing and the image of the *Fish* cutting into the *Oracle's* hull was clear in her mind, the rending noise and the sight of her ship rising from the sea then pulling free and reversing course. She didn't know how. She'd never crafted a spell like that. No one had.

She kicked free of the bedding, crossed to the windows and pressed her hands against the glass panes. The sheltered beaches of Luna's Cove lay ahead, the familiar run of pink sands, moss covered rocks and hills beyond. The *White Lily* lay anchored a short distance away. The tide was coming in and Brigit, on shore, lifted a crate from their dinghy, waded through the breakers and set it down above the high tide line, alongside the others.

Molly stripped to her under clothes, tied back her hair and walked quickly up the companionway to the rail. Troth and Tribolt, who were nearly inseparable, called to each other on the *White Lily*. The rest of the crew would be emptying the hold, readying the ship for repairs. She ought to join them. She would, but not yet. She needed to be alone.

They had taken the *White Lily* and sunk the *Oracle*, a ship of the king's fleet. Brigit had done a good job removing a shard from Tribolt's shoulder and Nick was no longer limping. And though it could be days, possibly weeks until the *Lily's* mast was repaired, they were safe and a good deal wealthier than when they left Auklet's harbor. It was the *Fish* that weighed heavily on her mind.

She took a breath and dove. Warmth surrounded her, the familiar weight of the sea. She plunged downward and kicked until her feet touched bottom. She frightened a large crab, pushed aside seaweed and scattered a swarm of angelfish, then arched her back and sprang upward. She shot to the surface, filled her lungs and dove again.

She felt her way along the *Fish's* keel, and forward toward the bow and now, as she surfaced and dove, she saw the phosphorescent light again, fainter than when the *Fish* rammed the *Oracle*, a remnant now, fading.

She had checked the keel in the past, more times than she could count, yet never saw a light. It emanated from beneath a sheathing, a layer that stretched fore to aft along the keel and part way up the bow. There were depressions and scorched boards where the few cannonballs Brigit couldn't stop had hit, but they were almost completely smoothed over. Her parents had built spells into the *Fish*. It healed and protected itself. She knew it was true. She lived daily with the benefits of those spells. They fixed the chinking. Repaired the sails. Greased the pullies, cleared the barnacles, but she'd never known how far they went. And this spell—the *Fish* taking control, defending itself—went deeper. It had been there all along, yet never had cause to emerge.

Take care of the *Fish*, they had said, and she'll take care of you. And she was more than grateful for those spells. Her life, and Evan's depended on them. But how was she supposed to take care of her ship when it kept secrets she had never known?

She surfaced and tread water. If she could see through the hills and land formations, the rim—the edge of the world—wouldn't be far away.

Behind her, in the opposite direction and a half mile from the beach, an army of towering rocks guarded the entrance to Luna's Cove. Waves crashed against the black spires, broke and sprayed. To venture past, a ship first needed to see the cove, and that was impossible. The rocks were hidden in a fog, impenetrable until it was too late.

Luna's Cove appeared on no map. No spyglass could see her. No ship—except under Molly's guidance—could reach her gentle waters. The cove protected itself and apparently, so did the *Fish*, more than the spells that protected against shipworms, or hardened the chinking, tarred the ropes and cleaned any metal. More than she'd understood.

She swam for the shore then walked barefoot past a tidal pool and around the far side of an outcropping where she wouldn't be seen. She sat and pulled her knees to her chest. Though Luna's Cove was near the ice, she knew little about the rim's nature. With a favorable wind and a spell to hasten the journey it could take no more than a few hours to reach, the distance so brief, she wondered they hadn't explored more often. Then again, she had so badly wanted to protect Evan, and not make the same mistakes her parents made, she had told herself it was bad luck to go there. But Senesh and Esty Sinclair were gone and the world was changing, and she had difficult, confusing decisions to make.

She had brought Evan to the guild halls, had him tested and declared a witch. She had fought and killed and hired a crew and brought them to Luna's Cove. All things her parents would never have done. Except, truth was, she didn't understand her parent's intentions. She never had. She was seventeen when they left yet they still treated her like a child, softening some truths, hiding others.

She had felt lost when she thought the *Fish* would go down, but that didn't make her childish. She had been frightened when she boarded the *White Lily*, but fear didn't mean she was weak. It was what she did with her fear that mattered. And right now, what mattered was not only learning how the *Fish* defended itself but finding a way to use it and build the safehouse she wanted.

They had a good start on the gold, and there was more in her house in Auklet. She thought of the stolen chest—it was still there, and she ought to retrieve it. The more she thought about it, the more sense it made. Bring the chest here, and close down the house. Auklet was dangerous. The governor was looking for her, and there could be survivors from the *Oracle* or *White Lily* who'd recognize her.

She thought of Davit Lake. Wasn't it possible, even likely, that if someone was searching for the *White Lily*, he would know? He lived on Murrock with the governor, but she had last seen him in the Gold Key in Auklet. What if he still frequented the tavern? The distance between the two isles wasn't far. He'd be in the thick of things. Anything she learned, the smallest tidbit, could be useful. It would help them plan routes, target ships, avoid the guild rats. She'd close up her house, and look for him when she was done, then bring the chest and whatever belongings she wanted to keep, back to Luna's Cove.

*   *   *

By afternoon the following day, the *White Lily* lay careened on the beach. Her portside gaped at clouds, starboard burrowed into the wet sand like a turtle unable to right itself. A web of pulleys and spliced ropes spurted from every block and bolt and hole, wrapped around the ruined mast and stretched upward toward the first strong line of trees. Damaged sails had been hauled to the beach; those that were still intact were carefully stowed. The wind had dried the planks and the newly exposed barnacles were sharp enough to slice Molly's skin.

When at last they stopped to sit around the fire, the sun was down and the moon a sliver in the sky. The crew was in high spirits and joking about the next raid. A bar of gold had been found beneath the captain's desk, and a small chest with jewels had somehow managed to wash up on the beach.

Earlier in the day, Molly had shown them the house where she and Evan and their parents lived when they weren't on the *Fish*. The entrance was tucked beneath an overgrown slope of moss and rock and hidden with spells, but once inside, the rooms let in sunlight and warmth. There were curving walls and high ceilings, soft carpets and living plants that arched between corridors. But though the crew admired the house and agreed to keep their plunder inside, they preferred to sleep in sight of the ships.

They were sitting around the fire and talking about destinations they'd try as soon as the repairs were done, and how they'd decide on their next foray. What sort of ship to take, and how they would give their shares away if that's what they wanted; hand off their coins to the first beggar who walked by if they damn well pleased. It didn't matter so long as the choice was theirs.

She wondered—not for the first time— why the crew was willing to follow her. She was the youngest and least experienced. They hadn't known her until Macklin brought them to her cellar. Yet they trusted her, and it wasn't only because she was paying them, or because she owned the *Fish*. Part of it, she reasoned, had to do with her craft, the rest with their own particular brand of loyalty and stubbornness.

Nick yelped as his fingers grazed the coals. He'd been checking the spit and he cradled his hand and Molly watched as Sally grew concerned. He moaned and she moved nearer, until she caught him staring at her open shirt. She rolled her eyes and walked away.

"What do you want me to stare at?" he pouted.

"Stare at the sea," she said. "Stare at Tribolt for all I care."

"He's not in love with me."

"Neither am I."

"But you will be. I'm working on it." Nick teased and started to sing: "*Oh beware the fancy sailor, Mistress Sigh. If he takes you to his bed, then be warned you'll never wed. Please beware the fancy sailor, Mistress Sigh.*" He glanced meaningfully at her, but she crossed her arms and looked away.

"*I'm a better man that he is, Mistress Sigh. If you take me for a husband, Mistress Sigh, from your kisses and your home, I will never need to roam. I will keep you for a treasure, Mistress Sigh.*"

Macklin nudged Molly's shoulder. He speared her a chunk of meat and passed it over. "You should eat," he said pointedly.

She picked at the meat while Macklin cut another slice. "Have you gone over the damages?" she asked.

"Aye. We'll need trees for a new mast."

"The tallest are to the west above the beach," Molly said. "You'll find cedar and cherry and oak. Cherry is good."

Macklin looked at her. "*We'll* find cherry," he whispered. "Where will you be?"

She didn't answer, and the others hadn't heard.

Tribolt raised his voice. "I like it here," he said. "No wharfage fees. No guild rats. Did you see the look in that captain's eyes when he realized the *Fish* wasn't on fire?"

"He'll spread the tale," Madinina said.

Nick said, "We'll be as famous as Night Watermen."

"Infamous." Tribolt laughed. "They'll beg us to join forces."

"Except we'll never find them," Sally said. "They don't take recruits. You have to be born a Waterman."

Molly looked up. "They take new crew," she said. "Just that you don't go looking for them, they come to you, and that's only with a recommendation from one of their own."

Macklin cocked his head. "And where did you hear that?"

"I don't know." She stared at the fire. "Somewhere. Everyone says it."

"What I heard," Troth said, "is that Watermen split their shares. We swore to do the same and we should. There's eight of us here counting Madinina, a compass rose. That's a good sign. You take two shares Molly, and we split the rest, equal shares all around."

Molly nodded, but she was only half listening. Where had she heard that about the Night Watermen? She hadn't made it up or learned it at the governor's palace. It could have been in one of the taverns where, for all she knew, half the patrons were Night Waterman. It wasn't as if they'd use real names.

She looked up. "I'm taking the *Fish* to Auklet," she said suddenly. "First light, tomorrow. I'll sail with the tide." *But how do I know so much about Night Watermen when I don't even know the spells on my own ship?*

The laughter fell away, and Macklin hurried to fill it. "We'll split the crew," he said. "A few of us wait here, the rest go with you." He glanced at Brigit.

"Our gunpowder's damp," she agreed. "I'll go with you. I know the sellers, the best supplies."

"No," Molly said firmly. "You'll stay together. I'll close the house in Auklet. It's a small thing. I don't need help. I'll sail straight back."

"The king will be looking for us," Tribolt said. "Shouldn't we wait longer, give them time to forget?"

"They won't be looking for one woman," she said. "I know how to hide."

The silence returned. People shifted. Poked the fire until finally, Sally spoke up. "It's her ship," she said. "Her choice. Let's decide on a location and a time to meet."

Macklin frowned. "All right, but I don't like it. Let's say we meet between the fifth and seventh day from now. The point off the narrow sound. We can do that can't we? Finish our work, send message spells if need be."

Molly rose. The fire was hot on her face. She felt resolved, not altogether wise but at least not foolish. "We'll make a pact before I leave," she said. *Our pact, not the Night Watermen's.* "A pirate's charter. Wherever we are, together or apart, it binds us. If anyone among us loses a hand or a leg or even a finger during a fight, that person will be cared for by the others."

"Aye," they agreed.

Sally came up behind Nick and rested her hand on his shoulder.

"If any one of us steals from the others," Brigit added, "or tries to run away without explanation, without warning, that person will be left on an island."

"But not without provisions," Tribolt said. "With food and a weapon and gun powder. Fresh water if there's none to be found."

"What of the punishment?" Troth said. "I won't swear to any charter that treats men and women the way the guild does. No lashing. No corporal punishment. No one is ever, no matter the crime, denied their craft."

"What if someone doesn't agree?"

"We vote," Macklin said. "All of us. You also, Madinina. You're one of us now. We vote our rules. We write our own charter."

Madinina had been quiet till then, too uncertain of her place to speak out. "Thank you," she said. "We vote the rules."

"Except for what Troth said." Molly raised her voice. "About the shares. I won't take more. Except for the *Fish*; she isn't counted. She's mine and my brother's. The *White Lily* belongs to you, so long as you're together. But we share the gold and spells. Whether you're bosun or gunner or navigator, ice or water, fire or sky, we are witches. Equal. We are not the guild to set one witch above another."

Macklin said, "Or to give more of a say to one over another. We swear on our charter and sit in council together."

"We swear on the gift of the stars," Molly said. "We take to heart the truths they gave us, not as the guild twisted them, but as they were meant to be. We are one people. We rejoice in the power we share. Say it. Repeat it."

They were all standing now, their faces shot with red and gold from the burning light. "*We are one people. We rejoice in the power we share.*"

"The gift of the stars flows through us."

"*The gift of the stars flows through us.*"

"The river of light did find us. We are free witches. The capacity for a witches' craft is not constant in any family. We will not have a society divided by those with stronger blood, those whose craft is weaker."

"*We will not have a society of those with stronger blood and those whose craft is weaker.*"

"We are free witches. One people, from the First Stars through the blood of all women. We are ice. We are fire. We are water. We are sky. We rejoice in the power we share. Swear it, swear it on the stars."

"I swear."

"I do swear."

"And I." One by one, they sealed the charter. *We are one people. We rejoice in the power we share.*

* * *

The Night Watermen's flagship *Akistra* lay waiting in rough waters off the northernmost point of Chriserin Isle. Two of their smaller ships, *Cosmus* and *Elaphe,* anchored nearby. Both were three masted galleons. Both flew the Night Watermen's double headed water moccasin flag with their own symbol centered within. A kraken on the *Cosmus;* a rat on the *Elaphe.* Both were dwarfed by the towering *Akistra.*

South and to the west, the dark cliffs of Chriserin formed a shadowed wall. Clouds covered the sky and the wind had been rising since before the moon came up. Oil lamps flickered across the *Akistra's* deck, blew out and flared again.

Davit Lake steered his borrowed catboat straight on toward the light. He called to Brittle, but the older man was hunched in the bow, head in his hands and too busy feeling miserable to answer his friend. It wouldn't be long now. The trip was taking less time than Davit expected. Even so, the fishwife they paid for the use of her boat and stabling their horses would be tapping her foot until they returned. Davit balled up a rag and threw it at Brittle's head. "Wake up," he called. "Light the signal lamp, will you?"

"As if I could sleep." Brittle grabbed the bulky duffle between his feet and pushed it toward Davit. "I'm too old for this," he moaned. "You're the sailor. You light the damn thing."

Davit lurched to grab the lamp before it broke. He unwrapped the oilcloth and pulled out the flint and striker. "You're a nuisance and a thief, Mr. Brittle and please, if you're going to vomit, do it over the side." He shook his head as the spark caught, waited, then raised the lamp above his head and waved it back and forth.

He lowered it, counted to five and waved it until a yellow light answered from high on the *Akistra's* top and in no time at all, the little catboat was bobbing alongside the *Akistra's* massive hull. Someone tossed a rope ladder down and Davit steadied it for Brittle. "Up you go," he said holding the older man's elbow. He waited till the older man reached the deck, then sent a chest up a rope behind him.

The Night Watermen's oldest, most revered, most crowded vessel was over a hundred and fifty feet long. She was fully rigged with four masts and heavy cannons on three gun decks. Smaller guns projected from the stern and bow and the rails high above. Paint gleamed. The figurehead's eyes glistened. Davit leaned back and picked out the light in the cook's galley.

If the *Akistra's* supplies had come in—the ship never made port—there'd be strings of garlic hanging from hooks, onions and figs, sausages and cheese. There'd be a cabin boy whose hands had been smacked at least twice that day for stealing a taste. Davit smiled at the thought. He, too, had been a boy on this ship, hid beneath tables and slept alongside cannons. He used to climb those shrouds and feed Lala and Stinky, the ravens that had the run of the ship and followed him about the deck and along the yards and anywhere he climbed with a morsel of food in his hand.

He watched the play of shadows, halyards and shroud and masts crisscrossing each other under the midnight sky. He listened to the Watermen's voices, knots of men and women drinking and playing dice, sharpening blades on whetstones, carving wood. And finally, with the memories eased into place and the point of this visit clear in his thoughts, he followed Brittle up the ladder.

He'd barely reached the rail when a huge, one armed man in a red shirt grabbed him and hauled him in. "Davit Lake!" he exclaimed. "You've been gone too long this time."

"Too long and too far, Mr. Brink." Davit slapped the man's shoulder. "And most of them places I never want to see again."

Another man tapped Davit from behind. He was dressed in ill-fitting clothes that looked part guild rat, part pirate. "Deesh!" he laughed. "Do I still owe you that gold piece or do you owe me?"

"You owe me," Deesh said and Davit pumped his hand and then the next man's, and then a comely, red haired older woman and a young girl dressed in a velvet coat who jumped on his back and tickled his neck. "Crowson! Mistress Stace! Lena!" He smiled as he was passed from one to the next, hugged and slapped and chided for being gone.

"You shouldn't ever have left," a man remarked.

"Sign a Waterman's charter," Crowson said, "and you go where you're sent. He's here, ain't he? That's what counts."

"But only for a visit, I'm sorry to say. Mr. Brittle wanted to trade." Davit looked past the small crowd to where Brittle had already thrown back the lid on his chest. People huddled in to see his wares: spells and jewelry, weapons and clothes. "Of course, it's real," Brittle bellowed. "That's lapis. And that's a ruby. That one protects against weevils. You'll never regret these." The ravens swooped to the rail. They cawed and Davit answered with a sound in the back of his throat.

Rough as the seas were, it was warm on board. Shirt sleeves were rolled up and arms clearly visible. Many were scarred; proof of how far the guild was willing to go to control the crafts. But scarred or not, witch or human, the Waterman's double headed snake was visible. The tattoo on a woman's forearm, a man's chest, the gems on many of their faces. Small, precious stones, they decorated cheeks, foreheads and chins. Not the guild's single line that ran in a structured order. These were patterns, no two alike, but all with the same meaning. We are Night Watermen. We are proud and we are free.

Davit caught himself staring and turned away. His own arm and face were bare. Always had been. Always would be. The choice had nothing to do with his regard for the Watermen and he didn't often think about it. The decision had not been his.

A woman appeared at the companionway and caught Davit's eye. Marissa Hope. She was older than Davit, but not a great deal. Her thick red hair was braided and her face freckled and she was more somber than most on the crowded deck. He noted the black handled dagger in her waistband, another in her boot; even among their own, the Watermen kept weapons in reach. "They're waiting for you," she said and looked past Davit to Brittle.

She smiled as he approached, and Davit was surprised to see the look that passed between them. She reached for Brittle's hand and he took it, stepped closer and they kissed. Davit's face grew warm and he looked away, then looked again.

What was it like, he wondered, to kiss a woman you loved and hold her? He'd been with women before, in the courts of Jamasak and other isles, but that was different. Love would be having someone's face and voice inside your thoughts, and the thoughts filling your head at the oddest moments. Whispering her name. Jenin Rose. He wondered who she was. How he'd find her again. He'd only met her the one time, in Brittle's shop; yet there she was, inhabiting his thoughts.

Marissa winked at Davit then nodded for him to follow. "Not you." She playfully pushed Brittle aside. "You wait here. I'm to bring him below but that's all."

"I'll be here." Brittle said, and poked Davit's chest. "And you, take your time down there. Don't hurry back."

Marissa led him through the companionway and down to a lower deck and stopped in front of an ornately carved door. There were images carved into the wood: the sun and moon and stars. They rode a ribbon of lights as they beat back a maelstrom of fanged fishes and tusked animals and fire breathing birds. "San Hesrin is here," she said as she rapped on the door. "Trading. You're just in time."

Inside, two women and two men were seated around a long trestle table. At the far end of the cabin, a sleeping alcove was tucked behind an arch. Statues of two-headed dogs carrying spears stood guard on either side.

The trader, San Hesrin, waited beside a chair. He was a dark-skinned man, broader and taller than everyone else. A single row of diamonds curved across the bridge of his nose and he was dressed in rich, fur trimmed clothes. Davit counted four open cases of firearms on the floor behind him. He glanced at Hesrin, exchanged a nod.

Draks Halo, seated at the end of the table, waited for Marissa to leave before opening his arms to greet Davit. He was older than San Hesrin, but looked stronger, battle tested and wary. His wife, Ayva Trill sat to his right. Krila Sand sat next with her husband Gryer Scarp. Together, they were the four captains of the Night Watermen, its fleet, its dealings, its beginnings, its plans.

Davit stepped into Drak's embrace and they slapped each other's backs and looked warmly at each other until Ayva stepped between. She was as tall as her husband but slender and she kissed Davit on both cheeks then took his face in her hands and smiled.

Gryer and Krila waited their turn then squeezed his shoulder and clasped his hand. They each had brown hair and brown eyes. Krila's were large and missed nothing. Her mouth was thin, her face a sharp oval. Her gray curls were held in place with beads that Davit had seen her throw and explode like bolts of charged gunpowder. He had seen them burn and maim.

"Sit, please," Draks said when their greetings were done. He was clean shaven, his gray hair still thick and curled to his shoulders. He wore a vest with a bandolier covered with strings of spells that clacked as he moved, and a silver medallion in the shape of a water snake hung around his neck. "It's been too many months," he said warmly. "Even if it is my doing."

"I'll remember you said that," Davit laughed, but he was serious as well. Though it was the king who sent him to the governor with the pretext of being his nephew, it was Draks Halo who positioned him to be near the king. Davit couldn't have said which of the postings he disliked more, the years in Jamasak or the months wasted with Navarr.

"Wine?" Ayva asked. "You must be thirsty." She filled a goblet and pushed a platter heaped with dried fruits and nuts, cheeses and breads nearer Davit's reach. "We have San Hesrin to thank for the wine," she said. "He brought it earlier today, along with the muskets and pistols."

San Hesrin lifted a satchel onto the table. It seemed ordinary enough, canvas with something hard and angular inside. Hesrin was a trader, one of many in the vast Watermen network. Unlike Brittle, he traded in weapons and spells that enhanced a gun's reach or strengthened a sword's bite. He wasn't a pirate, and he wasn't there for the fruit and cheese.

If there was a time when Ayva and Draks Halo hadn't been part of his life, Davit no longer remembered. Gryer and Krila had been on the *Akistra* as well the morning they reeled him in, a scrawny, shivering five-year-old adrift in a boat. Alone. Waving his arms and crying a tale of an old man who saved him from a fire, parents lost and a town, isle, details, even his name, lost forever.

It was Ayva and Draks gave him a new one, Davit, for the hoist they used to draw him from the sea, and Lake, because he kept repeating the one sound again and again. But he attached himself to them like a puppy to its master and for weeks whimpered if one or the other wasn't in sight.

There were a few more wrinkles around Ayva's eyes. Her brown hair was held in place with ivory combs that were sharp as daggers and she wore pearls and wide bracelets, necklaces with rare stones. He had once thought her the most beautiful woman in the world, a standard no one could reach. If that had changed, it had less to do with the wisps of gray in her hair and more that he had met other women of late, different women.

"It's good you're here," San Hesrin said as he drew a large, object from the sack. It was metal and rounded, and at first Davit took it for a bucket of some kind, until Hesrin turned it and he realized it was a helmet, partially encased in ice. Davit glanced about the table. "May I?"

Ayva nodded and watched closely for his reaction.

Draks said, "One of our ships picked it up a few weeks ago. It's rim ice so there's no chance of melting. We're giving it to San Hesrin in thanks for the inventory. Ten cases of muskets and pistols. Choose something, please, for me."

"That's generous, thank you. I will, but... This. This is interesting." He tested the helmet's weight. The top came to a point and the back was long enough to protect the wearer's neck. The front—if it weren't for the ice—would keep a soldier's face safe from arrows and swords, possibly even gun shot. "There's no guild mark," he murmured as he examined it. "But these markings inside, I can't read them, can you?"

"No, and there's no spell on it," Ayva said.

The helmet was heavy, though Davit couldn't say whether the weight was more from the ice or metal. "What are you thinking? Could it be a relic, from the time before the stars? Unless it's fake?" He looked up and caught Draks and Gryer exchanging a glance.

"It was found near Doshaget," Draks said. "But it could have fallen from most anywhere along the rim. Fallen into the water, floated along."

"There's a puzzle here, and you want me to figure it out?" Davit thought of the last time he had seen an object partially encased in ice. He and that young fellow broke into the guild shop. Melvin Goodeye. He was surprised he remembered the name. They'd had a few laughs, gotten drunk and talked. Improbable as it seemed, he felt as if they were kindred spirits and had much in common. And there was something else, something about the block of ice they'd picked up, but he couldn't remember. And no surprise there; he'd been drunk to the core and babbling.

Every school child learned about ice and the rim, and if the helmet truly was a relic, it meant that either the stars themselves had brought it when they discovered the isles, or it belonged to the First People and had somehow become encased in ice.

He wondered suddenly if Jenin Rose had come to Brittle not just to sell spells, but for relics? Brittle was known to have a few. He bought, sold and traded them in his shop and here on the *Akistra*. He remembered her eyes, flashing with… What had that been? Anger? Fear? Of what? Being found out? He often felt that way, as if he was hiding, even from himself.

Draks sipped his drink. "It began as a puzzle," he said, pacing. "But we found the answer and it's troubling. Another helmet just like this one was, coincidentally, found by the king. And now he's having it copied. He's making hundreds. Artice Makken is planning for war."

"War?" Davit glanced at their faces. He had hoped to be done with the king. A war would rock the isles, pit witch against witch, human against human and each against the other. The isles had always been united behind Jamasak. Whatever skirmishes there were had been against individual pirates and renegades and short-lived rebellions. Even the Watermen, a cohesive network of black marketeers, had never fought a full-scale war.

San Hesrin leaned forward, hands on the table. "Not just hundreds of helmets. Thousands. His witches are crafting copies. And it's not just Watermen he's fighting. It's the guild. He fears his power is waning. We all know the story. The stars promised a thousand years, and a thousand years has come. We all feel it. But we'll be ready."

"And how are we to prepare for a battle as large as that?"

"We're stronger than he thinks," Draks said. "And whether the king wants war or not, he shall have it." He turned toward San Hesrin. "We're grateful for the guns and information. But if you'll excuse us, I'd like to speak to my foster son. And take the helmet. It's yours. A token of our thanks. We want it seen. It will draw people to our side. We thought to avoid war. The king's brought it to us. People need to know. The thousand-year battle has begun."

San Hesrin nodded, made his farewells. "We hadn't heard from you," Draks said as soon as the door closed. "Does the governor suspect anything?"

"Navarr? Of course not. He's nothing. A fool. You probably heard about the ships that were taken? I was there when the crews trudged in. They were a sight, but they were walking on their own, most of them. A few didn't make it."

Gryer leaned forward. "We heard, but only a little. The *Oracle* had been requisitioned by the king when she was rammed by a carrack half her size, a skeleton crew, the captain no more than a boy."

Davit nodded. "Then you've heard most of what there is to tell. Both attacks were crafted. The survivors were very clear on that."

"Of course, they were crafted," Draks said sharply. "How else could a pack of renegades sink a king's ship?"

Ayva said, "We were told there were witches on board the *Oracle*, pressed into service. Did you meet any?"

Davit frowned. "No. But they might not have wanted it known."

"It fits," Krila said. "If these ships were crewed by press gangs, we might be able to turn them to our side? And here's another thing. Our spies tell us Artice Makken hasn't been in Jamasak in months. He's building a castle. No one knows where."

Draks said, "We hoped Navarr would lead us to the renegades. He's a greedy man. He wouldn't give up a chance at a prize."

"Navarr? Greedy?" Davit shook his head. "Perhaps, but not for money. He's satisfied with his income of taxes and guild fees."

Krila said, "Even so. He can make trouble. We need to find these renegades, before they take any more ships. We need them gone."

Davit pulled on his chin. "It could take time. The ship's flag was fake, and they gave names, but they weren't real."

Draks brought out a chart and unrolled it on the table. "As best we can tell, the *Oracle* went down here."

Davit leaned over his shoulder. "We'll watch for stolen goods. It's a start." He glanced around the table and it came back to him, the way each of the four filled in where the others left off. The way they were of one mind, working together these last… What? Twenty years?

He'd heard stories of how the company first met. Most agreed it was in the king's jails. They were witches, brought in separately on charges of conspiracy, inciting riots, burglary. There must have been some truth to it because once released, they scraped together the resources—a little too quickly for honest work— and obtained a ship. They traded that ship for a larger one, and eventually for the *Akistra*. He didn't know when exactly they became Night Watermen. Certainly, before they found him.

"This part about the castle," he said. "It doesn't make sense. Makken wouldn't keep it secret. He'd crow with pride."

"When did you last see him?"

"Six months ago. Before he sent me to Navarr." Davit paused. "Murrock's not far from where the ships were taken."

"The king doesn't know our strength," Draks said. "He doesn't know he'll be going against the guild and Watermen together. Think of it. The numbers. Our sea power and their witches. We'll sort out the isles later. Who rules where and how and who is free and such, but for now—"

"That helmet?" Davit asked. "Was it real?"

"Yes, of course." Draks sounded annoyed. "You saw yourself the ice didn't melt. But the story about the king crafting more? No. But we wanted San Hesrin to believe it and tell others. And we were curious to see what you'd think. Not to trick you, but if we could convince you—"

"Where was it found?"

"We're not really sure. It was bought and sold multiple times. What matters is that people believe the king is using witches against them."

"The ice is not melting," Gryer said impatiently. "If it were, the waters would rise and the isles would be obliterated and that, most obviously, is not happening."

Ayva touched his arm. "We have to be ready, Davit. We need you back at Makken's side. Contact him. Tell him you have new information. It doesn't matter what. Make it up. He trusts you."

"He is expecting word," Davit said thoughtfully. "I've been putting it off. I passed along the little I heard of the guild meetings in Mann Isle, but he already knew."

"Feed him something about these renegades," Krila said. "It doesn't have to be true."

"We need you," Draks said. "Your eyes and your ears. The king's afraid. He's weak, Davit. Our time has come."

*　*　*

By the time Davit found Brittle, he and Marissa were asleep on the weather deck. Their legs were intertwined and an empty bottle of rum near at hand. Davit tapped Marissa's shoulder and she carefully freed herself from Brittle's embrace and kissed him on the forehead.

Davit glanced to the east. There was no sign of a sunrise and he needed to catch the tide. He stepped over sleeping bodies, exchanged a few brief words with Brink and Deesh. Night Watermen were asleep in every corner, a few of the younger ones played a last round of Storm. A lone singer finished her verse:

> *Flow like a river, shine like the sea,*
> *Flow like a river, shine like the sea,*
> *Hasten the dark lights that set us all free.*
> *Sharpen your sword and strengthen your hand,*
> *Human and witch and woman and man.*
> *Raise high the rafters, hasten the grain,*
> *Thousand year star light shine upon us again.*

Brink helped them lower the empty chest onto the catboat. And between them, they hauled the drunken Brittle down the ladder until he was safely curled against the boat's curved sides.

Davit pulled in Brittle's arms and legs and found what passed for a blanket and covered him. It would be a few hours until they were back on land and though he would have appreciated a bit of company, Brittle was passed out again, snoring and dreaming of a smiling Marissa.

Davit checked the wind. He brought the bow sharply around, nudged the one small sail and was pleased when it gave him no trouble and filled with exactly the wind he needed. He'd been sailing over an hour when hills took shape in the fog. He shook off his drowsiness and adjusted the sail. But when he looked again, he realized it was a ship he had sighted, not land. He reached for his spyglass and looked again.

That was odd; the ship carried no flag, nor was there any marking on the hull and he was too far off to see a figurehead. It was a small ship, the first two masts square rigged, latten on the mizzen. He wouldn't have noticed at all if the clouds hadn't faded and the moon not come out.

He shook his head. He was spying again. Why did it seem that was all he ever did? All anyone wanted him for, but... What ship would be sailing so late at night? And without a lamp off her stern or bow? They were making good time, four knots, probably more. But something was strange here. He almost wished he could cast a spell to bring her near, or maybe a spell to see by? Witches did that and he sometimes, not often, wished he could, too.

"Wake up!" he called, and Brittle moaned and went back asleep.

He tacked to starboard and this time when he lifted the spyglass, he saw someone on the aft deck, one person, standing alone.

It was too far to know for sure, but… That was odd. The narrow shoulders, the posture. They reminded him of someone. He squinted, looked again. The figure was slight, young. It reminded him of the man—boy— he'd met at the palace, then again at the Gold Key inn. Melvin Goodeye. He had thought about him just now on the *Akistra*. But what was he doing alone on a ship and sailing without a light?

An odd thought fell into place. Melvin Goodeye had been at the palace the night Navarr's chest was stolen, and the very next morning he met Jenin Rose. What if Brittle was wrong about her? Or he was right, but in the wrong way. One of the men who'd stolen the chest from the governor's guards that night had been older, but the other was described as young and slight…

It was Goodeye who forced Jenin Rose to bring the stolen jewels to Brittle's shop! She wasn't responsible. No wonder she had been nervous. She wasn't the thief. Melvin Goodeye was. And though Davit couldn't figure how the two were related, he had a hunch that Goodeye was involved with sinking the *Oracle* and the *White Lily* as well. The timing was too close. And Goodeye had said he was human, but of course he was a witch. He remembered now the shock he felt, a sort of static—he didn't know what else to call it—when they touched the relic at the same time. Goodeye was lying and the proof was here, riding the waves in the midnight hours.

Oh, but this was good. He had something now, finally, to give Draks Halo and the governor and the king. The whole bloody lot of them and their lies. So many lies, he could hardly keep them straight anymore. But he was willing to bet the fancy pistol Draks Halo just gave him that

Melvin Goodeye would lead straight to Jenin Rose, and that was exactly where he wanted to be.

13

Introductions, Long Overdue

The iron gate across the back entrance to Molly's property was bolted when she returned, no sign of footprints or tampering. If anyone had come snooping these last few weeks, they'd covered their tracks. Not that she expected trouble; she was confident that no one had connected the incidents with the two ships to this quiet house on a courtly road. Even so, she had been wise to hide the seeing eyes above the hinges when she locked the gates. She climbed halfway up, snagged them and checked that their lids remained closed. And the ivy she'd stretched across the top; one touch that wasn't her own and it would have turned brown.

She glanced up and down road, then stepped inside and closed the gate. There was no sign of footprints around the hedges or leading to the shed or outbuildings. As far as she could tell, no one had tried to jimmy a door or break a window. Why then was she so jittery?

Yes, she had allowed the *White Lily's* crew to escape. But their hands had been bound and even if they freed the knots, they had no oars, no drinking water, no maps. They'd reach land eventually, or be picked up, but nowhere near Tars. The same with the *Oracle's* crew. Madinina had assured her that most of the witches, even those hired by the captain, had no love for the king and if they were questioned, they wouldn't know her name. They couldn't possibly trace her to this house.

She entered through a rear door. The furnishings— divans, assorted tables and chairs—were covered with sheeting. The caretakers had done their job well. There were the requisite washstands, pitchers and bowls. The kitchen counters were scrubbed. A large pot hung from a hook in the fireplace. She had accumulated a minimum of household possessions, no more than necessary to maintain the appearance of an ordinary home. A painting on a prominent wall held the image of a middle-aged woman with kind, reassuring eyes. If asked she could say it was an aunt or cousin. It lent an air of respectability. Normalcy. Enough, she hoped, to assuage suspicions and keep people from searching the cellar for hidden rooms, tunnels below the garden.

She opened doors, checked hallways and stood in the central courtyard. The glass domed ceiling echoed her footsteps. The fountains were dry. Everything intact. She opened windows in her bed chamber to let the air flow through then, on second thought, closed them again and pulled the latches tight. A family with five raucous boys lived in the house to the right above hers. And in the stone house opposite, an older couple lived with their meddlesome widowed son and infant daughter. The baby cried. The son sent invitations to dinners she did not accept.

And finally, when she was certain the house was safe, she lit a lamp and sprung the latch on an ornamental panel in the main hall. There were two ways to reach her cellar. From the garden tunnel or the hidden stairs and she hurried down, entered the cellar and quickly glanced around. Nothing had changed. Firearms hung on the wall to her left. Flint locks and older match locks. The blunderbuss she'd stolen from a guard in Hawley. The pistol with the jaw shaped like a dog's snout. The center wall was covered in a sunburst of daggers, below them were her short swords, axes, knives arranged by size. She kept the blades honed and the handles polished and she knew where each one had been purchased or stolen, traded or won.

She moved along the wall. The smallest dagger had come from a witch on Bulatt Isle. She had been in a crowded marketplace when the woman, well dressed but nervous, peeled back the cloth that covered her basket and showed the ebony handled blade along with the guild mark on her arm. "Four silvers," she whispered as the crowd pushed by. "Now. I can't wait. Pay me and it's yours." And Molly had.

The woman fled into the crowd and Molly never saw her again, but she carried the dagger in her boot for the better part of a year. It had cut the cords on a dozen purses, stopped a too-curious harbor master, and once—she smiled to remember the night—threatened a journeyman who chose a particular alley to piss in just as Molly jumped from a window with a jewelry chest in her hands.

She pulled the dagger from the peg, swung it in an arc. For years she had been collecting weapons, stealing jewelry and coins, waiting to be free. And now that freedom was near, why did one spell on the *Fish* trouble her so?

The answer was less about the *Fish* ramming the *Oracle*, and more about realizing that, having spent most of the last three years onboard the ship, she thought she knew everything about it. She didn't, and she should have. Her parents had kept their secrets closer than she realized. And if she hadn't known that spell was there, what else didn't she know?

She returned the dagger to its peg and glanced around. The last time she'd been in this room Macklin had been here and Sally and Nick and Brigit, Tribolt and Troth. She had used the knives to prove she was a witch. She'd thrown them, juggled them. But the spells were simple compared to what the *Fish* had done. Ramming itself prow first into the *Oracle* and pulling out unscathed. As if her parents had reached across time and protected her.

She sighed and took up the lamp and entered the smaller side room. Apart from a few new cobwebs, nothing had changed. She turned a slow circle and was surprised to see the governor's chest pushed up against the wall. She had forgotten it was here.

She felt an odd sentimental attachment to the thing, as if they'd been through a crucible together. She remembered the day they'd stolen it and the way Evan, at the last possible moment, crafted his fog. And she met Davit Lake at the palace, and again the next day at the pawnshop.

He liked to talk and drink a little too much, and he had sought out Melvin Goodeye when he wanted someone honest. That was what he'd called her. Him. Honest. He wouldn't be suspicious if Melvin happened to bump into him at the Gold Key inn and struck up a conversation, asked a few innocent questions. Was the governor still searching for the thieves? Was there news of another ship, sunk in deep waters?

She smiled as she planned the ruse. She crafted a quick spell to change her dress into Goodeye's shirt and trousers. Another that needed a bit more energy and attention to reshape the contours of her face, complexion. hair. Except for that one moment when they'd gotten drunk in the guild shop and her spell slipped, he'd been easily tricked. It shouldn't take long to reach the inn and find him. And for the first time in she couldn't remember how long, she smiled as she locked the doors and left through the rear gate.

*　*　*

The Gold Key inn was as dark and loud and crowded as the first time Molly visited, searching for Davit Lake that time as well. She stepped inside and was instantly swallowed in a knot of gruff, bawdy patrons. They jostled her and pushed her along until she ducked between two burly men and made her along the wall at the edge of the crowd. Even so, it was difficult to see. She was tempted to jump or stand on a chair, but people might notice, and she wanted to see Davit before he saw her. And besides, she reminded herself, jumping was not something Melvin Goodeye would do. He was a young and coming merchant. A little full of himself. A bit fawning. She coughed and lowered her voice.

She squeezed around a table full of men arguing over their dice, and past an alcove where two young women, their rumpled skirts pushed halfway to their waist, sat on the laps of older, well dressed men. Coins clinked along with the sound of laughter and she moved toward the counter that separated the outer room from the kitchens. And then she found him, Davit Lake, sitting with his chair tilted against the wall, black hair peeking beneath a hat, three men with him around the table.

He brought his chair down and they huddled closer. Molly edged around the counter for a better view. The man on Davit's right, the tallest one, had a thin, dark mustache. The one to his left was nearly bald. The third, facing her, had a hard face with small eyes and thin yellow hair and though none of them were in uniform, they were obviously soldiers, trained and armed. The tall one was a witch with two gems along his jaw. She wasn't sure about the others. They were large and muscular, arms thick as masts. Shells hung from their bandoliers and muskets leaned against their chairs.

Davit was dressed much the same as before, not in the lace he'd worn at the palace but in the clothes of a man trying to blend in. Dark trousers, linen shirt, a dull blue vest. Only his hat stood out, a black three-cornered thing with a bright feather. And, she had to admit, he was a fine-looking man with his dark hair falling across one eye and his mouth turning up when he smiled. But looks and demeanor didn't prove the kind of person he was, any more than her clothes proved she was Melvin Goodeye. For all she knew, the governor's nephew was obligated to sit with the soldiers, share a drink. But what was so interesting that kept them glancing at the door?

Her stomach knotted. If the soldiers were after the chest, they would be searching for the two guards who had snuck into the tunnel during the ball: Evan had kept his true face, and she was disguised as a short, older guard.

The soldiers scanned the crowd and she edged away… Right into another man's elbow. His drink went flying and he shouted, and Davit glanced up and out of the entire crowded room, saw her. He stopped talking, looked and looked again.

She straightened her shoulders, touched two fingers to her temple in greeting. Lake dipped his head and turned, said something to the soldiers. The bald one reached toward his sword. Another slipped his hand inside his vest. They glanced at Molly then quickly looked away. The three soldiers rose and disappeared, for toward an upper level, one toward the door. Lake collected his mug and a pitcher and worked his way toward her through the crowd.

"Friends of yours?" She nodded toward the soldiers. "They left in a hurry."

"What, them?" Davit's eyes were cold. He called for a boy to bring another mug. "They couldn't stay."

"Soldiers, were they?"

"I suppose." Davit watched her in a way she hadn't seen before. He glanced to her waistband, her vest, her boots. Looking for weapons, she wondered.

"We were just sharing a table," Davit said. "Said they were looking for a sail maker's shop." The boy returned with the mug and Davit took a drink and watched her over the rim. "You haven't been here of late?"

Molly laughed self-consciously. "I needed a while to recover after our last evening out."

"Oh. We did drink a bit, didn't we?"

"More than a bit, if I remember. Though I don't. Not usually. Drink, I mean. Those soldiers, they were looking for someone?"

"Were they?" Lake stepped around and blocked her view. "Do you remember that night we met?"

"We broke into a guild shop. I'm sorry, if there are debts—"

"Before that. At the palace. I asked if you'd share a drink."

"At your uncle's palace?" Molly wasn't certain where the conversation was leading, but it wasn't what she had in mind.

"My uncle, yes," he repeated impatiently. He glanced over his shoulder. "A chest was stolen that night. I'm sure you heard?"

"Did they find it?"

Lake stepped toward her. "There was a girl. She was seen frequenting pawn shops shortly afterward. She might be in trouble."

Molly blinked. Was he talking about her? In Brittle's pawn shop? She broke from his gaze and shook her head. "I'm sorry. I'm not sure I understand. What do you mean, 'trouble?'"

"I mean," he said tightly, "There were two men at the palace that night, disguised as guards. One older, one younger. It was dark, and reports weren't clear. They made it to the wharf and disappeared."

Molly glanced toward the entry. The path was blocked. The inn was crowded, chairs and benches full, people milling about, leaning against walls.

Davit said, "She didn't know the spells were stolen. She was forced to sell them. But the young guard… He was about your size. Did I mention the other incident? A king's ship was sunk. Not far from here. It could have been the work of the same man, narrow shoulders, trim build. Young."

Molly caught one of the soldiers making his way back down the stairs. The yellow haired one, though she hadn't seen him leave, entered through the main door. He drew a pistol and immediately, a circle opened. Patrons backed away.

"Stay where you are," he shouted. "Everyone, stay!" A woman gasped, and suddenly people were shoving chairs and toppling benches, rushing for the door.

Davit grabbed Molly's arm and dug in. Their eyes locked. But then, oddly, he hesitated, cocked his head and frowned. His grip lightened as he searched her face. It lasted no more than an instant, but it was enough. She yanked free, but he lunged and grabbed her arm again. His fingers dug in, hurting. "Where is she?" he demanded. "If she's hurt, I swear on every star—"

The crowd shifted. The third soldier pushed through the kitchen door, pistol raised. She was out of time.

She stepped toward Davit and his grip loosened just enough for her to twist and lean back and kick, her boot to his shin. He yelped, and Molly pulled free. She pushed her way into the crowd then dropped to the floor, hiding beneath a table as Davit ran by. He spun and turned left then right, shoving people aside as he tried to reach the door. She backed up, crawled between tables and chair legs, past skirts and spittoons, an orange dog that growled and bared its teeth until she murmured a spell and it lowered its head to its paws.

She paused for a moment, waited for her heart to quiet before popping up her head. Her arm was bruised where Davit grabbed her, but not enough to worry. The crowd was furious, no one listening to the soldiers. Behind her, a set of red curtains separated the run of private alcoves from the larger hall. She heard laughter and a sound like snoring. She dropped beneath the table, crawled toward the wall.

The curtain was guarded by a stout woman perched on a stool, arms crossed as she watched the ruckus. Molly pressed a coin in her hand. "Buy yourself a drink," she said, and the woman winked as calmly as if she did this every day. Molly glanced back and saw Davit grabbing one man, checking his face then releasing him and grabbing another. The woman pulled back the curtain and Molly hurried through.

Inside, two women, hardly more than girls, sat around a table set for a game of Walls and Water. Two older men were asleep behind them, chins on their chests as they slumped in their overstuffed chairs. The girls barely looked up until they realized Melvin wasn't there to serve drinks. The red headed girl on the right smiled slyly. "Soldiers out there?" Her eyes roved meaningfully over Molly's body.

"King's soldiers," Molly said. "Do you think you might…? Would you mind…?"

"Hide you?" the second girl finished. She pursed her lips and lowered her shawl to show a shoulder. "For a kiss, I might."

Molly opened the curtain a crack and peered out. Davit was on one side of the hall now, the soldiers on the other.

"You shy or something?" the girl asked, and Molly turned back around. The girl patted her lap. "You could go back out or stay and have a little fun. Isn't that right, Dory?"

The other girl winked. "We don't care much for king's men. They never like to pay. But we like you."

The red headed girl rose and before Molly realized, she had one arm around her shoulders and her lips pressed tight against her mouth.

Molly's eyes widened. She pulled away, but politely she hoped, with a peck on the girl's face. Behind them, the men continued to snore. The girl ran her hand suggestively along Molly's side, to her waist then her hip and around her rear and squeezed.

Molly glanced past her piled curls and ribbons and searched the room. A couch. A buffet piled with fruit and drinks. The curtained door and to her right—she slipped free of the girl's arms—an alcove and a narrow door. "Sorry," Molly said. "No time. You're very nice but, does that lead out?"

The girl pretended to pout. "But we just started to play." She caught her friend's smile and they exchanged a glance. The dark-haired girl went to the curtain, while the other produced a key, unlocked the door and hurried Molly through. "Come back when you have more time." She nodded toward the men. "Those two don't kiss near as well as you."

A moment later, Molly found herself alone on a side street behind the inn. The night seemed darker though hardly an hour had passed. Clouds covered the stars and the moon was nowhere in sight. Her left arm burned, and she rubbed it then pushed up her sleeve to see whether it was bleeding or merely bruised but there was no blood, no scratch where his nails dug in.

Instead, what she found was a flat marker, a tracking spell the size of her smallest fingernail embedded in her forearm: a black compass rose on a sliver of mother-of-pearl. Did he actually think Melvin Goodeye wouldn't have the wherewithal to find it, remove it before it was used?

She was furious. Insulted. The man was a fool if he thought some guild registered, Grimoire copied, boughten spell was all he needed to lead the king's men to her door. The tracker's base was embedded in her skin with a bezel with prongs, as if it was a jewel in a ring. She dug her fingernails beneath, winced and pried till it flew off, hit the ground and rolled away. Three small dots of blood remained.

She pushed her sleeve down, turned and heard voices, horse's hooves clomping on cobblestones on the main road and voices, shouting. Alert and cautious, she followed the narrow alley around toward the front entrance. Shots cracked and glass burst. The cog lights went out and the inn and nearby shops plunged into darkness. Men and women rushed through the doors, pushing and cursing and desperate to avoid the soldiers. They climbed onto horses and walked quickly into the dark and Molly walked with them, eyes and head forward, never looking back.

She was still angry as she unlocked the front gate and entered the house. It was dark and she lit a lamp, opened the false panel and hurried to the cellar.

There was no time to linger over questions of what to take, what to leave behind. She was done with the house; it was no longer safe, and she had to get to the *Fish*. That was the important thing. Grab whatever she could easily carry and sell. Gold, of course and weapons. Spells, however valuable, were more likely to raise questions if she was caught.

She moved from the main room to a smaller, side storage and set the lamp down and started emptying chests, throwing their contents into smaller bags and sacks. Piles grew on the floor. Platters. Jewelry. Spells. Small duffels she could carry up the stairs, larger double handled chests she could not.

She was furious, as much at herself as at Davit Lake. How had she ever thought she could trust him? The governor's nephew? A pampered king's man and who knew what else? She'd been a fool to go to the inn when she'd promised Macklin she'd do no more than clear out her valuables and return to the crew.

She kicked angrily at the stolen chest and kicked it again. The top flew open. Spells scattered and shells wobbled, and their contents fell loose. Craft wrought daggers that stretched like accordions. Sleeping dragonflies folded in shells. They rolled and bumped into walls. Cordials to turn saltwater fresh. Hair pins that grew into knives.

She kicked and sent them scattering across the floor. One landed against a small book and on impulse she picked it up. *The King's Grimoire* was written across the cover. She had found it on a shelf in the solar when she first leased the house. Covered in dust, replaced by newer versions, it could have been in the house for years.

She opened it at random and read the heading. *Spells to attract and repel.* And beneath that: *To Aid the Course of an Arrow, Dagger, or Stone in its Flight. The chant shall be: This day, under the Stars of ascendancy. (Metal; Stone; Wood; or etcetera) that reaches. Annealed. Exchange.*

The object shall be: A blade of grass, kissed by the wind in a following direction. Alternatively: A hair drawn from the scalp... Lacking that, a thread... {refer also to Repel (1) Sky (2) Water}. The gesture shall be: A sharp swing of the right hand, finger pointed... Failing that, a droplet of seawater in a catchment basin may be used...

Molly would have laughed had the instructions not made her so angry. Choices. When had the teaching masters ever allowed Evan a choice? Was this the best they had to offer? A guide to alternate attempts and failed gestures apprentices were expected to memorize?

She snapped the book shut and tossed it to a corner and returned to the larger cellar. She frowned as she studied the neat display of pistols, daggers and long guns arranged by size. She eyed one, a dagger with a slight curve to the blade. She didn't touch it, simply stared at it hanging there between the pegs and chanted: *This day, under the stars of ascendancy. Steel that reaches. Annealed. Exchange.*

Nothing happened.

She started again, this time pulling her arm back to add the gesture. *A sharp swing of the right hand, finger pointed, from the left shoulder drawing a line in the desired direction.*

Again nothing.

And when, she asked herself, was the last time anyone claimed that guild cogs were dependable? And why—except for collecting fees—would masters go to all the trouble of compiling Grimoires if their cogs barely worked? But if they didn't care, why add that ridiculous list of alternate spells along with flawed ones?

No wonder Evan was frustrated. She kept sending him back to the guild. He wasn't a bungling, half grown young man without the discipline to learn his spells. He was craftborn, damn it. Same as she was, not some tool for the guild. She had been too caught up thinking about a future that would probably never come, to understand the brother standing in front of her.

She was wrong about so much. The spells crafted into the *Fish*. Davit Lake befriending Melvin Goodeye. Evan earning a master's charter. Would she always get it wrong?

She raised her hand and pointed, first at the dagger then toward the ceiling. The blade flew from the wall, hit an overhead beam and stuck. The long sword next. She sent it flashing point first and it struck the floor, wobbled and buried itself. Again, and again she pointed, and blades circled and sped. She sent one flying toward the far wall. There! Another for the ceiling. Daggers. Axes. Swords. They flew and whirled, faster and harder, a blur of light. A rush of air.

No chant. No object. No gestures. Nothing but her own will crafting the spells as she'd always done. The way she knew how… Except… She stopped as she felt a hint of warm air on her neck. And a noise behind her back, quiet and controlled. She didn't breathe. Swords, daggers, broad axes hovered in the air.

Footsteps drew near, and a man's voice: "So it was you, all along?"

Molly released the knives and they fell with a clatter. She turned slowly around and faced Davit Lake, his pistol at her chest. "What was?" she asked. She locked eyes with him, forced herself to stay calm. She wondered if he was alone. She heard no footsteps on the stairs and none above her head, but Lake looked confident, even cocky.

"On your ship," he said. "I saw you, alone at night."

Molly waited. She willed her heart to slow, her hands not to shake.

"Or maybe it wasn't your ship? Was it hijacked? Did you steal it?"

She lowered her gaze. He carried a dagger in his belt, another tucked in his boot. He saw her looking and pulled back his vest, showed her the butt of another pistol.

"That's right," he said. "I forgot. You're not supposed to be a witch. Just an ordinary merchant's son. Melvin Goodeye. Who are you, really? And no lying this time. No stories. No pretending to be drunk."

Molly glared at him. She didn't like the way he kept staring, frowning and cocking his head. "I might not be Melvin Goodeye, but you're no governor's nephew, are you? And if I'm a witch…" She made a quick decision, "So are you." She glanced to the ceiling. The dagger was there, embedded in the beam. If she was fast enough…

"Me? A witch?" Lake snorted, but she caught a hesitation. He fixed his grip on the pistol. "You don't know anything about me."

She risked a glance to the beam. It won't work, she decided. By the time she freed the dagger, he'd have his shot. "So, you say." She wanted him talking, buying time. "You expect me to believe that a real governor's nephew would follow me to a cellar? That someone raised in Jamasak's court would prefer Gold Key ale to a noble's wine cellar?" She watched his eyes. He was lying. She didn't know why.

"I am not a witch," he said tightly. "You do nothing but hide and lie and cheat. You're pawns, the lot of you. A weapon for humans to buy and discard."

"Then how did you find me if not by your craft?"

"With a boughten spell. Right there on your arm. I didn't come here to listen to accusations."

"Only to give them? As if you know anything about me." Her eyes on Davit, Molly rolled up her sleeve and held out her arm.

He glanced down, saw the three dots of dry blood, the remains of his tracking spell. A frown crossed his face. "So, you pulled it out, but not before it led me here."

"I think not. It was you. You're a witch."

"I am not."

"Of course, you are. I threw the tracker away at the inn. You found me on your own. Or wait…" Her thoughts leaped again. "You don't know, do you? You're a witch and don't even know."

He started to say something, stopped and his frown deepened. He studied her face. He looked at her mouth, her dark eyes, the way she tied back her hair. His expression changed.

She felt self-conscious suddenly and tried not to touch her face. Was it slipping again, her spell? Was her real features showing? It had happened before, not only in the guild shop when she was drunk, but other times. Not even a craftborn witch could hold multiple spells for long. She lowered her arm, pushed down her sleeve. "What are you looking at?" she demanded.

"It's you. Your eyes. I mean…" He lowered his gun. "Who are you?"

She nearly laughed. He still thought she was Melvin. He was looking right at her and didn't know. But she had him now, a way out. It worked for Sally Yarrow and she might not be good at it, but she'd seen it done.

She slowly pulled the pins from her hair, ran her fingers through the strands and let them lengthen and fall like a cloak around her shoulders. And then her face; she touched it and the contours softened and changed. She blinked, and Melvin was gone.

Davit stared. "It was you? All along? You're Jenin Rose. There is no Melvin. You stole the chest—" He stepped toward her. "You have to get out."

"Get out?" That was the last thing she expected. "What do you mean."

"Leave. Run. They're coming."

"Who?"

"The governor's men. And the king's."

"They won't find me."

"It's too late. They know about your ship. They know you sank the *Oracle* and took the *White Lily*."

She thought of Macklin and the crew, Evan and the *Fish*, unguarded in the harbor. Her heart thundered against her chest. "You told them?"

"I thought you were Melvin. I would never have told."

She hesitated, long enough for him to reach out and pull her close. He lowered his face and pressed his lips against hers and kissed her. And for a moment, she didn't think to stop him. His lips were warm and searching and, though she didn't mean to, she let the kiss go on and kissed him back. She breathed him in, the thick, salt smell of his hair, his warm skin. He felt like a memory, come home.

He opened his eyes and they looked at each other. She remembered the first—and second—time their hands touched. Something in her, and in the relic as well, recognized his craft and reached out.

She stepped back. He was a witch, yet he'd brought the governor's men to her house? What if Evan had been here? What then?

She raised her hand and slapped him, hard across the face—that for the kiss—and a kick, for following her here. His pistol flew across the room and she pointed toward the dagger. It pulled free of the beam, flew to her hand and she lunged.

She was furious. She was a fool and all her plans, and the hopes of her crew were gone because of him. Because of her. The king's men were on their way.

She came at him with her knife, but he grabbed her wrist. She fell back with a feint, but he held tight and she tried again, and this time threw him off balance. Angry, furious, she walked him backward and pressed him against the wall, the blade to his face. He clenched his jaw and pushed back, but she held her ground.

The point bit into his cheek and he felt a burn, then blood on his face. He raised his arms and tried to throw her off. She caught herself but far away, up the stairs and in the house overhead, a door slammed. Glass shattered and footsteps pounded the floor.

Davit seized the moment and reached for her hand, but she fell back and kicked a stool in his path. He tripped and flailed his arms and Molly leaped at him. She kicked him in the side, and he fell then rolled to his hands and knees, but she was watching now. She raced from the cellar, through the hidden tunnel up through the shed and out again into the maze of her garden.

She vaulted for the rear gate, climbed it and dropped to the other side. There was no sign of Davit and she slowed and stole her way through the bushes and crouching low, made her way toward the front of the house.

Horses, wagons and soldiers filled the street. Her front door hung open and the shadowy figures of soldiers—five, ten, more than she could count—ransacked the house. They overturned tables and chairs and shattered windows with their rifle butts. She heard furniture breaking, wood smashing. She took one last look then turned for the wharf and the *Fish* and Evan. She had to get Evan before the governor and his guild rats reached him first.

14

The Castle Star

Davit stood at the bow of the governor's ship *Corona* looking out on a wall of fog. Unbroken, as far as he could see and high as the stars and he didn't like it. There was an odor, like the too-warm vapors of a hot springs and shadows across the waves, but where was that boat? The coordinates were correct. He'd copied them himself from the king's message.

He felt along his jaw. Jenin Roses' cut no longer burned. What smarted was the way she grew angry when she thought he betrayed her.

He'd give anything to know what she really thought. But he'd do it again. If she was standing in front of him right now, he'd kiss her perfect, incomprehensible lips and tell her that he hadn't stopped thinking about her from the moment they met in Brittle's shop. And she had kissed him back, hadn't she? Or was he imagining it because he wanted so badly for it to be true?

If only she had told the truth. He never would have told the governor he'd found the chest. Or led the soldiers to her house. Navarr would never let up until the stolen spells were safe and he could play at being a witch. Damn them all, humans and witches alike, for their envy and greed. And damn the stars for leaving him in this fix.

Someone called his name and he turned to find Hanra Ward, the *Corona's* captain motioning from the middeck. "Weather's rising," she called. "Our witches aren't having much luck against the waves. I'll warn the governor. We should turn back."

Davit shielded his eyes against the spray and made his way forward. Ward was a decent captain though her crew had more experience ferrying Navarr on afternoon jaunts than fighting heavy seas. "My uncle left orders," he said. "We're to wait until we meet the ship."

Ward pushed her dripping hair from her face. "Your uncle is seasick and hiding below deck," she said derisively.

Jeron Scrud suddenly appeared. He glanced dismissively past the captain and eyed Davit. "I've roused him," he said. "He's feeling better." He nodded toward the east and Ward and Davit peered into the distance. The fog was changing. The gray wall shifted, and a crack appeared, as if heavy curtains were sliding apart. A moment later a small rounded coracle with a single mast and arched prow slipped through and the fog closed behind it.

Someone shouted and a swivel gun screeched. The captain shouted to hold fire. The governor emerged from below and walked unevenly to the gunwale. "What's going on?" he called. "Are they here? Scrud? Did you tell them I was waiting?"

Harkin Navarr looked as out of place as a man could be. His carefully groomed curls were ruined. The frilled lace on his shirtsleeves dripped water and Davit didn't want to know what else. Scrud hid his expression, but Davit caught the disgust in his gaze, and the way he pretended not to hear.

It didn't take long for the coracle to reach the larger ship's side. There were two sailors on board, and they brought it alongside the hull and Captain Ward ordered a ladder thrown down. It took a bit of maneuvering to help Navarr over the side, and though Davit would have preferred Scrud not follow, he wasn't surprised when the tutor climbed down behind. Davit waited till he was settled then joined him on the thwart opposite Navarr.

"You Lake?" one of the sailors called.

Davit nodded, but Navarr took offense. "Governor Harkin Navarr," he announced. "We sent word."

The sailor pushed off the *Corona's* hull. He was an older man with dark eyebrows that joined across the center and he was not impressed. "So long as I got one passenger named Lake, it's not my business who else climbs aboard."

The *Corona* grew smaller and the smell of sulfur thickened around them. Scrud covered his mouth and Navarr's lips turned a sickly blue. The sailor in the stern adjusted the sail and the fog reshaped itself. Where Davit had thought it was a curtain parting to let them through, it seemed now they were sailing through a cavern with towering walls to the right and left and an opening at the far end and a ship, a single ship so large it was almost a city floating in the open sea.

The sailor laughed at Davit's surprise. "Your king awaits," he called. "Behold the *Castle Star.*"

Davit didn't answer. He'd been expecting the royal barge where he'd often dined with the king and his cousins, astrologers and advisors. Or one of Makken's pleasure ships with colored sails and music wafting across the decks and games and feasts that lasted for days but not this… This frigate larger than anything Davit had imagined. Its four masts raked the sky. Silk sails stretched on arms wide as a giant's. They caught the light and shone, and the entire ship glittered like a city of gold.

"I'd hold on if I were you," the sailor called. "The waves will be worse as we near."

Navarr clung to his seat. "I had no idea," he whispered to Scrud. "You're sure he knows we're coming? I mean to tell him about my spells."

"He's your kinsman," Scrud reassured him. "You mustn't worry."

Davit tried to ignore them. He needed to pay attention, commit everything to memory. The decks and number and size of the guns. How many soldiers there were; how many witches. He noted the sleek high sides and beak head and calculated how fast it might sail. Draks Halo and Ayva and Gryer Scarp and Krila Sand needed to be warned and not just about the size and strength of the ship but the king's intentions. Was he planning an attack, or was this 'castle' more about chest pounding and showing his strength?

The royal Makken family and the guild had jostled for power for generations. Draks believed the king saw the black market Watermen as no more a nuisance then the few unallied pirates that threatened his ships, that his real battle lay with the guild. But if the guild knew of this *Castle Star*, they hadn't told the Night Watermen—their newest allies— and Draks hadn't told him.

The helmsman maneuvered the coracle nearer the massive hull and a ramp emerged, a walkway—witch crafted most likely—that switched back and forth as it pressed against the sides. He secured the coracle to an iron ring and motioned Navarr to go first. Scrud, then Davit followed behind.

"I'm Davit Lake," he said, practicing his lie. "Ward of Rickjay Lynx, and of the King and I've done this before. I am human, not witch and certainly not a Night Waterman." *And thank the stars Jenin Rose escaped.*

He counted three gun decks. Twenty-five cannons aft, twenty-five forward. Lighter cannons along the sternpost, the lids painted bright. The governor reached the deck and Davit leaned out and noted the swivel guns mounted on reinforced rails, the cross bows and spears, hundreds of them stacked vertically inside the hull. A giant catapult was chained near the mainmast and there was a pyramid of what looked to be heavy rocks alongside. And with it, as if the king thought going to war was no different than any other fete, the entire weather deck was wreathed with wispy lengths of fabrics that draped across the lower ropes and yards and circled the masts. Songbirds trilled from the ratlines and hovered over flowers and there were fruits so ripe, they looked as if the least wind would shake them free.

And finally, Navarr and Scrud moved ahead and Davit found himself between two lines of soldiers, uniformed men and women carrying swords and blunderbusses, pistols tucked into belts. He saw no shells but there were witches, further back.

They clustered in groups of twos and threes and leaned against the gunwales and masts. Their faces were heavy with tattoos and gems. Most wore a short cloak pinned over their shoulders, a style he had not seen before. Black and gold and white, they were emblazoned with craft symbols. And behind them more armed soldiers, some with guns and others with blades and they seemed to be guarding the witches.

He looked away as soldiers patted Scrud's sides and felt inside his boots. They found a pistol in one, and a shell in another; they handed them off to a witch and Scrud moved on.

And finally, Artice Makken, Ruler in Jamasak and Descendent of the Stars stepped through a wide door in the quarterdeck. Soldiers stiffened and the king opened his arms wide, hurried to Davit and pulled him to his chest. "Finally, you're here. I've been waiting. Surrounded by fools."

"As have I," Davit answered. "But I'm here. It's good to see you, sir."

Navarr tried to move in, but Makken was already leading Davit to a quieter spot. "Be careful," he whispered. "I trust no one anymore. Not my council or captains, certainly not my witches and astrologers."

He glanced over his shoulder. "One thing is certain: something's happening. Here. We've tracked the dark lights nearly to the rim, I've plotted their course. They're fading elsewhere. Scarcely enter the domes. But you've heard all that before." He spoke rapidly, his ideas clipped and unfinished. "Tell me, has he signed a truce with the guild?

Davit tried to follow. "You mean Navarr? Not to my knowledge, sir. No."

The king seemed to have aged. His clothes, which were less formal than Navarr's, hung loosely on his shoulders. His hair was thinner, his balance unsteady.

Davit had expected the king to greet him with pleasantries, not this whispered talk of enemies and fading lights. But then, he hadn't ex-pected a vessel the likes of the *Castle Star*. It was a war machine, crafted and designed for a battle that, even with Draks Halo's warnings, he had never believed would come. "I have to apologize for not contacting you more often," he said. "Navarr wants very much to talk with you. He's a—"

"I know what he is. A fool and an indolent slug of a man. If he wasn't my wife's cousin, I would have replaced him years ago. But enough. I'll take you below and we'll steal a moment's peace. What do you think of my castle? Surprised?"

"I am, yes," Davit said, and the king beamed with pleasure.

He followed Makken to a lower deck and through a wide set of doors into a large open cabin. The floor was made of ice, he realized. Blue-white and smooth, glazed to a shine. It was carpeted along the edges for a walkway, and there were skins down the center that belonged to no animal he had ever seen. Huge, thick white pelts lay end to end across the ice. There were claws longer than a man's fingers, and heads with giant, empty eye holes. The cabin was warm and save for a row of ice-carved statues—life sized—of past kings and queens of Jamasak, it was empty.

Makken led him to an even larger hall with sentinels posted at the entry and men and women, none of whom Davit recognized, standing about, talking and drinking. The king's astrologers were there as well. They were dressed in white, tailored long coats for the men, tunics for the women. They glanced up, saw the king and stiffened.

Makken led him to a long table at the end of the hall. The ceiling overhead was crafted to resemble dark lights, streaming curtains of pale reds and greens that lit the table and chairs. They sat, Makken first then Davit, and though no hand touched the goblets in front of them, they were suddenly filed with drink.

Breathe, Davit warned himself as he raised his cup. *There'll be truth-sayers among the witches, less easily deceived than the king.* "To the castle," he called loudly.

"The *Castle Star*," Makken repeated and a boy hurried forward with an empty tray. By the time he set it down, it was filled with spirals of oysters and cheeses, crab legs and fruit. The king selected a pink claw dripping with butter. "You approve of my little ship?"

"I don't know what to say. And you were having this built the last time I was in Jamasak? Where? How did you hide it? I never knew."

Makken laughed. "You weren't supposed to. Nobody was. We built it off the coast, doesn't matter where. No one was allowed to leave, and I couldn't talk, not even to you. Not once we understand the extent of the guild's treachery."

The king paused as a woman approached, a witch with three red corundums and a diamond marking her temple. She was small with a boyish figure, striking and intent. Her dark hair was wiry and long, with a few wisps of grey. Her dress, a tapered sheath, was also dark. Only the jacket, stiff with mother of pearl, held any color.

"Ilenna," the king said. "You'll show my ward around the ship? And don't try to get out of it, Davit. I know that look. You're not going back with Navarr. I need you here, with Ilenna. She's one of my new Council witches. Most of these are. Ilenna Fran is my philosopher. She designed the ship."

"I'm honored," he said carefully. "But, sir. You really will have to excuse me. I hadn't planned to stay."

"I insist. Ilenna will show you the workings. They're crafted to her specifications. The shipbuilder's drawings alone are worth a day."

Ilenna stood behind Makken's chair. "The king gives me too much credit," she said. "There were scores of witches involved."

Davit dipped his head. He'd find an excuse to leave later, phrase it so the king thought it his own idea. "Of course, I'm curious to see the *Castle Star*. Everything about the ship."

"That's better," Makken said. "When you see what we've assembled, you'll understand."

"And there's more." Ilenna pushed a chair between Davit and the king. "Fifty caravels and twenty galleons. Warships to be built over the next five years. The heavy guns are new, their bores smooth. I've perfected the technique. The hulls are double walled. The masts will be of a single oak. Straight grained. Ringed with iron. Crafted, of course."

"Of course," Davit said. He glanced to the far doors. If he needed to escape, it would be easier in the dark. He'd need a boat, and a way through the fog…

Makken wiped his mouth. "A fleet," he said. "And no need for a shipyard or foundries. We have an army of witches and for that. I put the guild on notice. Send me witches and I'll pay with gold. Deny me, and I revoke your charter."

He looked to Ilenna. "I know, I know," he said. "They think I'm not aware of their treason. I ask for witches and they send journeymen with no more than a first mark." His face reddened. "Did they think I'd sit by and do nothing? They're traitors, all of them. Fools and thieves."

People were watching now. Voices hushed. Ilenna touched his arm and Makken collected himself. She seemed used to controlling the king though Davit knew, if she did not, her influence would last only so long as he allowed.

Artice Makken kept his favorites close. He promoted them, doted on them. Friends and lovers, philosophers, witches, wards. Davit counted himself among them. He'd caught the king's eye almost immediately after one of Draks Halo's spies introduced him. He survived by learning to please people, say the right thing and hide his true thoughts. He succeeded, though he wasn't always proud.

"Davit?" The king was looking at him. "I asked a question. I didn't send you away to lollygag around Navarr's gardens."

"Excuse me. Something caught in my throat." He drank and tried to think. He had planned to give Melvin Goodeye's name to the king, but it was too late for that. Jenin Rose had changed everything. He set down the goblet. "What did I learn…? About the governor, you mean?"

"The governor, the guild, anything," the king snapped. "Navarr's in the thick of it, isn't he?" He narrowed his eyes. "Wait. There's that look again. You think Navarr isn't capable of plotting? That doesn't matter. He's a puppet and I need to know who's pulling the strings."

Davit thought of Navarr pacing above them like a spoiled child, hardly aware the adults were carving up his world. He thought of Draks lying to San Hesrin and spreading misinformation, and the guild denying decent men and women the right to use their crafts.

But tell the truth and he wouldn't live till tomorrow. Lie and the king's witches would know. This newest philosopher or astrologer or engineer—whatever Ilenna was—would know in a moment. But if the king wanted the governor, that he could provide. "You mean with the chest?" he said. "The stolen cogs?"

"What cogs?" The king looked puzzled. "With the ice, damn it! What else are we talking about? There are relics; more every week. And most from this location, near the rim. Why? How? That's the question. Ilenna, show him the newest."

Ilenna passed a polished silver coin to Davit. In size, it was no different than most coins, but the image was like nothing he'd ever seen. One side held the face of man with his hair cut straight above his brows, a crown of laurel on his head. His draped garment was pinned with a jewel at one shoulder. There was writing on the opposite side, though he couldn't read it, and the letters were different from the angled scratch marks inside Drak's helmet. "Has anyone deciphered it?"

"Not yet," Makken said. "And it's not a cog. It doesn't do anything. It's a relic. Carried by the First Stars. We've been mapping the rim and finding a few as we go. One of our witches, a prisoner, found it. She knew nothing of its true value."

Davit nodded toward the white furs that scattered the floor. "Those skins," he asked. "You found them as well?"

"The white bears? Do you like them?"

"Are they relics?" He thought of Draks' trumped-up tale of the king crafting thousands of helmets in preparation for war.

The king raised a brow. "Of course, they're relics. Haven't you been listening? Something is happening. *Here*. Perhaps the stars placed a beacon here, centuries ago. The ruins of their home preserved for a thousand years in ice. Whatever it is, I mean to find out."

Davit pressed harder. "So, you found that many bears, but only the one coin? No, you said there was more than one."

"One bear," Ilenna said tightly. "The others are copies. Crafted. I'll wager you can't pick the real one?"

"No," he laughed her off. "I'm sure I can't. But… What of the Night Watermen? Do they have a hand in this?"

"They're thieves," Makken said. "Greedy and disorganized and certainly not a threat. Tell me about Navarr. You've been with him."

"Of course, constantly."

"Have you?" Ilenna raised a brow. "That's not what our witches say."

Davit paled. He started to protest then caught himself and waited.

"You've been spending a good deal of time at a certain Gold Key inn," she continued. "Twice with a young man, well dressed, slight. On one occasion you left together. Most recently, you followed him. Do you want to tell us who he is?"

Makken raised a brow.

Davit flexed his foot and felt the knife strapped to his calf. He could easily reach it, but then what? Even if he made it out of the room— which was doubtful— he could hardly swim back to the *Corona*. He straightened and met the king's gaze. "The man was one of my spies. I needed him. Navarr feared I was getting too close."

Makken leaned forward. "To what? By the stars, Davit, stop making me ask. He's with the guild? Is that it?"

"I don't think so. Or, if he is, I haven't seen it. He's afraid you'll find out he's a witch."

"Navarr?" The king made a face. "That's not possible." He glanced to his witches. They dropped their gazes and didn't speak. Makken snorted. "He's duping you. The man was tested. His blood would have shown. He's as human as you and I."

Davit pulled out the small, enameled shell he'd been carrying for weeks. He flicked the latch and a seeing eye rolled across the table. It blinked and a miniature shirtless Navarr appeared in front of them. Jaws clenched, the tension palpable as he urged his magic to raise two small rubber balls. There was no sign of Scrud or Brittle or Davit and the display of levitation would have been a fine accomplishment for a young apprentice. For a governor required by law to be human, it was not.

Makken smiled. "Have one of my captains arrest Mr. Navarr. He won't fight. He doesn't know how." Ilenna rose and Makken touched her arm. "But don't put him in the brig with the other witches. My wife would have my head."

He took a drink, set the goblet down. He seemed pleased with himself. "You understand, my boy, how much is at stake? I've assembled the strongest witches, and I will raise an armada the likes of which the isles have never seen. I will not let the guild, or anyone, destroy our peace. "I'm sorry I hadn't told you earlier. I needed to be sure."

"One thing more and I'll have someone find you a cabin for the night." The king lay his hand over Davit's, glanced at him, and frowned. "What? Anxious again?" He waited. "I'll have the truth, Davit. Don't push me."

"Yes. Well, you see…" Davit took a breath, let it out. "I didn't want to mention it. There is… There's a woman."

Makken's frown fell away. He pounded the table and laughed. "A woman? I never knew you to be shy. What? Do I know her? Were you afraid I wouldn't approve?"

"Somewhat, sir. It's complicated. You see, I know her name. Jenin Rose—" He hesitated, but the king kept smiling. "But I don't know where she's gone."

Makken laughed again. "Not to the arms of another man? She couldn't possibly be that foolish. Find her. I insist. But wait, tell me. Hair like silk, or dark and thick as a rope? I want to hear."

"She's beautiful," Davit said quietly. "A treasure. She has a way of flicking her head when she's angry and her hair moves like water. Or, not water. More like a dark fire."

"Ha! You've fought already." Makken crowed. "And you're going back for more. You tell this Jenin Rose I order her to do exactly as you wish. And so long as she wishes it too, I promise at least a few months' peace. Now, you'll stay the night. Tomorrow, you'll see my newest love, my *Castle Star*. Leave after that, but I want you back in a week. And bring her. I'd like nothing more than to meet the wily young woman who snared my favorite ward. That's an order. You're the only one keeps me laughing, Davit. You keep me young."

*   *   *

The upper deck of the *Castle Star* was a hub of activity, soldiers cleaning their guns, sailors climbing the ratlines, scurrying along the yards. Davit turned to get the lay of the ship. The wind was easy and the water nearly still. The sun had dipped below the horizon and he needed a quiet corner, if such a thing was possible. He glanced aft and was surprised to see a handful of sailors tying a large merchant vessel off the stern. The name *Swift Pace* was painted along the bow.

The new ship was broad with a high forecastle and higher stern and easily over a hundred feet long. Gruff shouting broke out on the upper deck and Davit pulled into the shadows and watched as soldiers emerged from below. Pistols drawn they prodded a long line of men and women off the *Swift Pace* and onto the *Castle Star*.

He caught the glint of a gem on one man's face, more on the limping woman next in line. They were witches and they were prisoners. He'd heard stories, but never seen such a thing. Their legs were shackled, hands tied. *Don't put Navarr in the hold with the other prisoners*, Makken had said and suddenly, Davit understood why.

Opulence above, hunger and the whip below. No wonder the king's witches were tense. He'd caught their furtive glances and remembered how the talking ceased. He had wondered if it was respect; he didn't think so now.

He turned back the way he'd come. Finding an isolated corner was more difficult than he'd guessed, and he trailed his hand along the rail and tried to look as if he had nothing more important on his mind than enjoying the evening breeze.

He had to get word to Draks. The Night Watermen had no idea Makken's so-called castle was actually a ship, and the king wasn't hiding. He was already at sea.

He didn't know whether Draks and the others would bide their time or call in the Night Watermen and launch an attack. Their ships were scattered across the isles, independent, but linked through a consensual network of traders, merchants, and contracts. But without information, without the coordinates, they were an easy target for the *Castle Star's* catapults and heavy guns.

Davit found a corner behind a set of stairs, made sure no one could hear him, and turned to face the sea.

He cupped his hands, lifted them to his mouth and thought of Jenin Rose. If he ever saw her again… No. Not if. When he saw her again, he'd ask how she disguised herself so convincingly. She might never have apprenticed in a guild hall, but from what he'd seen of her magic, she could have been a guild master. One of the best.

He wondered if he'd get a chance to tell her that she just saved his life. *There is a woman. Hair the color of fire.* He smiled at the thought. She'd probably shoot him for saying that, especially to the king.

He cleared his thoughts. *I can do this,* he told himself. *Send a simple spell. It doesn't mean I'm a witch. I've bought messenger spells before. Anyone should be able to figure it out. I've always had luck with wind, with weather. I can be lucky with this…*

The chant would be the coordinates, not for her house—she wouldn't be there—maybe the Gold Key? He looked for an object and noticed a splinter on a board. He pried it loose and cupped it in his palm. He'd need a gesture next. Some sort of flinging motion, like an arrow shooting across the sea. He raised his hand—

"I have a better idea than that, Mr. Lake."

Davit spun and found Jeron Scrud leaning against the stairs. "Are you following me?" he demanded. He flicked the splinter away and stepped from the wall.

"A little," Scrud admitted. "I find myself without an ally. The governor, as I'm sure you know, has been taken away. And the only man I know with his wits about him is slinking around in the dark trying to send a message to… Let me guess… The pawnbroker you brought that day? No. Night Watermen?" He glanced wryly at Davit. "Wait. Don't answer. It doesn't matter. But, allow me to help. I have a few messenger shells. Here, take one." Scrud opened his hand and showed two amethyst shells, their clasp dangling open."

Davit pressed his hands firmly to his sides. "Use that and every witch on board will find me before I draw a breath."

"Oh, I think not. They're quite busy keeping this barge afloat."

"Against their will," Davit said. "You're better off using those yourself and help the governor."

Scrud snorted. "He'll be fine. There's no law against being a human witch. It's not supposed to happen, but the world *is* changing. Navarr isn't capable of more than a few tricks. And yet, that he can accomplish that much—think of what it means."

Davit shook his head. Much as he disliked the governor, he mistrusted Jeron Scrud more. "If you're trying to make a point Mr. Scrud, get to it."

"I am, and you need to think. Whatever you were trying to do just now—and I've been around Navarr long enough to recognize it—I'm offering a working cog, for the simple reason that I want to survive. Take it, and perhaps you'll repay the favor someday. There's going to be a war, Davit. Humans against witches, witches against each other. No one's free anymore. A thousand years have passed, and you have to choose sides."

Davit stared at the shells in Scrud's hand, nodded and took one.

15

A Witch's Intention

The night was clear, the moon reflecting sharply on the water as Molly lowered the dinghy over the *Fish's* side. She climbed down behind it, released the chains and fixed the oars in the locks.

Westward, even at this late hour, Mann Isle's harbor was aglow with lights, too many to risk entering from that direction. She'd aim for the cliffs instead and come in from the east where she remembered the rocks from the last time she was here. The shoreline was craggy, but it would be easier to hide a small boat. She picked out a promontory and with the *Fish* anchored safe behind her, set to rowing.

The tide was pulling against her, and it would have been easier in the daylight, but easy wasn't what she needed right now. She needed speed. She needed to find Evan. Get him out of Hayden Hall and away from the guild masters and everyone else who tried to deny their craft. She'd had enough, damn them all. She glanced over her shoulder, marked the rock's position and blew a spell across the waves to speed her path.

She was worried. Evan hadn't answered any of her messages, and it could be nothing. He could be busy. Or preoccupied. Or angry. Or it could be the fault of that turncoat. That cheating, lying, pompous, self-satisfied drunkard, Davit Lake.

Did he really expect her to believe he wanted to help? When he was the one put the tracking spell on her arm, and claimed he wasn't a witch when obviously he was? She'd known it from the first time their hands touched—accidentally. At the ball and Brittles' shop, at the guildhall. It was a wonder he could look himself in a mirror, and not see the obvious truth. Yet he'd stolen into her house, summoned guards, kissed her and said *she* didn't understand?

Lights flashed near the harbor and the memory fled. There were ships, far more than she realized from the *Fish*. Smaller vessels anchored close in, larger ones further out. She counted fifteen then twenty tall ships with pointed bows and high stern castles and shadow lines where heavy guns sat. They were outfitted for war.

War? Against the king? She frowned and adjusted her course. Madinina said the *Oracle* had been requisitioned, that the king was using witches to craft weapons. And after decades without a major war, the guild was building a navy. The more she searched for answers, the more questions blocked her path.

She steered the dinghy into a hard landing, stepped out and took her bearings. There was a jumble of stacked rocks a few feet from shore. Riva was brightest in the northern sky, ten degrees west off the point. She tied off the boat, looked about, and crafted a cog light to find the path ahead, then started climbing.

She grabbed hold of bushes, pulled herself over scree and scrambled upward, past the switchbacks and into the taller trees and finally to the outer wall surrounding Hayden Hall. The ancient stonework was crumbling but she found Evan's rope exactly where they left it.

She drew a breath, concentrated on the cog light that still hovered in the air, and though she still might need it, put it out rather than risk being found. She yanked on the rope and tested its strength. She herself up and perched atop the capstones.

From there, she could see the lights at the main hall on the opposite side of the fields and though she had never been further inside than Ossian's chambers, Evan had shown her where the apprentices' attics were and how to find his window in the upper roofs. The younger boys would be asleep and though she couldn't very well check every bed, she would if she had to. If she searched and Evan didn't answer.

She owed him an apology for making him go back. Hayden Hall wasn't safe. It hadn't been before, and it certainly wasn't with those ships in the harbor. The guild had nothing worth teaching. Evan was right and she was wrong, and she was sorry it had taken so long to understand. He didn't belong here. They needed to build their new home together.

She dropped to the ground and raced across the shadowed field to the nearest shed. From there to a barn and across another yard till she reached the main hall and a window with the shutters open. She sprang for the ledge and squeezed inside.

Torches stuttered on the walls but there was no sign of guards, not along the narrow corridors, and not in the great hall where the hearth was already cold.

She took the stairwell leading to the boy's side of the attic, tried the first door and found a storage closet. The second room was filled with the sounds of breathing, the rustle of a blanket, four cots. Four tousled heads, none of them Evan's. She slipped back out.

In the last room, a tow-headed boy lay asleep in the cot nearest the door. He was younger than Evan, they all were. One skinny boy clutched his pillow, another had cheeks that were brown and smooth. Pity they didn't know how little the guild could teach them.

But what had they done with Evan? Switched sleeping arrangements? Or what if he was being punished? Or, what if… She stopped. She heard voices outside, not loud but urgent. She backed out of the room and hurried to a window at the end of the corridor. It was unlocked and there was a ledge outside, narrow but wide enough for anyone who'd grown up swinging from lines and spars the way she had. The way Evan had.

She was outside in no time, crouching on the ledge and looking down on the two people she had hoped not to see: Master Ossian and Warden Sanders. They were standing at the base of the stairs leading to the dome and a man and woman were with them, masters to judge from their robes, though she didn't recognize them. What surprised her more was finding the dome's roof drawn back.

She looked up and saw a pale stream of dark lights stretched across the sky. They were thin tonight, cloudlike, though for all the astrologers' predictions, it was impossible to know when they'd turn from a dull white to a river of red and green. It could happen anytime.

She moved and her hand came down on a pebble. It dug into her palm, stuck there for a moment, then fell and hit the cobblestones. Ossian glanced upward, and Molly flattened herself against the wall.

Sanders seemed impatient. He touched Ossian's arm, said something, and Ossian turned back to their work. He was crafting a spell. Molly recognized the cadence of a chant though she caught only a few words. Quadrants and something about latitude and maybe the word 'gate,' but she wasn't sure.

But if the words were odd, so was the way all four masters took turns saying the lines. She had never heard a cog tried that way, each taking one of the elements, water and sky, fire and ice. She caught something about coordinates and stars and ascendant and tried to hear more, but a pebble hit her foot and she froze.

She looked up, saw nothing then nudged it against the wall, so it wouldn't tumble. The masters were inside the dome now, but the lights had faded. They, watched the sky, grew impatient and stepped back out. Ossian seemed annoyed.

Another pebble hit and Molly's gaze shot up and this time she saw someone leaning out from the adjacent roof. A hooded figure, a girl motioning her to… What? Jump?

No! The girl pointed toward the inside corner of Molly's ledge.

Below her, the dome was closing. If they looked up just now, the masters would see her. The girl had flattened herself against the roof, but Molly was exposed.

She crawled toward the corner wall, found a series of notches in the brickwork and started climbing, one toe-hold at a time until the girl grabbed the back of her vest, reeled her in then pushed her down to hide. "Hurry!" she whispered. Her voice was low and serious. "They'll see us."

"Wait! Who are you?"

The girl glanced over the edge and frowned. Ossian, Sanders and the others were shoulder to shoulder below them. They shook their heads and glanced upward, not at the ledge but toward the sky. "They're trying to craft a spell," she said.

"I can see that, but why?"

"I'd laugh except it's serious. Four masters trying to summon the dark lights and they can't get it right."

Molly met the girl's eyes. She seemed smart and earnest, and she wasn't on Ossian's side.

"They've been at it all night. Ossian hoped his spells would be stronger because it's nearly solstice. But they're not. He left and came back with the others. They tried inside the dome. Outside. With a fire. Without. Best I can tell, he's summoning guild ships, trying to use the lights to carry his message."

"But the ships are already in the harbor?"

"He wants more. But we have to hurry. You're Molly, aren't you? I'm Cai. Evan's friend."

Molly opened then closed her mouth. Evan's friend? A girl? Evan had never mentioned a friend before… Though… Why not? It was possible. The girl, Cai, was near his age, strong willed, pretty with her chopped off hair. And prone to climbing rooftops and laughing at the masters. "All right, I believe you. Where is he? Hiding?"

"I was hoping you knew."

Molly froze and Cai reached out, touched her arm "He's safe. At least, I think he is. We'll talk. But we have to run."

Molly nodded, and they started across the peak. Cai was long legged, agile and familiar with the roofs. They jumped to a lower level, shimmied onto one ledge then down to another then dropped to the ground. A dog barked in the distance but there were no footsteps and they raced past the stables and across an overgrown field behind the teaching halls then back into the thick of the woods.

Cai stopped outside a tall, crumbling structure nearly hidden in an ancient stand of trees. Molly had passed this way, but never seen it. "Where are we?" she asked.

"An old storehouse. No one uses it anymore." Cai held her hand over the ivy-covered surface and a door swung open on rusted hinges.

She's a witch, Molly realized. Of course. And an apprentice. She pictured Cai racing across the field with Evan, laughing together. Her brother was no longer a boy. She was the one who had treated him that way, far too long.

They entered a plain, abandoned room. Cai motioned toward a candle she must have left there, and the wick suddenly lit. They stepped over missing floorboards and around upended tables and across the room to a set of stairs that groaned as they climbed. They reached the first landing, then another and Cai pushed open a door to a dusty attic. Inside, the beams were strung with bits and pieces of abandoned bird's nests. Damp, moldering books were stacked against the walls. Crates. Cobwebs. Narrow windows. The smells of another time. Only one table, heavy with thick square legs stood intact. Cai said, "I stumbled on it after Evan left. You're the first person I've brought here."

Molly glanced about. She felt empty suddenly, lonely. She'd been counting gold and risking the *Fish*, and telling herself it was all for Evan's sake while he was… Where? "He left?" she asked. Her voice was shaking; she forced herself to calm down. "Where is he? What happened?"

"I'm sorry. I thought you knew. You didn't get any messages?"

"No. You?" She waited for Cai's answer.

"A few, but none recently." There was a noise and Cai moved to the open window and peered into the dark. The nearby trees and thick foliage made it difficult to see but they heard dogs barking far away.

"I was planning to leave." Cai nodded at a table with several daggers and a gun case, powder horn and packets of food and a water skin. A pack leaned against the wall. "I was about to send you a message when the *Fish* came in."

"I'm sorry," Molly said. "I'm not following. Can we start at the beginning?"

Cai nodded and told her about searching the library for the Red Grimoire. About how Evan gave himself up so she and Reed—another friend—could get away and now Evan was trying to get to Carillon, but it would take longer than they planned. "Reed's going to be all right. Evan needs to know that. His family took him home. He could walk, a little, and he didn't want to go but didn't want to stay either."

Molly watched Cai as she spoke. She took in the odd cut of her hair, her gaze that was so determined. "The pebble you threw on the roof?" she asked. "You used a weathercraft spell to aim, didn't you? And the door? The hinges were rusted and I'm guessing you used an ice spell to open it. Ice and sky. And you lit the candle, that was fire. Small spells, or you couldn't have held so many at once, but that's not what matters. You're craftborn, aren't you? Like Evan. Like me. And you're hiding it from Ossian."

Cai shrugged; the questions didn't seem to surprise her. "It's easiest sometimes to hide in plain sight. Ossian never looked for what he didn't want to find. With me, with Evan, maybe others. The crafts are changing, not just here."

Molly nodded. "And when you tried to learn cogs the guild way, did they work?" Cai shrugged again and Molly caught more of what Evan must have seen. She was intelligent, strong and thoughtful, all at the same time.

"They worked sometimes, not always," Cai answered. "It's different for everyone and we learn what we can. Apprentices who bend metals have a difficult time with weather, but they still try. Without cogs we'd all of us, human and witch, be at the mercy of the elements. We—" She stopped as the sounds of barking grew louder.

They snapped to attention, glanced at each and nodded. The barking was unmistakable now, vicious and nearer as the dogs reached the trees.

Shouting followed and boots pounded the ground. Molly pulled out her gun, focused her attention and, quick as thought, the barrel was loaded, the pan and flint ready. Cai did the same, and by the time they grabbed a few more knives and the pack, Ossian's soldiers were at the walls.

They reached the landing, but too late as axes bit into the wooden door on the floor below. Rocks shattered the windows and glass shards flew like darts. They turned back for the attic, bolted the door and, standing alongside the window, peered outside.

Armed men and women surrounded the building and there were dogs everywhere, barking and sniffing the perimeter. "Is there a cellar?" Molly asked. "A chimney, a closet we could hide with a spell?"

"No. Nothing like that. But maybe…" She turned, and her gaze stopped on a rope coiled in the corner. "The trees," she said. "It's the only way."

Molly nodded and they carried the table across the room and stood it beneath the window. It was wider than the opening, and sturdy. Molly twisted one end of the rope around the table legs and knotted it securely while Cai fastened a weight to the other end. Cai grabbed a pack and they mounted the table and looked to the trees. The trunks were thick and strong. Heavy branches reached toward the wall outside their window.

Cai tested the rope. "I'll go first," she said. "I'll catch a branch, and we shimmy down the rope—" She stopped, looked to Molly. "Are you all right? You think you can do it?"

"Me?" Molly raised a brow. "I was wondering about you." They looked at each other and would have laughed if they had the time. Instead, Cai blinked and started a chant, but Molly touched her arm. "Wait," she said. "I have an idea."

She looked to the ground, to the tops of the soldier's heads as they searched the crumbling walls. She couldn't see Hayden Hall's main building, but it was there, as was the hill above them, and the sea far below, and further out, the *Fish*, waiting to carry them to safety.

She turned to Cai. "We do this together," she said, and Cai looked surprised, but only for a moment. She nodded and they drew a breath, both in unison.

Molly shut out the noise of the dogs, the footsteps pounding and blades scraping as they pulled from scabbards. She sharpened her senses until the wind was the only thing she heard. She felt it needle her needle her cheeks and lift her collar and move among the leaves, and she spoke to it. "Come play with the sky," she chanted. "Come with your dance and show us your game and carry our scent so far away, these men and their dogs will never know what trick you played."

Cai went next. "You are the wind and I am your chant."

"You are the force that moves through the trees."

"Your gesture the waves on the water."

"And this," Molly said, "my request."

"And this my request," Cai repeated.

They blew and their words floated upward, and the wind answered. It gathered and rose and swept across the sea. It played havoc with the waves and gusted above the cliffs and down toward the trees. It took hold of the rope as Cai threw and it answered their call.

The dogs came alert. They lifted their snouts and caught the stray wind. They yelped with excitement and bounded from the walls. The soldiers looked confused. They called into the darkness and ran after the dogs, away from the forest and toward the main hall.

Cai reached the ground first and Molly jumped next. They zigzagged through the trees, then out into the open again and toward the stone wall and nearly made it. They might have, except that the second line of Ossian's soldiers burst into the field. They carried torches and guns and a half dozen new dogs raced toward them.

A musket sprayed the ground and Cai tripped but Molly caught her arm and steadied her and they raced for the trees again. The soldiers were close behind, more dogs than people and Cai veered again. They ran though shadows and dodged boulders, down the steep hill as the dogs gained on them, barking and snapping and closer behind.

They slid and picked themselves up and ran again. Until suddenly, the trees gave way and Molly pulled to a halt at the edge of the cliff. She yanked Cai back to keep her from falling. They hung on an outcropping of moss-covered rocks. Far below, waves crashed and sprayed. She couldn't see the path and there was no easy footing and the dogs howled as they ripped through the underbrush.

Her heart hammered in her chest. The sea was rougher than when she rowed in and her small boat was nowhere in sight. She had time for one frantic wish that she'd left a light burning on the *Fish* then she squeezed Cai's hand.

"For Evan," Cai whispered.

"For Evan," Molly agreed.

Cai wriggled out of her pack. Molly pushed her knives and pistols more securely into her belt. The gunpowder would be ruined, but that didn't matter. She glanced back, saw a flurry of movement, a flash of teeth. She filled her lungs, squeezed Cai's hand, then leapt and sprang as far out as she could, out and down toward the dark water. She fell. And fell. And fell. And hit.

Hands, arms, then head; she entered the water. Arrow straight but hard, she plunged and felt sharp rocks scrape her arms and legs. She felt the water, thick and heavy and cold and she slowed then felt gravel beneath her feet.

She opened her eyes to find strands of dark kelp and shadowy, fleeting fish bodies. Pain squeezed her chest and she ignored it and pushed off the bottom, swimming until she burst free and gasped for air as a gun shot hit the water nearby. She felt bruised, but alive. She tread water and turned to look for Cai and didn't see her. "Cai?" No answer. "Cai?" She tried not to panic.

She plunged again but the water was murky and dark, and she surfaced and dove again, sweeping nearer the rocks this time, closer to the bottom, then higher, fighting the drag of her boots and clothes. Until, somehow, just as she feared that no one could possibly stay below so long, a form took shape, a torso, arms and legs suspended just below the surface. She sped toward Cai, pulled her to her chest. There was no resistance, no awareness.

Molly changed positions, kept one arm around Cai's chest and kicked toward the rocks.

She reached them, but her fingers slipped on algae and she found no grip. Cai's eyes were closed, her body heavy. The dinghy was too far to reach, and the shore wasn't safe from gunshots, but she saw something, a log, trapped in the lee of the rocks nearer the shore.

She swam for the log and caught hold and maneuvered Cai's limp form part way on, and started kicking, guiding them toward the *Fish*.

She was tired and her thoughts were muddied but she crafted enough of a spell to smooth the waves and fought the urge to rest. She swam without thinking, with no awareness of anything but the *Fish* like a beacon calling her forward and the need to move, one leg and then the other, her body supporting Cai's until finally, a shadow darkened the water. She kicked toward the hull and just as she was trying to figure out how to get them safely aboard, a rope smacked down beside her.

Relief washed over her. It was Macklin. They'd finished the repairs to the *White Lily* and come after her. She flexed her hands, forced her fingers to cooperate and maneuvered the rope over Cai's head. "Ready," she called weakly.

"Aye, ma'am. What's this you're hauling?"

Exhaustion seeped into her bones and she was too tired to answer. She tugged the line and Cai's limp figure rose. *Ma'am?* she wanted to ask. *Since when do you call me ma'am?*

It seemed as if hours passed before the rope returned. When it did, someone had retied the knots with loops for a seat. She murmured her thanks and worked her arms through and began to rise. Looking up, she hoped the figures on the deck belonged to her crew and not the strangers she thought she saw.

They did not.

They grabbed her and threw her to the deck and a boot came down on her back. She caught a glimpse of faces, men and women with long braids and bright clothes, the glint of weapons, swords and axes. Her face was pressed against the deck and she tried to move, and they allowed her to roll over, slowly. She came to her knees. A pinch faced, dark haired man held her arms while an older woman removed her weapons.

Another man held a gun at Macklin's back. He wore a flowery vest and incongruous lacy scarf. Macklin's hands were tied, his right eye swollen shut but he nodded when she looked his way.

Troth stood behind him. His arms were bound around the mainmast and he couldn't turn his face. She looked for Sally and Brigit, found them sitting on the deck with Madinina, their backs lashed together, legs outstretched. Nick, with a bloodied mouth sat a short distance away. Tribolt. She didn't see Tribolt. And Cai was nowhere to be seen.

She forced herself to sit taller, straighten her shoulders. "Who are you?" she demanded. "Macklin? What happened?"

"They came out of nowhere, boarded us just as was found the *Fish*."

"Trespassing," the man holding the gun said. "That's what you were."

"These are open waters," Macklin said.

"Says who?" The man slammed the butt of his pistol into Macklin's shoulder and he reeled and the man kicked him, in the side this time. Molly wrenched free, but the woman raised a gun. It was loaded, cocked and inches from her face. "Enough!" Molly shouted and raised her hands. "I have no weapons. But you're on my ship. Who are you? Where's the girl?"

"Simmer down," the woman said. She was tall, gray-haired, but not so old she couldn't put up a fight. "We've no interest in hurting these nice folks. Crew says your name is Molly Sinclair, Captain Sinclair, but more than that, they're not inclined to say."

Molly studied the pirates. Most carried pistols and bandoliers strung with an odd mix of shells and weapons. For all their tattoos, she couldn't tell how many were human, how many witch.

"What we're trying to figure," the woman said, "is who you really are. You're not guild. And you're not royal cause you wouldn't be swimming around in your trousers. You're not one of us, or we'd know."

"Where's the rest of my crew," she snapped back.

"Tribolt's all right," Nick called from behind her. "He took a bullet, but he's on their ship. They have surgeons."

He nodded aft and Molly turned to find the *White Lily* anchored alongside her ship. The masts were repaired, gleaming with varnish. The rails had been replaced and the hull no longer looked like a skeleton limped back from the grave. A new name, *Luna's Watch,* graced the bow, but she didn't feel relieved.

Another ship floated off its portside and Molly's breath caught at the size. Its masts scraped the sky. Its spars stretched cold as cannon barrels. And though she had tried to convince herself she didn't know who these pirates were, it wasn't true. They were Night Watermen and the ship, staring at her like a figure out of a dream, was their flagship *Akistra.* She straightened and hid her fear. "Free my crew," she said tightly, "and I'll talk to your captain."

The woman sneered. "Oh, you'll talk, missy. Though it's four captains not one, and I don't do anything without they say so."

Molly squared her shoulders. Her crew was alive. The Watermen had seized the *Fish* but hadn't stolen it. Perhaps she could stall them or negotiate until she knew what they wanted. "Here's my promise," she said firmly. "Free my crew and I won't put up a fight. I don't put up a fight, and you won't have to shoot me. I'll tell your captains who I really am."

The woman looked thoughtful, as if considering the offer, though Molly doubted it. Night Watermen were thieves and worse, and she hated everything she knew about them. *Be careful,* she warned herself. *Don't trust them.* Her parents never had. She remembered the way they used to hurry her and Evan into the *Ice Warden's* hold any time a Waterman ship so much as hailed them from afar…

Hailed them? She frowned. Out of what corner of her thoughts had that memory come?

She tried to remember more. There was hazy impression—she didn't know from where—of angry voices. Evan crying, their father running down to hush them, but there wasn't time to think. The woman lowered her gun. She motioned, and one after the other, Nick and Sally and Brigit, Macklin and Troth were cut free. They rubbed their wrists, shook out their arms and, at the Night Waterman's prodding, fell into line. Molly walked first, over the narrow plank onto the newly repaired *Luna's Watch* and across that deck to a ship she had hoped never to see.

16

And the Greatest of These is Ice

There were three ships that Molly would have known with her eyes closed and her hands tied behind her back: the *Fish* and her parent's *Ice Warden* of course, and to a lesser degree the *White Lily* or *Luna's Watch* as she was now named. None of them compared with the *Akistra*.

Its beam was wider than the three ships combined; its masts were ancient timbers, sails wide as clouds across the sky. And though there were three cannon decks, it seemed more a floating city than a warship.

There were lights everywhere, candles and lanterns and braziers burning on the weather deck. Ravens watched from the spars and people staring, as curious for a look at her as she was of them. The Night Watermen wore gems in their faces, more than the guild would have allowed. The men were marked with swirls of tattoos on their shoulders, necks and cheeks; women sported three vertical lines on their chin. And the clothes; they were a discordance of fabrics and colors, spider fine lace from Sophen, red wool from Mann. Some carried strips of fabric with the king's emblem like trophies dangling from their belts.

A red headed woman with long braids shoved Molly toward a companionway. Macklin tried to follow, but she jabbed her gun at his side and pushed him back. "I'll be all right," Molly said reassuringly, though she wasn't sure it was true.

They reached the lower deck and she glanced past the cannons hoping to find Cai or Tribolt but there was no sign of a sickroom and the red-haired woman shoved her again, down to another deck and a door so heavily carved she paused for a better look. In the upper corners, men and women—the First Stars—fought off armored beasts and fire breathing birds. It was like a storybook, each panel revealing a battle between the stars and strange creatures. Stars and an onslaught of warriors. Stars raising the isles and closing their world.

The woman rapped on the door. "It's Marissa," she called. "I have her."

The doors opened from within and Molly found herself in a long cabin full of men and women staring back at her. They carried pistols, cutlasses and daggers. Shells hung from their belts and around their necks and braided into their hair. A few were missing hands. A long table with four high backed chairs stood in the middle of the floor. Behind them were two men and two women.

The Night Watermen's four captains. Of course. They looked haughty and suspicious, as though they already saw themselves as judges and her a common thief. "Your name?" the man nearest her asked. His face was a swirl of tattoos and gems, his voice deep and unhurried, but with a hint of anger, waiting.

Breath, Molly reminded herself. She wondered if she should have lied about her name. She would lie if she had to, to protect her ship and brother and crew. She'd been doing it for years. Human and witch. Pirate and merchant. Jenin Rose and Melvin Goodeye. But she needed to know what she was lying about. "Molly Sinclair," she said, and the man turned to the woman who'd ushered her in.

"She said it on her own," she answered. "I swear. No one spoke to her."

"Sinclair?" he repeated, in a tone Molly couldn't place. "And you were spying on us. Is that correct?"

Spying? Was that what they thought I was doing?

The woman to his right touched his arm. She was the age her mother might be if she was alive, and tall and proud. Her face was lean, her chin strong. She carried a full set of master's gems, opal to corundum, on her temple. "It's a common enough name," Molly said.

"Is it?" The man raised a brow. "I'm told the *Fish* is yours? Is that correct? You have nothing to fear from answering."

Molly didn't believe him. "It is, yes," she said. "But you have me at a disadvantage. I've given you my name. I don't know yours?"

"Fair enough. I'm Draks Halo." He watched her closely. "You've heard the name?"

"I've heard of your ship and the Night Watermen of course, but not you." And yet, she did remember. Not his name so much as the apprehension she felt whenever Night Watermen were mentioned, a disquiet that had always been part of her. Like the verse she suddenly remembered singing to Evan when they were young: *Watch out for the Waterman's knife, the Waterman's fight, the Waterman's might. Never join the Waterman's night, or they'll bite you while you're sleeping.*

The apprehension came from her parents. They had instilled it in her the same way they'd taught her respect for the sea, to keep her craft hidden. It was the reason she grew uneasy when Macklin and the others spoke about their charter. Why she knew things about them she had never learned on her own. Her parents had known the Night Watermen. She remembered that now. They had stepped aboard the *Ice Warden* while she and Evan hid below, not once but many times.

"Tell me, how old are you?" Draks asked. His voice was calm and measured. He pushed a plate of fruit across the table, nodded at her to eat.

She ignored the food. The cabin was impressive, with heavy carvings on the walls, mounted weapons, paintings, vases. A curtain shielded an alcove with a man guarding one side, a woman the other. "Twenty-one," she answered.

"Young to be a captain," he mused. "But then, if you are in command, we ask again. What exactly were you doing in these waters?"

Draks Halo had the sharp eyes of a man who'd lived his life by his wits. His graying hair curled above his shoulders and he wore a vest and half cape stitched from the skins of a scaled animal, the *Akistra's* water moccasin most likely. He pulled it back and made sure she saw the two daggers in his belt, each with a shell embedded in the handle.

"These are open seas," she said. "And my ships are private vessels. I committed no crimes, trespassed on no one's property. And I might ask the same of you. Why are you here? What do you want?"

A murmur of disapproval moved through the cabin. "Look to your crew, Captain Sinclair," Draks said dryly. "You do not have the advantage here and I'm an impatient man, not a cruel one, otherwise they would all be dead, sinking to the ocean floor rather than nursing their wounds under my surgeon's care."

Molly glared back. She didn't like this man, his sarcasm and threats. "I have every right to search for my brother," she said tightly. "And I am looking to my crew. I demand to see the girl who came with me. Where is she?"

"What's this?" Drakes snorted. "Another Sinclair? How many are there?"

"Draks," the woman said calmly. "She has a right to inquire." She dipped her head. "Your companions are well, I assure you. We saw what you did, saving that girl's life. She's safely asleep. And your man, also. He suffered a knife wound but our surgeon reports the bleeding has stopped and the wound wasn't critical or deep. We would not, we do not believe in allowing anyone, stranger or friend, to suffer unnecessarily. Ask anyone here. They'll speak for themselves. They left their halls and merchant ships to join us. We are a free people."

The woman's voice was soft and musical and something in the way she spoke caught at the edge of memory. Draks. Draks Halo. Captain Halo. Her parents had spoken his name, most often in whispers and secret conversations when they didn't know she was listening from behind a chair. And this woman's voice, it was like a dream, so much like her mother's it caught her by surprise.

What had her parents been hiding? The Night Watermen had been fewer in number in those days. Her parent's ship, the *Ice Warden* could have out-sailed the hulking *Akistra* with no more than a thought.

Except… She had the timing wrong, she realized. She must have been around twelve when the *Akistra* was built. Their numbers had already grown. Before that, they sailed a smaller ship. The name came to her. *The Dawn.* It had a raven for a figurehead, black wings flush against the sides, more like the *Fish* but larger, and nothing like the *Akistra.*

"Tell us about this brother," the second man said. He was slighter than Draks Halo, less hulking thought his eyes were just as stern. "Is he another Sinclair?"

Molly straightened. "Tell me your names," she said. "I gave you mine."

The woman laughed. "Captains, friends; we forget our manners. The girl's brave. She is our guest and deserves an answer. Molly Sinclair, my name is Ayva Trill. Draks Halo is my husband. To my left stands Krila Sand, and Gryer Scarp her husband. Together we are the captains of the *Akistra.* And now, this brother of yours. Is he younger? Older?"

"Younger," Molly said. "He's on a ship, the *Swift Pace.*"

"I don't know that name. Ula?" Ayva looked to an older woman asleep in a chair.

The woman opened her eyes. Her mouth on one side hung lower than the other and one eyelid drooped. Her words were slurred but the meaning was clear. "There is a *Swift Pace,*" she said. "Registered out of Doshaget and owned by one Mere Doreth. It left Mann Harbor for Bulatt on the second, under Riva's Star."

Draks glared at Molly. "Which doesn't explain why you were slinking around Mann Harbor, spying. If you even have a brother."

"Oh, she does. She has a brother." Cai appeared. She clung unsteadily to the curtain outside the alcove. She hobbled a few steps, reached for a chair.

Molly started toward her, but a Waterman blocked her way. They had given Cai dry clothes, leggings and a shirt twice too large. Her short hair was disheveled, and she looked weak but unharmed.

"She's telling the truth," Cai said, and she coughed and needed a moment before she could speak again. "Her brother is Evan Sinclair. He was a stowaway." She turned to Molly. "They want money. That's all." She moved haltingly from the chair to the table. "Tell your Watermen to help us find Evan and you'll have all the money you want."

"They're thieves," Molly said. "There isn't enough gold in the seas to satisfy their greed."

"We need them, Molly. I can pay, and they'll let us go."

Draks glanced at Molly. "You don't know who she is, do you?"

"She's an apprentice, same as my brother."

"She's Artice Makken's niece. His sister's daughter to be precise, and she certainly can pay your ransom, or your ship's, or this brother's if need be." He turned to Cai. "And you don't know anything about her, do you? Babes in the woods," he chuckled. "That's what you are."

Molly frowned. It didn't matter who Cai was. Or it did, but she'd sort it out later. She had a lot of sorting out to do. Not only about enemies who turned out to be friends and strangers who may or may not be enemies. Or the way Cai was in love with her brother; she'd sort that out later too. But Cai was only part right. They did want money, but they wanted information more.

"You want to know about my brother?" she said, feeling her way forward. "He was apprenticed at Hayden Hall. I went there to buy out his charter, bring him home."

"Ah. She's talking," Draks said. "Very good. And where exactly is home? Ula?" Draks turned to the older woman. "What do you know of these ships? *Luna's Watch* and the *Fish*?"

"There is no *Luna's Watch*," she said from her chair. "But there was a *White Lily*. It was sunk. No. That's not right. It was taken. There's a smell of fresh varnish nearby. And the *Fish*..." She paused. "There is no *Fish* in any harbor master's log. Not by that name."

"It isn't registered," Molly said. "You won't find it. We took the *White Lily* and the last thing we wanted was trouble. If we'd known the *Akistra* was in these waters, we'd have stayed far off. You'll find notes in a log, in my cabin."

"You're the renegades." Ayva said. "It would be ironic, wouldn't it? If it were true."

Draks looked hard at Molly. "Thieving I understand. Makken's niece running away, I understand. But if you are lying and it's the king you're running to, we will find out. Gryer, do you mind? Search her cabin."

Gryer beckoned the two men nearest the door to follow, then hurried out ahead of them. Draks moved to the stern windows and stared toward the rising light. Krila motioned Cai and Molly to sit. She offered them food and water, and Molly took it this time. The cold drink helped clear her head, but though she couldn't remember when she'd last slept or eaten, she wasn't hungry.

Dawn was approaching. Another few days and the solstice would be on them. She was weary to the bone and jittery and she would have laid her head on the great slab of a table and slept, if only for a moment, but she couldn't. The three men returned surprisingly soon and Gryer pulled Draks, Ayva and Krila aside. Gryer seemed angry. He was holding something, the harbor list she assumed, until he turned and set the small model of the *Ice Warden* in front of her. "This is yours?" he asked.

"Of course, it's hers," Krila said. "It was in her cabin."

"Where she sent us," Gryer said. "She wanted us to find it."

"And why not? She told us her name."

"It could be a decoy?" Draks said.

Molly pushed herself from the chair. "I'm not a child," she said. "I can speak for myself."

"Then do it," Gryer snapped. "Explain how you came by this?"

"It was a gift," she said tightly.

"From who?" Ayva asked. "The *Ice Warden* sank years ago."

Molly opened then closed her mouth. She hadn't mentioned the ship's name, nor was it printed on the tiny bow. She glanced at the replica of her parent's ship. The sails were full, the line of tiny oars drawn in. The bow gleamed as if the paint was newly dried.

Draks' hand shot out. He grabbed her wrist, slammed it to the table. "Who are you?" he demanded. He bore down hard. "Who is your mother? Your father?"

Molly winced and tried to pull free, but Draks was heavier and stronger and he was hurting her and suddenly, she remembered him. Pacing the deck of the *Ice Warden*, looming over her father. Sometimes talking but more often arguing. And not just him but Ayva and Gryer and Krila. And not once, but many times. Evan was in his bed, too young to be afraid. Her mother hushed him to sleep and warned Molly to guard him. But she was curious, and their voices were loud, and she couldn't possibly stay below and wait. She crept up and watched from the stairs as Halo and the others drank their wine and ate their food and laid out plans she wasn't supposed to hear.

"*We need to try again,*" her mother said when they were gone. Her voice was urgent, troubled. "*You know it's there. The relics came from the other side. We're not the first to try.*"

"*But first we finish the new ship,*" her father said. "*We'll search after that.*"

Draks released Molly's arm. She started to rub her wrist then stopped. She refused to show any pain. "My father's name is Senesh. My mother is Esty. Senesh and Esty Sinclair."

"You're lying," Gryer snarled. "They're dead. How did you come by that… that toy?"

"They're not dead. You don't know that."

Gryer slammed his fist against the table and the *Ice Warden* wobbled and fell to its side. "If they're not dead, where are they? And don't pretend they're on the other side."

Breathe, Molly warned herself. *Stay calm.* They just admitted knowing her parents. And though they didn't know any more than she did whether they were dead or alive, they might know which route they took, or what they'd planned. "I don't know where they are," she said. "I'm telling the truth."

"Gryer, enough," Ayva said. "There are better ways to ask. Molly, dear—"

"No." Molly stopped her. "Don't placate me. You want information? We'll trade. Three years ago, on the 15th day of Teair, my parents left my brother Evan and me for the last time. They told us they were mapping the ice, but what they were really looking for, or whether they ended up shipwrecked or lost, I don't know. They left and we never heard from them again."

"That tells us nothing," Gryer said. "And they couldn't have hidden two mewing brats while we were sailing and fighting side by side. When last we saw them—"

"When last we saw them," Ayva interrupted. "It could have been for the very reason that Esty could no longer hide them. And your memory is off. They were no longer fighting beside us by then. They refused."

"They thought they were too good for us," Krila said. "That I remember."

"Why go to the trouble of hiding two children?" Gryer asked. "Why would we care?"

"We might not," Ayva said. "But others would."

Molly held out her arm.

Gryer glanced down. "No mark," he said. "She's not even an apprentice. Though how with Sinclair blood—?"

Krila shook her head. "Husband. Captain. I love you dearly, but you ask the wrong questions. Molly, you bear no guild sign but your brother is apprenticed?" Molly nodded. "Of course. You said he was at Hayden Hall. While a girl, a young girl that's a witch, needn't be tested. And with no guild sign, a craft can easily be hid. Is that what you've done?" Molly nodded.

"And you know," Ayva said, "That since your parents were witches, and so are you and your brother, that you are craftborn. Both of you."

"Yes."

"And your parents and their parents before them. A line unbroken. You said they were mapping the rim, which is true—we have several of their charts. They are fabulous. The work. The detail. No one else comes near. They longed to be free of the guild. We all do. But did you also know they thought there was a Southern Passage, a route through the ice where the First Stars entered?"

Molly had been standing. She sat down. She knew yet didn't know. She knew their maps were near to perfection and beautiful with their fabulous animals and the gates of gleaming ice to show the stars sailing through. She knew their warning; *Never tell anyone what you are, Molly Sinclair. Never tell them what you are or what you are doing.* For years, she had resented them for running away, for the time lost hiding and waiting in Luna's Cove.

"And if she's craftborn," Draks said, "Then of course they wanted to hide her. I'm surprised they let the boy apprentice."

"They didn't," Molly said. "That was my doing."

"Of course," Ayva said. "It would have gone against everything they believed. Nothing was more important to them than living free."

"It's what we all want," Draks said and he met Molly's gaze. "It's what we fight for. Stay with us, Molly. We'll help you find your brother."

"Stay with you?"

Cai's eyes widened. *No.* She mouthed the words. *They're lying.*

Molly folded her hands on the table. "A moment ago, you didn't believe who I was."

"A moment ago," Draks said, "everything changed."

Ayva sat beside her. "You could have a home with us. You'd no longer have to hide your craft." She reached for Molly's hands, but she pulled away.

"If you wanted the same things as my parents, why didn't you follow them?"

"We wanted to," Ayva said. "But they'd go off on their own and not tell us where. Did you know Senesh and Esty were with us at the start?"

"With you?" She knew no such thing. And yet… It could be true. It could have been when she was very young, or before she was born. She glanced around the cabin. Their wealth was obvious. Gold platters. Jeweled hilts. Gold on the chandelier. Gems and glitter everywhere. Her parents never spoke of money beyond their everyday needs.

"We were on a ship called *The Dawn*."

"You served together?"

"The six of us, yes. But we didn't serve on a ship, we owned it."

The four captains spoke quickly, and the story took shape. Draks and Ayva had met Senesh and Esty by chance at a guild hall, not apprentices but petty thieves—pick pockets in Draks and Ayva's case, burglars for Senesh and Esty though they claimed to steal only from the guild. They weren't proud of their thievery, but it was necessary. They were witches, renegades near the age Molly was now. Draks and Ayva were—had been—master witches until they refused to register their spells. Senesh and Esty were craftborn. All were forced to live in hiding.

Draks mistook Senesh for an ordinary thief, a young man down on his luck and trading illegal spells. He snatched his purse, ran off and stopped in an alley to gloat, only to find Esty waiting for him and Senesh out of nowhere, with a knife at his throat.

Senesh dared him to fight and Draks took the bait and by the time it was over, Drak's nose was broken, he'd lost a tooth and the four of them were comrades, brothers and sisters against the guild.

They introduced Esty and Senesh to Gryer and Krila and the six of them promised to share their take, bring in more witches, men and women willing to swear loyalty. They invented a name, Night Watermen, and swore an oath to someday destroy the guild and its stranglehold on the isles. Time passed. Their escapades brought wealth and wealth brought trouble and trouble brought the need for unity, a vast network of individual pirates, joining their cause. Some stayed apart, but most joined, agreed to their oath and became part of their web.

Molly frowned but listened and held quiet.

Word of their successes grew, and more people arrived. Witches for the most part, but human also. Men and women willing to leave their homes in an effort to destroy the guild and claim a heritage that was rightfully theirs. All but Senesh and Esty.

"The more we succeeded," Ayva said, "the more distant they became. There wasn't a single moment when they left us. They drifted away. We followed, even begged them to stay and help us fight, but by then they were infatuated with their own dreams. We didn't argue, we differed."

Molly weighed their words against her memories. The details were sparse, but they fit, at least around the edges. Except for one word, *infatuated*. It made light of their lives. Of everything that had happened. Call it an obsession, a mission, but an infatuation? No.

Then, dismissively, "There is no Southern Passage," Draks said. "Or if there was, it doesn't matter anymore. Not when we have a chance to end the king's reign." He leaned toward Molly. "Senesh and Esty were craftborn, the strongest of us all. You hate the king. Help us finish what they began."

"I'm not sure how to answer," she said. *Or if hating the king is reason enough to trust Night Watermen.*

"You'd no longer have to hide," Ayva said. "We offer freedom. The chance to be who and what you are."

Freedom? The word stopped her. How could they possibly know how often she dreamt of freedom, tried to imagine how it would feel? To talk openly about the way she shaped her thoughts into something physical? Rain and wind and waves and so much more. To explore the reaches of her craft and share with others. She thought of her crew and the oath they'd sworn. *We are one people. We rejoice in the power we share.*

Draks spoke gently, allowing her time. "We offer a safe home on the seas, a new ship outfitted as royally as befits a daughter of the Sinclairs."

Molly stiffened. His voice was beguiling, layered with lies. "I have a ship," she said firmly. "I want no other. And I was under the impression Night Watermen believe in equality. Full and equal shares."

"Exactly," Draks said. "Once the guild is dissolved and the king's army destroyed, you can choose any ship from their fleet. A palace to live in, or if you prefer, a guild hall all your own."

"I don't want those things," she said. "And the *Fish* is more than a ship, it's my home. I'd as soon cut off my arm as leave her behind."

Ayva shot a glance at Draks. "Of course," he said. "I didn't mean to imply… We'll provide you with a crew of Night Watermen. There are no finer sailors anywhere."

"I'm sure, but…" Molly tread carefully. There were layers here, secrets behind secrets and she couldn't puzzle them out. "I have a crew. We've sworn loyalty."

Ayva stood behind Draks. "But how many are you, dear? Seven? Against the king?"

"Ten," Cai said. "As soon as we find Evan."

"And your *Fish*? There are spells crafted into the ship, of course?"

Molly forced a smile. Ayva was guessing, hoping for information. "The *Fish* is well built," she agreed. "But the *Akistra* is a champion."

"She's built for war and war is coming." Draks said. He leaned back and stared at the cabin's ceiling, the carved sun and moon, dark lights and stars. "Your parents talked constantly about them, the stars and the people they found here. They believed that somewhere in the rim was a gate where the stars entered. It's there in their charts."

"I don't know what they believed," Molly said, suddenly angry. "But I know what they found. Nothing. They found nothing at all."

Draks sighed. "They were the dreamers among us," he said. "We were the thieves while they were the peacemakers. We were angry while they were hopeful, bursting with ideas. Even now, the words every new Waterman swears are theirs. We cut our fingers and pressed them together and swore, the six of us, that a time would come when the guild no longer controlled the crafts and the king no longer tithed every spell. We were a flame, but they were the spark.

"But sparks flare," he continued, "while flames grow. And the more we grew, the more Senesh and Esty's talk turned to doom and darkness and days when, no matter our efforts, the crafts would die.

"They brought ancient, molding books and calculations to prove their stance. Chunks of eternal ice and maps of legendary lands. They said the isles would sink. Or the waters rise. I'm not sure which disaster was supposed to strike first."

Draks stopped. He looked to the door as hurried footsteps drew near. A knock followed, loud and insistent, and a Waterman entered, a man missing three fingers on his left hand. "There's a ship," he announced excitedly. "The *Corona*. The wind's at her back and she's coming on fast."

Draks looked pleased. "Come," he said. "We want you to hear this."

Molly remembered the *Corona*—it was Governor Navarr's ship— and she rose but they held Cai back when she tried to pass. She nodded for Molly to go on, and by the time they reached the weather deck, the port rail was crowded with Watermen waving at the oncoming ship. Her crew was there as well. Madinina and Nick standing apart with Sally. They sent her wary questioning glances and she answered with a nod and a glance she hoped they understood. *Be ready. Trust no one.*

Draks opened a space at the taffrail and Molly pressed in beside him. The *Corona* was nearly on them, growing larger under a gathering sky. The wind picked up and she watched the ship tack as it approached. "Prepare for boarding!" Gryer shouted and the Watermen reached for ropes and pikes. Gryer jumped in to help with the lines and Draks waved toward the ship. Molly glanced about. Not a weapon had been drawn.

The *Corona's* regular crew held back. Their eyes darted warily over the ragged crowd smiling from the rail. And by the time Davit Lake climbed across and the Watermen shook his hand and called him by name, the sailors on the governor's ship looked as confused as she was.

Quickly, she slipped behind the mainmast. He was the last man in the isles she wanted to see, and Davit nearly missed seeing her, he would have, had not someone called his name and he turned and caught sight of her hair, a shoulder, and then her face before she was fully hid. She swallowed and realized how foolish she looked, like a child trying to hide. She stepped out, crossed her arms and glared.

"I thought that was your ship," he said but his voice was off. He put his hands on his belt, then his waist, his sides.

Ayva glanced between them. "You know each other?"

"No," Molly insisted, and it was true. She didn't know anything about him. She never had.

"We've met," Davit said. "Several times."

"Or course," Ayva said haltingly. "But since you can't seem to agree, perhaps you might save the private conversation for later?"

"You don't trust him, surely?" Molly blurted. "He's a kings' man. A spy. He—"

Draks raised his hand, "He's one of us, Miss Sinclair, there's hardly anyone I'd trust more."

"Sinclair?" Davit repeated. "What happened to Jenin Rose? How many names do you have?"

"You're the one that lied," Molly snapped. "I didn't sneak into your house with a squad of soldiers."

"And I didn't pull my sword on you."

"You lied about being a witch."

Davit's eyes widened and Molly froze. *That was wrong.* It was his choice whether to speak of his craft. Not hers.

Gryer glanced between them. "Enough of this," he snapped. "He's no more a witch than a king's man. Someone's been feeding you lies."

It was awkward, but she caught Davit's eye and he nodded back.

Ayva locked her arm in Davit's. "Of course, he isn't a king's man. He wouldn't be standing here if he was. But tell us, you were on the *Castle Star*?"

Davit grew serious. "Yes, and you have to change course. Makken's ship—"

"We will," Draks said offhandedly. "We'll send word to the *Elaphe* and *Cosmus.* But you should have told us you'd met a Sinclair. Did you know she has a brother?"

"His ship is larger than the *Akistra*—" Davit stopped. "A brother?" He cocked his head, blinked. "*The* Sinclairs? That's not possible. You said—"

"We didn't know. You were with us visits, but too young."

"Visits?" Molly was confused again. "What visits?" She would have known if Davit was on the *Ice Warden.* Though… She studied his face. If she could hide in the shadows and listen from the stairs, couldn't he?

Davit's voice rose. "Have you heard nothing?" he said angrily. "The king is here. His ship."

Draks stepped toward him. "You were on it? Where?"

"South of Tars. Not far from the rim. It's heavily armed, with catapults and cog fire. But it's only the one ship and they aren't expecting Night Watermen and the guild together."

"Summon our ships," Gryer said. "We'll meet at one of the nearby isles. The guild will follow. We'll make plans."

Molly thought of Luna's Cove. It was also near the rim. "Wait. The king's ship is near the rim? Where exactly?"

"Can't say for sure," Davit answered. "They could have sailed by now. They could be anywhere."

"You needn't worry," Draks said, misunderstanding. "We'll fight them anywhere."

"Of course," Molly said dryly. "The Night Watermen and guild together." It wasn't difficult to understand. They each had something to gain. But for all Ayva's protesting that they were interested in more than gold, it seemed that was all they talked about. Riches. Wealth. Power when Artice Makken was gone.

"Think of it," Draks said. "Artice Makken has council witches, we have guild masters. He has cannons, so do we. And with the spells on your *Fish* joined to ours, we can win."

"His arrogance is a weakness," Davit said. "He's hiding in a witch crafted fog, not expecting an attack. We can take him by surprise."

"Your *Fish* could lead our fleet.," Draks said eagerly. "With the spells the Sinclairs crafted into your ship, and you at the helm… You'll join us, of course?"

"Join you? No. Not until I find my brother."

Draks backtracked. "And we'll help," he said. "We'll make short work of this war."

"One skirmish," Ayva said, "If your *Fish* is anything like the *Ice Warden*—"

"But I know where he is," Molly insisted. "On the *Swift Pace*. He isn't trying to hide."

"The *Swift Pace*?" Davit frowned. "But that's a prison ship. I saw it, docked alongside the *Castle Star*. If your brother was on board—"

Molly froze.

"He isn't safe," Davit said. "The *Swift Pace* was holding witches. They'd been pressed into service and caught trying to flee."

"But you saw him? My brother?"

"No, I'm sorry. I don't know what he looks like."

"But you met him, at the governor's palace. He was the other guard. Black hair. He helped me steal the chest—" She stopped. She shouldn't have said that. And yet, how could it matter anymore?

"I'm sorry," Davit said gently. "All I know is that prisoners were taken off the *Swift Pace*, chained and loaded onto the king's ship."

Molly's thoughts raced. "Right, then. What if we go with that?" She turned to Draks. "I can't help you," she said. "I'm taking the *Fish* and going after my brother." She looked for Macklin, found him near the rail, behind the crowd. "My crew is free to do as they wish," she said loudly. "*Luna's Watch* is theirs."

Davit touched her arm and she stared at his hand. He pulled back. "It won't work," he said. "The *Fish* will be a beacon. The king's witches will feel it coming. They'll blast you from the seas."

"Then I'll take a smaller ship. I'll tow it behind the *Fish* until I'm close enough, then cross over and slip on board."

"It's the same problem," Davit said. "No one gets through the fog unless they're a friend."

"I'll take a cat boat. I'll hide it in a fog."

Draks grew thoughtful. "That could work. We'll help. Take one of ours."

Molly ignored him. She met Davit's gaze. "The king trusts you?" she asked. "Take me there."

"No!" Draks protested. "I need you, Davit. It's dangerous."

He whipped around. "But you'd send her?"

"That's not what I meant. She's a Sinclair. She's craftborn. She can fight."

"And I can't?"

"It's different. You're human. The king would crush you under his heels."

Davit tensed. "You wanted me to be human, remember? To place me near the king. And you're right. I don't have any craft. You made sure of that."

Draks' eyes widened. "I took you in—" he started, but there was a ruckus, loud voices and shouts and suddenly, Madinina forced her way through. "Leave her be," Molly called as Madinina pushed the Watermen aside. Her black hair blew behind. Her gaze was dark and steady. "Take me with you," she said.

"What? No." Davit looked to Molly. "It's not safe. Who is she?"

"One of my crew," Molly said. "She was on the *Oracle,* shackled in the hold. She jumped overboard to join us."

Gryer laughed. "You hear that. We'll make Watermen of your crew yet. Where were they taking you?"

Madinina said, "To the rim. Seems everyone's trying to get there." She turned to Davit. "I heard what you said, and you need me. You know the king, but I know his witches. They have no love for Artice Makken."

"It's plausible," Draks said, as if it was his to decide. "But your chances might be better if you try a spell."

Molly turned on him. "You want my ship?" she said suddenly. "Take it. On loan. In exchange for Davit and Madinina. But only until I return. I want their help to free my brother. Lend us a small boat and the *Fish* stays here. If neither of us comes back. If we die—" she stopped. Forced herself to breathe, say the words. "If we die, it's yours."

No one moved. There wasn't a sound beyond the wind and water. Draks watched her closely, searching for a lie. "And if something goes wrong? If you're held indefinitely? We, the Night Watermen, not your crew—they'll have *Luna's Watch*—we keep the *Fish*?"

Molly's eyes hardened. She looked to her crew and Macklin met here gaze, but there was no hint of an answer in his eyes. He respected her, but this was her choice. Her decision. Her ship.

She turned to Draks. "You said yourself the Sinclairs built the *Fish*. That's what you want, isn't it? Not me. My ship. While I want my brother."

"Done!" Draks cried. "You need Davit? Take him. Take what you need."

Davit blinked. He opened, then closed his mouth. He had just been traded but looking at him, Molly thought that, surprised or not, he just might want it.

She pressed her arms against her sides. Her hands were shaking, and she didn't want anyone to see. She may have made a terrible mistake and lost the *Fish*, but Evan was in danger and between Draks and Davit, it was clear who she trusted more. The sea and sky and her entire world had shifted.

17

Stars Align

It was an ill-wind that carried Molly toward the fog and the ship Draks Halo provided for the night crossing was little more than a hull with a main sail and jib, an altogether sorry trade for the *Fish*. But Davit and Madinina advised her to take it, not argue. It was a loan they reminded her, not a trade, and she had set the terms herself. Find Evan. Stay alive. Take back the *Fish*.

The words were like the parts of a cog and she repeated them as the fog rose before her. It was immense, even stranger than Davit described, a massive, swirling, witch crafted barrier of gray, black and white that sliced the sea in two. Though to call it a fog was no nearer the truth than calling the bucket Draks Halo gave them a ship, or the talk she'd heard aboard the *Akistra* the truth.

She shook her head in dismay. It was two days since Halo agreed to her plan, more than enough time to realize he had manipulated her and lied. She glanced past Madinina toward the lanterns flickering on the *Akistra, Elaphe,* and *Cosmos,* and other Watermen ships that joined them; carracks and barges, fire ships and rebuilt fishing boats and guild ships as well, more with each passing hour. They carried catapults and incendiaries, vats of cog fire and witches, so many witches with their spells to slow the wind and ease the currents and hasten the battle they seemed so much to want.

She was surprised how quickly the Night Watermen turned themselves from rivals into friends. At the ease with which Draks Halo changed his story then changed it again when he realized the *Fish* was within his grasp. They were allies so long as it suited his purpose though part of it, she admitted, was her purpose too.

Three months ago, on the equinox, this would all have seemed impossible. Today, with the winter solstice—the darkest day of the year—they were united against the king. But afterward? When the days grew long? Molly wondered if she'd still be able to build the haven she dreamed of. Her crew was growing and as soon as Evan was free, she'd have more than just the two of them to think about.

The boat dipped and she hung on as the wind drove them into the fog. Madinina clung to the till and Davit stood in the bow and scanned the dark, churning wall. His hair was soaked, and he was squinting but he was handsome, very much so, and she wondered if Cai thought Evan handsome too.

She had chafed at being left behind, but she'd hit her head and blacked out from the dive and was still recovering. And she was young; how could she possibly understand her feelings? Or Sally Yarrow? When had she stopped being annoyed by Nick's advances and welcomed them instead? Had he said something? Done something? Had they gone for a walk and Sally decided she enjoyed his boyish teasing? Had she kissed him? Where was the book that taught them to know these things?

"Look there," Davit called. "The water's churning, as if two currents are coming together." She peered into the dark and Davit turned, watched her a moment. "I was thinking about you," he said. "About that day we met at Brittle's shop."

"The first time you hit me?" She quipped then, not wanting to sound angry, tried again. "I mean with the door. The door hit me."

"Yes, the door." Davit looked at her. "I was sure I recognized you. And it was the same at the Gold Key, and even when you were Melvin Goodeye and we were sitting on the guild shop floor. It kept nagging at me, and some of it was my craft—I think you brought it out in me—not just the fact of it, but the longing for something that wasn't a lie. And the feeling also that I knew you, had always known you, from long ago."

Molly leaned toward him and listened. This was new for her, this kind of talk. Honesty. Openness. And she had felt the same, not just as if she had always known him, but as if she felt a flaring in her craft, as if it recognized him too. She hadn't seen it until she looked back, but the pieces were there.

"We were children," he said. "I remember visiting your ship with Draks and Ayva and you were hiding on the stairs. They didn't see you, but I couldn't take my eyes off you. They had told me your parents were bad people and I thought they were holding you prisoner. I was frightened for you, until I realized you were hiding, but you would never be anyone's prisoner. Even then. You're the only person I know who's truly free."

"Me? I've never been free. And if I were, I'd give it up in a moment to help my brother."

"That's what I mean. I've always done what I was told. Draks never wanted me to be a witch so I convinced myself that the things that happened to me, the things I made happen, weren't real. Navarr calls himself a human witch, and though I never wanted it to be true, I'm something like that; not so strong as you, but it's there. I can navigate in the dark, ease a wind. Follow you home." He took a breath, let it out. "I convinced myself that anyone could do those things. When Draks needed me to spy, I spied. For him, the king. Navarr. Even now. I'm here because Draks wanted the *Fish*."

Molly cocked her head. "And that's the only reason?"

Davit started to answer, but the wind suddenly changed. The bow dipped into the water; the hull shook. "Over there!" Madinina shouted. "Can you see?"

The fog had thinned. It changed into tendrils of mist and haze and soon, even that was gone. The water, dead ahead, was black. Islands floated where they couldn't possibly be. "What is that?" Molly called. "Not land?"

Davit stared ahead. "Ships," he said tightly. "They're ships. The king's gathered his armada. He tried to tell me, but his council witch stopped him. I should have known."

Molly saw them now. Scores of ships. No, more than that. They were drawn into a circle, a perimeter around the largest vessel of all, the *Castle Star* with sails beyond count and masts rising toward the sky. Something caught her eye and she followed it upward. The dark lights were changing. Ribbons of reds and greens and purple whipped northward overhead. "Winter solstice," she said. "The longest night of the year."

A moment later cannon fire from the other direction burst across the sea. "It's the *Akistra*," Davit said, surprised. "Draks is buying us time."

Molly looked right, then left. It was impossible to make out individual ships, and daylight was hours away, but she could see the separate navies approach in long flanks, the guild and Night Watermen, the *Akistra* firing from the north. The king's armada nearer the ice to the south. And somewhere beyond Makken's fleet, Luna's Cove—still hidden, she hoped— in a different sort of fog.

Volleys came from both directions now, a shot and then an answer, a concussion and a blast, but well off from their position.

They pulled the sails and, like a mouse slipping through a field of wheat, rowed below the towering hulls. Here and there a sailor peered from one of the king's ships, but their attention was northward toward the oncoming battle. No one thought to look down. No one noticed the slender shadow on the waves. And finally, though time seemed to slow, and her words echoed and died, Molly grabbed a cleat on the *Castle Star* and tied their little boat alongside.

There were handholds and ropes fastened from above and Madinina climbed up first then Davit. Molly followed and tried and failed to count the number of decks she passed, the rows of brightly painted gun ports, the carved wooden faces leering all about. She looked up and saw Madinina's legs dangling through a window then Davit disappearing inside. She waited her turn, then threw her leg over a sill and dropped into a lamp lit cabin somewhere on an upper deck.

Madinina had already opened the cabin door a crack and Molly hurried across the floor and peered over her shoulder into a teeming, chaotic passageway with uniformed men and women rushing about.

"You, Sregal. Fincher! Over here," a woman called. "You four to the bosun. Where's my damn gunner?"

They closed the door and Molly stood with her back against the wall, breathing hard. Judging from the look of the washstand, the large sea chest and heavy desk, they had slipped into an officer's cabin. Madinina searched the drawers and pulled out a set of ivory handled pistols. She checked the mechanism and sighted along the barrel. "I'll take these," she said and before Molly could stop her, she was gone, out the door and into the corridor, and Molly was alone with Davit.

His back was turned, and she moved along the wall and studied the array of weapons hanging on display. She pulled down a handgun with a gold handle, cocked, then released it, and tucked it in her belt. She found packets of black powder and helped herself to those and then a larger gun. She turned to show Davit and caught him unfastening his vest.

She stared and reddened as he wadded it up, tossed it behind the bed. He pulled an officer's blue jacket from a stand. He slipped it on and fastened the catches then turned and saw her eyes. "What's the matter?" he asked.

"Nothing, it's just—" Molly stifled a laugh. "I wouldn't know how to button that thing."

"If it troubles you—"

Molly pictured him taking it off again "No! Leave it on. You might need it."

"And you also," he said lifting a second jacket from the stand.

She hesitated, then set down the guns and took the jacket. She slipped her arms through the sleeves, but the cuffs reached beyond her fingertips. She tugged at the shoulders, and folded the cuffs, then stopped and gave it up. "It won't work," she said as she pulled the jacket off. "No one will be fooled."

Davit looked her up and down. She was wearing the same dark leggings she always wore, tall boots, plain shirt and vest, suitable for an ordinary ship, but the *Castle Star?*

"What's wrong?" she asked.

"Nothing, if you're on the *Fish* or *Akistra.* But here? The first person sees you will ring an alarm. Try again. I'll help."

"You don't need—" Molly stopped as he slipped the jacket over her arms and shoulders and ran his hands along the sleeves. His touch was firm and gentle, and she liked it. Liked that she didn't want to push him away or question her thoughts. She closed her eyes and felt his hands move across her arms. The fabric drew in and grew lighter. He tugged the hem, and she heard the rustle of silk and felt the coat ease itself closer around her hips. He was doing it. Him. Davit. Not her. The seams pulled in. The edges softened.

She held her breath as his hands followed the curve of her waist. Buttons fastened themselves and the fabric cinched. It molded itself over her breasts, softened and shaped itself. His fingers brushed the back of her neck and she opened her eyes. He moved toward her and she reached to meet his lips. They kissed, and this time it led to a second, deeper kiss that was all the better because she wanted it to happen.

When at last they pulled away, Davit looked dazed and surprised. "I didn't know I could do that."

"Kiss me or craft a spell?" she teased.

"Both. Either. I've spent a lifetime denying that I had any craft. And I've wanted to kiss you since the first time we met. But the jacket? It fits?"

She held up her arms and looked down. "No boughten spells?"

"As if you would have allowed it." Then, more seriously, "I'm not supposed to be able to do that," he said. "I was tested in a dome. The dark lights never touched me."

"Then they're blind. Or blame the dome. Or the guild. Or all of them. But… Davit, I have to go. I have to find my brother."

"*We* have to find him."

Molly met his gaze then kissed him again, a quick kiss on the lips and his face lit up. She stepped away, turned and opened the door to the sounds of gun fire, cannons on a lower deck, voices shouting along the passageways.

Madinina was waiting alongside the door. She motioned them to follow, hurry, and they were swept into a current of soldiers and sailors, and for everyone that looked stern and angry, two more seemed worried and afraid.

"We go down," Madinina said as they pressed through the crowd. "If your brother's a prisoner, he'll be in the lowest hold." They slowed when guards and crewmen pushed by, rushed when the way was clear and reached the lowest stairs as an explosion rocked the ship.

Lamps shook and boards rattled, and Molly grit her teeth and clung to the wall. The air was sour and stale and there were doors on both sides, locked and barred with metal grates covering small windows. Madinina raised a lamp and they tested bolts and put their ears to the doors until finally, they heard a cry, a woman's voice and then a man's, two men, gruff and loud at the far end of the passageway.

They moved slowly along, and Molly grimaced as she made out a wall with shackles and chains, metal rings hammered into studs and off to one side, as far from the night sky as anything could be, a dome of the stars. It was small, but intact, with the same half walls and rounded ceiling as any in a guild hall would be.

Startled, the guards looked up. Davit lowered his gun. "We're here to check the prisoners," he called gruffly.

"Says who?" one called back.

"Gander," Madinina said, pulling a name from her memory. "Short man, mutton chop beard."

The guards looked at each other, shrugged. "Don't know him, but he'd be up on the gun decks." A large man with a broad chest, the man took in Davit's clothes and smirked. "I thought you royals were all sheltered with the king."

"And we will be, as soon as we check the prisoners."

The second guard, a younger man, eyed Madinina. "I ain't seen you before, have I?"

"They're with me," Davit said.

Molly studied the dome. Everything about it was wrong. Not just its size, but that it was there at all. She touched a column; it was cold, and her fingers came away wet. *Not rim ice.* She turned to catch Madinina's attention and saw a woman half hidden behind the guards.

She thought at first the woman was standing there, then saw her arms. They were chained to the wall above her head. Her hair was matted, and fresh blood dripped from her face and along her neck. She was middle aged; her gaze was unfocused, confused.

Molly turned on the guards. "What are you doing?" she demanded. "Is she a witch?"

"Used to be," the heavier guard boasted. "Ain't one anymore." The table beside him was covered with knives and tools, pinchers, pliers, cutters and flasks and piles of open shells. Their contents were scattered. Four bloodied gems sat in a shallow bowl.

The woman moaned and the guard smacked her across the face. "Here, you want to try? Maybe you can change her mind. Who'd you say you was?"

"Davit Lake. King's ward." He clenched his hands into fists. "What's going on?"

The guard snorted. "Same thing we do to all the prisoners. Rip out their marks. Let them rot in the brig. Wait. I get it. You're looking for gems, aren't you? Forget it. You'll never sell these."

"Why's that?" Madinina asked "You planning to steal them your-self?"

"Nah," the guard gave her a look. "Don't need to steal. The king pays good money if we get a witch to give up her cogs."

"Shut up," the other guard snapped. "You're talking too much." He stepped toward Davit, puffed out his chest. "Get out. All of you. We got orders. I don't care who you are."

Behind him, the woman gathered her strength and spit. The guard flinched. He felt the back of his neck and reeled, but not before Molly drew her knife.

She lunged at the guard, and Davit went for the other. Madinina rushed in to shield the woman.

The fight lasted but a minute. Molly jabbed her blade at the guard's ribs, then bobbed and sidestepped and drew him away from the others.

He reeled and reached for one of his knives, but hit a corner of the table and shells, blades and gems scattered and rolled across the floor. He stumbled and Molly moved in. She pricked his chest with the point of her blade, and he froze and threw up his hands.

The other man grabbed a short sword and came at Davit. They lunged at each other, but Davit was lighter on his feet and slammed his fist into the man's face. He recoiled and Davit grabbed his wrist, banged it against a wall and his blade dropped to his feet. Davit picked it up and drew his gun.

He shoved the man to his knees, noticed a cord around his neck, tugged it and discovered a set of keys. He pulled them free and tossed them to Madinina and a moment later, she unlocked the woman's wrists and eased her to the floor. "Who are you?" the woman rasped.

"Friends," Madinina answered gently. "What's your name?

"Sura Yellen." She coughed and spit blood while Madinina held her shoulders. "I know you?"

"I think so. From Rayshell. A year ago? We were selling to the guild?"

"I remember. You were on the *Eastern Breeze*?"

Molly found a cup and water and helped Sura drink. "I'm looking for my brother," she said. "Fifteen years old. Black hair? He might be a prisoner?"

Sura nodded toward a door. "They keep us in there, but I can't say as I've seen him. It's dark. They pull us out one at a time. That key he's got; it's the only one. They want our crafts." She stopped, coughed then started again. "Be careful. Just because they're prisoners doesn't mean they're on your side."

Molly took the keys from Davit and examined the door. She ran her hand across the fittings and felt a warmth—heat—from a cog. It grew stronger, hotter, burning, and she pulled back her hand. *Find Evan*, she told herself. *That's first. Find Evan. Stay alive. Take back the Fish.*

The door rumbled suddenly. The floor shook and then the walls. Molly braced herself as, somewhere above, a cannonball hit the ship. She waited till it eased then, *Find Evan. Stay Alive. Take back the Fish*, she murmured, and reached again for the door.

She winced and forced herself to ignore the heat, slid the key in the lock, and whatever spell was there faded as a mechanism clicked and the door sprang open. She took a breath and with Madinina and Davit at her back, stepped through and found herself on a dimly lit landing with a short set of stairs leading down to the prison hold.

She blinked in the gloom, then spun as the door closed behind them. Davit lurched to grab it and Madinina went for the bolt, but too late. Davit ran his hand along the seams and Molly did as well but there was no inside knob, no bar or handle, no heat, or hidden lock.

They glanced warily at each and Molly slipped the key in a vest pocket, patted it to be sure it was there, then turned back around. That was when the smell hit her, the dank sense of rot and the sound of men and women moaning. Her eyes grew accustomed to the dark and where she had expected to see chains and bars caging the prisoners, she found men and women crowded into a huge, empty hold. Some were standing, others seated against the walls, some too weak for even that. Two men stood wrestling off to the side, a circle of onlookers goading them on.

Across the floor and up along the walls and decking overhead, a locking spell of iron mesh surrounded them all.

She started down the steps when a woman laughed derisively. "What's this? Pretty guards? Come to let us out? Let us out!" Her voice grew louder. "Let us out!"

A stave flew past Molly's head and she ducked, and Davit swerved, and the hold burst with sudden light and a hundred faces turned their way. But only for a moment, and the light blew out. "What's the matter, kingie?" A man shouted. "Afraid of a little spell?"

Molly took a step. "I'm no king's man," she called into the dark.

"Woman then," the man laughed. "Makes no matter. You're one of them."

She peered ahead, but the gloom remained, and it was difficult to see. The smell was awful and there were sick and wounded people everywhere. No sign of Evan, but he was here. She felt certain.

Madinina joined her on the step. "Sura Yellen sent us," she called. "She said you'd help."

"What'd you do with her?" a man cried and suddenly he was on the bottom step, pulling at Molly's arm. His fingers dug into her flesh and he tried to drag her down and she jerked free but his hand—his entire arm— came off and she teetered back. The man cackled as he stepped away and waved his real, intact arm for them to see. The arm in Molly's hand was no more than a splintered board.

She'd had enough. These people might be dangerous, but whatever spells they were still capable of crafting were limited, small and useless. She raised her pistol, shot overhead and the prisoners cowered as droplets of a dark, viscous liquid splattered their shoulders and pooled at their feet. Molly grimaced and slapped at her clothes, and Davit and Madinina did the same but the liquid, so far as she could tell, did no harm.

She stepped into a pool of slime ignored it, and it disappeared. "Evan?" she shouted. "I'm looking for a boy. Evan Sinclair?" She pushed her way through the crush of prisoners.

The cackling started again. "Pick me!" they called. "You can get in my pants."

"Quiet!" a man shouted. "They're looking for Evan. Sura Yellen sent them."

"No, you be quiet," another man called. "Sura's dead. They're lying."

Someone was singing.

> *Well its heave the ropes and set the sails,*
> *The stars are shining through the veil.*
> *The river flows, a witch is born.*
> *We craft our spells and sail at dawn.*
> *Thousand years begin anew."*

Others took up the song, but it came out more a dirge than a chanty.

"Molly?"

She glanced at Davit. Had someone called her name? She grabbed a woman by her collar. "Is he here? My brother. Where—?"

"Molly?"

She heard it again, a small voice. She let go the woman's shirt and pushed her way forward. The crowd pressed behind her.

"Molly, is that you?"

"Where are you?" she shouted.

"Here. By the wall."

A path opened and Molly looked down and found her brother sitting, his back against the wall. His knees were pressed to his chest. An elderly woman with long white hair leaned heavily against his shoulder. "I'm all right," he said softly. He put his arm around the woman's shoulder and helped her sit, then rose to his feet. He was shaking and unsteady and Molly's heart fell.

No, she thought. *You don't look at all right.* His face was bruised, hair matted. He looked skinnier if that was possible, but... He was whole and standing. She pulled him close and they held each other then stepped back. It felt like years since she'd seen him and she drank in his face, his eyes and hair and what seemed to be a new, determined edge to his mouth.

He started to say something, then saw Davit. "What's he doing here?"

"My name is Davit. Davit Lake."

"Governor's nephew. I know who you are."

"Evan, it's all right. He saved my life."

"No. It's a trap." Evan glanced worriedly toward the woman.

"He's not who we thought he was. If it wasn't for him, I wouldn't have gone to Hayden Hall or—"

Evan blinked. "You were at Hayden Hall?"

"I didn't know you left. I'm sorry. I—"

He grabbed her arm. "Was Cai there? Is she all right?"

"Yes. She's with my crew. I'm trying to tell you. We'll get you out. They're fighting." Molly's heart raced. Her brother had changed. He was more certain of himself, no longer a boy. She glanced over her shoulder. The crowd that had heckled her stood in a close circle. They were quiet. Respectful.

"Braithe?" Evan said to the woman. "Did you hear? We're leaving. Cai's waiting. I told you about her." He looked to Molly. "You have a key? Or a spell?"

The prisoners pressed close, their voices loud again. "They have a key," someone repeated, and the word quickly spread. "We're getting out."

"It's locked," Molly said. "The door's sealed."

"No matter." Braithe chirped as she played with the ends of her hair. Her voice was high and childlike. "The boy keeps the cog lights burning. Cleans the water. Brushes my hair. He does that. He does." She lowered her voice. "King Makken thinks our cogs are gone. But they're not. Evan brought them back."

"She's been here longer than anyone," Evan said. "I'd have been kicked to death if she didn't help me. There's no clean water and they keep it dark, but I figured out their cogs. The muck that keeps falling, it used to burn." He knelt down. "Braithe? Can you walk now? It's time to leave."

Her eyes brightened. "I'm going to hang him, you know, the king. Hang him till he rots. Give me my brush."

Evan found the mother-of-pearl hairbrush tucked in behind her legs. "Here you go," he said, and he took one arm and Davit took the other. Braithe winced as she stood, and the crowd opened to let them through.

Madinina rushed ahead to the stairs and Molly joined her, then faced the crowd. "They're fighting above," she called. "The Night Watermen and the guild against the king. We don't know which way it's going, but there are hundreds of ships out there, war ships from every side. But we'll find a way off this prison ship—"

"—Or go down fighting," someone called.

She looked to Evan. "Or go down fighting," she called back.

Someone clapped their hands, slowly and loud and the sound broke through the murmurs. "That's fine for thieves," a man shouted. "But she's not even a witch."

Molly peered into the dark. "Who's there?" she called. "Show yourself."

"It's the governor," Evan said quietly. "Harkin Navarr. Only he's not governor anymore."

Molly picked out Navarr, alone against a wall. He had stopped clapping and was worrying the buttons on his coat, touching them then circling his hands. The buttons glowed. Orbs of light they looked as if they had come free and were hovering in the air, following his hands. But only for a moment, and the lights faded.

"I thought they kept only witches in here," she said.

"That's all he does," Evan said. "All he can do."

"Let him rot," someone called. "He's a human witch. He's what's wrong with the world."

Molly thought of Navarr's glee as his guests dropped their cogs into his chest. He was a human witch, gloating as he stole their spells and hid his nature from a world that wouldn't believe such things could be true. She thought of Davit Lake, human like Navarr. An outlier like her. His hands touched with magic as he traced the curve of her waist. Whatever he was… It didn't matter anymore.

Madinina pulled Molly from her thoughts. "The door's too tight," she said. "There's no gap and I have nothing to pry with."

"Spells don't work on the door," Evan said. "Their wards are too strong."

Molly stepped in and traced her hands along the door frame and felt nothing, no ridge, no break or gap. The seal was as smooth as if it didn't exist.

Evan said, "There's not a witch in here hasn't tried to open it."

Molly nodded at Evan, but it was Braithe she noticed and the way she played with her hair and shaped the strands around her fingers. She was smiling, the only person in the crowded, frightened hold.

Molly knelt in front of the door and put her face to the floorboards. She ran a finger along the edge and felt air, a gap thinner than a fingernail. "Sura?" she called to the other side. "Can you hear me?"

A murmur returned.

"Stay there," she called, then she sat up and looked to Braithe. "Do you mind," she asked gently. "Could I trouble you for a few lengths of hair."

The older woman smiled. "I was hoping you'd ask. I told you we'd hang the king."

"Just a few strands," Molly said. "I won't need more."

Curious, Evan helped Braithe snap off a few lengths of hair. They were longer than his arm and white, and there wasn't a touch of magic about them.

Molly broke off a few lengths of her own shorter, dark hair and twisted them with Braithe's into a thread, then wove it in and around itself until it formed a thin rectangle. She placed it atop the real key and pressed until she had an impression, a copy equal in shape but thinner by far. She breathed on it then took away the real key, and a copy—a replica that was neither a spell nor a boughten cog—remained.

She worked it under the door, across the threshold and out the other side where Sura Yellen picked it up, used her own craft, and pressed the new key into the hole.

The mechanism shifted. The lock released, and Molly pushed open the door and instantly, the shock of cannon fire reached from the upper decks. The prisoners didn't care. They rushed from the hold and breathed in the air. It was sharp and gritty and carried a smell like freedom. They surged out of the hold and down the passageway, up the stairs and into the battle.

18

Warmth Walks Where I Walk

Molly was picked up in the press of shoulders, arms and bodies, of witches suddenly free and hungry to find someone, anyone, and make them pay for jailing them in that dark, rotting hole. It was a mob, and they carried her with them, her feet barely touching down as they overwhelmed the stairs.

She craned her neck and struggled to see Madinina near the front. Her fist was raised, and witches surrounded her. They shouted and called for rebellion, for blood and death and revenge. Evan was behind them and off to one side, slowed by Sura Yellen and Braithe's faltering steps. The older woman winced in pain one moment and laughed the next as she slowly climbed the stairs. Finally, at the top, the corridor widened, and Molly wrenched free and shouted to Davit. They pressed against the wall and let a score of prisoners, Harkin Navarr among them, past until finally, Evan caught up. They kept together as far as the next companionway but Braithe's legs crumbled and she sank to the floor.

Evan and Davit pulled her aside and Madinina glanced back. "I'll find you," she called as the crowd pulled her out of sight. "Free the crafts," the witches cried. "End the guild!" They grabbed axes and smashed water barrels. Crewmen scattered rather than fight while others—sailors and a few soldiers among them— ripped off their Jamasak jackets and grabbed staves and clubs, anything that resembled a weapon, and joined their side.

Molly stopped at a porthole and froze as she stared to the sea. Davit pressed in beside her. Daylight had come. Winter solstice. The shortest day. Lightening flared and thunder mingled with explosions. And through it all, below the skies and across the sea, the entire world seemed to be on fire.

Everywhere she looked there was smoke and flames. Scores of ships with their sails scorched and ruined. Masts shattered. Decks ablaze. She saw people leaping from spars, black dots of heads and arms flailing as they swam, desperate to reach their boats. She saw the king's armada, no longer massed together and protecting the *Castle Star* but divided and lost among the advancing ships, their defenses broken.

Yet… Most of the ruined hulks, so far as she could tell, were Watermen and guild. The king was winning. His fireships and towering catapults, witch-guided cannons and flaming arrows engulfed and overpowered Halo's fleet.

Davit shook his head. He saw nothing anywhere to give him hope until, suddenly, "Wait! Look there." He grabbed Molly's arm. "The *Akistra*. She's afloat."

Molly peered through the smoke. "I see her, yes. The foresail's down. They're returning fire, but…" her heart stopped as she searched the nearby waters. "I don't see the *Fish*."

Davit turned to Molly. Her clothes were disheveled, her hair a wild mass, and though the air was warm, he felt her shiver. "You would feel it, wouldn't you?" he asked. "If the *Fish* was gone? You would know?"

Molly wasn't certain. She had never truly known whether her parents were dead. Never woken from a dream or felt a sudden emptiness that told her they were gone. But then… How could she *not* know if the *Fish* had been destroyed? It would call her, wouldn't it, in some secret language, an echo spell all its own?

The guild ships were fighting back. A few Watermen vessels had broken through the king's formation, their cannons strafing the decks and taking a toll, and that was only what she could see through the narrow porthole. She counted five, six, seven king's ships with their flags in tatters, dead in the water or in flames. The battle was not yet decided.

She moved to another porthole and was surprised to find the ice nearer than she expected. They'd been heading southward—past Luna's Cove—while she was below. The fog had thrown her off. The towering sheets of ice caught the rising sun and mirrored the flames and dying ships.

And there was free floating ice as well, lone shimmering mountains that calved and drifted from the rim. It was an odd thing and she didn't like it. Didn't like that she couldn't tell which way the battle was going. That she couldn't find the *Fish* or *White Lily* and didn't know where her crew was or if they were alive and how they'd regroup if she ever found them.

Evan had roused Braithe and they started moving again but didn't get far when they heard gun shots and shouting. The corridor widened in front of a set of doors and they glanced right and left then took a chance and entered, Davit first, then Evan with Braithe and Sura Yellen and Molly behind. They stepped into a long cabin crowded with people and Molly had just enough time to notice the row of ice statues when, too late, she realized their mistake.

"Davit? Davit Lake?" A voice from the far end of the cabin called. Soldiers and witches, astrologers in white and courtiers in bright clothes stopped and glanced their way. Molly had never been in the king's presence—few outside Jamasak had—and she moved nearer as Artice Makken called again.

His high-backed chair was alive with branches and leaves, flowers in full bloom and colors bright as the sun. Behind him, a bank of windows—ice, not glass— let in a filtered light. Cannons fired on the upper decks and the tables rattled but Makken swept his hand as if nothing was the matter. "Davit!" he called. "Come here where I can see you. Finally! Someone's who's not afraid of a storm."

Davit took her hand. "Remember," he said, "you're Jenin Rose. You're human, not witch and… I may have told him…" He glanced away. "I left to find a woman."

"You what?" she started, but Davit was already gone. She craned her neck, trying to see and nearly hit the statue beside her, a queen shaped from ice, her dress gathered into folds. Frowning, she touched it, then stared at the moisture on her fingers. The same moisture as the pillars in the fake dome. How much of this star-forgotten ship was real, she wondered, and how much held together by the witches standing about the walls. Nearby the windows. Alongside the door. Everywhere she looked, holding their spells in place.

"Let the man through," the king called. "Let him breathe. And some-one bring wine." The king sounded cheerful, as if the battle outside had nothing to do with him. "Ilenna? Where are you? Davit's here."

Molly moved through the crowd until she saw a woman step from the huddle of white-robed astrologers and approach the king. She was dark and angular, and Molly recognized Ilenna Fran from Davit's de-scription. The king's philosopher. She had designed the *Castle Star*, and Evan's prison, and probably the frozen statues as well. "You see," Makken said. "He came back. I knew he would."

Ilenna said something, but her words were cut short as cannons fired and the deck groaned. Tension swept the crowd. "Damn!" Makken shouted. "Where are my witches? Quiet that storm! Davit, what did you say?"

Davit said, "I'm sure I told you. I did leave. I've only just returned."

The king looked confused. He nodded toward Ilenna. "She thinks I can't remember what I ate for breakfast, let alone how near the rim we are. Did I show you my maps?"

Footsteps rumbled outside the doors. Heads turned and the mur-muring grew agitated. Soldiers prodded everyone back against the walls and Molly ducked between two men and moved nearer.

Makken pulled on Davit's arm. "The *Castle Star*'s a fortress," he said. "I told them; it can't sink. But do they care? I have a castle picked out for you when we get home. Have you heard?" He raised his voice. "We're purging the guild halls. Restoring the crafts."

"Please not Navarr's castle," Davit joked. "Anywhere but that," but the king didn't laugh.

"Of course not," he said irritably. "I'll give you one of the guild's. Have I told you, they're hiding witches. Lying about the crafts." He stopped suddenly. "Wait." His eyes brightened. "Sly boy. You thought I'd forget. You found her, didn't you? Is she here, your sweetheart? Speak up. Don't deny me a few pleasures."

Davit scanned the crowd. He caught Molly's eye and motioned her forward, but suddenly, Evan was there as well. He grabbed her arm, held her back. "I'll be fine," she whispered. "But if anything goes wrong, find the *Fish* and get to the *Akistra*."

"The Watermen ship? Why?"

Molly looked at her brother. He hadn't seen Cai disappear into the dark waters. Didn't know about the trade she'd made with the Watermen, the *Fish* for his safety. "There's no time to explain. Just, if anything goes wrong, the Night Watermen will take you in. Cai's with them, and safe. She loves you."

He dropped his hand. "She said that?"

"She didn't have to," Molly said. "And we'll talk, but later. There isn't time."

She stepped forward and Makken saw her. "Finally!" he exclaimed. "Come here, come closer. She's perfect! Davit. Shame on you for hiding her. Tell us your name, dear."

The king looked older than Molly expected; his hair was white, his shoulders bent, face as wrinkled as any fisherman. *Go carefully*, she warned herself. *There's a trap here and Makken's not the only enemy.* "I'm Jenin Rose, sir."

"And such a rose," Makken said and Molly tried not to cringe. "Don't be shy."

She glanced to Ilenna. As erratic as the king was, she trusted her less. Ilenna's sharp gaze darted from Molly's face to her belt, her boots and vest, never resting. She passed judgment, moved along. She was still looking her over when a light flared through the windows and she turned—they all did—and tried to see. A vessel was floundering, and there was another ship behind it, nearly lost in the smoke and flares.

Thick though the windows were, Molly knew her ship. She recognized the castles and the curve of the *Fish's* bow, the line of her planks. Her heart skipped. It was the *Fish.* Her ship, emerging from the smoke. Sections of the bulwark were gone, and the main mast was leaning, but it was there, intact. And just ahead, the Night Watermen's *Akistra* with most of its sails billowing.

The *Fish* was on the inside nearer the *Castle Star,* the *Akistra* off its bow. There was no sign of *Luna's Watch* though with all the smoke and haze, it could be anywhere. She wondered where Macklin was and if Brigit was directing the *Fish's* guns or if there were Night Watermen on board.

"… Jenin?"

Molly pulled back.

"I asked if you and your husband would join me for dinner."

"Husband?" Her eyes widened and she flicked a glance at Davit. "Excuse, me, sir. We're not married."

"Of course, you're not," the king chuckled, but a commotion rose at the far end of the hall. Molly glimpsed Evan pushing his way toward the doors while a crowd of angry witches tried to break in. There was pounding, and the sound of axes cutting through wood. The doors flew opened and Molly thought she saw Madinina, but the king's soldiers were already blocking the way. There was brawling inside as well, and it was difficult to see who was pushing in and who was trying to get out.

"Turn around," Davit whispered. "Don't stare."

"It's just a storm," Makken said loudly. "And if anyone panics, I'll throw them in the sea myself." He leaned back in his chair and seemed to wither. "Witches. Soldiers. They're useless," he said, quieter now. "Frightened children. While I've found the source, and solstice is on us. Isn't that right, Ilenna?"

"Of course," Ilenna said. "That's exactly right, sir. We're near the rim."

"But the rim circles all the isles," Molly said before she could stop herself. "Why does it have to be here?" *So near Luna's Cove,* she thought, but she didn't say that aloud.

Ilenna raised a brow. "It's the guild that brought the battle here, not us."

Makken glared at her. "That's not true," he said. "We're here to find the relics. Renew the crafts. Here. The generations will begin again. It's why we've come."

"But why couldn't it have been Doshaget or Pyr?" Molly asked. Most all the isles are near the rim." *And why had her parents picked Luna's Cove? Was it because of the southern rim? Was something different here?"*

Ilenna ignored her. "We've talked about this, my lord. The guild wants you to believe that the appearance of all these new relics matter, but they don't." Her words were placating, and Molly wondered which of the two was in charge. Except that Ilenna was right in one thing: it didn't matter. She didn't need to be careful. She needed to get off this ship.

Makken's mind wandered again. "Davit, she's perfect," he crowed. "If she wasn't human, I'd name her to my council. I assume you've talked to her family. I can draw up papers; assure them you have certain privileges and properties. Tell me again where you were raised, child?"

Davit nudged Molly, but she wasn't paying attention. The guards had barricaded the doors, but the fighting had escalated and more of the witches inside were fighting alongside Evan. He grabbed a soldier by his jacket while a woman threw herself at the doors.

"Sophen," Davit answered. "She's from Sophen."

"Really? She doesn't sound like Sophen."

"Born there," Davit backtracked. "She's more recently from Doshaget. The journey wasn't far."

"From Jamasak it isn't far," Ilenna said. "And you didn't know where she was. And now you're here so quickly, along with the other ships?"

A jolt rocked the deck and the king grasped his chair. Gray smoke blew into the hall. The guards tried erecting a barricade, but it was overwhelmed as witches and crew and soldiers and courtiers pushed their way in while others fought their way out. She saw Evan jump on a soldier's back while a woman kicked the man's calf.

She couldn't wait. She lunged past the king and bounded toward the windows. She had no plan and knew only that they needed to get out. *Reach the* Fish. *Stay alive.* She kicked aside a table and sent platters of mangoes and grapes flying then jumped to reach the long bay of windows, touched one, and stopped.

She was right. They weren't ice. They were a cog, crafted to please the king and impress his enemies. Everything about the *Castle Star* was a fake, dying from its center. Same as the guild. Same as their cogs. She set her hand to the windows, and pushed her thoughts further in, inside the ice.

Eyes closed, her thoughts sharpened. She found the pattern of water and air that shaped the ice-like window. She felt the bonds of pressure holding it together and followed it with her thoughts, her craft, the heat of her blood. She thought of the sea that lapped against the real ice. Of rain that fell from clouds and water that evaporated upward. She thought of dampness and puddles and droplets of dew. Of sunlight filtering through waves, of water in all its forms. And the windows began to thin. Ice softened and pooled into droplets and disappeared.

Wind gusted through the empty panes and she opened her eyes to the flare of blue and yellow incendiaries, flaming arrows and ships on fire, lightening and rain. It was storming outside, and the horizon was a mass of rolling warships and angry waves. She filled her thoughts with a single image and reached toward the *Fish*.

"*Come find me,*" she chanted to her ship. "*Swim past the cannon fire. Sail past the arrow's sting. Warmth walks where I walk. Carry me home.*"

Lightening flashed and someone on the *Fish's* deck fired a cannon-ade and she saw figures on board. People running about. She saw the fish, the figurehead, open its eyes—

And they grabbed her, the king's soldiers. They wrenched her from the broken window and dragged her across the floor. She pitched and kicked, but they were large men and they knocked her down and shoved her to her knees in front of the king. The floor, she noticed wryly, was wet and cold.

Two more guards surrounded Davit. One of them, a boy, looked more frightened of the king than of Davit. The other, a woman, pressed a blade against his throat.

"Leave him!" Molly shouted. She tried to stand but one of the guards kicked her down and she winced and tasted blood. "Leave him," she repeated. "It's me you want."

"So, it seems," Ilenna said. Her voice was flat and hard. "Who were you talking to?"

"It's not even ice," Molly said. "Anyone could have broken through."

"Anyone didn't. You did. And you didn't answer my question." She grabbed Molly's chin, pinched hard and forced her to look up. "No gems? I have a prison full of your sort."

The king looked annoyed. "Leave her alone. You can see she never apprenticed."

Ilenna let her go. She loomed over Molly. "What then?" she demanded. "Your parents too poor to test you in a hall?"

"Enough, Ilenna," the king said. "We haven't time. If she's a witch, then she's been lying to Davit." He motioned to the guards. "Back away, all of you."

Molly was released and this time when she tried to stand, no one stopped her. The two who'd been holding Davit exchanged a glance and took a slow step back, then another, then turned and fled with others for the doors.

The light outside was changing. Shadows darkened the water and the sky was gray. Molly saw the *Fish*, sailing dead on for the *Castle Star*.

Its mainsail filled the windows. The bow pointed directly toward her. She had called and the ship answered. It was sailing directly at them.

Her thoughts reeled to the last time the *Fish* rammed a ship and she stood helplessly by as it climbed the *Oracle's* hull. Timbers split and the deck buckled. The *Fish* saved itself, but the *Castle Star* was far larger. Her ship would never survive…

She spun and craned her neck and searched for Evan. She had to reach him, now, before it was too late.

Ilenna stepped toward the king. "You can't keep searching for relics."

"I don't have to," Makken answered flatly. "The ice is thinning. The thousand years begin again."

"And how is that supposed to happen?" she scoffed. "There is no other side."

Soldiers and witches were backing away behind them. Molly looked to Davit. "Get Evan," she said. "Find Madinina. Hurry!" He was gone in an instant, and no one stopped Molly as she rushed for the windows. The smoke had momentarily thinned and the *Fish* was nearer, closing the gap. Its wooden eyes opened and stared at the *Castle Star.* "No!" she shouted. "Get back!"

She saw Macklin on the forecastle, Brigit loading a musket, Nick scrambling up the ratlines. She couldn't see Tribolt or Troth and didn't know if Sally was alive or if Cai was with them, but the ship had been hit. Her stomach lurched. Streams of smoke drifted across the deck. A ragged hole gaped in the boards. The binnacle was gone, and sails flapped useless from the yards. The foremast was shattered and leaning. It looked too brittle to stand.

Evan was suddenly beside her, and Madinina then Davit with a soldier on his heels. He spun and wrestled the pistol from the man's grip then slammed the butt against his shoulder. The man staggered back then faltered and tripped and did not try again. "Where's Braithe?" Molly asked. "And Sura Yellen?"

Evan shook his head. "Sura joined the others. Braith's gone. But Molly, it's all right. She said… She said she was free." He stopped as he saw the *Fish* coming toward them. He stood there a moment, not moving, then, "Cai!" he shouted desperately. Then louder, again, leaping for the window; "Cai! I'm here."

"Evan?" A girl's voice called across the water. "Evan? Where are you?"

His face fell as the *Akistra* appeared behind the *Fish*. Archers stood along the gunwale and storms of flaming cog arrows flew at the *Castle Star*. Dark smoke billowed from the lower cannon ports and Night Watermen ran furiously about putting out fires, working what remained of the sails while the *Fish* sailed forward.

Molly pushed Evan aside as a spray of gunshots strafed the upper decks and the *Akistra* fired and fired again. Cannon shots flew and catapults launched fiery boulders. The *Castle Star* groaned and returned fire.

The *Fish* slowed. It came no closer. Molly craned her neck and gauged the distance, and though the *Castle Star* sat higher in the water, their window was on a lower deck. The distance between them too far to jump, but if she grabbed a rope and swung…

She shouted and caught Nick's attention. She motioned to the line still fastened near his feet and motioned again to be sure he understood. She climbed to the sill, threw her leg over the edge and Evan climbed up alongside her. She watched as Nick tied the line off above his head, fastened a weight and checked the knots.

She leaned out, stretched her arm. "*Come,*" she chanted as he heaved the line. "*Swim past the cannon fire. Sail past the arrow's sting. Reach for these waiting hands. Carry us home…*" and caught it.

She passed the rope to Evan. There was shooting above them, muskets and smaller guns spraying the *Fish's* deck. The *Castle Star's* heavier guns were aimed at the *Akistra* and swinging across, they'd be open targets, but they had to try.

Evan wrapped his ankles above the metal hooks and kicked off. Molly pushed and he swung low across the water, higher as he arced toward the *Fish*. He reached it and hovered over the deck until, glancing down as he started to swing back, he let go the rope, dropped and hit the deck and rolled.

Nick retrieved the line, threw it again and Madinina crossed over, and Davit after that. The line came back, and Molly caught it and glanced, one last time, at the king. He was sitting on the floor now, alone and leaning heavily against his chair. His face was cut, and he put his hand to his cheek, stared at the blood. Ilenna was nowhere to be seen. She was dead perhaps, lost in the spiral of smoke or maybe she had deserted with the crowd. Heavy guns roared from the upper decks. Smaller guns popped and cracked in the halls.

Molly stood and balanced on the sill. She wrapped her hands around the rope. "*Sail past the arrow's sting,*" she chanted. "*Swing above cannon fire. Fly now my craft-wrought line. Carry me home.*" She leapt…

…And had just enough time to wonder why the *Fish* hadn't rammed the *Castle Star,* and for one glorious moment, she was flying.

She felt as if time had slowed and her ship's foremast wasn't ruined and the shots flying around her could do no harm. She looked for a sign of the phosphorescent glow on the *Fish's* keel. It wasn't there. Instead, a shadow stretched across the hull, between the waterline and cannon ports, a shadow she had never seen before.

And it came to her, an understanding that had taken all this time. Her parents hadn't abandoned them. They hadn't run away. They were desperate to understand what was happening, here at the end of the thousand years. They had built the *Fish* to be their guards, their eyes and ears watching over her and Evan should anything happen to them. It was a weapon. The lesser spells, those that cleared barnacles and tightened the chinking and strengthened the sails, were crafted to renew themselves. If the greater spells had been hidden, it was only because they hadn't been needed before.

She landed amidst a volley of gun fire, stumbled and rolled and tried to right herself and fell again. "I'm all right," she called as she pushed herself up on her hands. Her crew was there. They raced about the deck with their arms over their heads as boards shattered and spars toppled and fell.

She tried to rise, but a shock of pain stabbed her side and she collapsed and lay there and listened for the sounds of the rudder turning, lines slipping through blocks. They didn't come. The *Fish* was dead in the water.

She was past exhaustion and her entire body ached, but she was back on the *Fish*, and they were together. Her ear was pressed against the deck and the hum and vibrations were different than she'd ever heard. Not silent—the wind still hit the ruined sheets; waves still rocked the hull—but the *Fish* didn't answer.

She lifted her head and stared toward the sea. It was dotted with ships, most of them smoldering, too damaged to sail. She thought of her parent's *Ice Warden*, how wonderful it would be if suddenly, at that very moment, its bow came riding across the waves. It would be larger than the *Fish*, at least she thought so. There was so much about her parent's ship she no longer remembered.

She clenched her jaw and forced herself to sit. She thought of the ship model the Watermen had made so much of. The details were perfect, even to the *Ice Warden's* oars. They were straight and long. Exactly below the gun deck where she'd seen the shadow line on the *Fish* just now and wondered why the keel light hadn't returned.

Keel lights and weapons. Shadows and oars.

Molly blinked. She turned, straightened her legs then stood and started running. Davit watched her, and Evan and Cai and the rest of the crew. They called, asked if she was hurt but there was no time to answer. She threw back the shattered hatch cover and jumped to the deck below. She landed in a crouch then straightened and paused while her eyes adjusted to the dimmer light and found them, exactly where Senesh and Esty Sinclair had left them for her to find. A part of the planking crafted between shadows. A line of oars built straight and true and never needed until now.

She ran the length of the deck, down along the starboard wall, back on the port. She jumped over cannons and fallen barrels and masses of ropes, scarcely lifting her hand from the wood as she ran.

She thought of the replication spells she used when she stole jewelry. The finding and hiding spell that disguised the oars was not so different. A trick of one board touching the next, the true shape hidden, the new shape smoothed over.

Her fingers swept the boards as she ran and she could almost feel them, the long shafts and rounded handles waiting in the shadow until she'd circled the deck and the full strength of the spell passed through her, out from her fingers and into the wood.

The ship changed at her touch. Not silently but with a grating sound as if it had a voice of its own. Boards lengthened and stretched. Portholes opened. Oars extended, and with and no need of human hands to guide them, dipped deep in the water and pulled against the churning waves.

The *Fish* began to move. It pulled from the *Castle Star*'s shadow and away from the *Akistra's* towering sides. Molly reached the upper deck and the first hard drops of rain hit her face. The brief solstice day had faded, and dark lights shimmered across the sky. The last thing she was aware of was the sound of cannon fire grown faint as the *Fish* sped away. An explosion and then a pause, an answer and a pause.

And lightening, she remembered that later. She remembered Harkin Navarr climbing in a boat. Scrud was there as well, and others. Women and men, soldiers, Watermen and witches. The sea was dotted with people fighting for a handhold, a seat on a boat, anything they could cling to among the skeletons of burning ships. The *Akistra* was still afloat, as was the massively disabled *Castle Star* and she thought she saw *Luna's Watch*, though she was never sure.

The deck rocked beneath her and the oars drew a steady rhythm. She didn't know their destination, only that they were leaving the battle behind and the dark lights were out. She would remember that later; bands of color pointing toward the south, brighter, stronger, fiercer than she'd ever seen. And the rain; it was cold this near the rim. Its touch brought a deep, fearful chill.

19

Solstice

Thousand Years Begin Again

It was the cold that woke her, more than the hard deck or the rough blanket someone had drawn across her shoulders. She raised her head and listened to the waves slapping against the hull and the wind in the tattered sails, but no cannon fire. No battle sounds. They were safe, at least for now.

Molly gathered the blanket and tried to stand but settled for sitting. The sky had cleared, but it was still dark. Lanterns hung from the ship's walls; not many, but enough to walk the deck without stumbling. Was it over, the fighting? Were Draks Halo and Ayva Trill still alive? Or the king? It felt strange to have slipped away before the battle was done and not know which way it had gone.

She turned and saw Evan first then Cai. They were sitting with their backs against one of the few lengths of bulwark that hadn't been destroyed. Their shoulders were touching. They were holding hands. She watched for a moment, the easy way they leaned together, their faces open even amid the ruin. Macklin and Davit were gathering charred boards, piling them out of the way. Brigit stood just beyond, and Nick was climbing the mainmast. Something about it looked off, a crack maybe or a damaged yard? Not so serious as the ruined foremast, but something?

Sally noticed her sitting and hurried over. Her hair was tied back, and she looked tired but unharmed. Always the navigator, she had been watching the southern sky. "Where are we?" Molly asked.

"South and east of Luna's Cove. We're drifting with the current. Are you all right?"

"I think so, yes." Molly rubbed her face then looked across the water and stared.

Ahead and off the starboard bow icebergs floated freely, small flat pans and sharply angled towers, some the size of houses, others human sized like sentinels marking the way. Molly had seen free-floating ice before, not often and usually from a hilltop on Luna's Cove, but she had never been so near the rim. Never seen so many calved and floated blocks. And the wall itself… It stretched east and west ahead of them; a towering wall too high for anyone to see over. Too deeply encased in magic to cross. Too ancient and riddled in tales to understand.

The ice was beautiful in its starkness, palettes of grays and shadows and fissures caught in the moon's reflected light. But where on maps it was drawn as a simple line circling the isles here, even in the scant light, it was far more complicated. Braided streams of running water flowed across exposed rock beds. There were fault lines and dark caverns, impossible to say how deep.

She turned to see the wake; it was small, but the wind was picking up. She didn't know the currents here, but with the foremast down and the lateen sails ruined, unless someone crafted a spell to change their course, the ship would carry them into the rim. "What happened with the oars?" she asked.

"Gone," Sally said. "They disappeared as soon as we were out of danger. You could have blinked and missed the whole thing. Did you really not know they were there?"

"I didn't," she said truthfully, and she might have said more, but Davit approached with a water skin. She reached for it, caught the way his eyes softened, and the worry eased as he saw she was all right. She answered with a smile, and Sally glanced teasingly between them until Macklin and Brigit and the others gathered around.

Much of their stores had been destroyed, Madinina reported, barrels smashed, drinking water down to half their supply. The hull was strafed, the stern castle nearly gone. The hold was leaking, and they had patched some of the holes, but there were more to find. Oddly enough, the *Fish* hadn't taken care of them. It seemed to be resting or gathering strength for whatever came next.

Molly glanced across their faces. They looked worn and bruised but surprisingly hopeful and pleased to find themselves alive, the ship afloat, even in its damaged state. "Where's Troth?" she asked suddenly.

"He's hurt," Tribolt said. "Sleeping below. He took a wound to his leg. It's deep but I cleaned it best I could and gave him a dose for the pain."

"Some bloody fool shot him," Macklin said, "Just after we took back the *Fish*. Tribolt's hardly left his side."

"Of course," Molly said, and she touched Tribolt's arm. "Go to him. Do what you can; we need him well. And the *Fish*? I never heard. How did you win her back?"

"That was the easy part. You were hardly gone when they boarded the ship, Gryer Scarp and a dozen Watermen drooling with greed."

"I abandoned my ship," Molly said. "I should never have done that."

"You saved your brother's life," Macklin said. "You couldn't have done that staying behind. And besides, we stole her back, didn't we? They ransacked everything after you left. Your cabin. The hold. Powder stores. You're not gonna like what you see, but whatever Scarp was looking for, he didn't find. Least ways their hands were empty when they came back, and they didn't look pleased.

"After that, the fighting started, and they were too busy to worry about us. We stole on board, convinced the few fellows left behind that they didn't want to be there. We were making plans when the *Fish* started moving. We didn't know what was happening until we realized it was you—" He stopped suddenly.

There was a snap and a tremor. They jumped back and craned their necks as the uppermost section of the main mast groaned then cracked, high above the cap. "All hands!" Molly shouted and they raised their arms and ducked as lines snapped loose and a section of the topmast teetered then snapped again. It dropped, caught in a web of lines and hung precariously above their heads. "Bring it down," she shouted. "Grab the lines before the yards fall!"

Try a cog," Evan shouted, but it was too late.

The stays snapped, then the shrouds. The topmast slid and dangled and fell again until somehow, thankfully, it snagged and stopped with one end caught in the lines, the wider end scraping the deck.

Molly's heart pounded as she circled the broken pole. It was tapered and easily ten feet long, flat across the break, surprisingly smooth to the eye, and hardly worn.

There was a long silence then, "We could make for Auklet?" Evan suggested. "Or Luna's Cove? Repair it there."

Tribolt agreed. "Capstan bars might help. I've used them before, like splints to span the break. Might not hold in rough seas, but it will get us to land and a new timber?"

Molly didn't answer. She touched the base, then quickly pulled back her hand and stared. She'd caught a splinter. It was needle thin and small, and there was a drop of blood. She looked to the pole again, to the flat bottom and smooth sides. Nothing was marred or cracked. She pulled out the splinter then, more carefully, felt along the edge.

She probed deeper this time, pushed away the outer world until she found it, the real wood, shattered and ragged with shards. She thumped the wood. "Evan," she said slowly. "I think it's hollow."

Macklin stepped closer. "Can't be," he said. "No one builds a hollow mast. It would be too weak."

"I know, but—" Molly walked around the remains of the standing mast. She looked at the collar and brackets and bolts that secured the giant timber in place, then upward along its length and down again to where it passed through the deck. She looked to her brother. "Do you remember that first spell you found? The morning after we stole the chest?"

Evan nodded. "The replicator? I was holding it, but the points were sharp, and it got away. We chased it." He glanced about. "It turned into a barrel. Then a rope. Then disappeared into the mast."

"I think it's still there," Molly said. "A sheathing, along the length." She shook the hanging pole, not hard, but enough so there was a rattling sound, like soot falling in a chimney. She stepped back and stared as layers of torn shards sprouted from the wood and the replicator fell away. It separated itself from the mast and became a ball again, spiny as a sea urchin. The instant it was gone, the topmast fell. The lines snapped and it hit the deck, bounced once then stopped.

There were noises inside. Scraping sounds, then a sudden rush as shells fell from the hollow cavity and scattered across the deck. And not only shells but packets and papers, charts and weapons, pistols and knives, instruments and relics covered in ice.

They glanced at each other and stared, then started gathering them up and calling out. Cai found a spyglass and thought it broken until she twisted the wider end and the glass suddenly cleared. Macklin found an arrow with a point shaped from stone. They examined tools and turned over instruments that made no sense. Sally found a round, brass device the size of her fist and there was a needle under glass and markings around the edge. She turned and the needle moved. "It's pointing north," she called, and showed it to Nick while Davit inspected a shaft that was long as his arm and held a crosspiece that slid along the length. He raised it toward the ice, then skyward trying to figure it out.

Evan found a map and he and Molly held it and turned it until the drawings of plump, curly haired children with wings were upright.

There were ships with crosses on their sails, and sea serpents in the corners, but two giant land masses that looked as if, were it not for the sea dividing them, they could be pushed into one immense island that dwarfed all the others.

And along one coast, a dotted line led north to what she guessed was their archipelago, though the isles were misshapen and there was no sign of Jamasak or a rim of any kind. But there was a gate, arched and wide, approximately where Luna's Cove might be.

Evan said it first. "Do you think they're alive?" he asked. "On the other side?"

Molly let go of the map and Evan rolled it up. "No," she said. "I used to, but not anymore. They would have come back. Though, I think now the *Ice Warden* made it to the other side."

"And maybe they came back and forth, and left us this map. Or someone from the other side found their way here and gave it to them?"

"Maybe. One of those. But it doesn't mean they're alive over there." She watched her brother. "What do you think?"

"About what…? Oh." Evan met her gaze. "You're asking if I want to—"

"Follow. Yes. I am. Our parents weren't running from the guild, I've figured out that much. They were searching, not hiding. They knew— they all did—the thousand years were ending. The crafts were changing. What magic the first men and women brought here is finished, like a cog that's good for three times and no more. The Night Watermen chose to stay and reap whatever power remained. Our parents wanted more."

"And what about wanting to build a home somewhere? You'd give that up?"

"The isles will still be here when the war is done. And we have the *Fish*, so we're already home."

The ice was drawing nearer, fissures widening as they watched. Evan didn't answer with words, he didn't have to. He clasped the map to his chest and hurried to show Cai. And no sooner was he gone but Davit was at her side. She would understand if he wanted to go back. The Night Watermen had raised him, given him purpose. What did she have to offer but a chance to turn his back on everything he'd known?

He nodded toward Evan. "That map, it was from the other side, wasn't it?"

"I think so. Yes. But I don't know how my parents came by it." She paused, took a breath and reached toward his hand. "I mean to find out."

"It's important," he said. "Finding out. Do you mind if I come with you?" He reached out and she closed her hand over his, and they stood quiet for a moment, their fingers twined together.

Daylight was coming, a pale light widening in the east. Molly glanced aloft. The sails were in shreds and the mainmast broken, but the *Fish* was steering itself again, carrying them toward the ice. Or maybe it was the current. Or some magic in the rim. Or another spell her parents left behind.

She used to wonder if the stars would ever return and if they did would they come riding their ships on a river of lights the way guild claimed. She wondered where they really came from, and whether the questions her parents tried to answer had more to do with the stars or the crafts, or simply the other side?

Evan leaned on the rail with Cai and Macklin, everyone pointing. Davit hurried to join them, and Molly followed and stared at the oddly shaped ice formations surrounding them now. Small and flat, large and craggy, they floated alongside the *Fish*. Something moved, a lean, dark shape, a sea mammal of some kind, resting on a pan of ice. Its eyes caught the light and it reared its head then shook itself and dove into the sea.

Molly looked to her crew. Their eyes were wide, mouths agape. "Forward or back?" she called. "I'm going in. I need to know what's on the other side. But there's still time to meet another ship, let you off, if that's your choice."

No one hesitated. "We already swore," Macklin called, and the rest of the crew urged him on. "We're with you. And whatever waits, we share as well."

There were more of the creatures now. They ware dark and sleek with round eyes and short legs and flippers. They basked in the growing sun and lay there, unafraid of the people or ship. A few splashed into the sea. They swam ahead then looked back.

A fissure just ahead of them came into view, its towering walls shaped of ice and rock. The *Fish* adjusted its course and steered dead on for the opening and Molly caught her breath at the size of it, the walls of ice and rock rising on either side. She glanced to Davit, to Evan and Cai and Macklin and the crew, and one by one, they answered with a nod.

The current eased. The wind died and the cavern narrowed around them. The air turned cold, brittle and sharp. Molly raised her hands, pointed at her ship, and blocks clattered and lines that had been torn grew whole again. Her thoughts flew to the lower deck, to the boards that shaped the hull and the keel that held it strong and she reached them with her craft. Portholes opened. Oars extended and dipped into the still water and pulled. Far ahead, the light grew brighter and she saw signs of shipwrecks, ancient boards jutting from the cavern walls, too old to belong to her parent's ship, but she would keep searching. The *Fish* opened its eyes and looked south.

#

Acknowledgments

The idea for this book began with an action figure— a three inch tall woman with black hair, a pistol in one hand, saber in the other. She's dressed as a pirate and I named her Molly, after one of the characters my father made up in the stories my brothers and I begged him to tell when we were kids.

The Molly Sinclair in this book owes her thanks to Tania Clucas for sharing her thoughts no matter what odd hour I called. And to a certain group of people: to Terry Boren first, for being an honest and insightful beta reader and to Jim Ruppert, Spencer Ruppert and Jasmine Johnson; to Eric Heyne, Alex Fitts and Annabel; David Marusek; Rich Carr; Burns Cooper and Sandra Boatwright; and my husband Luke.

The enjoyment and sustenance I gained from our gatherings seem far out of proportion to what we were actually doing every Sunday, from episode to episode and season after season: eating, drinking and watching our way through *Game of Thrones* and talking about any topic, related or not, under Alaska's ever changing sun. Authors, professors, and friends. This book would be far poorer without you.

Meet the Author

Elyse Guttenberg followed the highway north from New York to Fairbanks, Alaska when she was in her 20's, and has been living and writing there ever since. She received a Fellowship in Literature from the Alaska State Council on the Arts, and her first novel SUNDER, ECLIPSE AND SEED was shortlisted for Best First Fantasy from the International Association for the Fantastic in the Arts. SUMMER LIGHT and DAUGHTER OF THE SHAMAN are prehistories set in Alaska, 2000 years ago. When she's not writing you can find her building rock walls in the summer and wielding her appropriately sized chainsaw in winter.

Visit her website and learn more at www.elyseguttenberg.com

If you enjoyed THE POWER WE SHARE
look for Elyse Guttenberg's other titles:

On the frozen shores of Alaska's distant past, a young woman
yearns to be a shaman.

Desired by a powerful shaman and in love with a stranger cast out of his home, Elik fights for a way to save her people and reach her destiny. But will the old shaman relinquish his claim? Will the spirits reveal their secrets before the harsh winter closes in?

"Anyone interested in Alaska's Natives will find much to like in this book and anyone interested in good, factually correct fiction will find it irresistible." -- Alaska Magazine

The saga of one woman, chosen by the spirits and called on
to save her people.

Elik's quest to become a shaman continues as she joins her husband
in his search for revenge against the man that murdered his father.

Traded. Separated. Alone. Elik finds herself caught between vengeance
and unimagined love in a new land where starvation must be met with
courage and hope can be found only through the magic of the shaman
song coiled inside her.

She can enter dreams and travel the land,
But can she stop a nightmare before it destroys the world?

When Calyx's father banishes her to the temple at Aster, it's an answer to her prayers for now she will be trained to watch and speak the dreams of others. But learning the ways of a jarak dreamer is more difficult than she imagined, and time is short.

While priests scheme and a jealous queen stands in her way Edishu, the gods own nightmare, longs to escape his prison and conquer Calyx through her dreams. Now one woman stands alone to protect her people from an ancient prophecy and a dread rule.

Thank you so much for reading THE POWER WE SHARE, and I hope you enjoyed it. If you have a minute, please consider leaving an honest review on you favorite site. Readers' reviews, even more than professional ones, make all the difference in helping books get found. Contact me on my website at www.elyseguttenberg.com. It means a lot to know that readers are finding my work.